PHANTOM
HOLLOW

BOOK TWO

# NEVER
# LOOK
# BACK

A NOVEL

# KATHY
# HERMAN

Best-Selling Author of *All Things Hidden*

# Praise for
## *Never Look Back*

"*Never Look Back* picks up speed, racing around twists and turns, so you have to hang on tight until the end. Now I need to read the next book in the series."

> —LAURAINE SNELLING, best-selling author of the Red River of the North series and the Dakota Treasures series, as well as *The Brushstroke Legacy*

"Once again, Kathy Herman creates a world full of intrigue and suspense, full of characters easy to love, with poignant emotional and spiritual threads that transcend story and touch hearts. I cheered for Ivy and Montana and their story of hope and second chances. Don't miss *Never Look Back*!"

> —SUSAN MAY WARREN, award-winning author of *In Sheep's Clothing*

"Two lives tangled in past mistakes. A relationship no one approves of. A vicious attacker with an escalating agenda. *Never Look Back* is a powerful story—and an exciting read!—of how God can work for good even in the midst of evil."

> —LORENA MCCOURTNEY, author of the Ivy Malone Mystery series

"Kathy Herman creates real characters dealing with real problems. Her novels contain unexpected moments that leave the reader wanting more. *Never Look Back* is no exception."

> —JANET BENREY, coauthor of *Glory Be!* and *Gone to Glory*

"In *Never Look Back*, Kathy Herman crafts an intriguing story about fresh starts and the depths of God's forgiveness. With likable characters and an unlikely villain, *Never Look Back* makes for a truly entertaining read."

> —MARLO SCHALESKY, author of *Veil of Fire*

"Grab hold for the twists and turns of Kathy Herman's compelling suspense, filled with complex characters, vivid setting, and a red-herring plot."

> —GAIL GAYMER MARTIN, author of *Michigan* and *Finding Christmas*, a Booksellers Best Award winner.

"Kathy Herman just keeps getting better. The deep characters, heartfelt story line, and escalating drama in *Never Look Back* left me wanting more. Congratulations, Kathy!"

—CRESTON MAPES, author of *Nobody*

"Kathy Herman has created a vivid sense of place in *Never Look Back,* an absorbing tale of suspense and intrigue filled with characters to root for—and remember."

—MINDY STARNS CLARK, author of the Smart Chick Mysteries and the Million Dollar Mysteries

"*Never Look Back* is another page-turning mystery that will make you wish you lived in Jacob's Ear. These characters are sure to welcome you in, offer you a cup of coffee, and ask you who you think is the villain. And if you think you know, think again. This one can fool even the most brilliant amateur sleuths among us."

—WANDA DYSON, author of the Johnson-Shefford Case Files Suspense series

### Praise for the
### Phantom Hollow Series
### by Kathy Herman

"*[Ever Present Danger]* is a thrilling ride full of surprising twists and turns."

—ROMANTIC TIMES BOOKCLUB

"*Ever Present Danger* is another page-turning mystery. Kathy has a special way of creating characters you can root for."

—ARMCHAIR INTERVIEWS

"Be prepared to stay up late as you get to know the people of Phantom Hollow—a place you'll want to visit again and again."

—CAROL COX, author of *Ticket to Tomorrow* and *Fair Game*

"*Ever Present Danger* has all the tightly woven drama, excellent characterization, and suspense Kathy Herman's readers have come to love."

—HANNAH ALEXANDER, author of *Grave Risk* and *Death Benefits*

# NEVER
# LOOK
# BACK

PHANTOM
HOLLOW

BOOK TWO

# NEVER
# LOOK
# BACK

## KATHY
## HERMAN

MULTNOMAH
BOOKS

NEVER LOOK BACK
PUBLISHED BY MULTNOMAH BOOKS
12265 Oracle Boulevard, Suite 200
Colorado Springs, Colorado 80921
*A division of Random House Inc.*

All Scripture quotations are taken from the Holy Bible, New International Version®.
NIV®. Copyright © 1973, 1978, 1984 by International Bible Society. Used by per-
mission of Zondervan Publishing House. All rights reserved.

The characters and events in this book are fictional, and any resemblance to actual
persons or events is coincidental.

ISBN 1-59052-922-7

Published in association with the literary agency of Alive Communications Inc.,
7680 Goddard Street, Suite 200, Colorado Springs, CO 80920, www.alive
communications.com.

Library of Congress Cataloging-in-Publication Data
Herman, Kathy.
      Never look back / by Kathy Herman. — 1st ed.
          p. cm. — (Phantom hollow ; bk. 2.)
      ISBN 1-59052-922-7
      I. Title.  II. Series.
PS3608.E762N48 2007
813'.6—dc22

                                                        2007022697

Printed in the United States of America
2007—First Edition

10  9  8  7  6  5  4  3  2  1

*To Him who is both the Giver and the Gift.*

# ACKNOWLEDGMENTS

IN THE WRITING of this story, I drew from several resource people, each of whom shared generously from his storehouse of knowledge and experience. I did my best to integrate the facts as I understood them. If accuracy was compromised in any way, it was unintentional and strictly of my own doing.

I owe a debt of gratitude to my friend Will Ray, professional investigator, state of Oregon, for taking time to give his input on forensic evidence, crime-scene investigations, autopsies, and background checks. Will, thanks for your willingness to answer my questions thoroughly and in a timely manner.

A heartfelt thank-you to Paul David Houston, former assistant district attorney, Nacogdoches County, Texas, for explaining the procedure involved when a prisoner is released from jail; and to my friend Danny Tyler for explaining the role of Colorado marshals in small-town law enforcement.

I wish to extend my heartfelt thanks to my sister and zealous prayer warrior, Pat Phillips, and my online prayer team for your amazing support. How God is using you!

Thanks also to Kim Prothro, Deidre Pool, Susie Killough, Judi Wieghat, Mark and Donna Skorheim, Pearl Anderson, my friends at LifeWay Christian Store in Tyler, Texas, and in Nashville, Tennessee, and the ladies in my Bible-study class at Bethel Bible Church for your many prayers for my writing ministry. It means so much.

To those who read my books and those who sell them, thanks for encouraging me with e-mails and cards and personal testimonies about how God has used my words to challenge and inspire you. He uses you to bless me more often than you know.

To my novelist friends in ChiLibris, thanks for sharing so generously from your collective storehouse of knowledge and experience. It's an honor to be counted among you.

To Julee Schwarzburg and the staff at the newly formed WaterBrook-Multnomah Publishing Group, thanks for all you do to get my books on the shelves. I look forward to becoming part of the "family."

To my editor, Diane Noble, thanks for helping me to tighten the story and to keep my characters true—and for being a cheerleader! I so enjoy working with you!

To my husband, Paul, who reminded me when I thought I would never make this deadline that Nehemiah rebuilt the wall around Jerusalem in only fifty-two days, thanks for never letting me forget that God can multiply my time and isn't bound by deadlines. You are such an encourager!

And to my Father in heaven, how I thank You for allowing me the privilege of writing stories that challenge and bless Your people. I pray that the truth of Your Word woven into this story will come to life in the heart of every reader, and that not one will be left carrying the guilt of sins Your Son died to remove.

# PROLOGUE

JOHNSON MCRAE TUCKED his gun in the waistband of his trousers and stepped over the three corpses that lay sprawled on the warehouse floor, trying to decide what he wanted to have for dinner.

He bent down and retrieved the black velvet pouch that now belonged to him alone and entertained thoughts of the lavish lifestyle that awaited him. A smile tugged at the corners of his mouth. Why was it that now, when he could finally afford to dine in the finest restaurants on the planet, he was craving a Big Mac and fries?

Probably just as well. Why risk being seen in a public place when he could get what he wanted using the drive-through? Only four thieves in North America were capable of pulling off a heist this sophisticated, and the cops knew he was one of them. He wondered how long it would be before they discovered what was left of the other three suspects he had just eliminated—or if they ever would. What reason would anyone have to come to this abandoned warehouse?

Johnson stepped back and stole one last glance at the lifeless trio that had helped to make him a rich man. "So long, suckers. Like they say, 'There's no honor among thieves.'"

He picked up the battery-operated lantern that burned brightly atop a plastic crate and used it to light the way back to the entrance. He slid open the rusty door just enough to squeeze through and closed it behind him.

Johnson put on his sunglasses and walked over to the getaway van he had rented with one of several ill-gotten credit cards. He dropped the lantern on the front seat and put the van in neutral and released the brake, then pushed the van into a wooded area where it couldn't be seen from the road.

He brushed his hands together and stood thinking for a moment. Had he forgotten anything? Every detail had gone according to plan—except for the unfortunate encounter with the gallery security guard. A dead body would likely ensure that the cops would turn up the heat and maybe even involve the feds. Which meant he needed to find a place to lie low and let the hype die down.

A grin stretched his cheeks. Colorado was invigorating this time of year. He might as well enjoy a little R and R till it was safe to deliver the rare jewels to his contact in Argentina—and walk away with the entire six million dollars.

Johnson heard voices and turned. Through the trees, he spotted two boys on bicycles coming down the unpaved road.

*What are they doing here?*

He hurried back inside the warehouse and squatted behind a stack of shipping containers wrought with cobwebs. He waited for several minutes, then saw daylight as the entrance door slid to one side and a pair of short silhouettes filled the opening.

"I've been in here before, Patrick, and there's no ghost," the taller boy said. "I don't care what those guys swore they saw."

"Well, somethin' freaked 'em out," Patrick insisted. "Anyway, the sign said no trespassing. I don't think we should go in."

"Chicken."

"I'm not chicken, Kenny! I don't wanna get grounded, okay? My parents told me not to come down here."

"Well, *I'm* not gonna tell them. You going in with me or not?"

Patrick shook his head. "You go, if you're so sure there's nothin' in there."

"Okay, you big baby. Watch this."

Kenny stepped inside, his hands cupped around his mouth. "Hey, spook, you big white bag of hot air, we're over here! Come and get us!" He snickered, his hands held defensively in front of him as if he were prepared to execute some debilitating karate move. "See? I told you there's no ghost in here."

"Good," Patrick said. "Then let's go."

"I say we walk all the way through the building and prove it's no big deal. Then we go get those wusses and do it again to show we've got more guts than they do."

"I don't know, it's pretty dark…"

"There's enough light if we leave the door open. I could always go get your little sister. I'll bet she's not scared."

There was a long stretch of silence, then Patrick tentatively stepped inside.

"Good man." Kenny gave Patrick a slap on the back. "Come on. I'll go first."

Kenny moved slowly down the center of the massive warehouse, Patrick closer than a shadow.

"There's nothing in here but empty shelves," Kenny said. "If we go down this aisle, we'll run into the back door."

*Not without tripping over those dead bodies, you won't,* Johnson thought. *The last thing I need is the two of you running to the cops before I can get out of town.* He picked up a nail, threw it into the dark vacuum, and heard a tinkling metallic sound when it hit the concrete.

"What was that? Did you hear that?" Patrick said.

"It's just the wind. It blew something into the door. Keep moving."

"We should go back. What if those guys really *did* see a ghost?"

"They didn't," Kenny said, sounding less convinced. "Don't freak on me. We can do this."

Johnson got up and moved surreptitiously behind the boys, knowing what he'd have to do if they discovered the bodies.

"I can't see where I'm going," Patrick whined.

"See that crack of light in front of us? That's the back door."

*Too bad you're never going to reach it!* Johnson waited until the boys were just a few yards shy of where the corpses lay, then rushed them from behind. He grabbed the necks of their T-shirts firmly and bellowed a fiendish laugh that reverberated in the blackness.

The boys screamed, their arms flailing, as he tightened his grip and relished the adrenaline rush.

"Don't fiiiight me!" Johnson roared, the cadence of his voice decidedly ghoulish. "I'm going to let you liiiive! Run! Run awaaaay while you can and never come baaaack, or next time will be your laaaast!"

He made a 180-degree turn, maintaining a choking grip on the necks of their T-shirts, and gave the daredevils a hearty shove toward the front entrance, his sinister laughter nipping at their heels.

The pair dashed toward the light and scrambled almost cartoonlike to squeeze through the door at the same time, then hopped on their bikes and hightailed it up the unpaved road.

Johnson laughed till he cried, wishing he could have seen the expressions on their faces. He waited sixty seconds, then poked his head out the entrance and looked up the road, satisfied the scared boys were long gone. He stepped outside and slid the door closed, still chuckling and trying to remember the last time he'd had that much fun.

He put on his dark glasses and trudged into the woods, past the van, and down a gentle slope in the direction of the Wal-Mart parking lot, where the *real* getaway car awaited him.

He wondered what the parents of the traumatized boys would make of their sons' ghost story and was sobered by the thought that if those kids had caught even a glimpse of his face, there would be five dead bodies on the warehouse floor instead of only three.

1

IVY GRIFFITH APPROACHED the last gray security door and pressed the release button, her heart galloping and her legs as wobbly as a foal's. She glanced up at the camera as she had been instructed to do, waited until she heard the lock disengage and the alarm sound, then pulled the door open and entered the public sector of the Tanner County Jail—a free woman!

She was surprised to see so many people scurrying about. Feeling a little lightheaded and suddenly wishing she had eaten breakfast, she made her way over to the far wall and leaned against it. She blew the bangs off her forehead and forced a smile for two female deputies eying her.

*Lord, please don't let me pass out and make a scene. I just want to go home!*

"Ivy! Over here!"

She turned toward the unmistakable voice and spotted her father in the congested corridor, his hand waving in the air. She hurried toward him, zigzagging around several people before she finally caught up to him and lost herself in his embrace.

"Let's go home, honey," Elam Griffith finally said. "It's over."

*Over.* How the thought excited her! She had paid her debt to society and wanted nothing more than to move on with her life.

Ivy walked arm-in-arm with her father to the exit door and stepped outside into the bright November sunshine. She inhaled deeply, drawing in the fresh mountain air, and whispered a prayer of thanks. She wondered how long it would be before any of this seemed real.

"Well, I'll tell you one thing," Elam said. "Montana was too wired to sleep last night. That boy can hardly wait to see you."

"You explained why I didn't want him to come down here, didn't you?"

"Sure, but I really don't think it would've bothered him. All he's talked about for weeks is your coming home."

"I just didn't think it was necessary to saddle a seven-year-old with the memory of his mother being released from jail. I want him to remember this day as my *coming home,* not my *getting out.*"

Elam smiled. "Well, however he looks at it, I expect that little scamp has his nose pressed against the living-room window. Let's not keep him waiting. Come on, the Suburban's parked across the street."

"He seems to be thriving," Ivy said. "Every time we've talked, he's gone on and on about all the things he's involved in. You and Mom have done a great job with him. I can never thank you enough."

"No need to thank us, honey. We love Montana and have gotten really close to him. But he needs his mother."

Ivy got in the Suburban and looked out at the towering San Juan Mountains that encircled the town of Jacob's Ear with postcard beauty. "After six months in that place, you can't imagine how wonderful it is not to be looking through iron bars."

"I suppose I can't," Elam said. "But it's sure great seeing you dressed in your own clothes instead of that orange jumpsuit."

"I promise you I'm going to give away everything in my closet that has even a speck of orange in it."

"Good, because your mother can hardly wait to take you shopping. She's already mapping out some elaborate strategy for hitting all the after-Thanksgiving sales."

"Is she planning a big Thanksgiving dinner?"

Elam chortled. "Are you kidding? We'll need to take both cars into town when she does her grocery shopping. Rusty and his family are driving in from Albuquerque. Our Thanksgiving table will be full for the first time in ages."

Ivy wished she shared her father's enthusiasm but wondered if she would even know her brother after all this time. And how he would react to all the trouble she had caused?

Elam started the car and pulled onto Main Street. "By the way, I ran into Mr. and Mrs. Hadley at the post office the other day. They were polite but never mentioned your getting out."

"Do you think they've forgiven me?"

"I honestly don't know."

Ivy sighed. "It had to be devastating when they found out I covered up their son's murder. Ten years is a long time to live with the false hope that he'd be found alive. And I let them believe it."

"I'm sure it was, honey. But you can't undo what was done. You served your time."

Ivy looked over at Jewel's Café as they passed by and noticed the green and white gingham curtains still framing the windows. "How's Jewel?"

"Same old spitfire. She'd like you to come back to work for her."

"Really? That's surprising."

"Oh, you know Jewel. She looks at the heart. It's irrelevant whether you were away on vacation or did time in jail. She was happy with your work and has a job for you anytime you want it."

"What a sweetheart. I enjoyed working at the café, but I can't make a living waiting tables. I've got to figure out something else."

"Funny, but your mother and I have been discussing this very thing." Elam stroked his mustache. "We wondered if you'd consider being in charge of registration at the conference center. It pays three dollars more an hour than you were making at Jewel's, and we'd let you and Montana live in one of the chalet cabins as a perk. Interested?"

"Are you serious?"

"Absolutely. And full-time staff get medical insurance. It's up to you, but we think it's a good option."

Ivy sat stunned, gratitude knotting in her throat. "I…I never dreamed you'd let me work at the camp."

"Why not?"

"I have a criminal record now. You've got nice Christian people coming in and out of there. Just doesn't seem appropriate."

"Baloney. It's appropriate if I say it's appropriate. For crying out loud, Ivy, you recommitted your life to Christ. Besides, your mom and I own the place, remember?" He turned to her and winked, the corners of his mouth twitching. "You'd be good at it. Give it some thought."

As they drove out of the city limits and onto Three Peaks Road, her father waved at someone in a red pickup, then put his cell phone to his ear. "Carolyn, it's me… Yeah, it went fine. Only took us a minute to hook up… She looks great… I know he's champing at the bit. Tell him we're about fifteen minutes from home…"

*Home.* Ivy nestled in the heated leather seat, her heart racing with hope. She looked out across Phantom Hollow at the jagged, snowcapped peaks that still took her breath away, confident that Montana would grow up loving and respecting this unspoiled beauty the way she had—and that her parents would be the stabilizing force in his life.

She closed her eyes, the sun warming her face, and let herself dream about what the future might hold. The idea of living with her son in their own home and finally being able to support him was very exciting, even if it was possible only because of her parents' generosity. She wasn't about to pass up her dad's job offer, but she wondered if the Three Peaks staff would resent his hiring a family member—worse yet, one who'd been in jail—with no job experience beyond waiting tables.

"Dad, how do Jake and Brandon feel about me coming to work at the camp? I mean, it sounds like you pulled rank on them."

"Think so, do you?" Elam's tone was playful. "Why don't you let them speak for themselves? Take a look…"

Ivy opened her eyes as the car slowed and finally stopped in front of the entrance to Three Peaks Christian Camp and Conference Center. Huge yellow ribbons had been tied on either side of the stone entrance, and all along the road beyond staff people stood waving yellow streamers.

"Welcome home, Ivy!" they shouted, almost in unison.

"Oh, Dad…" Ivy put her hand over her mouth but was unable to keep the tightness in her throat from turning to sobs.

She heard Brandon Jones's unique whistle above all the cheering, but as the car inched forward, all she saw was a blurry mass of smiling faces.

"Hey, Mom! Over here! Mom!"

Ivy's heart leaped. She wiped her eyes and surveyed the wall of well-wishers until she spotted Montana jumping up and down and waving his arms in the air. She flung open the door and ran to him, then picked him up and twirled him around in a circle before planting kisses all over his cold, soft cheeks.

"I've missed you so much!"

Montana giggled, a jack-o'-lantern smile taking up half his face. "Do you like our surprise?"

"I *love* your surprise!" It was a million times better than their being reunited at the jail.

"It was Kelsey and Brandon's idea. Cool, huh?"

"Very." Ivy felt a hand squeeze her shoulder and looked up into the most loving gaze she'd ever seen. "Mom…" Ivy threw her arms around her mother and just let the tears go. "It's so great to be home."

"There's been such a void since you left," Carolyn Griffith said. "This family just isn't complete without you."

*Family.* The word warmed her down to her soul, like hot cocoa on a blustery day.

Before Ivy could let go of her mother, she was completely enveloped in a group hug. When everyone finally let go and stepped back, her gaze fell on Kelsey Jones's radiant face.

"Guess you can you tell we're glad to see you," Kelsey said.

"Goodness, I never expected anything like this." Ivy laughed and cried at the same time. "Montana said this was Brandon's and your idea."

Brandon Jones smiled, tongue in cheek, and reached for Kelsey's hand. "What can we say? We're just a couple of party animals."

Ivy moved her eyes from person to person, touched by the acceptance she saw on all their faces.

"Elam said you might like to work registration," Jake Compton said. "I really need someone to take it over ASAP. Brandon's been pinch-hitting since summer camp ended, but he's really lousy at it."

Brandon elbowed Jake in the ribs. "Okay, Ivy, you going to get me off the hook here? If you don't come on board, heaven only knows how long I'll have to put up with this abuse."

"Mom, *take* the job!" Montana said. "You should see the house we get to live in. It's got this really cool loft that can be my room."

Ivy brushed her fingers through her son's thick auburn hair and reveled in the moment, hoping she wasn't going to wake up in her bunk at the county jail and realize she'd been dreaming.


Sheriff Flint Carter sat at his desk scanning the arrest listings in Friday's edition of the *Tri-County Courier,* hoping nothing would happen between then and five o'clock to interfere with his having a relaxing weekend. He heard footsteps in the hallway and glanced up just as Lieutenant Bobby Knolls appeared in the doorway.

"There you are," Flint said. "Did you follow up on that tip?"

Bobby blew a pink bubble and sucked the gum into his mouth. "Yeah, we spent all morning searchin' the area around Jacob's mine. Sure would help if the caller had told us what we're supposed to be lookin' for. If there is somethin' suspicious goin' on out there, we sure couldn't find it. Seemed like a big waste of time. So anything interesting goin' on here? Was Ivy Griffith released?"

"At nine o'clock this morning. I feel really good about it."

"Some folks think it stinks that she only served half her sentence."

"Tough. Her time was reduced exactly the same as every other inmate rewarded for good behavior. Until the taxpayers are willing to approve funding for a bigger jail, they're just going to have to live with our system of two days' credit for each day served."

"Yeah, if we kept every inmate for the duration of his sentence, we'd have to start usin' office space and chainin' them to the radiators."

"Exactly. So let the whiners put their tax money where their mouth is."

Bobby stepped inside Flint's office and leaned against the wall, his arms folded across his chest. "Actually, I think it's more personal than that. A lot of folks want someone punished for Joe Hadley's murder. It's almost like they don't even remember that it was Ivy's boyfriend and two of his teammates that did it. Since those guys are dead, she's the only one left to blame."

"The girl was guilty of covering for her friends. She's not a murderer. And in all my years as sheriff, I've never seen anyone else voluntarily come forward ten years *after* the crime and insist on being charged, even though the statute of limitations had run. Ivy asked for the maximum when she could've walked." Flint took off his reading glasses and laid them on the desk. "People should try cutting her some slack."

"Let's hope they do. Think you and Elam'll ever be friends again?"

"I don't know, Bobby. It'd be awkward trying to go back to the way things were before I put his daughter in jail."

"Have you ever talked to him about it?"

"I meant to. But things got busy over the summer, and time got away from me."

"Are you goin' to?"

"What's with all the questions? Have you finished your end-of-the-week report yet?"

Bobby unfolded his arms and walked over to the doorway, then stopped and spun around. "Look, Sheriff. It's really none of my business. But it's a shame that you and Elam haven't spoken since Ivy went to jail. You were just doin' your job. He wouldn't have respected you for doin' less."

"Go back to work, Bobby."

"Most guys never have a close friend like that. Maybe you shouldn't let it go so easily."

"I never said anything about letting it go. I just said it was awkward."

Bobby held his gaze, one eyebrow arched. "Then why don't you deal with it so it won't be?"

# 2

JEWEL SADLER TURNED on the Closed sign at Jewel's Café and walked over to the town's centenarians, Deke and Roscoe, who had split an order of Sunday's roast beef special and then taken small bites off opposite ends of a slice of orange cake for the past forty minutes.

"So which of my two favorite customers gets the bill tonight?" she said.

Deke raised his hand. "You can put it on *my* tab."

Roscoe lifted his faded dark eyes, his hand to his ear. "Say what?"

"I'm payin'," Deke hollered. "It's my turn."

Roscoe gave a nod, then pushed back his chair and ever so slowly rose to his feet. "I'll git it next time."

*Sure you will.* Jewel chuckled to herself. She had been running tabs for these two old geezers for twenty years and had yet to collect a nickel.

Jewel helped Deke get his arms into the threadbare down jacket she was sure he'd been wearing since she bought this place. "Okay, you're good to go."

"Come on, you ol' coot." Roscoe flashed Deke a grin, revealing a row of stained teeth. "We best be gittin' home before the snow starts flyin'."

"Want me to drive you?" Jewel said.

Deke pulled on his Denver Broncos stocking cap. "Nah. We been gittin' around on foot fer a hunerd years. God willin', we'll manage for another hunerd."

Jewel went over and opened the door for the two old guys and thought of her own dad, who would have been ninety-eight this month. "Good night, fellas."

Roscoe tipped his coonskin cap. "See ya tomorrow."

"Mighty fine eatin', Jewel." Deke patted her shoulder. "Mighty fine."

She closed the door and locked it, then rang out the cash register and put the money in a zippered bag. She strolled through the swinging doors and across the kitchen into the back office, where she heard a gentle knock on the alley door.

"Come in."

The door opened, and a familiar form stood in the threshold. "You really should keep this door locked."

"Ivy!" Jewel rushed over and threw her arms around Ivy Griffith and rocked her from side to side. "It's so good to see you, doll! I heard on the news that you got out Friday."

"I've been with my family all weekend. Montana would hardly leave my side. I knew you'd be closing up about now and thought I'd slip in and say hello."

"I'm glad you did. So when are you coming back to work?" Jewel leaned back and looked into Ivy's eyes and knew the answer. "Don't want your old job back, eh?"

"That's not it. I loved working here, but I need to make enough to support Montana. My parents asked me to take over registration at Three Peaks. We can live in one of the chalet cabins rent-free as a perk, and I'll also get medical insurance. I can't afford to turn it down."

"Of course you can't." Jewel patted the old vinyl chair next to her desk. "Why don't you get comfy, and I'll get us some hot chocolate."

"That sounds great. But I can get it."

"Just sit there and let me pamper you for a change."

"Okay. I'd like marshmallows in mine, please."

Jewel pulled the chair from behind her desk and rolled it over next to Ivy's, then went out to the hot chocolate maker, filled two mugs, and added a scoop of miniature marshmallows to each.

"Here you go, doll. Be careful. It's really hot."

"Thanks. Mmm…the aroma brings back such pleasant memories. Mom always made hot cocoa for Rusty and me after school. If only I could go back to those days and live my life over again with what I know now."

"Would be nice, but I think we all learn the hard way. I'm just sorry you had to go to jail. I hope it wasn't too awful."

"The worst part was being away from Montana," Ivy said. "And coming to grips with why I ended up there. Sometimes I still can't believe I made a pact with Pete, Reg, and Denny not to tell anyone they killed Joe Hadley. Can you imagine the emotional roller coaster we put his parents on?"

"You were a high-school kid. Sometimes teens get talked into doing things and don't know how to get out. It's a crying shame."

Ivy looked at Jewel, her round gray eyes seeming to beg for understanding. "I'm sure some people will always wonder if I was involved in the murder and not just the cover-up."

Jewel reached over and patted Ivy's knee. "Well, I'm not one of them."

"I know. It means a lot that you believe me." Ivy took a sip of hot chocolate. "I wasn't sure how you'd react when it all hit the news. I wanted to come tell you myself, but I was afraid you'd never want to see me again."

"Not true. I was heartsick. Sure explained why you stayed away all those years."

"Do you realize I've wasted almost a third of my life?"

"Listen, doll. When you get to be my age, ten years will only amount to a smidgen. You've got plenty of time to turn things around. Best thing you can do is shift into forward and never look back."

Ivy opened the front door of her parents' home and was hit with the delicious smell of something baking.

Before she even got her snowy boots off, Montana had his arms around her waist, his face aglow, and was gazing up at her with those puppy eyes that looked remarkably like her brother's.

"Me and Grandma made Frosty-the-Snowman cookies. Wanna try one?"

"Sure. Talk about perfect timing, have you looked outside?"

"Yeah, we might get six inches of snow! Maybe I won't have school tomorrow."

Ivy tousled his hair. "Don't count on it. It takes a pretty big storm to close the schools around here. But you can play in the snow when you get home."

"Can we get out the sleds and race down that really steep hill like you and Uncle Rusty did when you were kids?"

"Sure. But I warn you, I'm fast." Ivy pinched his tummy. "And I show no mercy. I used to beat Uncle Rusty all the time."

"Grandma said he's coming here for Thanksgiving and bringing Aunt Jackie and Tia and Josie. They're my cousins. I never had cousins before. Or even an aunt and uncle."

Ivy took her finger and touched his freckled nose. "There're a lot of things we never had before that we'll get to enjoy now."

"Yeah, like our own house with a loft that's gonna be my room."

"That too. Okay, lead me to the cookies."

She followed Montana into the kitchen and went over and stood by her mother. "I had a really nice visit with Jewel. She understands why I want to take the job at Three Peaks."

"I had a feeling she would."

"How cute these are." Ivy picked up a snowman cookie and bit into it. "Yum."

"We did good—huh, Mom?"

"I'll say."

"Montana cut them out and decorated them." Carolyn licked the icing off the spoon and set the bowl in the sink. "We just used my plain old sugar cookie recipe."

Ivy lifted her eyebrows. "There's nothing 'plain old' about your recipe. These are to die for."

Carolyn chuckled. "Don't do that. There are three dozen of these just waiting for you and Montana to gobble up. Then he wants to make some in the shape of a pumpkin."

"Good. I gained twelve pounds when I was in jail. I'd like to gain another twelve."

"The extra weight looks good on you, honey. You're starting to get your shape back."

"Thanks. But you do realize if I keep this up, I won't be able to get into any of my clothes?"

Carolyn smiled. "That's what after-Thanksgiving sales are for."

Ivy felt a tug on the bottom of her sweater.

"Mom, I'm gonna go take my shower," Montana said. "Would you listen to me read before I go to bed?"

"Sure. Is *Green Eggs and Ham* still your favorite book?"

"Kinda. But I can read lots of books now. You'll see." He dashed out of the kitchen and up the staircase.

"I can't believe how responsible he's become," Ivy said. "You and Dad have done a great job with him."

"Montana's a great kid. It didn't take much doing. I think having our church family loving on him has been a big plus."

Ivy studied the giant snowflakes collecting on the window. "I'm a little nervous about seeing Rusty. Ten years is a long time. It's weird trying to picture him as a veterinarian and married with two little girls."

"Oh, they're so adorable. Dark curls and deep blue eyes. They're the spitting image of Jacqueline. Rusty's going to be surprised at how much Montana looks like him. The two could pass for father and son."

Ivy smiled. "Eerie, isn't it?"

"Pretty amazing."

"Mom…how has Rusty dealt with all the trouble I've gotten into over the years? You and Dad keep dancing around it."

There was a long pause, and Carolyn began to arrange the cookies in the bottom of an oblong Tupperware container. "He's struggled with it."

"Can you be more specific?"

"He was angry that you dropped out of college and didn't tell us where you were. And that after we paid for your drug rehab, you disappeared again and didn't contact us until you got arrested and put back in the program."

"Does he know what I was doing for drug money?"

Carolyn nodded. "We never held back anything."

"No wonder he's distant. He must think I'm a real sleaze."

"Don't say that, honey. I think he's worked through the saga of your drug addiction. But I'm not going to lie to you. He can't accept that you covered up Joe Hadley's murder—or that you were in jail."

Ivy's heart sank.

"Now, don't get upset. Rusty adores you. After a few days of us all being together, it'll be like old times."

"What if it isn't? I *have* done some pretty awful things, and I'm anything but the little sister he remembers."

"Ivy listen to me." Carolyn tilted Ivy's chin upward and held her gaze. "You have to leave the past in the past. What you did isn't who you are."

"Tell that to Rusty."

"I'm saying it to *you*. Have you already forgotten what Pastor Myers said in his sermon this morning? God doesn't keep a record of sins we've confessed. And neither should we."

"I believe that. So why do I still feel guilty?"

Carolyn leaned forward and pressed her lips to Ivy's forehead. "It might help if you'd stop replaying in your mind everything you did wrong and start focusing on how to do things right."

"Mom, I'm ready!" Montana voice rang out from the top of the stairs.

Ivy paused for a moment, encouraged by her mother's words. "You're right. I think I'll start by spending some quality time with that little munchkin of mine."


Brandon Jones chased his giggling wife up the front steps of their log home and stuffed a fistful of snow down the collar of her ski jacket, evoking a girlish squeal he was sure the Comptons could hear across the street.

"Okay, okay," Kelsey said, laughing so hard she could hardly catch her breath. "We're even."

"That's what you think. A bucket of snow dumped over my head deserves more retaliation than this." Brandon lifted his eyebrows several times and laughed wickedly. "Not to worry, my little pretty. I'll wait for a moment when you least expect it to get my revenge. You don't know the meaning of the word *cold*."

Kelsey stomped her feet on the porch and stepped inside on the floor mat and quickly got out of her ski jacket and brushed the snow off the back of her neck.

"You have to admit it was funny," she said, removing her boots. "I would've preferred a good snowball fight, but this dry snow won't form a ball like the kind we had in Raleigh."

"We'll see if you're as amused when it's my turn to get even." Brandon pulled off his snow-caked stocking cap and dropped it on the mat along with his gloves. He took off his ski jacket and made a face when he felt water trickling down his bare chest and back.

Kelsey started laughing again. "Why don't you put on a dry shirt and go stand in front the fire? I'll bring you a bowl of chili. That'll warm you on the inside."

"Smells terrific. I'm starved."

"It'll just be a couple minutes."

Brandon walked down the hall and through the bedroom in his stocking feet and tossed his flannel shirt in the bathroom sink. He put on the heaviest sweatshirt he owned, then went into the living room and stood by the fire, smiling in spite of himself.

How he loved being married to Kelsey! Their first anniversary was coming up the week of Thanksgiving, and he wanted to surprise her with a special gift, though he hadn't been able to think of anything yet.

Kelsey came out of the kitchen and set a tray on the coffee table.

Brandon went over and flopped on the couch next to her and said the blessing, then sat forward and rubbed his hand together. "This smells great! Let's get down to some serious eating."

Kelsey handed him the container of shredded cheddar cheese. "Funny how last Sunday night, we were sitting here discussing how Ivy would be home by this time next week—and she is."

"Brandon stuffed a saltine in his mouth. "I'm glad she agreed to take the job."

"We haven't really talked about it, but I assume you're confident she can handle registration?"

"Sure, why not? She's smart. And we saw firsthand when she worked at Jewel's how well she could juggle orders and keep a warm and friendly attitude toward customers. If she can use those same skills to supervise registration, it'll be a win-win."

"Do you think Jake hired her just because she's Elam's daughter?"

"Let's just say that Jake would never have considered her if she *wasn't* Elam's daughter. We have an unofficial policy against hiring anyone with a criminal record. But this is a unique situation. We all know Ivy's circumstances, and Jake's willing to give her a chance."

"Well, he couldn't exactly say no to Elam, either." Kelsey took a spoonful of chili and blew on it. "I'm thrilled she took the job. I'm looking forward to working with her. When does she start?"

"Nothing's in concrete, but probably a week from tomorrow. Jake suggested she take two weeks to get moved and settled in the new place, but Ivy's insistent that she's been sitting around for six months and is ready to get busy." Brandon wiped his mouth with a napkin.

"Truthfully, getting her and Montana moved should be a snap. Since the chalet's already furnished, we'll only be moving clothes and a few odds and ends."

Kelsey sprinkled a spoonful of shredded cheddar on her chili and seemed to be lost in thought. After a moment she said, "I don't think anyone on staff has a problem with Ivy's being hired, do you?"

"No one's said. Then again, who would be bold enough to admit it?"

# 3

ON THURSDAY AFTERNOON Ivy sat in front of a crackling fire in the living room of her new home, thinking that her mother and son should be arriving at any moment. She heard a car door slam, and her pulse quickened. She pulled back the curtain and saw her mother's Jeep parked out front and Montana trudging through the snow, his stocking cap pulled down to his eyebrows and his grin the size of Texas.

She jumped up and scanned the room one last time to make sure things were just the way she wanted them, then opened the front door and waved, realizing that this marked the beginning of a new chapter in their lives.

"Grandma said we're already moved in!" Montana exclaimed.

Ivy stepped back and let him squeeze past her. "We thought it would be fun to surprise you when you got out of school."

Montana paused just long enough to make a quick sweep with his eyes, then kicked off his boots and darted over to the ladder and climbed up to the loft.

"This is so cool!" he hollered.

A few seconds later he appeared at the railing, his weight resting on his elbows. "What's that yummy smell?"

"I made brownies for you and Grandma."

"Yay!"

Ivy winked at her mom as Montana scrambled down the ladder. "Take it easy, Tarzan. All I need is you breaking a leg."

Carolyn went into the kitchen and started opening cabinet doors. "Do you remember where you put the napkins?"

"Mom, sit down and let me serve you for a change. You want coffee, milk, or hot cocoa?"

"Coffee sounds good. If you'll have some too."

Ivy glanced over at Montana, who stood looking up at the stone fireplace that dominated the far wall. "What would *you* like, sweetie?"

"Milk, please. Can we have a fire *every* day?"

"Well, we've got plenty of firewood stacked up out there. It'll be your job to bring it in. Pretty cozy, huh?"

"I *love* this house!" Montana held out his arms and twirled around. "It's fun having one humongous room instead of lots of smaller ones."

"It's obvious we hit a home run with number one grandson," Carolyn said. "I hope it doesn't take long for *you* to adjust to the open concept. It's not as private."

Ivy's mind flashed back to her jail cell. "Are you kidding? It's amazing just having a place of our own. We can't thank you and Dad enough for letting us live here. I can always go to my bedroom if I need a little space to myself."

Montana took his thumb and pointed to himself. "But *I've* got the funnest room. I've got *two* beds, so I can have sleepovers. And Kelsey's gonna make me curtains that have deers on them." He went over to the table and crawled up in a chair. "What kind are you gonna get, Mom?"

"The curtains that are already here will do just fine."

"But your dad and I have already arranged for Kelsey to get with you and make window treatments," Carolyn said. "That's going to be our housewarming gift."

"You've done enough."

"Nonsense. It would thrill us to see you make this place your own. We want you to pick out new furniture too."

"There's nothing wrong with the furniture," Ivy said.

"I know, honey. Jake wants to use it to replace damaged pieces in the other chalets. We really want you to start fresh by having your own things. This is not a cabin for guests anymore. It's your home."

Ivy set a plate of brownies on the table, her eyes brimming with tears. "I never imagined having all this. I don't even know what to say."

Carolyn reached over and took her hand. "You don't have to say anything. Just let us do this."

Sheriff Flint Carter pulled up in front of Jewel's Café and spotted Elam Griffith's maroon Suburban parked across the street. He sat for a moment, wondering if this was a mistake. A cigarette sounded really good about now, even though he'd kicked the habit years ago.

He got out of his squad car and walked inside and nodded at Jewel Sadler. "I'll have coffee when you've got a minute."

"I've got a fresh pot. Be right there."

Flint made his way to the back where Elam sat, his elbows on the table and his hands wrapped around a coffee mug.

"Hey," Flint said.

Elam acknowledged him with his eyes. "Why don't we cut to the chase? Just tell me what it is you wanted to talk to me about."

Flint pulled out a chair and sat, thinking no matter how many times he had rehearsed the answer, it never sounded adequate. "For starters, I wanted to say how pleased I am that Ivy's out of jail. She was a model prisoner and certainly earned an early release."

"You didn't ask me here to say what we both already know."

Flint looked into Elam's eyes and saw the same anger he had seen the last time they'd had a one-on-one. "Look...it's been six months since we had a civil conversation. Don't you think it's time we cleared things up?"

"Why? Things seem crystal clear to me: You wanted to finger the class-reunion shooter and didn't give a rip whether my daughter got victimized in the process. You betrayed our friendship when you allowed her to be interrogated without even asking if she wanted an attorney, especially knowing her drug history. Didn't sit right with me then. Still doesn't."

Flint made a tent with his fingers. "What would you have done, Elam? We were finally starting to connect the dots in the two cases and had reason to believe that Ivy knew the three class-reunion victims had murdered Joe Hadley ten years ago—and probably even knew who had murdered *them*." Flint lifted his eyes. "We were right."

"Fine. You got what you wanted. Ivy did her time. And since Joe Hadley's killers are dead and the nut case who shot them is in prison for life, you can run for reelection."

Jewel came over and set a mug of coffee and a plastic pitcher on the table. "Here you go. Either of you want something sweet to go with it? I just took a batch of cranberry muffins out of the oven."

Elam shook his head.

"Nothing now," Flint said. "But why don't you wrap up a half dozen for me to take home?"

"Sure thing." Jewel patted his shoulder. "Sorry to interrupt."

Elam's eyes seemed to be following Jewel as she walked away, and then he turned his gaze on Flint. "What did you hope to gain by talking to me?"

"I hoped we could come to a mutual understanding that I was just doing my job. Believe it or not, I gave Ivy the benefit of the doubt every step of the way. The feds wanted to push her a lot harder." Flint picked up his mug and blew on his coffee. "And just so you'll know, I respect her for having had the courage to admit the truth about what happened to Joe Hadley and for *not* cutting a deal. She could've walked. The girl's got grit. She deserves a clean slate."

Elam looked out the window, seemingly to hide emotions that were just under the surface. "Yeah, she does."

"Maybe it's time we all made a fresh start. I hate the bad blood between us. My son and your grandson are best friends. We can't keep avoiding each other. Believe me, they notice."

Elam tugged at his mustache. "You won't have to worry about it after today since Montana doesn't live with me and Carolyn anymore. He and Ivy moved into their own place. You prepared to let your son hang out at the home of someone who's done time in your jail?"

"You think I'm worried about what people think?"

"I'd be surprised if you weren't."

Flint exhaled loudly. "Could we just stick to the subject? Are we or are we not going to put the past behind us and start living in the present?"

At eight forty-five that night, Ivy heard a car pull up out front and then a gentle rap on the door. She peeked out the window, saw her dad standing on the stoop, and hurried to open the door.

"Come in out of the cold. You want something hot to drink? I could make us some tea."

Elam brushed the snowflakes off his sleeves. "No, thanks. Like I said on the phone, I'll just be here a few minutes. I wanted to wait till Montana was asleep."

"Well, he's out like a light. *Loves* his new room. I just can't thank you and Mom enough for letting us live here."

"It's the least we could do, honey." He kissed her cheek, then laid his coat on the back of a chair.

"Sit down and tell me what's on your mind. You seemed a bit subdued earlier when you and Mom were here for dinner."

Elam sat on the couch in front of the fire. "By the way, your fried chicken was as good as your mother's. I was impressed."

"That's because she gave me a blow-by-blow over the phone on how to make it."

He reached over and put his hand on hers. "It's nice seeing you happy."

"Thanks. For the first time in ages, I actually feel almost normal. So what'd you come to talk to me about?"

"Flint asked me to meet him at Jewel's this afternoon. Seems he's feeling awkward that we've been avoiding each other since you went to jail. I think he'd like things to be the way they used to be."

"I'm glad. You two were good friends."

"*Were* is about right."

"Dad, you're not still holding a grudge because he interrogated me without a lawyer present?"

He shrugged. "Maybe."

"I could've asked for one. I just didn't. But I never revealed anything during that interrogation that incriminated me. My confession later was completely voluntary."

"That's beside the point. Flint knew you could hang yourself at any moment and should never have left his friend's daughter that vulnerable."

"But I wasn't his friend's daughter at that point. I was a suspect...and I did know something. It's not as though he just had it in for me."

Elam played with his fingers. "It's not like I *enjoy* feeling this way. I know I should forgive him and put it behind me, but I'm not ready to do that."

"Well, at least he's made an overture. Maybe it's going to take time to let it go."

"I'm not sure I want to let it go."

Ivy studied her father's profile and, for the first time, noticed how pronounced the lines around his eyes were. "Dad, why did you come over here to tell me this? You could've told me on the phone."

Elam turned and looked at her, a strange emptiness in his eyes. "I think I just needed to eyeball someone and admit that I'm struggling with it. Your mom has put it behind her and gets annoyed with me when I bring it up."

"Have you talked to Pastor Myers?"

"No. I've pretty much shut it all up inside. I know my attitude's wrong, but I don't know how to stop feeling this way."

Ivy hugged the couch pillow to her chest. "So how did you leave the conversation with Flint?"

"He said the ball was in my court. That he'd be there if and when I'm ready to put it behind us. I think I mumbled something about not holding his breath, and then he left."

"Was he mad?"

Elam shook his head, his eyes fixed on the flames in the fireplace. "No, he seemed sad. Thing is, I don't even care. How's that for cold?"

# 4

THE FOLLOWING TUESDAY, Brandon Jones finished reading the *Tri-County Courier* and laid it on the table in the guest registration area. He walked down the hall and into the administrative offices of Three Peaks Christian Camp and Conference Center, then flopped in a chair next to Kelsey's desk and waited for her to stop typing.

"What are *you* grinning about?" she said.

"Ivy's doing an amazing job. She's only been at it since yesterday, and you'd think she'd been working registration for years. I'm thrilled to be out from under, but I'm even happier for her. Really, she's much better at this than any of us expected."

Kelsey swiveled her chair and faced him. "I really want this to work out for her. She seems so proud to finally be a part of something."

"I think it's a slam dunk. By the way, Elam had a brainstorm. There's this organization in Denver called My Brother's Keeper that finds jobs for recovering substance abusers who are new Christians. He asked Jake to contact them and hire a couple guys to work through the winter months to get the cabins refurbished."

"What a neat idea."

"Yeah, I thought so too. They'll be here the Monday after Thanksgiving."

"I wonder where Jake plans to put them? The lodge is booked with that women's retreat."

"We'll figure out something. But I have something more exciting than that to discuss with you."

"Really? What?"

"How would you like to fly back to Raleigh and celebrate our first anniversary at that charming lake house where we spent our honeymoon, and then drive down to Seaport and spend Thanksgiving with my family?"

Kelsey's eyes seemed to search his. "You're serious."

"Of course I'm serious."

"Jake's not going to let us both take off with such short notice."

"Well, guess what? I've already cleared it with him *and* reserved the lake house—assuming, of course, you're interested. I can always cancel."

"Don't you dare!" Kelsey got up and sat in his lap, her arms wrapped around his neck. "What a wonderful surprise! I'm ecstatic!"

Brandon relished her excitement for a few moments. "Jake told us to take off the entire week of Thanksgiving. We leave this Saturday and don't have to be back at work for *ten* days!"

"This is so unexpected. I never even considered you could get time off with Ivy still in training."

"Jake's going to arrange for someone else to work with her, but next week will be dead around here anyway." Brandon pulled Kelsey a little closer. "I'm thrilled I got the lake house. And I'm also jazzed about spending Thanksgiving in Seaport."

"Me too. I can hardly wait to see Ellen and Guy! I want to see everything: the People's Clinic, Gordy's Crab Shack, Weezie's house, the cave where you and Cade rode out the hurricane, and—"

"We'll have time to see it all, honey. And I can hardly wait to stroll barefoot on that white sandy beach. You can pack your bathing suit and leave your snow boots in the closet."

Late that afternoon, Ivy stood behind the registration desk and checked in two ladies who had arrived for a three-day writers conference.

"You're all set. Here's your group's schedule of events and a room key for each of you." Ivy set a map of the facility on the counter and explained the layout of the grounds and the location of the meeting rooms and dining hall. "Can I answer any questions for you?"

"I think you've about covered it," the older woman said.

"Feel free to call the front desk if you have questions later. You ladies enjoy your stay."

Ivy watched as the women left and wondered if their smiles would have been as friendly had they known she'd just gotten out of jail. She turned to Brandon. "I'm really enjoying this."

"I can tell. Everyone on staff is proud that you're picking this up so quickly. Of course, you haven't lived till you've had the experience of checking a large group in or out. It can get pretty crazy. But I doubt it's really any worse than the café was when you had a big crowd."

"You just have to greet the person in front of you and not worry about anyone else for that moment. By the way, Kelsey told me about your anniversary plans."

Brandon smiled with his eyes. "Should be great. Plus we're excited about seeing my family. I hear yours is getting together for a big Thanksgiving dinner."

"Yeah, my brother, Rusty, and his family are driving in for the long weekend. Mom's in her element, I can tell you that."

"I think it's wonderful you'll all be together again."

"It really is, but it seems a bit surreal. I mean, I haven't seen my brother in ten years. And I've never met his wife and daughters."

"All the more reason to be excited."

Ivy reached up and put her hand on the back of her neck. "Truthfully, I'm a little nervous. Keep in mind that while my brother graduated from college magna cum laude and then got his veterinary degree, I was shooting up and can hardly remember a thing. And most of what

I can remember, I wish I couldn't. It's not like we have a whole lot in common."

"He's your brother. Can't have any more in common than that."

"I guess. After I shamed the family, somehow I don't see him receiving me with open arms."

"Just be yourself. You and Rusty were close growing up. You just need time to reconnect."

"I hope you're right. I'm sure not expecting to pick up where we left off." Ivy sighed. "But I'd give anything if Rusty and Montana would hit it off."

"How could they not? Montana's a great kid. I'm jealous. I'd love to be his uncle."

Ivy smiled without meaning to. "For all practical purposes, you are. You've been such a positive role model. He looks up to you."

"Thanks. Maybe he and his uncle Rusty can do some guy things together. I would think that since Rusty's surrounded by two little girls and a wife, he would welcome a little male recreation."

The door opened, and a great-looking guy in a handsome leather jacket headed to the registration desk.

"My name's Luke Draper. I've reserved one of the chalets."

Ivy pulled up his reservation on the computer screen. "I'm showing an open checkout date. Is that correct, Mr. Draper?"

"Luke. And yes, it is." His smile revealed a set of perfect teeth. "I'm looking forward to soaking in the quiet and beauty of the area."

"Well, you came to the right place," Ivy said. "It's our off-season at the camp, and it's pretty quiet around here unless you're attending a conference. But there's plenty to do in the area if you want to stay busy. This is a popular cross-country skiing destination. The snowmobiling is wonderful. We have terrific ski slopes within easy driving distance. Plus the narrow-gauge train from Durango to Silverton runs all year long."

"Thanks, but I'm not much into *doing* at the moment. I came here to get some work done. And I'll probably spend my downtime communing with nature and getting to know the area through the lens of my camera."

"Okay, Mr. Draper…Luke. Let me show you on the map where your chalet is located."


Jewel refilled the sheriff's coffee and noticed the snow was coming down so slowly that the giant flakes appeared to be suspended in midair.

"I love it when it does that," she said.

Flint took a sip of coffee. "It's pretty, all right. But I'm a summer kind of guy. Not really looking forward to more snow."

Jewel laughed. "Then you're living in the wrong place, my friend. Can I get you anything else?"

"No, thanks. Why don't you take a break while there's no one else to wait on?"

Jewel went over to the cash register and watched the sheriff move a spoon back and forth in his black coffee for several minutes. "Flint, it's none of my business, and you don't have to answer if you don't want to, but what's going on with you and Elam? It's obvious something's wrong."

He pursed his lips and then lifted his droopy eyes. "It's a long story and not something I want to get into. We've got some differences I'd like to put behind us, and he's not ready to do that. And may never be."

Jewel came over and stood by the table. "Are you sure? You two have been friends an awful long time."

"I gave it my best shot. Wasn't good enough."

"You don't know that. Maybe something you said will keep working on him. I've known Elam since he was a kid, and it's not like him to be so bitter."

"Who said anything about him being bitter?"

Jewel felt her face get hot and knew she was blushing. "Okay, I overheard most of what you guys said, not that I was trying to eavesdrop. Oh, who am I kidding? Of course I was. But I won't say anything. You know that."

"What it boils down to is that I chose to interrogate Ivy without legal counsel while she was willing to talk. No attorney worth his salt would've let her open her mouth, and she was my only lead. I did what I had to."

"I know that. But so does Elam. Give him time."

"It's been six months. The longer it goes, the harder it is to know what to say."

"Have you talked to Ivy?"

Flint shook his head. "No, but our boys are best friends. I'm sure I'll be running into her, either at our house or hers."

"I didn't get the impression she blames anybody for anything. She accepts full responsibility for her part in covering up Joe's murder."

"Well, as long as Elam chooses to blame me for taking advantage of her, we'll never be friends again."

The door opened, and a good-looking young man in a black leather jacket stepped inside. "You open for business, ma'am?"

"I sure am. Why don't you sit wherever you'd like, and I'll get you a menu. You staying over at the Phantom Hollow Lodge?"

"No, I checked in at Three Peaks for some much-needed R and R, and the thought of sharing the dining hall with all those conference attendees was a little overwhelming." He smiled. "My name's Luke Draper."

"Jewel Sadler. Nice to make your acquaintance."

Jewel went over and picked up a menu and glass of water and stopped at Flint's table. "Don't give up on Elam. I'm going to make it a prayer concern of mine that you two work things out."

"I appreciate that. But like Elam said, don't hold your breath."

Jewel walked over to her new customer, set the glass on the table, and handed him the menu. "There you go, Luke. If you're interested in tonight's meat-loaf special with cheesy mashed potatoes and home-style green beans, it should be ready in about forty minutes. Includes a dinner salad, homemade rolls, and bread pudding. But I can get you anything else on the menu right now."

"Actually, the meat-loaf dinner sounds excellent. Maybe you could bring me an order of fries and a cup of black coffee. I'll just read my newspaper till dinner's ready." There was that winning smile again.

"Coming right up." Jewel walked past Flint and winked. She wondered if Ivy knew this fine specimen of a man was staying at the camp.

# 5

ON THE AFTERNOON before Thanksgiving, Ivy stood at her computer behind the registration desk and felt a blast of cold air as the main door of the lodge opened and closed.

"Hey, girlfriend," Suzanne Compton said. "I'm here to relieve you. Sorry I'm late. My pies took a little longer to get done than usual. You probably thought we all left you high and dry."

"I knew someone would be here. But I'm not in a huge hurry to leave. Montana's at Mom and Dad's, and my brother hasn't arrived yet. I thought you and Jake were going to your in-laws' for Thanksgiving."

"We are. But we're not driving up there till tomorrow morning."

Ivy lifted the hinged section of counter and let Suzanne in, and then walked through to the other side. "You sure you're okay by yourself?"

"What's there to do? I think we have all of three guests until Monday." Suzanne smiled, a twinkle in her eye. "I heard about the hunk with the open checkout date—who *wasn't* wearing a wedding ring."

"Don't even go there. A classy-looking guy like that would never be interested in someone with my history."

Suzanne's expression was playful. "Be open-minded. You never know what God may have in store for you."

"Just don't try to help Him along, okay? Have you heard from Brandon and Kelsey?"

"Funny you should ask. Brandon called Jake this afternoon to wish us all a happy Thanksgiving. Sounded like he and Kelsey had a very special anniversary and are looking forward to a big family gathering tomorrow. And so are you. Scoot. Have a wonderful weekend."

"Thanks. You and Jake do the same."

Ivy pushed open the heavy wooden door and stood under the overhang, looking out at the snowcapped peaks and the western sky streaked with orangey pink. She went over to where the Jeep was parked and slid in the front seat, torn between the excitement of being reunited with her brother and the fear of his disapproval. She didn't expect their relationship ever to be the same. Too much time had been lost. But could she win his affection? Would he be able to see her as his little sister and forgive the past mistakes she so desperately wanted to put behind her?

Ivy turned into the long, steep driveway that led up to her parents' log home at the base of the snow-covered foothills about two hundred yards from the entrance to Three Peaks.

As she got closer, she spotted a vehicle parked in the circle drive in front of the house. Her brother's Lincoln Navigator. Her pulse began to race.

She pulled up behind Rusty's car and turned off the motor just as Montana ran down the front steps and over to her driver's side window.

"They look just like that picture on the frigerator!" he said.

"Have they been here long?"

"Not very. Grandma's making apple cider, and after dinner, we get to eat the pumpkin cookies I made."

Her son's wide eyes sent joy through her. He had never experienced a big family gathering like this one. "Are the girls as adorable as Grandma said?"

"I guess so." Montana rolled his eyes. "They want me to go everywhere with them. I've been holding them on top of Sasha for doggyback rides."

"That sweet pooch is such a good sport."

"I think Uncle Rusty doesn't trust Sasha yet because he made us stop."

"Well, let me get out of here and go see everybody."

Ivy grabbed two pink and white polka dot gift bags off the seat. She opened the door and let Montana lead her by the hand up the steps to the front door, where her dad stood waiting with two little girls.

Ivy squatted in front of her nieces and felt an unexpected surge of emotion. "You must be Tia," she said to the taller one. "And you're Josie. You're even more beautiful than your pictures."

Tia held up four fingers. "I'm this many. But Josie's only three."

"I know. I'm your aunt Ivy. And I've been waiting a very long time to meet you. I brought you a surprise." Ivy handed each of the girls a gift bag. "Go ahead. You can open them."

Tia quickly removed the tissue paper and reached inside and pulled out a pink purse with an image of Snow White on the front. Her indigo eyes danced with excitement, and she clutched it to her chest.

Josie smiled shyly and took out an identical purse and slipped the slim strap over her shoulder.

"Can you tell Aunt Ivy thank you?" Elam said.

"Thank you," they said simultaneously, their singsongy voices suggesting they had been schooled in the art of politeness.

Ivy stood and put her lips to her father's ear. "My heart's about to pound out of my chest. Where is everybody?"

"Out in the kitchen." He tilted her chin and held her gaze. "Be yourself, honey. They're just family."

Ivy followed her dad into the kitchen and spotted her brother sitting at the table next to a dark-haired beauty with stunning blue eyes. She inched toward them, feeling as if her shoes were made of cement, unable to recall a single word of the salutation she had rehearsed over and over in her mind.

"I...I can't believe you're really here," she heard herself say. "I mean, that we're both here. Together. You haven't even changed that much. Well, other than you're grown-up. We both are." Ivy blew her bangs off her forehead. "I can't believe I'm chattering like a parrot. It's just so wonderful to see you."

Rusty stood and gave her a cold hug. "Nice you could make it."

*Nice I could* make *it?* She looked up at him, trying to discern what he meant and willed away the disappointment that tightened her throat. She didn't know what she had expected him to say. But that wasn't it. "I've missed you so much," she finally said.

Rusty's face remained expressionless. "I gave up on that emotion a long time ago. But it's good to see you."

"It's nice to finally meet you, Ivy." Jacqueline extended her hand.

"Thanks. Same here. Your daughters are gorgeous."

"They are, aren't they?" Rusty said. "Just like their mother." He slipped his arm around Jacqueline and pulled her closer.

"Well, there is *someone* who looks just like you." Ivy winked at Montana, who was beaming.

Rusty didn't say anything or respond in any way, and the kitchen was suddenly pin-drop still.

"Who wants apple cider?" Carolyn asked, louder than she needed to.

"I do!" Montana hurried over to her. "I'll carry it over to the table for Tia and Josie because I'm bigger."

Rusty glanced at his watch. "Actually, I think we'll pass. The sugar might spoil the girls' appetites this close to dinner."


Ivy lingered over dinner with her family around the dining-room table and listened to Rusty describe the good and the bad of his veterinary practice. She was trying not to get paranoid about the way he seemed to distance himself from Montana.

"My love for animals started right here," Rusty said. "We had such great animals growing up. I still remember the names of all the horses. My favorite was Lightning. And the cats…we must've had a hundred. Ziggy's the one that used to curl up at my feet at night."

"And don't forget Zeke," Elam said. "You hardly went anywhere without that ol' dog."

"My mom told me all about Zeke." Montana set his glass on the table, a milk mustache framing his mouth. "He was a cyber husky like Sasha."

Ivy smiled. "*Siberian* husky, sweetie. And boy, did he love Rusty! The rest of us were chopped liver."

"I've done my best to forget about Zeke." Rusty shot Ivy a piercing glance. "He'd been there all my life, and then suddenly he was gone. I grieved so hard I thought I'd die, till my feelings finally went numb. Now I don't think about him *at all*. Frankly, it's a huge relief."

Ivy studied Rusty's blank expression. Had losing Zeke been *that* traumatic? Then, almost like a sock in the stomach, it hit her. Her brother wasn't talking about Zeke. He was talking about her.

Montana wiped his mouth and folded his napkin next to his plate. "So is the reason you didn't want Tia and Josie riding on Sasha because she reminds you of Zeke, and you don't wanna get sad again?"

Rusty kept his eyes fixed on his empty plate. "That had nothing to do with Zeke. I just didn't want the girls to get hurt."

"I'm really strong, Uncle Rusty. I wasn't gonna let them fall."

Rusty lifted his eyes and finally looked directly at Montana, his stony expression tearing Ivy's heart as if he'd lashed her with a bullwhip. "I hear what you're saying, but I don't really know you—"

"*Yet,*" Ivy quickly added. "Montana's very responsible with little kids. And he's been so excited to finally meet his cousins. I think if you watch how gentle he is with them, you'll see there's nothing to worry about."

Carolyn pushed back her chair. "Why don't I serve up the cherry cobbler?"

"I'll help," Ivy said. "Montana, would you bring the dirty plates over to the sink?"

Montana collected the plates, and Ivy noticed that her brother seemed to avoid looking at him. She went over and stood beside her mother and said barely above a whisper, "Why is Rusty acting so hateful? Can't he see how hard Montana's trying to win his affection?"

"He's just tired," Carolyn said. "It was a long drive from Albuquerque. He'll be himself in the morning."


Ivy laid the book Montana had read to her on the nightstand. She listened while he said his prayers, then tucked the covers around him and kissed his cheek. "Good night, sweetie."

"Mom...why is Uncle Rusty mad? Did I do something wrong?"

"Absolutely not. You were a perfect gentleman, and I was very proud of you. I think he's just exhausted because he drove a long way to get here."

"He's not fun like I thought."

"Well, you don't really know him yet. He and I used to have a lot of fun when we were growing up."

"Yeah, like riding horses...and playing in that freezing cold waterfall...and always beating him to the bottom of that humongous hill on your sled."

Ivy smiled. "*Almost* always."

"Uncle Rusty acts like Grandpa did when we first moved here. He mostly pretends I'm not there."

"Oh, sweetie, I'm sure it's not on purpose."

All of a sudden Montana's puppy eyes turned to dark pools. "He wasn't scared Tia and Josie would fall off Sasha's back, because I was holding on really, really tight. He just didn't want them to play with me."

Ivy's heart sank. "I'm sure that's not it."

"Yes, it is. He said they could have apple cider and then said they couldn't when I asked Grandma if I could carry their cups to the table." A tear trickled down his cheek. "He doesn't like me."

"That's not true. You're so lovable there's no way he could not like you. He was just grouchy because he's tired."

"You think he would let me pull the girls in my wagon? They can't fall out."

"We'll see. But I want you to be your polite self, no matter how Uncle Rusty acts. Remember he and I haven't seen each other in a very long time, and he might still be angry with me for the bad choices I made when I was doing drugs."

"I used to be angry too. But I'm not anymore."

Ivy brushed the hair off his forehead. "I know. And I'm so glad. I love you."

"I love you too." Montana sat up and hugged her tightly and then lay back down. "Good night, Mommy."

"Sweet dreams." Ivy turned off the lamp, thinking he hadn't called her Mommy since his last birthday when he announced it sounded too babyish.

She climbed down the ladder from the loft and flopped on the couch, the old guilt and condemnation lurking just beneath the surface, and wondered if it were even *possible* to let go of the past.

She grabbed a couch pillow and hugged it to her chest, determined to figure out a way to protect Montana from Rusty's misdirected anger.

The phone rang and she jumped, her hand over her heart, and quickly picked it up. "Hello."

"It's Dad. You okay? I could tell you were ready to cry when you left."

"I'm all right," she said, just above a whisper. "I expected Rusty to act weird with me, but I was totally unprepared for his cruelty toward Montana. The poor kid was so excited to meet his cousins and did everything he could to make a good first impression. It's like Rusty went out of his way to make him feel like he didn't belong."

"Your mom tried to tell you it might take Rusty a while to warm up."

"I know. But he hurt Montana's feelings, and that's where I get my hackles up. If Rusty's got issues with me, fine. I deserve it. But don't pick on an innocent seven-year-old who wants a family so bad he can taste it…" Her voice failed, and she choked back the emotion.

"Honey, don't cry. I had a heart-to-heart with Rusty and told him how he came across and that I didn't appreciate his attitude. Things'll be better tomorrow after we've all had a good night's sleep. Your mother's laying out a spread you won't believe, and that'll set a festive tone. It's going to be a great Thanksgiving."

"I hope so." Ivy wiped the tears off her cheeks. "But that sweet little boy doesn't deserve to be rejected because of my mistakes. I'm not going to sit by silently and let Rusty hurt him again."

# 6

IVY AWOKE TO DAYLIGHT filtering in through the transom window
and the sound of cartoons echoing from the TV in the living room. She
glanced over at the clock and saw that it was only seven thirty.

She pulled the comforter up around her neck and nestled in the
warmth of her bed, wishing she could spend a quiet Thanksgiving at
home with Montana and avoid the risk of getting trapped at her parents'
house if her brother chose to be difficult again. How she hated feeling this
way! Especially after missing so many holidays and family gatherings
when she was either high or consumed with getting the next fix—days,
weeks, months, and years that added up to an entire decade she could
scarcely remember.

She turned her gaze on the framed photograph that graced her
nightstand and studied the faces of the two precious gifts that were salvaged from those locust years: her son, whom she hadn't been able to
bring herself to abort, yet hardly knew existed the first four years of his
life. And an angel named Lu Ramirez. There was no doubt in Ivy's
mind that had it not been for Lu's removing Montana from the squalor
and caring for him under her own roof, he would probably have died
of neglect.

She blinked the stinging from her eyes, sad that all her memories of him were sketchy until after she was released from rehab the last time. But by then, Lu had begun to mold Montana into the caring, sensitive, thoughtful little boy Ivy had come to treasure more than anything in this world.

Her bedroom door slowly opened, and her son appeared in the doorway, dressed in Spider-Man p.j.'s., his thick auburn hair falling into bangs just above his eyebrows, freckles sprinkled on his cheeks. For a split second she was transported back to her childhood, and Rusty had come to wake her so they could watch their Saturday-morning TV programs.

"Mom?" he whispered.

"I'm awake, sweetie. Come in."

Montana climbed in the bed and curled up under the covers next to her. "I have an idea for a surprise. But I need to know if it's okay."

"All right. Tell me what you're thinking."

"I wanna bring you breakfast in bed—as my Happy Thanksgiving present."

Ivy smiled. "And what'd you have in mind?"

"Well, I'm good at making English muffins and jelly. And I figured out how I wanna bring it. So can I?"

"Sure."

Montana threw back the covers and raced out of the bedroom.

Ivy heard him opening and closing drawers in the kitchen and then inhaled the wonderful aroma of bread toasting. She sat up and propped the pillows behind her, thinking this was a perfect way to start a day of thanksgiving.

*Lord, I love this child so much. Thank You for the way You protected him all the years I couldn't. Thank You for Lu, and all she meant to us. I'm happy she's rejoicing in Your presence. Tell her I miss her.*

*Help me to be the mother Montana needs, and teach him to trust You to be the Father he needs. And help us both to find all kinds of ways to be grateful today.*

A couple of minutes later, Montana came through the door, ever so slowly, carrying a shiny new baking sheet with both hands. "Here's your Happy Thanksgiving surprise, Mom!"

Wearing the proudest grin she had ever seen, he set the baking sheet on her lap.

"How beautiful, sweetie! Let's see what I've got here...a buttered English muffin with grape jelly. Orange juice. A sliced banana. And a cherry Pop-Tart. Perfect!"

He crawled up on the other side of the bed. "I'm glad you like my surprise."

"Mmm...I love your surprise. Not only was it thoughtful, it tastes really good."

Montana folded his arms across his chest and gave a firm nod. "Thanks. Grandma taught me how to cook."

Ivy put the plastic cup of orange juice to her lips to cover her smile and tried to look sufficiently serious. "She sure did."

"But I didn't make coffee. I'm not supposed to do that."

"Oh, I can make some later. This is great without it."

Montana beamed. "What time are we going to Grandma and Grandpa's?"

"We're supposed to be there around eleven. Did you taste my heavenly hash? I finished it last night."

"Uh-huh. It tastes yummy. I'm making something for everyone too."

"You are?"

"Yeah, I'm almost done. I made turkeys by tracing my hand, like we did at school. I just need you to help me spell the names so I can put the right one on each picture."

"How nice of you to think of everybody."

"I made Uncle Rusty's very carefully, and I didn't color outside the lines, not even a little bit."

Ivy's heart sank. "Sweetie, it's very nice that you drew turkeys for everyone. But please don't feel like you have to make Uncle Rusty's better than everyone else's."

"Maybe if he sees how good I did, he'll like me."

Ivy turned and brushed Montana's hair with her fingers. "Uncle Rusty will like you just the way you are. You don't have to be perfect."

"Well, I'm still giving him the very bestest one."

Jewel wiped her hands on her apron, delighted to see the café was nearly filled to capacity, and glad she'd had the foresight to schedule in two waitresses to help handle the Thanksgiving rush.

The door opened. Luke Draper came inside, and the door closed behind him. He looked around, then waved at someone.

Jewel hurried over to him, a menu in her hand. "There you are. I wondered if you'd be coming in. I know Three Peaks doesn't serve Thanksgiving dinner."

"Actually, I heard the best turkey and dressing in town is right here."

Luke flashed a smile worthy of a toothpaste ad, and she wondered if he'd been using those fancy whitening strips she'd seen advertised.

"I don't know about *best*," she said, "but most everyone is asking for seconds."

Luke placed his hands on his lean middle. "Well, I'm starved. And turkey and dressing is one of my favorite meals. I assume you've got some pumpkin pie to go with it?"

"Heavens, yes." Jewel waved her hand. "And pecan, cherry, lemon meringue, sweet potato, and Dutch apple—all homemade. The all-you-can-eat turkey dinner is ten ninety-five, and that includes dessert. I've got a table available over there by the window."

"Thanks, but Deke and Roscoe invited me to join them," Luke said. "We met down at the hardware store, where they were telling tales around that old potbelly stove. What colorful characters."

Jewel laughed. "You got that right. I'll be right back with your dinner. They're sitting there by the moose head."

The door opened again, and Jewel saw Lieutenant Bobby Knolls come in. She raised her hand to get his attention. "Be right there. You wanted four pies: two pumpkin and two pecan, right?"

Bobby blew a pink bubble and sucked the gum back into his mouth. "Yes ma'am."

Jewel went into the back room and got the four boxes of pies she had charged out earlier and slid them on the counter with a paid ticket, then turned to one of the waitresses. "Rita, would you take this out to Lieutenant Knolls for me? It's already paid."

Jewel filled a plate and added an extra scoop of dressing and took it out to Luke and set it in front of him. "There you go. Let me know when you're ready for seconds." She noticed that Deke and Roscoe were still working on the dinner they had split. "You guys need anything else?"

"I'd sure like a little more of them candied yams," Deke said.

"Say what?" Roscoe put his hand to his ear.

"I'm gittin' more yams. Want some?"

Roscoe shook his head. "Nah, this is good home cookin'. But I'm savin' room for punkin pie."

Jewel smiled and turned to Luke. "By the way, I've been meaning to ask you if you've met Ivy Griffith out at Three Peaks?"

"A little sandy blonde with intriguing eyes?"

Jewel nodded. "That's the one. She used to work for me."

"Really?"

"And she's single, in case you were wondering."

The corners of Luke's mouth twitched. "You don't say?"

"Well, I just thought that a young man such as yourself with all that time to kill might be looking for a nice young lady to spend some time with. Ivy's a real sweetheart."

Ivy sat in front of the fire in her parents' living room and took the last bite of pumpkin pie on her plate, relieved that the day had been relatively pleasant, even if it didn't live up to the warm, intimate gatherings she remembered from years ago.

"Mom, everything was delicious—*better* than delicious." Rusty stood behind his mother and massaged her shoulders. "I won't need to eat again for a week."

"I'm glad you enjoyed it," Carolyn said. "But something tells me that you'll be out in the kitchen picking through the leftovers before the sun goes down."

"I will." Montana pointed to himself with his thumb. "Mom said I could have *two* pieces of pumpkin pie, and I only ate one."

"Thanks again for the picture," Elam said. "That's the finest looking turkey anyone's ever drawn for me."

Carolyn nodded. "Really special, sweetie. Thank you."

Montana's foot jiggled nervously. "I really *really* worked hard. And I didn't even color outside the lines on Uncle Rusty's."

Ivy locked gazes with her brother. "You can't imagine how excited he was to give it to you."

"Really?" Rusty said. "I got sidetracked and forgot to look at it. I think it's on the window seat in the kitchen."

Montana jumped up. "I'll go get it so you can see how good I did."

Ivy waited until Montana was out of earshot and then said, "He's trying so hard to please you. He's never had an uncle before."

"That's not my fault," Rusty said flatly. "I'm not the one who left."

Ivy hated that she was blushing and was relieved when Tia ran into the living room.

"Daddy, would you help us get our babies out of the closet? Me and Josie put them in there for a nap, and the door won't let us back in."

"Sure, angel." Rusty scooped Tia into his arms. "Daddy knows a trick that will get that stubborn door to open. I had the same problem with it when *I* was your age."

"You did?"

"Yes, but not for long." Rusty put his lips to her neck and blew till she giggled. "Come on, let's go rescue your babies."

Ivy heard them reach the top of the stairs just as Montana came back in the living room.

"Where's Uncle Rusty?"

"He'll be back in a minute. The girls locked their dolls in the closet."

"That door always gets stuck. Grandpa showed me how to get it open. Want me to go tell Uncle Rusty?"

"That's nice of you, sweetie, but he knows how to do it."

Montana crawled up on the couch and nestled next to Ivy and seemed to be studying his picture. "I hope he likes this. I've never done a picture this good before."

"I think your turkeys are clever," Carolyn said. "I put mine on the refrigerator."

A grin spread slowly across Montana's face. "You're running out of room, Grandma. You save all my pictures."

Ivy heard playful, growling noises coming from the upstairs bedroom, and the girls squealing and giggling. Her heart ached for Montana, who sat quietly beside her and held his prized picture on his lap.


An hour later, Ivy saw Rusty sitting by himself on the front steps. She zipped her ski jacket and went outside and flopped down next to him. "We need to talk."

"About what?"

"About my son's feelings, for starters. Montana could hardly wait to give you the picture he'd made. And when he realized you hadn't even looked at it, he went after it and waited for you to come back downstairs. And then all he got from you was a dismissive comment. I realize it's just a drawing, but would it have killed you to show interest in something he worked so hard on?"

Rusty exhaled, his breath turning to vapor in the early evening chill. "I don't know what you want from me. You waited until the kid was seven years old to tell us he even existed—and now you expect me to be his instant uncle. It doesn't work that way."

"All I'm asking is that you treat him with the same kindness I've shown your girls."

"I never asked you to buy them presents or take on the role of *Auntie Ivy.* That was your doing."

"Would you rather I say and do things that hurt their feelings and leave them feeling as if they mean nothing at all to me? Because that's exactly what you're doing to Montana."

Rusty looked out toward the mountains that were silhouetted against a flaming western sky and said nothing.

"No matter how angry you are with me for my mistakes, it's not right to make Montana feel as if he's not a valued member of this family. He's a sweet, sensitive little boy who would love nothing more than to win the affection of his uncle Rusty. Can't you see that?"

"Well, excuse me for not wanting to be 'uncle on demand'! If you were so concerned about him, why did you let him go all that time without knowing his family? The only reason you came back here was to sponge off Mom and Dad because you knew you couldn't support yourself when your friend Lu died."

"That's not fair, and you know it!" Ivy paused and lowered her voice. "I needed to face my past and make things right, and I had to come back to Jacob's Ear to do that. I knew if I told the truth about Joe Hadley's death and my part of the cover-up I'd be going to jail. I needed Mom and Dad to make sure Montana would be okay."

"You've been a drain on them for the past ten years, and you're still taking. When are you going to start giving back?"

Ivy blinked to clear her eyes but felt the tears spilling down her cheeks. "I'm trying, Rusty. I've been out of jail less than a month. I'm working full-time at Three Peaks. It's going to take time."

"Why don't you get Montana's father to help with his support instead of expecting Mom and Dad to give you a car and a place to live?"

"I don't know where he is."

Rusty rolled his eyes. "Do you even know who he is?"

"Montana's *my* flesh and blood, and his part in this family has nothing to do with who fathered him!"

Rusty got up and started to go back inside. "I promised myself I wouldn't get into this conversation with you."

Ivy jumped up and grabbed him by the arm. "Well, as long as we're in it, why don't we clear the air?"

Rusty spun around, his eyes turning to slits. "Okay, you want me to level with you? I stopped feeling anything for you a long time ago! I've had all the hurt I can take where you're concerned. Mom and Dad have spent more money trying to get you straightened out than they did putting me through college. And what do you have to show for it? You've got a criminal record, an illegitimate son, and absolutely no direction for your life. I can only imagine what kind of emotional baggage your son is carrying around, and I'm uncomfortable leaving him alone with Tia and Josie. There, I said it!"

"You don't have to yell. I know I made all kinds of bad decisions, but Montana is the best thing that's ever happened to me. Lu was like a mother to him when I was doing drugs. He's been loved and nurtured, and he's exceptionally thoughtful and caring. If you'd open your eyes, you'd see that. Mom and Dad adore him."

"That's their choice. But I refuse to feel like the bad guy because I don't want to deal with your baggage."

*How dare you refer to my son as* baggage! Ivy took a slow, deep breath and let it out. *Lord, don't let me say something I'll regret.* "Rusty, I've never stopped loving you and can't tell you how many times over the years I wanted to call. I hope someday you'll let me share my story. I never meant to hurt anyone. But for now, can we at least agree to treat each other's children the way we would want our own to be treated?"

Rusty's gaze seemed to ice over. "I'll be polite to the kid, but I'm not going to open myself up for another disappointment. After everything you exposed Montana to, he's bound to start acting out. I'm not going to get burned twice, and I don't want my girls getting close to him either."

The door opened, and their father came out and stood on the porch. "We can hear you two arguing clear out in the kitchen."

"We're just getting *real* for a change," Rusty said.

Elam's eyebrows formed a dark, bushy line. "Ivy, why don't you go help your mother put some leftovers in containers for you and Montana to take home? I'd like to get *real* with your brother about a few things."

# 7

Ivy tucked Montana into bed, then climbed down the ladder and lay on the couch in front of the fire, trying not to feel guilty for enjoying her new surroundings, in spite of her brother's complaint that she was always taking from her parents and never giving back.

At least the day hadn't been a total loss. Her mother's Thanksgiving meal was delicious, and the conversation around the table was light. Montana was chatty all day and didn't seem to notice Rusty's indifference until after the incident with the drawing.

*I can only imagine what kind of emotional baggage your son is carrying around, and I'm uncomfortable leaving him alone with Tia and Josie.*

The implication of Rusty's words had cut even more deeply than she had let on. Why couldn't he see that his nephew was just a sweet little boy who desperately wanted his uncle's affection—not some dysfunctional time bomb waiting to explode?

Ivy breathed in and blew it out. How could she expect Rusty to understand what a positive influence Lu and her parents had been on Montana?

She heard a gentle rap on the door and figured it was her dad coming by to tell her how his "getting real" with Rusty went.

She flipped on the porch light and opened the door. "Come in, Dad."

"Your brother's completely beyond reason," Elam said as he squeezed past her. "Too much pent-up anger."

Ivy followed him over to the couch and sat next to him.

"How much of our argument did you hear?"

"Enough. I heard Rusty say he was uncomfortable letting Montana around Tia and Josie. That ticked me off, and I set him straight. I also told him your mother and I love Montana the same way we love those girls, and he'd better get used to it."

"Could you tell what's bothering him the most?"

Elam tugged at his mustache. "I'm not even sure *he* knows. But the bitterness goes deep. I don't see this being resolved over the holiday weekend. Sorry, honey."

"It means everything to me that you defended Montana."

"Rusty was completely out of line. It was all I could do to keep my mouth shut when he blew off Montana's picture, but I didn't want the boy caught in the middle."

"Thanks for that. At least Montana wasn't in earshot when I confronted Rusty. He doesn't know anything about it."

"Did he have much to say about Rusty's reaction to his picture?"

"No, but I think it really hurt him. He so desperately wants male affirmation."

"Well, that's what *I'm* for."

Ivy put her hand on her dad's. "I know. And you're great with him. I just think he wants the same kind of response from Rusty. How's Mom handling it?"

"Oh, she's trying to keep the peace, same as always. But she put the drawing Montana gave Rusty on the refrigerator with the others. I guess it's her own way of making a statement."

"The last thing I want to do is cause a rift between you and Mom and Rusty."

"Well, your brother's calling the shots. Either he can start dealing with his anger or go pout by himself. I've done what I can. The ball's in his court."

"Dad, I'm disgusted with Rusty too. But this is a lot for him to deal with all at once. And statistically speaking, Montana *should* be messed up, so we can't really blame Rusty for being wary. He just hasn't been around Montana enough to realize that he's surprisingly well adjusted."

Elam shook his head. "That's no excuse for cruelty. I'm not going to sit back and watch him hurt my grandson. Or my daughter, for that matter."

"Did you tell Rusty that?"

"Yeah, among other things. It wouldn't surprise me if he packs everything up and heads back to Albuquerque tomorrow."

"Oh, Dad. I'm so sorry things escalated to this level."

Elam took her hand in his the way he used to when she was little. "Guess it depends on how you look at it. I think I stayed pretty calm, considering. I just told your brother that I'm not going to allow him to take out his unresolved anger on you or Montana, and that you're just as much a part of this family as he and Jacqueline and the girls are. He's going to have to make a choice whether he can accept that or not."


Jewel turned on the Closed sign and went over and sat at the table with Luke Draper, who had been lingering over coffee for the past two hours.

"You going to be able to sleep with all that caffeine in your system?" Jewel asked.

Luke half smiled, his hands wrapped around a jumbo mug. "Caffeine doesn't usually keep me awake. But it's not like I have to be up at the crack of dawn and hit the floor running."

"Sure was nice of your board of directors to give you time off."

"They didn't *give* me time, Jewel. I haven't taken a vacation in three years. They wanted me to recharge my batteries, and they insisted I take a working vacation and put the polish on my new business plan."

"You seem so young to be obsessed with work. How old *are* you?"

"Thirty-seven."

Jewel waved her hand. "You're just a kid. What is it you actually do?"

"I'm the CEO of Leland and Sorrels, a computer software firm in Denver. It's a fast-paced, high-pressure, eighty-hour-a-week job that pays great and keeps me challenged." Luke flashed that movie-star smile. "I'm not sure I even remember how to stop working and just relax."

Jewel leaned forward on her arms. "You really should get to know Ivy, what with you being here by yourself and all. She's a native and can show you all the places this area is famous for."

"I'm not into the touristy stuff. And I really don't enjoy skiing. I'd much prefer to take my camera and go hiking. But this is the wrong time of year for that."

"Not if you go by snowmobile. You can rent one at Three Peaks. In fact, ask Ivy to take you out. She knows that area like the back of her hand. It's a wonderful way to see natural beauty you'll never be able to spot from the road."

Luke took a sip of coffee. "I'll keep that in mind. But photography isn't the kind of thing I need a companion for."

Jewel smiled to herself. *In other words, mind my own business and stop with the matchmaking.*


Flint opened the refrigerator door, pulled out a platter of leftover turkey and a jar of mayonnaise, then walked over to the kitchen table. He opened the bread wrapper and took out a couple of slices, then wrapped it up again.

Why hadn't he been able to get in a holiday mood, even when he sat down to Betty's gorgeous Thanksgiving table and the scrumptious meal she had prepared? He had managed to be pleasant, say a respectable prayer, and carve the turkey. He had even gorged himself like everyone else around the table, then hooted and hollered during the Broncos football game that followed. But it felt as though he were only going through the motions.

"I knew you'd be into the leftovers before the night was over." Betty came over to where he was sitting and put her hand on his shoulder. "Got everything you need, or can I get you something else?"

"Wouldn't mind a small dish of dressing to go with my sandwich. And a glass of milk. Your dinner was fabulous, hon. You really outdid yourself."

"Thanks. Everyone seemed to enjoy it." Betty put a scoop of dressing in a small dish, then put it in the microwave and turned it on. "And I think our parents had a good time."

"Yeah, till the Broncos lost."

"They forgot all about it after I served the pumpkin pie. And did you see how much Ian ate? I had no idea a seven-year-old could hold that much." Betty was quiet for a few moments, and then set a glass of milk on the table and sat down in the chair next to Flint's. "You've tried so hard to be pleasant all day, but I can tell something's bothering you."

Flint cut his sandwich in two and placed it on a napkin. "I guess I'm still down about Elam's unwillingness to forgive me."

"You've been friends too long. He'll come around eventually. I wonder what kind of Thanksgiving he and Carolyn had with Ivy home for the first time in years?"

"I'm glad she's out of jail. That girl's not a criminal at heart. I feel bad she wouldn't strike a deal with the DA, though. Living with a criminal record won't be easy." Flint took a bite of his sandwich and savored it for a moment. "Have you thought about the political fallout of letting Ian spend time at Montana's house?"

"I suppose there are those who won't be comfortable with it. But those little guys are two peas in a pod, and I can't see severing their friendship because Ivy served time for something that happened clear back in high school. She's certainly a responsible parent. Montana's a sweetheart. It's obvious he's been well cared for."

"You realize this might not play very well when it comes time for me to run for reelection?" Flint wiped his mouth with a paper towel. "And Ian's liable to get his feelings hurt if someone smarts off about it."

"Well, if that happens, we'll just have to use it as an opportunity to teach him how unfair it is not to forgive people when they're working hard to change. But as far as the election goes, I'm willing to chance that you'll win based on your track record. After all, you did solve Joe Hadley's murder and also the class-reunion shooting. People won't forget that."

Ivy climbed up the ladder to the loft and tiptoed over to Montana's bed to check on him, surprised to hear him sniffling. She knelt down next to his bed and spoke softly. "Sweetie, what's wrong?"

Montana curled up in a fetal position and didn't answer.

"You know you can talk to me about anything."

There was a long stretch of silence, then Montana rolled on his back. "Why didn't my dad want me?"

Ivy combed her fingers through his hair. "We've already talked about this. It's not that he didn't want you. He couldn't take care of you, just like I couldn't when I was doing drugs."

"Why doesn't he ever come to see me now?"

Ivy held her son's gaze, wondering if there would ever be a right time to tell him. "I'm sure he doesn't know where we are. But if he knew you, he would love you."

"You always say that." Montana's tears trickled down the sides of his face and onto his pillow. "But Uncle Rusty doesn't."

"Uncle Rusty's still angry with Mommy about bad choices I made a long time ago. And that makes him not want to act interested in anything that's important to me."

"I gave him the very bestest picture I ever drew, and he didn't even say if he liked it."

"That was rude. Mommy and Grandpa talked to him about it."

Montana folded his arms across his chest and pursed his lips. "Oh, man. Now he'll be mad at me."

"He seems mad at everyone right now."

"Except Tia and Josie and Aunt Jackie."

"That's true. But aren't you glad? It would be really sad if he treated them the same way he's been treating the rest of us."

"Yeah, I guess so." Montana was quiet for a moment and seemed to be pondering something. "Can I have Ian over for a sleepover, since we don't have school right now?"

"Sure, if it's okay with his parents."

"His dad's the sheriff, and his name is Flint. Isn't that a cool name?"

"Yes, it is. It's great to have a name you don't hear all the time. That's why I named you Montana."

"Did my dad like that name?"

"He was gone by the time you were born, remember?"

"Oh yeah. What job did he have?"

"He never told me."

"Well, what was his name?"

"Would you stop asking all these questions and just go to sleep?"

Montana's eyes welled again, and she instantly regretted using an angry tone with him.

"Mommy didn't mean to snap at you. I'm just mad at myself for taking drugs and not being able to remember a lot of things."

"The drugs made you forget my dad's name?"

Ivy gazed into her son's questioning eyes until her vision became blurry and the tears began to spill down her cheeks.

Montana sat up and put his arms around her. "Don't cry, Mom. It's okay. I don't hafta know his name. I just think about him sometimes."

# 8

IVY SPENT THE NEXT day with her mother and Jacqueline, taking in all the after-Thanksgiving sales and trying not to let her discomfort at leaving Montana in the care of his grandfather and uncle weigh on her.

When they finally arrived back home, she spotted Montana riding his sled down the steep hill she and Rusty used to play on. Sasha was barking playfully and chasing him.

The front door opened, and her father came out on the porch to greet them, a toothy grin appearing just below his mustache. "So how much did it cost me for you girls to save me money today?"

"We saved you a small fortune at that new mall in Mt. Byron." Carolyn smiled at him with her eyes and started pulling sacks out of the Jeep. "We got Ivy's new wardrobe off to a good start—and our Christmas shopping. It was a highly productive trip."

Elam chuckled. "Aren't they all?"

"So what did you guys do all day?" Carolyn said.

"Rusty and I took the grandkids to Jewel's for lunch, then took the snowmobiles out. I let Montana drive mine."

"I'll bet he loved that," Ivy said.

"He's good at it too. Rusty and the girls seemed to have fun, but I think we wore them out. They're all three sacked out on the couch."

Ivy waited until Jacqueline and her mother went up the front steps and into the house and then asked her father, "How *was* Rusty?"

"Polite. But he never let the girls out of his sight and wouldn't let them go sledding. Said he didn't want them to get sick."

"Baloney. He doesn't want to leave them alone with Montana."

"Well, at least he didn't pack up and go home mad like I feared he might. He's making an effort."

"So was he nicer to Montana?"

Elam tugged at his mustache. "Not exactly. They just didn't interact. Montana stayed pretty close to me and let me do the talking. And so did Rusty. That part was a little awkward. But at least Rusty wasn't hateful or condescending."

"Well, wasn't that grown up of him?" Ivy hated the sarcasm in her voice. "When are they driving back to Albuquerque?"

"In the morning."

Ivy sighed. "I suppose I should try one more time to clear the air before he goes. I may not see him for a while, and I really don't want this hanging over us."

After dinner Ivy found Rusty alone in the library reading the newspaper. She closed the door and sank into a leather chair, her arms folded.

"What'd I do wrong now?" he said.

"Nothing. I just don't want you to leave tomorrow with all this unresolved anger between us."

Rusty turned the page and didn't look up. "What do you want me to do about it, Ivy? I feel what I feel. It's not like I can change that."

"Then tell me what you're feeling so I can at least address it."

"You don't want to know."

"Yes, I do. I've lost ten years with you. I don't want to waste another day."

Rusty folded the newspaper and laid it next to him on the sofa. "Why is it always about what *you* want? What about what I want?

Or what Mom and Dad want? You broke our hearts. You expect me to just forgive and forget and leave myself wide open for you to do it all over again?"

"I would never do that."

"But you're a liar. So how can I believe anything you say?"

Ivy bit her lip. "Rusty, please. We have to start somewhere. I don't blame you for not trusting me. I let all of you down. But people change. All I'm asking is that you give me a chance to prove myself. Mom and Dad have, and we're doing great."

"Yeah, and you're *still* sucking them dry. Look, they can do whatever they want. But I cut you out of my life a long time ago. I'm not about to set myself up to get hurt again."

"I promise I'm not going to disappoint you anymore." Ivy blinked to clear her eyes. "I've been clean for three and a half years. I'm back in church and walking with the Lord. Trying to get reestablished here in Jacob's Ear. I've kicked the addiction."

"Oh, and you think it's just the addiction I'm disgusted about? Tell me how I'm supposed to hold my head up in this town when everyone knows my sister witnessed Joe Hadley's murder and covered it up for ten years? It's unconscionable that you let the Hadleys suffer all that time."

"I know. Sometimes I can't believe it either." Ivy exhaled audibly. "If I hadn't been high, I would've tried to stop the guys from beating up on Joe. That's the burden I have to live with. But I'm not a monster. And I did my time. All I'm asking for is a chance to prove I've changed."

Rusty's gaze was steely cold. "You still don't get it, do you? I don't want to care about you anymore, or the kid you should've never had. I'll be polite for Mom and Dad's sake. But as far as I'm concerned, I don't have a sister."

An hour later, Ivy stood at the front door with Montana, loaded down with sacks of clothes her mother had bought her—and with the harsh realization that her brother was leaving in the morning with all the bitterness he had brought with him.

"Here, let me help you with that," Elam said. "I'll run these out to the car while you say good-bye."

Ivy handed her father the sacks, aware that Rusty kept shifting his weight from one leg to the other. She reached over and hugged Jacqueline. "It was nice to finally meet you. Maybe I'll see you again at Christmas."

Jacqueline looked over at Rusty and then at Ivy. "I imagine we'll stay close to home because of the girls. We want them to enjoy Christmas in their own house. But hopefully, we'll see you again soon. Nice meeting you, Montana."

"Thanks," Montana mumbled, his hands deep in his pockets.

Ivy bent down and hugged Tia and then Josie. "Bye, girls. I'm so glad I got to see you."

"I like my pretty purse," Tia said.

"I'm glad." Ivy took her finger and touched both girls on the nose, then stood up straight and looked at Rusty, wishing she could shake the indifference out of him. "Have a safe trip home. Let's stay in touch."

Rusty nodded, but his eyes said no.

Ivy hugged her mother a little longer than usual, then went down the front steps to the car, feeling condemned and angry.


Ivy let Montana in the house and went back to the car to get the rest of the sacks. She saw someone waving from the street and realized it was Luke Draper.

"Hi, Luke. You out for a walk?"

"A *brisk* walk. Trying to burn off the calories I've consumed this weekend."

"Did you have a nice Thanksgiving?"

"I did. Jewel was a fine hostess. And I enjoyed her turkey dinner with a couple old duffers named Deke and Roscoe. You know them?"

Ivy laughed. "Everyone does."

"I heard them swapping stories down at the hardware store, and we got to talking. They invited me to join them at the café for Thanksgiving dinner. Gave me quite an education about this town."

"I'll bet." Ivy picked up as many sacks as she could carry and struggled to close the car door.

"Can I help you with that? Seems like a lot for a petite gal like you."

*Petite* sounded a lot nicer than *skinny.* "That'd be great. Thanks."

Luke trudged through the snow and took the sacks from her arms, then went up on the stoop and stomped the snow off his boots.

Ivy held open the door. "You can just put them there on the kitchen table."

Luke's gaze flitted around the room. "Looks just like the place I'm renting. You live here year-round?"

"Yes, a lot of the staff does."

"Anything else I can help you with?"

"That'll do it. Thanks."

"By the way," Luke said, "Jewel mentioned something about the camp having snowmobiles available for guests."

"That's right. Come to the front desk, and we'll get you set up."

Luke seemed to study her for a moment. "Any chance *you* could take me out? Jewel said you know this area really well."

"Sure. I can take you on some awesome trails that offer incredible views of the mountains. I'm off work till Monday. If you want to go out this weekend, let me know."

Luke smiled. "Thanks. I'll get back to you."

Ivy waited a few seconds after Luke left and then pulled back the curtain and watched him trudge back up to the road. Was it possible that a guy like that found her attractive? Maybe he was just lonely. Why else would he spend Thanksgiving Day down at Jewel's?

# 9

Brandon Jones opened the door to the administrative offices of Three Peaks Christian Camp and Conference Center and let Kelsey go in first.

"So the lovebirds *are* back," Jake Compton said. "How was the big anniversary trip?"

"Hey, if you'd noticed our tans, you wouldn't need to ask." Brandon flashed Jake an exaggerated grin. "We had a *great* time."

"It was a wonderful, unexpected break," Kelsey said. "Thanks for letting us take the time off."

Jake patted her shoulder. "Not a problem. It's been dead around here. But it's going to be a more-hectic-than-usual Monday, I'm afraid. We've got eighty-five ladies coming from Grand Junction for a Baptist women's retreat. And those two guys from My Brother's Keeper are due in sometime today. I'm anxious to get them started on renovating the cabins."

"Where did you decide to house these guys?" Brandon said.

"In Deer Run. It's the easiest cabin to get to. When they're finished refurbishing the other cabins, we can move them into one of those and do Deer Run last."

"How long do you think it'll take them to complete the project?"

"Several months," Jake said. "We should've done it last year. At least now we'll be sitting pretty for next summer's campers."

Brandon glanced over at the schedule board. "You want me to keep working with Ivy today? She practically had registration down pat before I left on vacation."

"I think she's got it, but I'd feel better if you stay within earshot till she gets the new group checked in. We don't want to scare her off."

"I don't see that happening. Registration can't be any more taxing than juggling all those customers down at Jewel's. I think she's great at multitasking."

"Good, that's exactly what we need." Jake looked at his watch. "Why don't you head over there and do some role-playing and make sure she's comfortable with the procedures? I doubt the ladies will start arriving until after lunch."

"Whatever it takes to get Ivy to run with it. I can hardly wait to pass the torch."

"I know. And once she can run registration by herself, I've got a big computer project for you to work on."

There was a knock at the door.

Brandon turned and saw two young men standing there. "Can we help you?"

"I'm Don Freeman," said the one with glasses. "And this is Rue Kessler. My Brother's Keeper made arrangements for us to come help you refurbish some cabins?"

"Man, that was fast," Jake said. "We weren't expecting you till much later in the day." He introduced himself and Brandon and Kelsey to the newcomers.

"We were told we were on the clock starting today," Don said. "So we drove as far as Mt. Byron last night so we could be here first thing."

"My kind of guys." Jake nodded toward his office. "Follow me, and I'll get you started on the paperwork."

Brandon watched them disappear into Jake's office and then turned to Kelsey. "They seem nice. I don't know what I was expecting."

"Did you notice that Rue fellow never made eye contact?" Kelsey said.

"He's probably self-conscious that we all know he's been in rehab. Or he's just shy. Why are you frowning?"

"I'm just not as comfortable about this as you and Jake seem to be."

"Why didn't you say something before now?"

Kelsey glanced over at Jake's door. "It's really not my place. Besides, it's hard to fault Elam for wanting to give these guys a second chance."

"The worst that can happen is they won't work out. In which case, we haven't really lost anything, *right*?" Brandon kissed her on the cheek. "See you at lunch."

Ivy stood at the registration desk enjoying the roaring fire in the stone fireplace while waiting for her computer to boot up. She saw Brandon exit the administrative offices, his face three shades darker than when she last saw him.

"You look terrific," Ivy said. "I guess you and Kelsey had a great time?"

"A *fabulous* time! Everything was perfect. I hired a gourmet cook to serve us dinner and a quartet to play chamber music at the lake house where we spent our honeymoon." Brandon's grin spanned his face. "It was a major splurge, but it was worth it to see that Cinderella sparkle in Kelsey's eyes."

"Sounds incredibly romantic. I'm glad you got to go."

"Me too." Brandon put his hands in his pockets, his feet rocking from heel to toe. "Kelsey and I thought about you on Thanksgiving and wondered how it went with your brother."

"It was all right."

"Just all right?"

A blush warmed her face. "Mom cooked an absolute feast. That part was great. It didn't go that well with Rusty, though."

Brandon lifted the hinged section of counter and walked through to the other side. "What a bummer. I had such high hopes it would."

"Oh well."

"You can tell me to mind my own business, if you want, but I'm curious what went wrong."

Ivy shrugged. "It's a long story. Suffice it to say that Rusty hasn't forgiven me for anything. And he wants nothing to do with Montana."

"Why not? He's such a great kid."

"I know. But in all fairness to Rusty, he hasn't been around here to see the changes in me. He's afraid to open himself up to more hurt. I can understand that."

"But what does that have to do with Montana?"

"You'd have to ask Rusty." Ivy manufactured a smile. "I know you didn't come over here to listen to my problems. Are we going to do some more training?"

"I think you've got it nailed. But let's review the registration procedures before our eighty-five lady guests start arriving—just to be sure."

Ivy envisioned a line of arrivals backed up to the parking lot, and her pulse began to race. "It's been a few days since I've done any of this. I hope I don't panic and forget everything I've learned."

Brandon smiled. "Relax. I'm not expecting you to do this by yourself the first time."

At five o'clock, Ivy gladly turned the registration desk over to Suzanne Compton and went out the front door wondering if she had handled the bulk of the afternoon check-in without coming across as a bumbling employee-in-training.

She spotted Rue Kessler dumping a shovelful of snow onto the heap already lining the sidewalk. "Are they ever going to let you off?"

"As soon as I'm done here," Rue said. "Feels good to be busy."

"I'm Ivy Griffith. I work the registration desk. We met earlier today, but I'm sure you don't have all our names committed to memory."

Rue stopped and leaned on his shovel and finally looked at her. "I remember yours."

Ivy took the chance to study his face. Early thirties. Dark hair. Dark eyes. Not bad looking. Judging from his ruddy, leathery complexion, she guessed he might have been in rehab for a drinking problem. "Is Rue your real name or is it short for something else?"

"It's not short for anything. It was my mother's maiden name."

"I like it."

"Thanks." Rue started shoveling again.

What was it about him that made her uncomfortable? "Guess I'll see you around," she said. "I'm done for the day."

"Your dad owns the place, right?"

"Yes, but he doesn't run it. Jake Compton's the administrator."

"Jake seems like a great guy. I appreciate him giving us a break. It's hard getting hired once people know you've been in rehab."

"Any idea how long you'll be working here?"

"Four months. Maybe five."

Ivy saw the headlights of a car and recognized it as Luke Draper's red Corvette. He waved at her and she waved back. He was probably on his way to eat dinner at Jewel's. She wondered why he hadn't come by over the weekend and let her take him out on the snowmobile.

"Who owns the Vette?" Rue asked.

"A guest."

"I saw him driving around earlier and didn't figure he was here for the *women's* retreat." Rue smiled and suddenly didn't seem so strange.

"Actually, the chalets are available for rent during the off-season. Jake likes to keep the place filled up year-round."

Rue picked up another shovelful of snow and tossed onto the pile. "Seems smart. So you live in Jacob's Ear?"

"Actually, I live here at Three Peaks with my son. He's seven."

"I remember when my nephews were that age. They're ten and eleven now. I like kids."

"Me too. And mine is probably famished. I need to pick him up and get him over to the dining hall. You know they're serving dinner from six until seven thirty, don't you?"

"Yeah, I'll be heading that way."

Ivy went over and got in her car, aware that he hadn't taken his eyes off her.


Brandon walked in the dining hall with Kelsey and spotted Rue Kessler and Don Freeman sitting at a table near the mammoth rock fireplace that dominated one wall.

Brandon made his way over to the table. "Hey, guys. Kelsey and I thought you might like some company for dinner. It's got to be a little weird in here with all these ladies."

Don Freeman let out a hearty laugh. "I dig women, but this is downright intimidating. Have a seat. We were just waiting for the buffet line to thin out before we take our turn."

Rue, his arms folded on the table, sat looking around the room.

"So how'd the first day go?" Brandon said.

Don's face lit up. "Great. We inspected the cabins and got the materials and paint ordered. We can pick up most of it tomorrow and get started. Can't tell you how good it feels to get back to work."

Brandon looked at Rue. "How'd *you* do?"

"Fine. I'm good with whatever you all want done. I'm a jack-of-all-trades and don't even mind shoveling snow." He shot Kelsey a quick glance and then looked at his hands. "Your hazel eyes are like my sister's. Only her hair's red."

Brandon made small talk for the next ten minutes, and then he followed Kelsey, Rue, and Don through the buffet line and back to the table carrying a tray filled to capacity.

"I have a question for you," Don said to Brandon. "We were told Mr. Griffith contacted My Brother's Keeper looking for workers. Usually MBK is out knocking on doors, trying to convince someone to hire us. How'd he know about the organization?"

Brandon took a sip of iced tea. "I'm not sure exactly. But he knows someone who's been through drug rehab and is doing really well. He wanted to open a door for somebody else who's looking for a fresh start."

"Well, we sure appreciate it."

Rue agreed with his eyes and took a bite of a barbecued chicken leg.

"I'd been waiting weeks for a job," Don said, "but Rue had just been accepted into the program when Mr. Griffith called. And since both of us know painting and carpentry work, the head honcho was pretty fired up that she could offer our services as a team. We're gonna do a good job for you."

"I'm sure you will." Brandon split his roll in two and buttered it. "So you guys have done this for a living?"

"I was a construction foreman," Rue said. "I can do just about anything you want. I'm good with my hands."

"Me too." Don pushed his glasses closer to his face. "I'd like to have my own handyman business again someday. Maybe having this reference will get me moving in the right direction."

"Hey, Ivy and Montana just walked in," Kelsey said. "Why don't we ask them to join us?"

Brandon waved them over to the table. "You remember Don and Rue, don't you, Ivy?"

"Sure."

"Guys, this is Ivy's son, Montana. Montana, this is Don. And Rue. They're going to be helping us fix up the cabins before camp starts again."

"Cool," Montana said. "If you need to know where stuff is, I can show you."

Rue looked up, his expression suddenly warm and friendly. "So you know this place pretty well, eh?"

Montana bobbed his head. "I know where all the cabins are and what's in all the buildings, even more than my mom does. And I know how to get to the bestest fishing spot…and where there's this really cool trail in the woods that leads to some humongous rocks you can climb."

"No kidding?" Rue winked at Ivy. "If it's okay with your mom, I'll take you up on your offer. A kid in the know has to be pretty important around here."

"He's very important around here," Brandon said. "Helps me all the time."

Montana turned to Ivy, his face beaming. "I could come right after school. Grandpa could bring me."

"Oh, sweetie, that's really nice of you. But Rue and Don can't just stop everything in the middle of the afternoon and go exploring. They have a huge project to finish. We need to let them work."

"I'm sure we can allow time for that," Brandon said. "In fact, I think it'd be neat if the guys would take Montana under their wing and teach him how to use some of the tools." He felt Kelsey kick him under the table and wondered what he'd said wrong.

"Well, he's certainly old enough to learn." Rue took a gulp of milk. "My granddad had me putting up fences when I was his age."

"I'm a really good learner. And I already know how to be careful with Grandpa's tools. Can I, Mom?"

"We'll talk about it later," Ivy said.

"Can't you just answer now?"

"Sweetie, let's go get in the buffet line." Ivy bent down and whispered something to him.

Rue put down his fork and wiped his mouth with a napkin. "I expect your mom'd feel more comfortable if she got to know me and Don first. After all, we're strangers."

Montana frowned and smiled at the same time. "That's what *she* said. But how can you be strangers if you work here?"

"A stranger is anyone we don't really know," Ivy quickly interjected. "It can even be someone nice. We've talked about this before."

Rue looked at Ivy and then at Montana. "Your mom's right. Parents should get to know the people their kids spend time with. I would."

"Do you have kids?" Montana asked.

"No, but I'm an uncle. And my sister's very picky about who my nephews spend time with."

"How old are your nephews?"

"Ten and eleven."

"Wow, that's much older than me. I'll be eight March 18."

Ivy fiddled with the collar on Montana's ski jacket. "I appreciate your sensitivity, Rue. I'm sure you and Don are very nice men. But you can understand how important it is that I teach Montana to exercise caution with strangers, especially now that he's getting more independent. Why don't we just let things evolve over the next couple weeks?"

"Believe me, we get it," Don said. "Once a guy's been in rehab, you aren't sure whether you can trust him or not."

Ivy's face flooded with heat. "That's not what I meant. I just—"

"It's okay." Rue held up his palm. "Say no more. I completely understand."


Brandon followed Kelsey out of the dining hall and down the snowpacked street toward their house.

"Okay, Kel. Go ahead and let me have it with both barrels."

Kelsey threw her hands in the air and kept walking. "What were you thinking? You can't just set up somebody's kid to work with complete strangers without even asking his mother! Couldn't you see Ivy was graciously trying to say no?"

"Sure, after you kicked me. I just don't get why she'd give a second thought to Montana spending time with anybody here at the camp."

Kelsey stopped and turned around. "If we had a young son, would you let him spend time alone with two adults we hardly knew?"

"For crying out loud, Kel. They're recovering substance abusers. Not perverts. We did the same thorough background check on them as we do on all the camp counselors we hire. And you've never questioned whether any of *them* are fit to be around kids."

"Fair enough. But I think you owe Ivy an apology for putting her in an awkward position. It was her call. Not yours. She shouldn't have had to explain herself in front of Montana."

"Yeah, I feel bad about that." Brandon caught a whiff of burning firewood and wished they had just stayed home and had a quiet dinner by themselves. "Ivy knows I'd never put Montana at risk."

"Of course she does. But you should've stayed out of it and let her decide what she was comfortable with. If the truth were known, Rue makes *me* uneasy. I get the feeling he's hiding something."

Brandon rolled his eyes. "Like what? How about giving the poor guy a break? He's self-conscious enough about going through rehab and having to start all over again. Don't read more into it."

# 10

By THE TIME Friday rolled around, Ivy had officially assumed the title of registration coordinator and was feeling more relaxed with the other members of the Three Peaks staff.

She stood behind the registration desk entering customer comments into the computer, and looked up when she saw Suzanne Compton coming to relieve her for lunch.

"You'd better hurry over to the dining hall," Suzanne said. "They're serving the cook's special sausage pasta, and it looks like the place is filling up fast."

Ivy glanced up at the clock and suddenly realized she was hungry. "I can't believe it's lunchtime already. The morning just flew by."

"That's a good sign. Jake said you're doing great."

"Thanks. I'm really liking it." Ivy grabbed her purse and her ski jacket, then lifted the hinged portion of the counter and let Suzanne squeeze past her.

Ivy walked out of the lodge and over to the dining hall. She pushed open the heavy wooden door and was hit with a blast of warm air and a cacophony of voices. People were scurrying to and fro, but over their heads, someone waved her direction.

It was Brandon. He was by her side before she had taken three more steps. "You're welcome to sit at our table. There's room for one more, and it may be your best shot."

Ivy glanced around the room. "Thanks. Looks like all our guests decided to show up at once."

"I think the conference leader put in a plug for the pasta. Better get in line. I'll save your place."

Ivy got through the buffet line faster than she anticipated and carried her tray over to the table where Brandon sat with several other staff people, including Rue Kessler.

Ivy ate her lunch and listened with interest to the banter being exchanged between the seasoned members of the staff, all too aware that neither she nor Rue had contributed to the dialogue.

Finally, Brandon glanced at his watch and stood. "Sorry. I've got to get back. I've got a meeting I'm not quite ready for."

"I've got to go too," said someone else.

One by one the staff people finished eating and left the table until Ivy and Rue were the only two still seated.

Rue lifted his eyes and smiled sheepishly. "Hello again."

"Looks like we're the last of the Mohicans." Ivy reached for her dish of tapioca pudding and set it on her empty plate. "When do you have to be back?"

"Not for twenty-five minutes. Jake insists that we take a full hour for lunch."

"Where's Don?"

"He was in the mood for a sub sandwich and drove into town."

"So do you like working here so far?"

"I do. Everyone's been helpful. The work's satisfying too. Don and I finished the carpentry and plumbing work on the first cabin. All we have to do now is paint. The others should go faster, now that we have the hang of it."

Ivy took a bite of tapioca and savored it, thinking he must be feeling as awkward about their conversation the other night as she was.

"I've heard nothing but raves about your work. Jake and Brandon couldn't be happier."

"Well, that's good to hear."

"Haven't they told you?"

"Yeah, but if they're telling other people, that's *really* a good sign."

"I suppose it is." Ivy started to say something and didn't, and then decided she might never have a better opportunity. "Listen, I hope you and Don weren't offended that I wanted to get to know you better before I let Montana spend time with you."

"Not at all."

"Just so you'll know: I didn't decide that because you've been through rehab."

"Maybe not consciously."

"Look, I doubt anyone on staff would ever mention this to you, but I've been through drug rehab myself and have been clean for three and a half years. So believe me, it was not my intent to judge you."

Rue looked up at her but didn't say anything.

"I think I overreacted the other night because I've recently become a single parent," Ivy said. "Frankly, the responsibility scares me to death."

"I understood exactly where you were coming from. You're smart to teach Montana to be cautious of everyone he doesn't know."

"I appreciated your backing me up." Ivy pushed her bowl aside and folded her arms on the table. "I'm probably overprotective. It's just that Montana's father isn't around. And I hear all these horror stories… Anyway, Brandon reminded me that you and Don were put through the same scrutiny as all the other staff people we hire. I should've known that."

Rue's expression softened. "Hey, it's okay. You were just being a good mom."

*A good mom.* Had anyone ever referred to her that way before?

"Well, I guess I'd better head back," Rue said. "Can I walk you to the lodge? It's on my way."

"Sure."

Ivy got up and made her way toward the exit, surprised when Rue hurried ahead of her and held open the door.

He followed her outside and stood looking up at the bluebird sky. "Supposed to be clear tonight."

"Is that significant?"

Rue smiled. "I'm a stargazer. Can't get enough of it. When the skies clear and I can get away from the city lights, I don't get much sleep."

Ivy was distracted by a man quickly approaching on the sidewalk and realized it was Luke Draper.

"I'm glad I spotted you," Luke said. "I stopped by registration, and the gal said you'd gone to lunch. Sorry I didn't get back to you about the snowmobiling. I got pulled into the chess tournament at the hardware store and had no idea what a big deal it is. That Deke is a legend—a hundred years old, and he almost never loses. Anyhow, the playoffs are this weekend, and I don't know when I'll get around to snowmobiling. I didn't want you to wonder why I hadn't come by."

*Of course I wondered. But it's obvious where I rank on your priority list.* "It's no big deal. Actually, I've been busy."

"Oh, good. Then I don't feel so bad." Luke blew on his hands and rubbed them together. "It's strange…when I checked in here, I'd forgotten how to relax. But getting a taste of the simple life is recharging my batteries. I haven't missed work. In fact, I'm considering buying a time-share so I can get away more often."

"I'm happy for you. Keep me posted on the tournament."

"I will." Luke turned and started to cross the street. "Have a nice weekend."

"Thanks. You too."

"Isn't that the guy who drives the Vette?" Rue said.

"Uh-huh. He's a higher-up in some computer firm and took time off to keep his board of directors happy. I don't think he expected to actually like it here."

A smile spread slowly across Rue's face. "Reminds me of the old TV comedy where the rich guy leaves his New York penthouse and buys a farm out in the boonies. The actor's name was Eddie Albert. What was the name of that show…?

*"Green Acres."* Ivy smiled without meaning to. "His wife was hilarious. And there was a pig named Arnold Ziffel that watched TV. I loved that show."

"Same here. Whatever happened to stuff that's just plain funny?"

"I don't know. But that sure was." Ivy glanced at her watch. "I need to get moving. I've only got a few minutes."

"Yeah, I need to hoof it or I'm gonna be late."

Ivy walked as fast as she could up the street, Rue keeping pace, and stopped in front of the lodge. "I'm glad we ran into each other. I feel better having cleared the air about the other night."

"Yeah, me too. Maybe we can go get coffee sometime. I heard Grinder's is the best place around."

"I'd like that."

Rue flashed a boyish grin and then said, "I need to hurry. Talk to you soon."

She watched him jog up the hill and realized she was really looking forward to spending more time with him. And that he didn't feel at all like a stranger.


The sheriff sat at his desk eating a ham-and-cheese on rye and reading the newspaper. He heard a knock and looked up. Lieutenant Bobby Knolls stood in the doorway.

"I didn't expect you back till after lunch."

"Sorry to interrupt yours," Bobby said. "But I wanted you to know we finished our follow-up on the second anonymous tip. Still didn't find whatever *suspicious activity* our caller made reference to out near Jacob's mine. I'm thinkin' someone's messin' with us. Both calls were made with a prepaid cell." Bobby blew a pink bubble and sucked it back into his mouth. "The only thing out there was Huck Maxfield and his cats."

"Where do I know that name from?"

"His grandfather was Gus Maxfield. Used to shoe horses."

Flint nodded. "Yeah, that's it. So Huck's living with him now?"

"No, the old man died last July, and Huck inherited the place. I don't know what it looked like before, but it's a dump now."

"I didn't know Gus passed away. So what's his grandson like?"

"One weird dude. Grins all the time—nearly drove me up a wall. Hair sticks up all over. Clothes are filthy. I doubt if he's had a bath since the old man passed. He's obviously not cookin' with all his burners, but he seemed harmless. Doesn't have an arrest record."

"Were you able to get inside the house?"

"Oh yeah. He let us in and told us to go through anything we wanted, then sat on the floor in the livin' room, cats crawlin' all over him, and played the jew's-harp while we walked through the place. Which was nastier than a Dumpster, I might add. Reeked of cat urine and sour garbage. I don't know how the guy can stand it."

"Do we need to get animal control out there?"

Bobby shrugged. "The cats seemed attached to him and looked surprisingly well fed."

"What about Huck?"

"He wasn't wastin' away either."

Flint sighed. "I wonder what our anonymous caller wanted us to see that we're missing?"

"Beats me. But till I have more to go on, I think it's a dead end."

"All right, Bobby. Stay on top of it. Thanks for the update."

Bobby stood silent for a moment, his hands in his pockets, and then said, "Anything changed between you and Elam?"

"It's none of your business."

"I know. But I care too much not to ask."

Flint sighed. "Tell you what. If it does, you'll be the first to know."

—

Ivy pushed open the front door of the lodge at ten after five and headed for her car.

"Ivy, wait up!" She recognized Rue's voice and saw him getting out of an older model Ford Explorer.

He hurried over to her. "I was hoping to catch you before you left for the weekend. If you're serious about wanting to have coffee with me, how about meeting me at Grinder's tomorrow morning? I'm completely flexible on the time."

Ivy hoped her expression didn't give away that she was having second thoughts. "I doubt I can get a baby-sitter that quickly."

"That's all right. Bring Montana with you. I heard Grinder's has all kinds of sweet rolls and pastries."

"I doubt we can make it before eleven. Montana loves Saturday cartoons, and it's the only chance I have to sleep in."

Rue nodded. "Eleven sounds perfect. Especially if I'm gonna be up half the night looking at stars."

"I can't believe you'd really stay awake for that. Makes me shiver just thinking about standing out in the cold night air. When it gets dark, all I want to do is sleep."

"Not me. I might miss something."

"Like what?"

"Well, besides everything in the night sky, the stillness. But certain things can be experienced only when it's dark."

"Give me an example."

"Well, it's the only time we can hear crickets, coyotes, or owls. It's when opossum, deer, and lots of other wildlife come out. Only in the dark does a snowy landscape seem to give off light of its own. When it's dark, moonbeams can make any body of water look like a gazillion diamonds. And fireworks can turn the sky into a kaleidoscope of fiery color. And Christmas lights can turn an ordinary street into a wonderland. If it weren't for the dark, candlelight dinners wouldn't be romantic. And you would've never heard of Thomas Edison, and—"

"Okay okay, I get the idea." Ivy laughed. "I've never looked at it that way. I've always been a little afraid of the dark."

"Why?"

"I'm not sure really. I guess when I was little I thought vampires and werewolves and everything creepy and evil thrived at night—and in my closet. There's still something sinister about the dark."

"Doesn't have to be. I think nighttime gets a bad rap."

"Well, you've certainly given me something to think about." Ivy opened the door to her Jeep and climbed into the front seat. "Enjoy your stargazing. I'll see you at Grinder's tomorrow morning at eleven."

# 11

NESTLED UNDER THE down comforter her parents had bought her, Ivy didn't want to open her eyes and spoil the sensation of drifting between sleep and wakefulness. In the quiet she could faintly hear cartoons playing on the TV in the living room and was reminded that it was Saturday and she didn't have to be anywhere until eleven. She thought about Rue Kessler and wished she hadn't agreed to waste part of her weekend on a guy who hadn't been out of rehab long enough to be dateable.

Suddenly the TV was louder, and Ivy sensed that her bedroom door was open. She kept her eyes closed and tried not to smile as she listened for the shuffling of slippers on the hardwood floor and felt someone climb into her bed.

"Who dares to enter my castle?" she said in her storybook voice.

"Me!" Montana let out a husky laugh.

Ivy opened her eyes and tickled his ribs, relishing the sound of his giggling and realizing how much she had missed it when she was in jail.

After several seconds she turned on her side, facing her son, and waited for him to quiet down.

"Can you see the clock?" she said. "What time is it?"

Montana raised himself up on his elbow and looked over her. "The big hand is on the one, and the little hand is on the eight. So…it's five minutes after eight o'clock, right?"

"That's right. Good job. Are you hungry?"

"I had two bowls of Cheerios and a banana," he said. "Want me to bring you some?"

Ivy took her index finger and traced his eyebrows. "That's very sweet of you. But I think I'll get up and make coffee and save room for a special treat."

"What is it?"

"Well, later this morning, you and I are going to a coffeehouse called Grinder's and meet Mr. Rue. You remember him from the other night?"

"Yeah, you said we had to know him better before I could spend time with him and that other guy."

"Right. This'll be a fun way to get to know him and…have a strawberry cream cheese Danish." Ivy lifted her eyebrows up and down several times. "Your very favorite."

"Yay!" Montana sat up and climbed out of bed. "I'm gonna go watch more cartoons so the time will go really fast!"

The phone rang, and Ivy groped the nightstand and picked up the receiver.

"Hello."

"Did I wake you?" her father said.

"No, I'm just lying in bed. What's wrong?"

"Your Mom and I are down at Jewel's and just heard that Deke and Roscoe are in the hospital. An intruder broke into their house early this morning and beat them up, then made off with a money jar. Unbelievable. People are outraged."

"Were they seriously hurt?"

"No one seems to know. But how much abuse can their hundred-year-old bodies withstand?"

Ivy exhaled into the receiver. "Poor things. How'd you find out about it?"

"A polished-looking young fella came in a few minutes ago, and I've been listening to what he's telling Jewel. He looks mad enough to spit nails. I've never seen him before, but I get the impression he's close to Deke and Roscoe. Maybe he's related to one of them."

"Does he drive a red Corvette?"

"I don't know, but I see one parked outside."

"It's probably Luke Draper," Ivy said. "He's a guest here at the camp and has gotten really fond of them. Just yesterday he told me about a chess tournament Deke's involved in at the hardware store. The playoffs were supposed to be held this weekend…Dad, you there…?"

"Yeah, sorry. I was trying to hear what he was saying to Jewel. Sounds like he's about to head over to the hospital now. Listen, honey, the waitress just brought our breakfast. Why don't I get back to you as soon I know more?"

"Okay, thanks. Call my cell. I'm going to be in and out today."

The sheriff paced in front of his desk, his hands in his pockets, his ire turning to sweat.

"Bobby, what heartless piece of garbage would pick up a fire log and brutalize two old men over a jar of *nickels*?"

Investigator Bobby Knolls leaned forward in his chair, his hands turned to fists. "The kind that's gonna be a pleasure to put away. Not that we have squat at the moment. We've gone over the house with a fine-tooth comb. No prints. No DNA. We got a mud sample off the carpet, but I don't expect that to tell us anything other than the guy didn't wipe his feet."

"Tell me about your conversation with the victims."

"Roscoe's disoriented from the pain medication and hasn't been any help at all. But Deke remembers bein' pulled out of bed and into the livin' room and made to stand next to Roscoe. He thinks the perp was taller than either of them, dressed in black from head to foot, including a ski mask and gloves—so much for distinguishing marks or characteristics."

"Would he recognize the perp's voice if he heard it?"

Bobby shook his head. "Perp never said anything, just picked up a log and started poundin' them with it until they collapsed on the floor. Then the guy went out in the kitchen, picked up the jar of nickels, and stepped over them on his way out the front door. Deke managed to crawl over to the phone and dial 911. He remembered the clock strikin' three."

"The perp didn't ransack the house?"

"Nope." Bobby popped a pink bubble. "Far as we can tell, all he was after was the jar of nickels. And he knew right where to find it."

"Who would've known about the nickels?"

"You mean other than anyone who ever listened to the banter down at the hardware store? It's a game with these two. They convert all their spare change to nickels. And every time that big ol' jar is full, they make a production of takin' it over to the Indian reservation and playin' the slots and seein' how long they can make it last. It's hard to say who all knew about it."

"Could've been someone looking for easy drug money."

Bobby shrugged "Those nickels wouldn't buy much, and it's odd he didn't hit any other houses. He sure didn't have to beat the tar out of two old duffers to get it. The sicko *wanted* to hurt them."

"Did Deke notice what color the perp's eyes were?"

"No. Just that he wore a ski mask. He was so scared, I'm surprised he remembered as much as he did. The poor guy's got a broken arm, cracked ribs, and a big gash on his head. Roscoe's nose is broken, and somethin's wrong with his back. I expect by tomorrow the bruisin' will tell the ugly truth about the poundin' they took."

Flint went over to the window and looked out across Phantom Hollow at the jagged, white peaks of the San Juans. "Those sweet old guys have been icons in Jacob's Ear since I was a little kid. Deke taught me how to stand up for myself when I was in the fifth grade and the class bully kept stealing my lunch. I've never forgotten that. It's probably one of the reasons I chose law enforcement—to help the helpless." Flint glanced at his watch and turned to Bobby. "And now it's my turn to help him. I want whoever did this. Knock on doors. Get in people's faces. Do whatever you have to. Find this creep and bring him in. I'm going over to the hospital to check on Deke and Roscoe."

Flint walked down the long, shiny corridor of the Tanner County Medical Center to room 114 and rapped gently on the open door. He saw a young man he didn't recognize sitting in a chair near two beds where Deke and Roscoe lay.

The young man looked up, then rose to his feet. "Hello, I'm Luke Draper."

"Sheriff Carter." Flint shook Luke's hand, his eyes fixed on the old men's battered faces and the monitoring devices they were hooked up to. "You a relative?"

"Just a friend. I'm here on vacation and overheard these two telling tales around that potbelly stove at the hardware store." Luke smiled. "I was captivated by the folklore. We've shared a few meals together, and they pulled me into a chess tournament this week. Deke was about to win it. The playoffs were supposed to be today and tomorrow."

Flint nodded. "I heard about that. Where are you staying, in case we need to ask you some questions?"

"I'm out at Three Peaks."

"Are you going to be here awhile yet?"

"A few weeks. Actually, I'm on a *working* vacation."

"What company do you work for?"

"Leland and Sorrels. We're a software solutions outfit. I'm the CEO." Luke handed him a business card. "Funny…when I first arrived here, I didn't think I even remembered *how* to relax. But after I discovered Deke and Roscoe and they introduced me to some of the locals, I've enjoyed getting to know people. This is a unique community."

Flint nodded toward the two patients. "You've been with them a lot lately. Any idea who might've done this?"

"No clue." Luke's expression suddenly turned somber. "It's good I didn't walk in on it, or you would've had to lock me up. Hard to say how I would've reacted if I'd caught the bottom feeder who did this."

"Yeah, I know what you mean. How'd you find out about it?"

"Went to pick them up. We were supposed to have breakfast at Jewel's and then head over to the chess tournament. When I got there, a neighbor told me what happened."

"Have Deke or Roscoe said anything to you about what happened?"

Luke put his hands in his pockets, a row of ridges forming on his forehead, and related what Deke had told him.

"That's exactly what he told my deputies," Flint said. "Ever heard them talk about the nickels?"

"Sure, that's how they save up to go play the slots. There couldn't have been enough in that jar to have precipitated a vicious attack like this."

"Did you notice anyone suspicious hanging around when you were involved in the chess tournament?"

"Not really. Folks came and went. I didn't pay a lot of attention. I was watching Deke's every move. The guy's a legend. Ever see him play?"

Flint smiled. "He's shamed me more than once."

There was a knock on the door. Flint turned and saw Jewel Sadler walk into the room.

"How are my guys doing?" she asked.

Luke went over and put his arm around her. "They're asleep. I warn you: they look really bad. But the doctor thinks they're going to be all right."

Jewel went over and stood between the two beds and didn't say anything. Finally, she turned around, her lower lip trembling, and wiped the tears off her cheeks. "Flint, you have to find the monster who did this to them."

"Believe me. I'll do everything in my power."

Flint sensed someone watching him. He quickly glanced into the hallway, then back again, pretending he hadn't seen Elam and Carolyn Griffith standing there. He offered Luke his hand. "I really should get back to work. Thanks for watching after these gentlemen. I may need to talk to you again as the investigation progresses."

"I'll help any way I can, Sheriff."

Flint took a slow, deep breath, bemoaning the fact that he couldn't avoid passing Elam on his way out. He walked into the hallway and stopped in front of them. "Hard to believe there are people capable of this, eh?"

"We're just sick about it," Carolyn said. "We'll only stay a minute, but we wanted to hold their hands and let them know we care, you know?"

Flint stole a glance at Elam. "That's very kind of you. Well, you'll have to excuse me. I was just on my way back to the office. Nice seeing you."

"Good seeing you," Carolyn said. "Say hello to Betty."

"I will."

Flint walked down the empty corridor toward the exit, the squeaking of his rubber soles on the shiny tile almost as irritating as Elam's indifference.

Ivy took a bite of her sweet roll and then a sip of hazelnut coffee and savored the complimentary flavors. "So what time did you finally get to bed?"

Rue Kessler sat back in the booth, his hands wrapped around a coffee mug. "I got back about three but was too wired to sleep. It was stupendous out there last night. Crystal clear. Orion was about as easy to pick out as I've ever seen him. Both Dippers too."

"How come you like stars so much?" Montana said, his mouth chock-full of sweet roll.

"I just like the night sky, the night air, the night sounds, the contrast of light and dark—all of it." Rue took his finger and wiped a drop of cream off the table. "It's not as much fun without my telescope, though. I'm really disappointed I forgot to bring it."

"I've seen the Big Dipper before," Montana said, "but I've never even heard of Ryan."

"That's Orion—pronounced o-RI-uhn. The Great Hunter. He's a lot harder to see. Orion is a constellation that includes two of the brightest stars in the sky. One of those stars is called Betelgeuse."

"Beetle juice?" Montana cocked his head, a tentative smile tugging at the corners of his mouth. "For real...?"

"Cross my heart. The other is called Rigel. If you could measure across Rigel, it would be about sixty times larger than the sun and at least forty thousand times brighter."

Montana put his hands to his cheeks. "Forty thousand? I can't even count that high. If it's bigger than the sun, how come it looks like a tiny dot?"

"Because it's about eight hundred light-years away."

"How far is that?"

Rue leaned forward on his elbows. "Well, if you were on a jet going five hundred miles an hour, you would have to fly for 1.34 million years to travel just *one* light-year. And remember Rigel's about eight hundred light-years away. That means it would take you...well, longer than any of us can even imagine."

"Wow! It might take longer than my whole life!"

Rue's smile turned his eyes to slits. "And you know what else is amazing? Our sun is a star too, and it's exactly the right distance from earth. A little closer or a little farther away could make it impossible for us to survive. Realizing things like that makes it easy for me to believe that God's behind it all."

"I believe in God. I asked Jesus into my heart," Montana said.

"So did I. And now it's even more fun to look at the things He made."

"Could you show me what beetle juice and Rigel look like?"

Rue glanced up at Ivy. "Whenever it's okay with your mom. I'll show you a diagram first so you can see what Orion looks like and how to spot Betelgeuse and Rigel."

"I really wanna see them. And I like being up late," Montana said. "I've stayed up till midnight before, haven't I, Mom?"

"Yes, you have." Ivy looked at her watch for the umpteenth time and wondered why she kept doing that. "Sweetie, you need to finish you hot chocolate so we can go run our errands while we're in town."

"Okay."

"Speaking of town, I have a question before you go," Rue said. "Can you tell me where Jacob's Ear got its name?"

Montana looked at Ivy, his eyes pleading. "Can I tell?"

"Sure. Go ahead."

"My grandpa said people used to mine gold here. One of them had the name Jacob Tanner. He was very rich from finding so much gold, and everybody knew him. But one day nobody knew where he was, so a lady named the widow Thompson went to his house to find him. She looked everywhere, but all she found was Jacob's ear on the back porch!" Montana grinned, his mouth framed with a chocolate mustache. "Everybody thought Bigfoot got him. They didn't know there's no such thing."

"Is that right?" Rue took a sip of coffee, not quite able to hide his smile.

"Actually," Ivy said, "a little folklore was more intriguing than saying a bear got him. The legend stuck, and so did the name. The chamber of commerce loves it. It's certainly a tourist draw."

"It's unique, all right. I about cracked up when the big wig at MBK told Don and me we were gonna be working in Jacob's Ear. That conjured up all kinds of images."

"Hey, what if they would've found Jacob Tanner's *toe*? The town would be named Jacob's Toe." Montana giggled. "Or Jacob's Nose. Or Jacob's Pinkie. Or what about Jacob's Lip?"

"I think somebody's had too much sugar." Ivy reached over and tousled his hair, surprised and pleased at how relaxed and enjoyable the conversation with Rue had been.

"I'm glad we did this," Rue said. "Now I know two very nice people in Jacob's Ear. Maybe we can do this again sometime soon."

# 12

IVY RANG THE BELL, then pushed open the front door of her parents' home and was hit with the wonderful aroma of her mother's tangy chicken stew.

"It's just me," Ivy hollered as she stepped into the foyer.

"We're in the kitchen!"

Ivy slipped off her ski jacket and laid it over the back of the couch, then went into the kitchen, where her dad sat at the table reading the newspaper and her mother stood at the stove, stirring the stew.

"Where's Montana?" Elam said.

"Outside playing with Sasha. We've been in the car a lot today, and he needs to burn off some energy." Ivy sat at the table across from her dad. "I got your message that you went to the hospital and saw Deke and Roscoe. It's hard for me to believe someone actually beat them up."

Carolyn shook her head and put the lid on the pot. "It was a hard dose of reality seeing them that way. But I'm glad we went. Flint was there. Jewel, too. She said to give you a hug. And we met Luke Draper. You were right. He's the man who came into the café and talked to her. Seems like a really nice young man."

"Yeah, he is. Did Sheriff Carter tell you any more about what happened, or if he has any suspects?"

"We didn't exactly talk to him," Elam said. "Just spoke in passing."

Carolyn turned around, her arms folded. "Well, *one* of us did."

There was an awkward stretch of silence, and Ivy sensed she had come at a bad time. She took a Ritz cracker out of the wrapper and bit into it. "Montana and I did something fun today. We went to Grinder's and spent some time getting to know Rue Kessler."

Elam lifted his eyes. "Oh?"

"He's into astronomy and told us all kinds of fascinating things about the constellation Orion."

"Why would you start a relationship with someone who's got the same bent for addiction?"

"It's not like I'm going to marry him, Dad. We just had coffee. He's really nice and very attentive to Montana. Heaven knows that child could use a little male affirmation after the way Rusty treated him. And just so you'll know: Rue wasn't addicted to drugs. He's a recovering alcoholic."

Elam's silence spoke louder than any words of disapproval he could have uttered.

"Dad, you're the one who wanted to hire him. Do you think it's right for me to ignore him when he doesn't know anybody here? That doesn't seem very Christian to me."

"I didn't say anything about ignoring him, honey. I just don't think it's a good idea for you to date him."

"Like I said, we enjoyed a cup of coffee and conversation. It was hardly a date. And Montana invited Rue to come to church with us in the morning. Rue's a new Christian, and he needs to find a church while he's working here."

Elam's expression softened. "You're sensitive and caring, Ivy. I just think it'd be wise for you to take it slow for a while. Get used to the new job. Get settled in the new house. Spend time with your son. Figure out who you are *before* you pursue a relationship."

"I'm not pursuing anything. But I'm not going to put a damper on Rue's taking an interest in Montana either. I prayed the Lord would send someone into our lives to bolster that kid's self-esteem. Who's to say he's not an answer to prayer?"

Elam gave her a you-should-listen-to-dear-old-Dad look. "It's impossible for me not to feel protective of you after all you've been through. So many of your troubles resulted from getting involved with the wrong people."

"I know, but I'm twenty-nine years old now. How am I going to learn to stand on my own unless you let me try?"

Elam took her hands in his. "Okay, I'll back off. Just put some of that wisdom you've been acquiring to good use, okay?"

The phone rang, and Carolyn reached over and picked it up. "Hello... Actually, she is... Hold on a second... Ivy, it's Brandon Jones."

Ivy took the receiver from her mother. "Hey, what's up?"

"I know this is last minute, but Kelsey and I decided to invite some of the Three Peaks staff over for Mexican food tonight. Would you like to come? We're going to get out the dominoes and play Mexican Train."

"Sounds like fun, but I don't know if I can get a baby-sitter that fast."

"Then bring Montana. He knows everybody."

"What time?"

"Sixish."

"Okay, thanks. See you then." Ivy handed the phone back to her mother. "Brandon and Kelsey have invited some of the staff over for Mexican food tonight. Sounds great. I don't think I've had Mexican food since Lu died."

"You need us to watch Montana?" Carolyn said.

"I have the option of bringing him with me."

Carolyn swatted the air. "Go have some fun with your friends. Maybe we'll drive into town and look at Christmas lights and then come back here and play Uno. Or Elam can play the piano and we'll make up silly songs. Montana gets a kick out of that."

Elam smiled sheepishly. "The things I do for that kid."

"Maybe I should hang around, Dad. Sounds pretty entertaining."

Carolyn laughed. "You have no idea just how entertaining, especially if Sasha starts howling."

"Are you sure you don't mind? I don't know what time I'll be back to pick him up."

"Why don't you just let him sleep here tonight?" Carolyn said. "I'll bring him home after breakfast in the morning so he can shower and get ready for church."


Flint sat in his office eating a sausage pizza with Lieutenant Bobby Knolls and Investigator Buck Lowry.

"What it boils down to is we've got zip." Flint took a wadded up napkin and wiped his mouth.

"Other than I'm pretty convinced that no one livin' in Jacob's Ear is capable of this," Bobby said. "We need to take a hard look at outsiders. Tourists. County employees. Gamblers. Boys at the high school and junior college. Whatever the perp's motive, he didn't have to assault two defenseless old men to steal that jar of nickels."

"Be glad they're alive." Buck picked up a slice of pizza and blew on it. "People have killed for less."

"Yeah, well, if Deke and Roscoe weren't in such good shape, the poundin' they took might've killed them."

"Still might," Flint said. "We don't know what health issues might result from this. Let's back up and talk about the neighbor for a minute. She told you she heard a car motor running sometime during the night."

Buck nodded. "Right. But she had no idea what time it was, and she never saw the vehicle, just remembered that it sounded big, like a truck or an SUV. Which describes nearly every vehicle in town."

"Even an idiot wouldn't drive up to the house he's gonna rob." Bobby sprinkled grated cheese on his pizza. "I doubt it was the perp's vehicle she heard."

"This reeks of angry young punk. What about Maxfield's grandson?" Flint said.

Bobby stopped chewing. "He's plenty weird, but he didn't come across as angry. But he's fifty, maybe fifty-five. Not a kid."

"Any idea what he's doing for money?" Flint said.

"No. But judgin' from the way he looked, I doubt he's holdin' down a job."

"Yet he appeared well fed."

"Yeah, he did." Bobby's eyes locked on to Flint's. "Maybe it's time to find out how Huck's supportin' himself and all those fat cats."

"I'll ride out there with you," Flint said. "I want to eyeball this character."

Flint got out of Bobby Knolls's squad car and sized up the dried-up old shanty he would never have recognized as Gus Maxfield's place if it hadn't been for the name on the mailbox. A late-model white Chevy pickup was parked out front.

"You weren't kidding about this place being a dump," Flint said. "Let's go see what the grandson has to say. You do the talking, Bobby. I'm just here to observe."

Flint trudged through the snow around a rusted-out Chevy Malibu, an old toilet bowl and sink, and all kinds of blacksmith tools and household appliances that were strewn about the property. He followed Bobby up the warped wooden steps just as an unkempt man, dressed in dirty coveralls and holding an orange and white striped cat on his shoulder, stepped outside on the porch.

"Huck Maxfield, I'm Lieutenant Bobby Knolls. I talked to you the other day. This is Sheriff Carter. We'd like to ask you some questions."

"About what?"

"A robbery."

"I don't know anything." Huck held open the door, a Gomer Pyle smile on his face, and motioned for them to go in.

Flint nearly gagged from the smell of garbage and cat urine. Something white and furry darted in front of him, and he almost tripped.

"Sit there, if you want." Huck pointed to a dilapidated brown couch covered in pet hair and then sat on what appeared to be an old vinyl car seat. "What robbery?"

"Two old gentlemen were beaten and robbed sometime last night or early this mornin'. Happened in Jacob's Ear, on Tanner's Ridge Road. Know anything about that?"

"You think I did it?" Huck reached into his matted, unruly hair and dug at his scalp.

"We're just gatherin' information. Were you in town yesterday?"

"I'm in town almost every day."

"Was that a yes?"

Huck nodded. "But I didn't beat up those two old guys or take the jar of nickels."

"How'd you know about the nickels?" Bobby's eyes narrowed. "We never told the media what was in the money jar."

"I heard about it at the feed store when I picked up a bag of food for my cats. Ask the guy with the white beard who works there. He's the one who was talking about it."

"Where were you last night?"

"Home. Same as every night."

"I don't suppose anyone can verify that?"

Huck's grin grew wider. "Mr. Whiskers here, but unless you speak feline, you'll need an interpreter."

"I'm not in the mood for clownin' around. Just answer the questions. Where do you work?"

"I'm between jobs at the moment."

"What'd you do before?"

Huck hesitated for a moment and then said, "Why should I have to tell you that?"

"Just answer the question."

"Huh-uh. I have rights."

"You wanna play hardball?" Bobby leaned forward, his hands clasped between his knees. "Because we can continue this conversation down at the station. Why don't you save us both a lot of time and just tell us where you used to work."

"Because it has nothing to do with this." A black cat with a white tip on its tail rubbed against his leg, then jumped up on the car seat and nestled in his lap.

"Is that so? How're you payin' for that nice truck parked outside if you're not workin'?"

"The title's free and clear."

"So what's the big deal about tellin' us where you got the money? You got somethin' to hide?"

"Not at all. I'm a private person. And you don't have the right to know my personal business."

"We do when we're investigating an assault and robbery."

Huck scratched the cat's ear. "Search my house, if you want. And my truck. Or anything I've got. But I'm not volunteering my personal business."

Ivy sat on one end of the couch in front of a crackling fire at Brandon and Kelsey's house, reveling in the victory of having just won all three games of Mexican Train.

"Have you no mercy?" Rue laughed and flopped down next to her. "If I didn't know better, I'd swear you were a ringer."

Ivy smiled without meaning to. "Actually, I hardly ever win. Feels kind of good."

"I wouldn't know. I was in *last* place. So what's Montana doing tonight?"

"My parents are keeping him. He loves being at their house."

"I sure did enjoy talking to the two of you today. He's a great kid. I'd really like to take him out and show him how to spot Orion—when you feel comfortable, of course."

"Oh, I think I'm there, Rue. Like I told you the other day, I over-reacted because the whole single-parent role scares me. The truth is, Montana could benefit from what you have to teach him as well as from the male attention and affirmation."

"Does he ever get to spend time with his dad?"

"His father's never been part of his life."

"Oh. I just assumed he was, since you said you'd recently become a single parent."

Ivy felt her face get hot. "It's a long story. Let me give you the short version: for the first four years of Montana's life, I was spaced out on drugs. A precious woman named Lu Ramirez would come get Montana and take care of him at her place. After I got clean, Montana and I lived with Lu, and she took care of him while I worked. Lu died last spring. And now, for the first time, I'm completely responsible for him. I really do feel like a single parent."

"I can see why."

"Don't get me wrong, my parents are wonderful with him. And my dad is a good male role model. But Montana can't win my brother Rusty's heart. And it's devastated him."

"They don't get along?"

"Rusty won't give him a chance. He's still angry with me for the years I was addicted to cocaine and meth. He's cut me out of his heart and doesn't want to let Montana in."

Rue shot her a knowing look. "Yeah, I get it. My family has issues with me, too. I don't know how long I have to be sober before they'll trust me again."

"Sorry, I didn't intend to dump all that on you. But if you're going to spend time with Montana, it's good for you to know."

"Does that mean you're going to let me take him out to see the stars?"

"Sure. As long as it's not on a school night."

"Why don't you come too?"

Brandon appeared at the couch and handed Ivy and Rue each a small bowl. "Cinnamon ice cream with honey drizzled on top. Hope you like it."

"Thanks," Rue said. "Sounds different."

"Anybody want coffee?"

"No, thanks," Ivy said. "I'm afraid it would keep me up all night."

"I'd love some." Rue winked. "I'm afraid I might fall asleep."

Flint sat in his easy chair, half watching an old John Wayne movie on TV and mentally cataloging everything they knew so far in Deke and Roscoe's case. He didn't trust Huck Maxfield, but he didn't have anything on him either. Just to be safe, he directed Bobby to order a thorough background check.

"If Huck won't tell us what he's hiding, we'll let the report tell us."

"Are you talking to yourself?" Betty stood in the doorway, her eyelids heavy.

"Apparently so. I was deep in thought. Why aren't you sleeping?"

"Other than the fact that whoever beat up two helpless old men is still out there?"

"Hon, why don't you let me worry about the perp? We've rarely had two assaults by the same guy. It was probably a kid looking for drug money. And with all the hype he's caused, it's likely that he's moved on."

"Well, 'likely' doesn't make me feel very good. So who's Huck?"

"Gus Maxfield's grandson. I doubt the name means anything to you, but Gus was a well-respected farrier in his day. Huck's been living in his grandfather's house since the old man died last summer."

"Why do you think he's hiding something?"

"He's just strange, that's all."

Betty folded her arms and leaned on the doorframe. "Define strange."

"Gomer Pyle grin. Clint Eastwood eyes. Homeless-man hygiene. Owns a million cats. His place looks and smells like the county dump."

"You suspect him?"

"We're just fishing at the moment. Huck's only been in the area for a few months, and we believe it had to be an outsider that hurt Deke and Roscoe. But nothing points to him."

"Can't you lock him up on health violations or something, just till you know for sure?"

"Hey, will you stop worrying? Remember, you've got an armed bodyguard at your house."

Betty came over and sat in his lap, her arms around his neck. "But I'd feel better if my armed bodyguard would come to bed where I could snuggle next to him."

"No one's going to break in here."

Betty held his gaze, the corners of her mouth turning up.

"Ahhh…I get it. You'd just prefer to have your bodyguard in closer proximity." Flint reached over and turned off the lamp, then moved his lips ever so slowly toward hers. "That's what I love most about the job."

# 13

IVY ARRIVED AT GRINDER'S Coffee House thinking Rue must be growing on her. Why else would she jump at the chance to be with him a third time that day? She saw him waving from a corner booth and a moment later slid in on the other side.

"I guess we know which of us has the heavier foot," she said.

"Actually, I've only been here a minute. I took time to gawk at the Christmas lights. Very pretty." Rue turned and looked out the window. "For some reason I thought a town this size would close up after dark."

Ivy laughed. "Well, not during the holidays. Ever since the slopes opened at White Top and Mt. Byron, more and more people are opting to ski in this area instead of Telluride. Most of them end up in Jacob's Ear, either to shop or eat. The tourist trade is off the charts in every season compared to when I was growing up."

"Have you always lived here?"

"I was born and raised here, but I lived in Denver the biggest part of the past ten years."

Rue leaned forward on his elbows. "Denver? That's where I'm from."

"I knew that. What part of the city do you live in?"

"Right now, I'm living in a halfway house near downtown. I used to live near Capitol Hill, back before they started to clean up the area and bring it back."

Ivy smiled. "So did I—during the three years I was clean. Lu and I and Montana rented a small apartment in an old house on Eleventh."

"Really? In the late nineties, me and some guys I worked with rented a house not far from there. Ever heard of a bar called Irving's?"

"Sure, I've been there a hundred times. How weird is that? We might've passed each other and never even knew it."

"Well, that's where I lived after work. All my buddies hung out there. We played pool. Threw darts. Watched ESPN. Had a few laughs and way too much beer. I never thought I had a drinking problem. As time went on, I started having a few beers over lunch, but the booze didn't affect my ability to do my job. It wasn't till after my mother passed away that it got out of control, and I ended up in rehab a few months later. Anyway, I've been sober since January 8 of this year."

"Feels great, doesn't it?"

Rue nodded. "Amen to that."

"Was your mother ill?"

"No." There was a long pause, and Rue stared at his hands. Finally he said, "It was a huge shock. Kind of hard to talk about."

"I'm sorry. I understand. Lu died of leukemia just weeks after she was diagnosed. I miss her terribly. She was like a mother to Montana *and* to me. I'm still not over it."

"So is Lu's dying the reason you came back here?"

Ivy felt her pulse quicken and was glad when the waitress came over to the booth.

"What can I get you two?"

"I'll have decaf," Ivy said.

"A double espresso for me." Rue smiled at her. "I'm gonna have one of those big chocolate chip cookies. You want something?"

"No, I'm still full from dinner."

"All right," the waitress said, "I'll be right back."

Rue folded his arms on the table. "Where were we? Oh yeah. We were talking about why you came back to Jacob's Ear."

*Just tell him everything and get it over with.* "I wanted to mend my relationship with my parents…but there was a more urgent reason. I needed to tell the sheriff about something I'd been holding inside since high school. It's probably more than you want to know, but if I don't tell you, you're bound to hear it somewhere else." Ivy lifted her eyes and looked into Rue's. "In January of my senior year, I witnessed my boyfriend and two of his teammates kill a classmate of ours, Joe Hadley. They didn't intend to kill him. An argument turned ugly, and the guys ganged up on Joe and started hitting him, then Pete put his hands around Joe's throat and squeezed until he went limp. The other guys finally pulled Pete off him, but Joe wasn't breathing."

"But someone tried to resuscitate him, right?"

"They were so panicked, I'm not sure they even thought of it."

"What about you?"

Ivy felt the truth scald her cheeks and wondered if owning it would ever get easier. "I'm ashamed to say I didn't do anything. I had smoked pot mixed with PCP because I flunked my calculus test and was so whacked-out that I couldn't really react."

"Were they high too?"

"No. They just were scared of what would happen to them. They had the presence of mind to get a shovel and bury Joe's body, then the four of us made a pact never to tell anyone. I wanted to—so many times—but I was too ashamed. And scared. We all left for college that summer, and I started using blow and meth to numb the guilt and was in and out of rehab for years. But when I finally got clean and stayed clean, I knew the only way I'd ever be free of it was to tell the truth."

"So did you?"

Ivy blew the bangs off her forehead. "Yes, this past spring. And then I served six months in jail for failure to report a felony. I was just released last month."

"You just got out of jail?"

Ivy nodded. "Shocked?"

"Yeah, kind of. But I'm glad you told me."

Rue seemed to stare at nothing, his fingers tapping the table. Finally, he locked gazes with her and said, "Must've been awful for you, trying to keep that kind of secret."

"You have no idea. Look, I'll understand if this changes your opinion of me. But I thought you should know."

"Well, it didn't change my opinion of you. Don't forget I live in a glass house. I'm a firm believer in not throwing stones."

Ivy made a tent with her fingers and rested for a moment in the relief she felt. "You're the first person I've talked to about this that didn't already know. Thanks for not making me feel like trash the way my brother Rusty did."


Brandon put soap in the dishwasher and turned it on for the second time that night and turned to Kelsey.

"It was fun having everyone here. The food was great." He pressed his lips to her cheek. "You're a terrific cook and a wonderful hostess."

"You know I enjoy doing it," Kelsey said. "Did you happen to notice how chummy Rue and Ivy were?"

Brandon laughed. "Nooo. Did I miss something?"

"Didn't you see them talking? They were totally engrossed for at least thirty minutes."

"So?"

"Something about Rue makes me uncomfortable. I told you that the other night. I certainly don't think it's smart for Ivy to get involved with a recovering alcoholic when she's a recovering drug addict. How old is Rue anyway?"

"Uh, thirty-four, if I remember right."

"He looks older."

"What makes you think Ivy's interested in him or vice versa? We're the ones who invited them here."

Kelsey reached up in the windowsill and felt the soil in the oblong copper planter. "It's just a feeling. Ivy's extremely vulnerable right now and shouldn't even consider beginning a relationship with anyone."

Brandon threw up his hands. "So now you've got the poor girl starting a relationship with him? Honey, this is totally unfounded. Get a grip."

"I admit it sounds presumptuous, but Ivy shared with me the cruel things Rusty said and the way he treated Montana. It was obvious she was devastated and feels condemned all over again. She needs to allow time for the Lord to bind up her wounds and heal the broken image she has of herself. Or she's liable to settle for less than what the Lord wants for her."

"Meaning Rue Kessler?"

"There's no way for me to know that. I just wish she wouldn't get involved with him right now."

"You're not her mother, Kel."

"And I really don't want to come across as if I have all the answers. I could be wrong."

"Then again, since you're the one who convinced her to recommit her life to Christ, maybe you could get away with giving her advice. She seems to look up to you."

Kelsey pinched a couple of dead leaves off the green plant and set the planter in the sink. "Giving that kind of advice is a sticky wicket. There's always the chance she'll miss my point and just think I'm putting Rue down."

"The worst she could do is not take your advice."

Kelsey's hazel eyes widened. "No, the worst she could do is stop speaking to me and make things uncomfortable at work."


Walking out of Grinder's and over to her car, Ivy was thinking how foolish it was that she hadn't worn the new down coat her mother bought her instead of the flimsy pink ski jacket because it matched her sweater.

"What a day," Rue said, his breath visible in the icy night air. "We sure covered a lot of ground."

"You're a good listener. I'm glad we talked."

"Yeah, me too." He looked up into the night sky. "Sure you don't wanna get away from the city lights and see what you've been missing?"

Ivy pushed her hands deeper into her pockets and tried to keep her teeth from chattering. "Thanks, but I'd like to go home and turn up the heat and get a good night's sleep. Sunday school starts at nine."

"What time is church?"

"Ten thirty."

"Why don't I meet you and Montana at the front entrance at ten twenty?"

"Okay. You remember how to get there?"

"Go east on Three Peaks Road until I run into it."

"That's it. Woodlands Community Church is almost exactly ten miles from the camp and just outside the city limits."

Rue pushed the button on his watch, and the face lit up green. "Well, it's not quite eleven, and that crisp clear sky is just too good to pass up. I'm gonna head back toward the camp and find a spot to pull off. Want me to follow you? You probably shouldn't be driving back in the dark by yourself."

"Thanks, but I'll be fine. I want to enjoy the Christmas lights for a few minutes. See you in the morning." Ivy started the car and slid the temperature lever over to bright red and waved good-bye to Rue.

She pulled out of the parking lot and onto Main Street, enamored with the town's holiday personality that hadn't changed much in the decade she was away. As far as she could see on both sides of the street, the historic brick buildings and each window and doorway were outlined in twinkling white lights.

She smiled as Rue's comment came to mind. *Only in the dark can Christmas lights turn an ordinary street into a wonderland.*

Her eyes were drawn to the blue lights that covered the bandstand in Spruce Park, and above it, seemingly suspended in air, a huge white star—just the way she remembered it as a kid.

In front of the courthouse the two giant old blue spruce trees had been overlaid from top to bottom with myriad twinkling colored lights and topped with a white star. To her dismay, three whimsical lighted snowmen had replaced the life-size manger scene her father had donated to the city when she was little.

A row of foil-wrapped packages had been strung above each intersection. And on the snowpacked street, two horses fitted with custom Santa hats clip-clopped in opposite directions, each pulling a red sleigh filled with late-night sightseers.

Ivy noticed a festive wreath on the door of Dilly's Deli and assumed the new owners had remodeled the inside after buying it from Pete Barton's mother.

She wondered if Montana had seen the Christmas lights and tried to picture him with her mom and dad singing silly songs around the piano while Sasha howled. She held that image in her mind for a moment and considered what a contrast it was to the stiff politeness that had permeated the house over Thanksgiving weekend. She was relieved that Rusty wasn't coming for Christmas, and she could already imagine how exciting it was going to be for Montana to cut down a real Christmas tree—and on his grandparents' property.

*Lord, thank You for Mom and Dad and everything they've done for us. What a blessing they are!*

Ivy glanced in her rearview mirror and didn't see Rue's headlights. Just as well. She didn't need or want him to feel responsible to escort her home.

What if she had confided too much in him? Maybe if she'd just kept quiet about going to jail, he never would have found out. Then again, Montana was bound to mention it. Or someone on staff at the camp. Wasn't it better to get it out in the open than to risk being embarrassed if

Rue found out and confronted her with it? She wondered if he had been truthful about not thinking less of her.

Ivy drove out of the downtown and slowed when she passed by the familiar powder blue Victorian house on the corner of Main and Palmer. She noticed Jewel Sadler's Oldsmobile parked in the driveway, lights on inside the house, and lighted wreaths in every window. She was surprised that Jewel was up this late and wondered if she was worried about Deke and Roscoe. It suddenly occurred to Ivy that she'd been so preoccupied all day that she'd scarcely given them another thought since she left her parents' house.

She decided that tomorrow she would stop by the café and see if Jewel could add any details to what her parents knew about the attack.


Jewel lay on the couch, wrapped in an afghan Kelsey Jones had made her and watching the tail end of a Jimmy Stewart movie. Her eyelids grew heavy, and she decided she would never last through the umpteen commercials that would precede the ending she'd already seen a dozen times before.

She got up and unplugged the lighted wreaths in the living-room windows and glanced over at the Tiffany lamp that her late husband had bought her for no particular reason, other than she had fallen in love with it. She went over and ran her fingers along the glass, still able to picture Melvin's beaming face, and wondered which of them had received the greater blessing.

"I wouldn't take a million bucks for this, Mel."

For a moment he seemed so close she thought she heard him breathing. This house was alive with his presence, and even after twenty years of living in it alone, she couldn't imagine ever selling it.

She pulled the chain on the lamp and turned toward the staircase, which was softly lit by the lights outside.

All at once she felt an explosion in her head and excruciating pain reverberating through her body. Her knees gave way and dropped her to the floor.

She lay sprawled on her back and struggled to get up and felt a powerful blow on her shoulder. And then her arm. Her ribs. Her leg.

"Stop!" Jewel held her hands defensively in front of her and saw someone in a black ski mask, seemingly a man, standing over her, a fire poker grasped in his gloved hand. She thought of Deke and Roscoe and braced herself for another onslaught of merciless blows.

But the assailant just stood there, his eyes visible through the holes in the ski mask. She saw him blink. In the dim light she couldn't tell what color his eyes were. Only that they were fixed on her.

"Please, take whatever you want," she heard herself say. "There's money in my purse. Jewelry upstairs."

The man shook his head from side to side.

"Tell me what you want."

The attacker raised the poker high over his head and held it as if he were relishing the thought of inflicting more pain.

Jewel clamped her eyes shut, determined not to add to his demented pleasure by showing fear or begging for her life.

*God, please don't let me die this way! Not in this house. Not in the shadow of Melvin's love.*

She lay motionless, her body racked with pain, and waited. Why didn't he just finish her off and get it over with? She was aware of her heart pounding, the cuckoo clock ticking, the masked man breathing—and then the fire poker hitting the wooden floor with a loud clank.

*He's leaving!*

Jewel heard footsteps on the creaky floor and opened her eyes just as the assailant straddled her and began hitting her in the face with something hard, each dizzying blow sending shock waves through her head.

She tasted blood and felt herself slipping away and wondered if she would still be breathing when the attacker was through with her—or if she was going to end her days as a murder statistic.

# 14

FLINT NESTLED IN HIS easy chair in the predawn quiet, reading the Sunday paper. He winced when his cell phone vibrated, then picked it up and read the number on the display. "Yeah, Bobby. What's up?"

"We responded to a 911 call and found Jewel Sadler beaten and lyin' in a pool of blood on her livin'-room floor," he said. "Said some guy in a ski mask worked her over. Looks like he used a brass fire poker and a glass paperweight. Judgin' from the look of her injuries, I'd say it happened a few hours ago. She's lost a lot of blood, but the EMTs think she's gonna be okay. She's on her way to Tanner County Medical Center."

Flint's heart sank. "Did she call it in?"

"The caller was male. Used a prepaid cell. Said a lady was in dire need of emergency help and gave Jewel's address, then hung up. Probably the same perp who did a number on Deke and Roscoe."

"Was she sexually assaulted?"

"She doesn't know. We'll know more later."

Flint sighed. "Who is this sick monster who gets off on brutalizing defenseless old people? And why'd he change his MO and call for help?"

"I doubt it was out of remorse. Probably wants us to know he's in control."

"Was Jewel robbed?"

"Her house wasn't ransacked. Her jewelry box is in plain view on her dresser. And her purse had forty bucks cash in it. She'll have to tell us if somethin's missin', but there's an empty table with a doily on it here in the livin' room. Jewel has whatnots and knickknacks everywhere else. Seems odd this one's empty."

"Did you ask her about it?"

"Not yet. I was more interested in gettin' a description of her attacker before the EMTs got her doped up on painkillers. Buck Lowry's on his way over here with a team to collect evidence. I'll go over to TCMC and wait till Jewel's able to talk some more."

Flint rolled his head in a circle. "Okay, Bobby. Tell Buck I'm on my way. When I'm done there, I'll meet you at the medical center."


Flint walked in the front door of Jewel's home and saw Buck Lowry standing next to a pool of red on the hardwood floor near the staircase, and a team of investigators moving about the house, gathering evidence.

"Fill me in," Flint said.

Buck came over and stood next to him, his arms folded. "Looks like the perp let himself in by breaking a window on the back door. We don't know if he was already inside when the victim got home and waited to make his move, or whether he broke in just before the attack. We do know the victim had been home at least long enough to change into her pajamas. We found two weapons on the floor: a fire poker and a lead crystal paperweight. Both belong to the victim, and both contain traces of her blood and hair.

"What about prints? DNA?"

"We dusted the weapons and that little desk over there, where we believe the perp found the paperweight. Also the knob on the back door, but I doubt we'll find the attacker's prints. If this is the same sicko who beat up Deke and Roscoe, I doubt we're going to find any of his DNA on the victim or in the house. But if there *is* anything here, we'll find it."

"Did you check her answering machine?"

"Yes, no messages."

"What about the café?"

Buck nodded. "Marshal Redmond just called, and the place is neat as a pin. No sign of an intruder. Nothing on the victim's calendar to indicate she was meeting anyone or going anywhere besides home."

"Okay, keep me posted. I'm going to go listen to the tape of the caller's voice, and then I'll be with Bobby at the medical center. I can't believe three elderly victims, personal friends of mine, were attacked on my watch, and we can't produce a single clue to help us nail this creep."

"You shouldn't take this personal, Sheriff."

Flint turned and walked toward the front door. "Too late!"

Flint stood with Bobby in the hallway outside the waiting room at Tanner County Medical Center. He glanced at his watch without noticing the time. "I wonder what's taking so long. Surely, the doctor knows something by now."

"Want me to go find us something to eat?" Bobby said.

"My stomach's upset. But if you're hungry, go ahead."

"The only thing I'm hungry for is gettin' the cuffs on this creep so he can't hurt anybody else."

Flint nodded. "I keep mentally replaying the caller's voice on that 911 recording. I'm convinced his southern accent was phony. The guy's just playing with us."

A door opened into the waiting room, and a man in a white coat came out and looked around, then acknowledged Bobby with his eyes and walked out into the hallway.

"Dr. Bronson, this is Sheriff Carter," Bobby said.

"Yes sir. I recognize your face." The doctor offered Flint his hand. "I'm relieved to report that Ms. Sadler's injuries are not permanent, at least the physical ones. She's lost a lot of blood and suffered multiple lacerations and contusions consistent with the beating she took. She's going to be very weak and sore, and the bruising and swelling is going to look much worse over the next few days. The good news is, she has no fractures. She does have a concussion, but it's not severe. We've admitted her and have started her on two pints of blood. We'll watch her closely for the next few days. Providing there are no complications, she should make a full recovery. If this woman were a cat, I'd say she just used up one of her nine lives. As horrible as it sounds, she's extremely lucky."

"No evidence of sexual assault?" Flint asked.

Dr. Bronson shook his head. "No. But the animal that did this deserves to be kept in a cage. I hope you get him off the street."

"Don't worry, we will. Did she say anything to you that we should know?"

"She didn't talk about what happened, if that's what you mean. But she was well aware of the time and upset she wasn't able to open the café."

Flint smiled. "I'm sure she was. Then in your opinion, Jewel's clear-headed enough to tell us what happened?"

"Not necessarily. It depends on how she reacts to the Demerol we gave her and whether or not she's disoriented and confused as a result of the head trauma. Don't be surprised if it takes a few hours or even a few days before she's able to recall everything that happened and put it in sequence. I will say she seemed pretty alert to me."

"Can we talk to her?" Flint said.

"As long as you don't push her too hard and don't stay more than ten minutes. She's in room 104."

Dr. Bronson shook hands with Flint and Bobby and then disappeared through the same door he had come out of.

"All right, Bobby. Let's go."

Flint started down the same shiny corridor he had walked the day before and stopped at room 104 and knocked softly on the open door. "Jewel? It's Flint. Lieutenant Knolls is with me."

Flint stepped inside and over to the bed where Jewel lay, her upper body elevated, her head resting on a pillow. She was hooked up to two IV drips; one contained clear liquid and the other blood. He tried not to let his face reflect the rage he felt or that he hardly recognized her. He reached out and squeezed her hand. "How're you feeling?"

"I've got a doozie…of a headache," Jewel said, her cut and swollen lips hardly moving. "First time in twenty years I wasn't there…to open…the café."

"You'll be back there soon, good as new." As slow and thick as her speech was, he needed to get the facts before the Demerol knocked her out. "Jewel, we hate to bother you when you feel so bad, but we need to be sure we're on the right track. Can you tell us again what you remember about your assailant?"

"He wore a black ski mask…never said a word…packed a wallop."

"You sure it was a man?"

"Had broad shoulders…like a man."

"Short or tall?"

Jewel's glassy eyes grew wide, almost as if the question amused her. "When you're on…the floor…looking up…everything…seems tall."

Flint smiled to himself. "Good point. Can you tell us what you remember about the attack? Every detail could be important."

"I was watching a movie…got sleepy…turned to go upstairs…felt like the roof fell in on my head. A man in a ski mask kept hitting…me with something. I…I told him to take my jewelry…purse. He shook his head… That's not what he wanted." Jewel's chin quivered.

Flint took her hand in his. "It's okay. Take your time. Did he say what he wanted?"

"I don't remember… He hit me in the face… I heard a siren…and voices…bright lights…loud noises." Jewel shook her head. "I'm not much help."

"Sure you are," Flint said. "Dr. Bronson said it might take a little while before you remember everything. You just rest. We know the guy hit you with a fire poker and a lead crystal paperweight. We found those weapons at the scene. You confirmed that he fit the description of Deke and Roscoe's attacker, so we have that to go on. And we have his voice on the 911 call he made."

Jewel stared at him blankly. "He called 911?"

"At 5:34 this morning."

"Well...doesn't that...beat all?"

"Listen, Jewel. The only thing I want you to be concerned with is getting better so you can get back to the café. We're going to put away the guy that did this to you."

"I have a question," Bobby said. "It doesn't appear the guy broke in to rob you. He didn't take your diamond jewelry or the forty bucks in your purse. But there's a small table in the livin' room close to the couch that's bare except for a white doily. Was there somethin' on it?"

Jewel moved her gaze from Bobby to Flint and back to Bobby as if she didn't quite understand the question. Suddenly, her eyes welled and she closed them, her head rolling from side to side on the pillow. "No. He can't have that. Not that..."

Bobby looked at Flint and shrugged. "What was on the table?"

"A gift from my husband...a Tiffany lamp...not worth much...but it meant everything to me."


Flint walked outside TCMC, Bobby on his heels, and drew in a slow deep breath of fresh air and let it out.

"I never get used to the cruelty," Flint said. "Wasn't it enough that he beat the poor woman? Did he really have to steal the one possession that meant the most to her?"

Bobby unwrapped a piece of bubblegum and popped it into his mouth. "It's another way our perp's showin' he's in control. Same as takin' Deke and Roscoe's money jar. Want some gum?"

"No thanks."

"What's drivin' *me* nuts is how the guy knew what would rattle her chain if he took it from her. Her husband's been dead for what, twenty years? I doubt Jewel goes around talkin' about a lamp he gave her."

Flint's cell phone vibrated, and he took it off his belt clip and read the number on the display.

"Yeah, Buck. How's it coming?"

"The only prints we found on the weapons used in the assault were Ms. Sadler's," Buck said. "Same with the doorknob. No great surprise. We're still going through everything we collected, but this guy's good. I doubt if we're going to find his prints or DNA. However, we did find something interesting: strands of orange hair—feline. According to a long-time neighbor, Ms. Sadler never owned a cat."

Flint looked over at Bobby. "Thanks, Buck. I just figured out my next stop." He put the phone on his belt clip. "Investigators found orange cat hair at the scene. Jewel's never owned a cat. Let's go talk to Huck Maxfield and turn up the heat."

Bobby blew a pink bubble and sucked it into his mouth. "Okay. But orange cats are a dime a dozen. And just because Maxfield knew about the nickels in the money jar is no great shakes either, since the manager at the feed store confirmed what he told us. We don't have a solid reason to suspect him in either assault."

"Yet!" Flint said louder than he meant to. "I don't trust the guy, and I'm not waiting around for his background check to come through on Monday!"

"All right, let's talk to him. But can you honestly imagine Huck Maxfield being vicious?"

"Well, let's just see how he reacts when we wipe that smirk off his grimy face."

Flint glanced up and saw Luke Draper walking briskly toward him.

"I just went to Jewel's for lunch," Luke said, sounding out of breath, "and there was a note on the door that the café is closed until further notice. A reporter hanging around outside told me someone broke into Jewel's house and beat her up. Is she going to be okay?"

"The doctor says she is." Flint put his hand on Luke's shoulder. "But brace yourself. She looks bad."

"First Deke and Roscoe, and now Jewel." Luke clenched his jaw. "Was the guy after something?"

"We can't really discuss with you the details of the investigation."

"Well, did she give you his description?"

"She did. And we think it could be the same perp who broke into Deke and Roscoe's."

Luke made a fist and punched the palm of his other hand. "I'd love to go after this scumbag."

"Don't get any wise ideas about lookin' for this guy on your own," Bobby said. "Or you might end up in the same shape as your friends."

Luke's eyes turned to slits. "Well, at least he'd be dealing with someone who could fight back."

"We're going to get him, Luke," Flint said. "Go on in and sit with Jewel. She's in 104. I know she'll be glad to see you."

Flint followed Bobby up the warped wooden steps to Huck Maxfield's porch and knocked on the frame of the torn screen door.

A few seconds later, Huck opened the door, unkempt as before, a grin revealing the unsightly tartar buildup on his teeth. "You back?"

"We'd like to talk to you about somethin' else," Bobby said.

"All right." Huck held open the door.

Bobby squeezed past him and Flint followed, repulsed anew by the stench of body odor and the pungent smells in the house.

Huck reached down and picked up a gray cat, then sat on the car seat and nodded toward the dilapidated brown couch. "Sit, if you like. What is it you wanted to talk about?"

"Jewel Sadler. Know her?" Bobby said.

"Can't say as I do."

"Ever eaten at Jewel's Café in Jacob's Ear?"

Huck shook his head, his hand scratching the cat's ear. "I don't eat out."

"Really? You do your own cookin'?"

"TV dinners." Huck's grin widened. "I'm particularly fond of Hungry Man meat loaf with mashed potatoes. What does my choice of food have to do with Jewel…what did you say her last name was?"

"Sadler. She owns Jewel's Café. Someone broke into her home last night and beat her up."

"Wasn't me."

"Where were you between 9:00 p.m. and 5:30 a.m.?"

Huck scratched his matted hair. "Asleep, I think. Of course, since I wasn't awake to verify it. I'm just guessing."

"How about you cut the cutesy commentary and just answer the questions," Bobby said. "Were you in Jacob's Ear yesterday?"

"Yeah. I went to the grocery store."

"What time?"

"After supper, around eight o'clock. The receipt's on the kitchen table if you want to take a look."

"And you expect us to believe you drove all the way back out here, put the groceries away, and were in bed asleep by nine?" Bobby rolled his eyes.

Huck's face turned red, but his grin remained fixed. "I might be wrong about the time. I didn't know it was going to be important, or I would've paid closer attention. Maybe it was earlier than eight. Does it really matter?"

Bobby leaned forward, his hands clasped between his knees. "Yeah, it does, Huck. You see, we found orange cat hair in the victim's house, and she's never owned a cat."

"And that makes me a suspect?" Huck laughed. "How many people in Tanner County own an orange cat?"

"Well, probably a lot. But we've had two anonymous phone calls in the past month suggesting that the sheriff's department should be aware of some suspicious activity near Jacob's mine. Guess what, Huck? You're the only one out here. Any idea what the caller was tryin' to tell us?"

"I don't have anything to hide. Search whatever you want: my house, truck, shed. I just want to be left alone. I don't bother anybody. And I don't know anything about that Jewel lady being robbed."

"Robbed?" Bobby got up and walked over to Huck, his arms folded across his chest. "Who said anything about robbed?"

"Well, I...I assumed she was, same as those two old-timers."

"Nice save, Huck. But I'm not buyin' it." Bobby leaned over, his nose not more than twelve inches in front of Huck's face. "You like beatin' up on defenseless old people? Is that what turns you on?"

"No."

"Did you break into Jewel Sadler's home and assault her?"

"I told you I didn't."

"The cat hair tells a different story."

"We both know better than that." Huck set the gray cat on the floor, and a calico cat immediately jumped up on the back of the car seat and rubbed against his neck.

"Have you spent time in the South, Huck? Did you think fakin' that southern accent on the 911 call would throw us?"

"I have no idea what you're talking about."

"Ever bought a prepaid cell phone?"

"No. I don't even know what one looks like." Huck rose to his feet, the grin finally gone from his face. "I'm done talking to you guys. If you want to search the premises, knock yourselves out. If not, you know the way out."

Flint locked gazes with Bobby, then got up from the couch and arched his low back. "We'll be in touch."

# 15

ON SUNDAY AFTERNOON, Ivy sat at her kitchen table with Rue. She was enjoying a cup of hot chocolate and thinking this had been one of the nicest weekends she could remember since moving back to Jacob's Ear. Rue had gone to church with her and Montana, and then the three of them had spent the afternoon riding snowmobiles and exploring the south end of Phantom Hollow.

Montana and Rue had hit it off much better than she ever imagined, and she was surprised to find herself vying for Rue's attention.

Montana climbed down the ladder from the loft, carrying a thin box under his arm. "Who wants to play Chinese checkers with me?" He flashed Rue an impish grin. "I warn you, I'm really good."

"Think so, eh? Well, here's what I'm really good at!"

Rue grabbed Montana and put him in a headlock, evoking a playful shriek. He tickled the boy's ribs until he was belly laughing so hard there was no sound. Rue finally stopped, and the two of them sat back and tried to catch their breath.

Ivy relished the laughter and the sight of her son having so much fun.

"Okay, champ." Rue opened the Chinese checkers box. "Sit down here and let's see how good you are. Ivy, you in?"

"Sure." She glanced up at the kitchen clock. "Why don't you stay for dinner? I've got chicken and vegetables in the Crockpot. We usually eat dinner around six."

"I wondered what smells so good," Rue said. "I'd love a home-cooked meal. Thanks."

"My mom cooks really good stuff." Montana made a fist and pointed his thumb at himself. "And *I* make the bestest English muffins and jelly. My grandma taught me how."

"I love English muffins and jelly. Maybe you could show *me* sometime." Rue winked at Ivy.

"Okay." Montana opened the packs of marbles. "I'm blue, you can be white, and Mom can be yellow."

The phone rang, and Ivy got up and picked up the receiver. "Hello."

"Honey, I've been trying to reach you most of the afternoon," her mother said. "Didn't you get my messages on your cell?"

"Sorry, Mom. We were out snowmobiling, and I never even thought to turn it on. What's wrong? You sound upset."

"She's going to be okay, but someone broke into Jewel's house last night, and she was badly beaten. Much the same scenario as what happened to Deke and Roscoe."

Ivy leaned against the countertop and blinked away the images that popped into her mind. "I can't believe this. What time did it happen?"

"Between the time she got home from work and five thirty this morning when the 911 call came in."

"I drove by there last night around eleven," Ivy said. "Her Olds was in the driveway, and all the wreaths were lit in the windows. I thought it was odd the lights were still on."

"That might be important. You should tell Flint."

"How did you find out Jewel'd been attacked?" Ivy said.

"Your dad and I went to the café after church and found a sign on the door indicating the café is closed until further notice. When we passed by Jewel's house, we saw the yellow crime-scene tape and turned around and went back. Her neighbor told us what happened and that

Marshal Redmond and the sheriff's deputies had been there all morning gathering evidence and asking questions. That's all we know, other than she's been admitted at TCMC and her condition is stable."

"Why don't you call Flint and find out exactly what happened?"

There was a long pause, and then Carolyn said, "Your dad refuses to talk to Flint…and I don't want to embarrass either of them by getting in the middle."

"I wish Dad would just forgive Flint and go on. I'm the one who got interrogated without an attorney present, and I'm not even mad at him."

"I'm with you. Elam knows exactly how I feel, but it's not my fight."

There was a long pause.

"Well," Ivy said, "if no one can tell me how she is, I'll go find out for myself."

Forty minutes later, Ivy left Montana with Rue in the waiting room of Tanner County Medical Center and headed down to room 104. She slipped inside and stopped just short of the bed, thinking for a moment that she must have been given the wrong room number.

The sleeping patient bore no resemblance to Jewel Sadler. All exposed flesh was badly discolored with varying shades of black and blue. One eye had been blackened, and her upper lip split and swelled twice its normal size. Around her head, layers of gauze resembling a do-rag had been wrapped so that not a strand of her hair was visible.

"Jewel?" she whispered.

The woman's eyes moved under her eyelids and finally opened.

Ivy stepped over to the side of the bed, her hands gripping the rail, and looked into the kind, unassuming, blue eyes that could only be Jewel Sadler's.

*What did that monster do to you?* Ivy was unsure if she had said the words out loud or merely thought them. Her vision blurred, and she felt Jewel's fingers touch hers. She opened her hand to receive them.

"It's okay, doll," Jewel said, barely above a whisper. "I'm already…on the mend. I'll be…out of here…before you know it."

"Sheriff Carter will get whoever did this!" Ivy said, almost as if saying it out loud would remove any doubt. "Does it hurt?"

"Only when I…move…or breathe…" Jewel's eyes lit up the way they did any time she was trying to be funny.

"I'm serious. They're giving you something for pain, right?"

"Strong stuff…makes me sleepy."

"Did you see the guy who did this?"

"I told Flint…he wore a ski mask."

"It's beyond me how anyone could do this to another person."

Jewel pushed her tongue along the inside of her lips as if her mouth were dry. "Could be worse… I'd hate to be…his dog."

"How you can joke about this?"

"Notice I'm not…laughing."

Ivy got quiet for a moment, Jewel's hand in hers, and thought about how fragile life is and how the assault could just as easily have ended in tragedy.

"I'm going…back to work…soon," Jewel said.

"You can't worry about the café right now."

"What else…have I got…to worry about?"

Ivy heard a knock on the door and turned just as Luke Draper came into the room with Rita and Laura, waitresses at the café.

"How's our girl?" Luke said.

Ivy lifted her eyebrows. "Determined to go back to work."

Luke pulled up a chair, his arms folded on the bedrail. "We had a feeling you'd be thinking that way, so we came as a united front. No one wants you back at the café any more than we do. But Rita and Laura can keep it running while you're getting better. And I'll bring my laptop and do my work down there. That way I can taste all the specials and report to you if they take any shortcuts on those delicious recipes of yours."

Jewel smiled and then winced. "You rascal."

"I'll even wait tables if you need me to. Jewel's Café does *not* need to close."

Jewel shook her head, her eyes dancing. "You're…something else."

"Rita and I can take turns opening and closing," Laura said. "Don't worry about a thing. But I can tell you right now, we're *not* letting him wait tables."

"Chicken." Luke chuckled. He took his cell phone off his belt clip and looked at the display screen. "Sorry, I need to take this. It's one of the board members—no doubt checking to make sure I'm not working on Sunday night. I'll be right back." He got up and ambled toward the door, the phone to his ear. "Hello, Raymond…no, actually I'm not…"

Ivy glanced at her watch. "Jewel, I need to go. Montana's in the waiting room with a friend. As soon as you're feeling better, he wants to come see you. He adores you and is so upset about what happened."

"Okay, doll…hug him…for me."

"I will." Ivy squeezed her hand. "I'll leave you in good company. I'd like to go see Deke and Roscoe for a minute."


Ivy sat in front of a crackling fire in her living room, the dishwasher humming behind her, and tried to shake the image of Jewel's, Deke's, and Roscoe's battered faces. She heard the front door open and felt a blast of cold air sweep across her shoulders.

"Mom, I saw it!" Montana came in and flopped on the couch next to her. I saw Betelgeuse! And Rigel! The Big Dipper too! Rue helped me find them. It was so cool!"

"We walked about a hundred yards away from the lights," Rue said. "It's amazing what you can see right out your back door. I can't wait to show him a diagram of Orion. It'll be even more fun when he knows what shape to look for."

"You *boys* have had quite a day," Ivy said.

"It's been great." Rue looked down at Montana. "But tomorrow's a school day. I need to hit the road and let you get ready for bed."

Montana's eyebrows formed a straight line. "Can't you stay and play Chinese checkers one more time? Pleeease…"

"I'm afraid not, champ. Your mom made it clear that it's lights out at eight."

"Sweetie, why don't you go take your shower?" Ivy said. "There might be time for one more game before eight."

"Okay!" Montana climbed up the ladder and looked over his shoulder. "I get to be blue again!"

Rue sat in the rocker. "Wish I could bottle all that energy."

"Thanks for showing an interest in him," Ivy said. "He's eating up the male attention."

"Well, it's not hard. He's a great kid to be around—a lot more polite than my nephews were at his age. And not at all spoiled. I don't know how you pulled that off, but you've done a good job with him."

"I'd like to take credit, but I think our having only the bare necessities for most of his life had everything to do with that. My friend Lu was the one who taught him manners and to be caring and thoughtful from a very early age. I hardly remember anything about him until he was four. I still feel so guilty about that."

"If you believe God's forgiven you, why are you beating up on yourself? He's still a great kid, so you're doing something right."

Montana scrambled down the ladder wearing only his underwear, pajamas tucked under his arm, and headed for the bathroom. "I'll be right back."

"I can't tell you how good it makes me feel to see that child happy and excited," Ivy said. "He's been through so much in the past few months: first moving here, starting a new school, then Lu dying, my going to jail, and now my brother Rusty's rejection. My parents have been wonderful with him. And it's been good getting plugged in at church. Yet I feel helpless to deal with the void he feels because his father's not part of his life."

"I'm really sorry he's been through all that. It's a pretty heavy load for a seven-year-old."

Ivy nodded. "But looking on the bright side, he loves school and gets along well with other kids. My parents and everyone here at the camp make a great extended family. And we love living in the chalet. We've never had our own place before, and Montana thinks having his bedroom in the loft is about the coolest thing in the world."

"It's real homey. I can see why you like it so much."

"Thanks. It's a palace compared to the scroungy apartments we rented in Denver."

"I get the feeling you don't have many pleasant memories of Denver."

Ivy stared at the flames dancing in the fireplace. "I really don't." *And you'd run the other way if I told you* everything.

The bathroom door opened, and Montana rushed into the living room dressed in Spider-Man p.j.'s, the hair at the nape of his neck wet, the clean smell of soap emanating from him. "It's only twenty till eight o'clock."

"You really want me to beat you again?" Rue said.

"No, *I'm* the champ. I won five times. You only won one time."

"Five to one? I'm worse at this than I thought." Rue rose to his feet. "Come on, Ivy." He held out his hand and pulled her to her feet. "We might as well share the humiliation."


Flint walked in the front door of his house, feeling spent and thinking a hot shower sounded great. He went into the bedroom and saw Betty lying on her side of the bed, a pillow propped behind her, reading a book.

"Hi, hon." Flint kissed her cheek. "Sorry I didn't make it home before Ian went down for the night."

Betty took off her reading glasses. "You've had quite a day."

"Fifteen straight hours and nothing solid. I hate it."

"I'm sorry. How's Jewel?"

"Looks like someone threw her under a Mack truck. As if beating the poor woman wasn't enough, the loser went for the jugular and stole a lamp her late husband had given her. Not money. Not jewelry. A Tiffany lamp she's real sentimental about."

"Was it valuable?"

"Jewel said it wasn't. She cried when Bobby told her it was missing."

"Why would an intruder take that and not her valuables?"

"How should I know? I'm just the lowly sheriff who hasn't got a clue what's going on."

Betty got up and put her arms around his neck. "Don't get down on yourself because you haven't solved this yet. It's the darnedest thing I've ever heard of."

"Buck's investigators found a couple strands of orange cat hair at the scene. Jewel's never owned a cat, so that could be important. Thing is, Jewel could've transported cat hair home on her coat or clothes. Or anyone who walked in her house could've brought it with them. Anyhow, it gave Bobby and me a good excuse to talk again with that nut case I told you about—the one with the bazillion cats."

Betty sat on the end of the bed. "You suspect him?"

"I wouldn't go that far, but I've got a bad feeling about him. He's new in the area and keeps to himself. He doesn't have a record. But after those two anonymous calls alerting us to suspicious activity out near Jacob's mine, my antenna's up. We're doing a background check and should know more about him by tomorrow or Tuesday."

"The cat hair would bug me."

Flint sat next to Betty and took off his shoes. "It's interesting, all right. But the guy absolutely doesn't care if we tear his place apart. He's given us a green light to look through everything he's got—house, truck, shed. Why would he do that if he had something to hide?"

# 16

Ivy put Monday morning's issue of the *Tri County Courier* on the coffee table in the lobby of Three Peaks Lodge and lifted the hinged counter and walked through to the other side.

Kelsey came in the front door, Brandon on her heels, and brushed the snowflakes off her parka. "Hey, girlfriend. How was the rest of your weekend?"

"Really good, thanks. Other than the horrible news about Jewel."

"We're just sick about it. Can't imagine who would do such a thing. We heard the café's going to be open, though."

Ivy nodded. "I went to the medical center to see Jewel last night, and Rita and Laura came in with Luke Draper just as I was leaving. They told Jewel not to worry about a thing, that they're going to keep things running."

The corners of Brandon's mouth turned up. "Does *they* include Luke?"

"No. He was just kidding around," Ivy said. "But you should've seen Jewel's eyes light up when she saw him—and it wasn't the Demerol. He's really good with her."

Brandon blew on his hands and rubbed them together. "I hate to change the subject, but I think I'll get a fire going in the fireplace. We've

got a new group arriving late this morning, and the temperature's supposed to drop fifteen degrees when that cold front moves through."

Kelsey started to go back to the offices and then turned around. "We
saw Rue sitting with you at church yesterday. Did you change your mind
about Montana spending time with him?"

"I overreacted to that," Ivy said. "Rue is *so* nice. The three of us
spent some quality time together, and he's incredible with Montana,
even has him hooked on astronomy. We went snowmobiling yesterday
afternoon, and Montana finally got to show him around the grounds.
Of course Rue acted like it was the first time he'd seen any of it and
complimented Montana for being such a good tour guide. Then he
came over and played Chinese checkers and had dinner with us. He
even sat with Montana in the waiting room at the medical center so I
could slip in and see Jewel."

Kelsey looked at her blankly for a moment. "Wow. I had no idea."

"What do you mean?"

"I'm just surprised you're spending so much time with Rue after your
discussion just a week ago about being cautious and letting things evolve."

"Well, I had to rethink that," Ivy said. "Rue obviously passed the
background and drug tests or he wouldn't be here. And if he had applied
for a job as a camp counselor, other than his age, we wouldn't have a valid
reason not to consider him, right?"

Brandon knelt in front of the fireplace and lit the starter log. "I'd like
to see him sober a lot longer first."

"It's been almost a year. But it's *always* going to be one day at a
time for both of us." Ivy bit her lip and entered her password into the
computer.

"Hey, look," Brandon said. "If I overstepped just then, I'm sorry. It's
really none of my business."

"Don't say that. You guys are like family. If it hadn't been for Kelsey,
I might never have recommitted my life to Christ. But I really do have
good sense. Yes, I've made lots of mistakes, and I've grown from each one.

Believe me, the last thing in the world I want to do is jeopardize Montana's happiness or my own. But I have to think ahead."

"Of course you do," Kelsey said, "but you've been through the mill this past year. It might be good to get comfortable with all the life changes you're facing before putting emotional energy into a relationship."

"I would hardly call what I have with Rue a *relationship*. I'm not closing my heart to the possibility that it might develop into one. I'll be thirty in May. I'd like to get married and have another child. It's not like I've set up a timetable. I've asked the Lord to open and close doors. The deepest desire of my heart is that Montana doesn't have to grow up without a dad just because I messed up."

Kelsey came over and leaned on the counter. "I really do understand that. And I didn't mean to upset you."

Ivy wiped a tear off her cheek. "I know. I'm a little ouchy when it comes to people second-guessing my decisions, probably because I feel so guilty about the past. I want people to believe in me."

Brandon came over and stood next to Kelsey. "Feeling protective of you doesn't mean we don't believe in you, Ivy. It's just a fact that once we fall for someone, we tend to see only the positives. It makes sense to allow time to consider the pros and cons of beginning a relationship *before* emotions ever enter in."

"I understand what you're saying, but I think we've established that Rue is an okay guy. I think I'm capable of taking it from here."


Flint sat at his desk reading the background report on Huck Maxfield. He heard a knock at the door and glanced up over the top of his glasses.

"Come in, Bobby. I'm done reading."

Bobby walked in and flopped in a chair. "How would you like to be saddled with the name Huckley? No wonder the guy's messed up."

"Hey, it's better than Huckleberry. I don't know what I expected to find, but not this. Huckley James Maxfield. Age fifty-three. Graduated from the University of Missouri at Columbia. Worked thirty years as an elementary schoolteacher in the Kansas City area. Retired in May of this year, which means he gets a nice pension. Which also means he doesn't need to steal a jar of nickels or a Tiffany lamp."

"Why wouldn't he just tell us he'd been a schoolteacher? What's he hiding?"

Flint shrugged. "Nothing that I can see. Maybe he really is just a private person like he said. He left his teaching career in good standing. Divorced in 1985. No kids. No alimony. Owned his home until June of this year. No credit-card debt. No lien on the truck."

Bobby popped a pink bubble and sucked the gum into his mouth. "On paper the guy's Mr. Citizen."

Flint looked at the photo on Maxwell's Colorado driver's license. "So what made him go from being a respectable member of society to living like a homeless man in a garbage heap in just six months? Maybe he's bipolar and off his meds."

"Nah, my wife's uncle's bipolar. He has episodes of bein' really hyper and talkin' too fast and then episodes of bein' withdrawn and anxious and unreasonable. Maxfield's demeanor's consistent, right down to the plastic grin."

"Which, you may recall, finally disappeared when we started talking to him about the prepaid cell phone."

"Yeah, but I'd pushed all his buttons. There's really nothin' there to make me think he's involved in the assaults. You want me to keep diggin'?"

Flint took off his glasses. "Not right now. I want you to go check out all the lodging places in the area. Get the name, address, and license number of every male guest who was registered the night of the attacks. See if that leads anywhere."


Ivy decided to go home for lunch and avoid the possibility of ending up at a table with Rue and Kelsey and Brandon. She picked up her mail at the office and then went out the front door of the lodge, her Polartec hat pulled down over her ears, and cut through the icy wind toward the chalet. Of all the days to decide to walk to work instead of drive!

It hit her that Christmas was only three weeks away and she needed to make plans to take Montana out to cut down a tree. She remembered where she had stashed the box of Christmas ornaments she had brought with her from Denver and wondered if it would be depressing to hang them on the tree now that Lu was gone.

Her thoughts flashed back to the artificial tree Lu had bought at the Salvation Army thrift store when Montana was four. It was new and still in the box, but it wasn't very tall or all that real looking. And every ornament the three of them put on it they had made themselves. It wasn't much, but it was enough. And though Lu would never admit it, Ivy was sure she had traded her cultured pearl necklace for it.

She couldn't imagine that a fresh-cut tree, even one decorated with all the specialty ornaments her parents would insist on buying, could ever be more beautiful.

Ivy trudged through the snow to her front door and unlocked it. She put the mail on the kitchen table and reached in the refrigerator for the container of leftover chicken and vegetables, put it in the microwave, and set the timer for three minutes.

She sat at the table and sorted through the mail and saw an envelope with a return address of Albuquerque, New Mexico, and figured it must be from Rusty.

She slid open the envelope and pulled out a handwritten note.

Ivy,

    Mom and Dad are pressuring us to come home for Christmas, which I already told them at Thanksgiving we're not going to do. Jacqueline and I want the girls to have Christmas in their own house. Now Mom and Dad are insisting that the four of you drive here the week <u>after</u> Christmas so we can all exchange gifts.

I resent being put in the position of being the bad guy. But the truth is: I don't want to spend any part of the holidays with you and Montana. I have too many bad memories associated with past Christmases when you were gone. And too much resentment associated with your return. Exchanging gifts under these circumstances is a big sham I'm not willing to get involved in.

I'm writing you because I don't think Mom and Dad are hearing me. I suggest you convince them not to make the trip—or to make it without you two. I see no reason to drag them into the reasons why.

Rusty

Ivy let the tears roll down her cheeks and onto the paper, guilt and condemnation piercing her heart all over again. If God had removed her sins as far as the east is from the west, how was it that other people, her own brother included, had no troubling picking them up and flinging them in her face?

Brandon sat in his office working on his computer when he heard a knock on the door and saw Rue Kessler standing there.

"Hey, Rue. Come in."

Rue stepped inside but remained standing. "As Don and I were leaving the dining hall, a Lieutenant Bobby Knolls approached us and asked a number of questions and wanted to know our whereabouts at the time of those beatings. Said you told him where to find us."

"I did. Please don't take it personal. The sheriff's department is questioning all male guests who were staying in the area over the weekend because of the assaults. No one is singling you out."

"Sure seemed like it to me. Don blew it off, but I didn't like Knolls's attitude. I told him the truth, and he snickered and wrote something down. I got the feeling he doesn't believe me."

"What'd you tell him?"

"The truth. I'm into astronomy and was stargazing up on Tanner's Ridge all night Friday and got back around 3:00 a.m. Saturday. It was one of the clearest nights I've seen in ages. Then on Saturday night after I left your place, Ivy and I met at Grinder's and talked till 11:00. After that, I drove back toward the camp and pulled off on road G-7 and spent another couple hours stargazing. I'm not making this up. I even took Montana out after dinner last night so he could see the two brightest stars in the constellation Orion—Rigel and Betelgeuse."

Brandon smiled. "Hey, I'm impressed."

"Well, the lieutenant wasn't. He just smirked, like he thought it was the stupidest alibi he ever heard. He asked if I'd been using a telescope, and I told him that I forgot to pack it when I came here. He wanted to know if anyone could vouch for when I got back to the cabin. Don said he heard me come in both nights but never looked at the clock."

"I'm sure it's no big deal."

Rue sat in the chair next to Brandon's desk. "It's a big deal to me when I can't prove where I was when those two old guys were beat up. And I can't prove where I was when Ivy's friend Jewel was attacked either, and she just happens to live down the street from Grinder's."

"There's no way Lieutenant Knolls suspects you, Rue. He's just doing his job."

Rue looked at his hands. "He asked if I've been drinking again."

"And you told him no, right?"

"Yeah. I've been sober almost a year. But how would he even know to ask me that?"

"I explained the role of My Brother's Keeper in recommending you guys for the refurbishing project."

"The lieutenant thinks it's odd that both attacks came the weekend after Don and I arrived."

"Well, it's the weekend after lots of other guys arrived in town too. I think Don had the right idea by blowing it off."

"I don't want any trouble, Brandon. I've got a crack at a construction foreman job when I get back to Denver, but I need a good reference from Three Peaks to cinch it."

"Unless there's something you're not telling me, I can't think of any reason why you won't get it."

# 17

IVY CAME OUT the front door of Three Peaks Lodge, the north wind slapping her face, surprised at how much colder it felt. She pulled her scarf up around her ears and her hat down, and walked briskly toward the car, glad she'd had the foresight to drive instead of walk back to the lodge after lunch.

"Ivy, wait!"

She recognized Rue's voice and turned around and saw him jogging toward her.

"I missed you at lunch," he said, sounding out of breath.

"I needed to take care of something at home, so I decided to eat last night's leftovers."

"Why do you look so down? Did you have a bad day?"

Ivy exhaled, her breath a cloud of white vapor. "I got a letter from my brother, Rusty, that has me pretty upset."

"What's the deal?"

Ivy paraphrased what she could remember of the letter, her eyes brimming with tears, her chin quivering. "I deserve his rejection. But Montana sure doesn't."

Rue put his arms around her, and Ivy yielded herself to his embrace, feeling surprisingly comfortable and considerably warmer.

"No one who's making an honest effort deserves that," Rue said.

"In some ways, I can't blame Rusty. I did some pretty despicable things when I was shooting up, and he hasn't been around to see the changes in me. Drugs turn a person ugly from the inside out. It's probably easy for Rusty to write me off since I don't even look like the same person."

Rue leaned back and looked into her eyes. "Well, the new person that's emerging is beautiful." He took his thumb and wiped the tears off her face. "Take one day at a time. That's all you can do."

"I'm not sure that's good enough for Rusty."

"Well, it's good enough for God. You can't worry about Rusty."

Rue's compassionate gaze seemed to melt all her defenses. He tilted her chin and moved his lips ever so slowly toward hers until she could feel the warmth of his breath. The sound of snow crunching under someone's feet caused her to turn, her eyes colliding with Brandon's.

Ivy felt the heat rush to her half-numb cheeks. She put her hands deep into her coat pockets. *So much for trying to convince Brandon that I'm not in a relationship with Rue.*

"Good night. See you guys tomorrow." Brandon whistled as he stepped off the sidewalk and walked over to the other side of the street.

There was a long, awkward pause, then Rue lifted his eyes. "I'd better let you go pick up Montana. When you're in a better frame of mind, we need to talk about something that happened to me today."

"Regarding what?"

"You really need to get out of this cold."

"At least give me a little hint."

"Okay. A Lieutenant Bobby Knolls was waiting for Don and me when we came out of the dining hall today. He wanted us to account for our whereabouts the nights those beatings happened."

"That's crazy."

"I know that, but I don't really have an alibi either."

Ivy shivered, her teeth chattering. "Why don't you come over for dinner around six thirty, and we can talk after Montana goes to bed?"

———

Flint sat at the dinner table and enjoyed a second helping of roast beef, carrots, and potatoes without saying a word about his day. Finally, after Ian finished eating and went upstairs to call Montana, Flint reached over and put his hand on Betty's.

"Great dinner, hon. I needed something good to happen today. Sometimes I think I'm going to have to get out of law enforcement if I want to live to a ripe old age."

"No breaks in the case, eh?" Betty said

"None. It's so frustrating. We got the report back on Huck Maxfield. The guy was a Missouri schoolteacher, of all things. Retired in May of this year, after thirty years, and sold his house. Was issued a Colorado driver's license in July and gave Gus's address as his own. No credit-card debt. His truck's paid for. Nice pension. All Huck inherited from his grandfather was that old shack. He's either really sentimental or has a screw loose to want to live in that dump. Either way, we have nothing on him."

"Back to square one," Betty said. "How maddening."

"Then Ivy Griffith called to say she was in town on Saturday night and remembers driving past Jewel's house around eleven and seeing the lights on and the Christmas wreaths still lit in the windows. She thought it was odd at the time and that it might be important. Which it would, except that the EMTs determined the attack happened four to five hours prior to their arrival, which would put it somewhere between twelve forty-five and one forty-five. We went back and talked to Jewel again. She still can't put the entire sequence together, but she did remember watching an old Jimmy Stewart movie and deciding there were too many commercials as it got closer to the end. She remembers unplugging the wreaths in the windows and starting to go upstairs to bed when she felt the first blow. We checked, and the movie started at eleven and ran until two, so what she remembers is consistent with what the EMTs said."

"But does that really help you?"

Flint took a sip of hot tea. "It might help us narrow down a list of suspects. We believe the perp targeted all three victims, but we can't figure out why he didn't take something valuable. If he just gets off on brutalizing old people, why bother taking anything at all?"

"I don't know, but I'll bet every senior in town is scared to death and wondering who's next."

"Marshal Redmond asked for help, so I've got a couple of our cruisers working the streets. But I'm not sure that'll be enough to deter our perp, assuming he's still out there."

Ivy stood in front of the fireplace, warming her back and watching the snowflakes accumulating outside her picture window. The mantel clock played half the Westminster chimes and then stopped.

"It's eight thirty," she said to Rue. "I'm going to go check on Montana. I'll be right back."

Ivy climbed the ladder to the loft and walked softly over to Montana's bed. The sound of his deep breathing told her what she needed to know. She bent down and pressed her lips to his warm cheek. "Sweet dreams. Mommy loves you."

She climbed back down the ladder and sat in the rocker. "He's out like a light. Thanks for helping him with his homework."

"It was fun listening to him spell his words. He didn't miss any."

"Believe me, he was tickled you noticed. Okay, before we get off on a rabbit track, finish telling me about what happened today."

Rue leaned his head against the back of the couch and looked over at her. "Like I told you, Lieutenant Knolls questioned Don and me about our whereabouts the nights of the attacks. I explained exactly where I was and what I was doing, and Knolls acted real smug about it. I got the strangest feeling that he suspects me."

"Oh, come on, Rue. That's insane."

"Yeah, but it could look like I was conveniently out of pocket during the times the beatings took place. I sure can't prove what I was doing. And I *was* in the neighborhood the night your friend Jewel was assaulted."

"You and everyone else out looking at Christmas lights. I'll just tell the lieutenant I knew exactly what you planned to do both nights. It's not like you invented it."

"What if he thinks I told you all that just to cover my tail?"

"Rue, stop being paranoid! You haven't done anything. You should talk to Brandon."

"I did. Right after it happened. He said not to take it personally, that the sheriff's department was questioning all male guests who had stayed in the area over the weekend."

"Well, there you go," Ivy said. "What did Don think about all this?"

"He blew it off. Nothing bothers him."

"Don't forget the burden of proof is on them, not you. I have a feeling this is more routine than you think."

"Yeah, I've heard that before."

"What do you mean?"

"I've seen people get railroaded, that's all. I've worked so hard to stay sober and get my life back. I just don't have the energy to deal with being falsely accused of something this serious and then having to fight to prove my innocence."

Ivy sensed that he had left the word *again* off the end of his sentence.

Rue got up and stood by the fire, his thumbs hooked on his jeans pockets, his expression somber. "I'll be thirty-five in June, and I'm ready to move on with my life. When I get back to Denver, I've got a crack at a construction foreman job. I hope to find the right woman and settle down. I want a house. Kids. Soccer games. Dance recitals. Piano lessons. Little League—the whole ball of wax. I wanna have the neighbors over for backyard cookouts. And the pastor for Sunday dinner. I'd like to take the kids camping. And to the zoo. And the Grand Canyon. But more than anything, I hope to grow old with the same woman and live long enough to celebrate our fiftieth wedding anniversary. I guess I want it so badly that

I'm scared something'll happen to mess it up…" Rue coughed, seemingly to stave off emotion that was right under the surface. "Maybe that's too pie in the sky."

"Not at all. And any man willing to work for all that deserves to have it." Ivy glanced out the window, thinking there was a lot more depth to Rue than she ever imagined. "Looks like it's stopped snowing. Can I get you something warm to drink? Hot chocolate? Coffee? Tea?"

"Thanks, but I should probably go. I never intended for this to turn into a poor-me session."

"I didn't take it that way. I appreciated the honest dialogue and will be praying about everything we talked about. Why don't you at least have something hot to drink before you go?"

"Actually, a cup of hot tea sounds great."


Brandon put the TV on mute as a commercial interrupted the ten o'clock news, all too aware that Kelsey had been quiet since dinner.

"Honey, you can't live Ivy's life for her," he said.

"I know that. But why didn't she just admit she was in a relationship with Rue and tell us to mind our own business?"

"I may have misread what was going on."

Kelsey rolled her eyes.

"All right. But how much personal information would you be willing to divulge to friends that opposed what you were doing?"

"That's not the point. Ivy's proven she's not the best judge of character. Her misguided loyalty to Pete Barton nearly ruined her life. And then, just seven months ago, she almost fell for the guy who killed him."

"*Almost* doesn't count. And in all fairness to Ivy, Bill had us all fooled."

"That doesn't make me feel any better. Ivy's vulnerable. She desperately wants to be in a loving relationship, but I'm not even sure she's healthy enough to draw someone like that."

"What you're saying is, she's no prize."

Kelsey's cheeks turned pink. "What I'm saying is, she's not ready."

"We might as well get gut-level honest, Kel. With her history, Ivy's not likely to attract the Luke Drapers of the world."

"I guess what I'm trying to say is that a month out on her own as a single mom doesn't qualify her to be half of a healthy relationship. Ivy needs time to figure out who she is and what she can bring to a relationship. My fear is that she's going to settle for—"

"Someone who's been as messed up as she was?"

"Exactly."

Brandon put his arm around Kelsey. "Honey, it would take a remarkable man to be willing to pick up Ivy's baggage unless he'd carried some of his own."

"Maybe so. But I can't believe in my heart that the Lord's will for her—and let's not forget Montana—is to hook up with someone who will have to spend the rest of his life trying to stay sober."

"Ivy has to spend the rest of her life trying to stay clean. What's the difference?"


Ivy got up from the kitchen table and put the coffee mugs in the dishwasher.

"I'm really glad you came over," she said. "I can't tell you how refreshing it is to have a man talk to me from his heart. That hasn't happened very often in my life."

Rue half smiled. "To tell you the truth, I don't usually find it easy to be this open. I probably overreacted to the lieutenant's questions, but thanks for letting me get it out. Sure beats sitting by myself with a bottle of whiskey, not that I have any intention of going near the stuff again."

"Good. It would be a shame if that woman you plan to spend fifty years with never got the chance."

Rue put on his coat and zipped it. "Thanks again for everything. The Lord really used you tonight."

"We're even then, because He's been using you, too."

The room was suddenly pin-drop still. Ivy stood facing Rue and sensed he was going to kiss her.

Rue cupped her face in his hands and gently pressed his lips to her cheek and then again and again as he moved his mouth ever so slowly to her ear. "Good night," he whispered.

The sensation of his breath in her ear turned her skin tingly, and Ivy surrendered to his embrace and the warmth of his lips melting into hers. Soon restraint gave way to eager, prolonged kisses that grew in intensity until she finally pushed away from him, her heart pounding like the wild, rhythmic beat of a tribal drum.

Silence filled the space between them like an airbag after a collision.

Finally Rue said, "Believe it or not, I didn't plan that."

"Neither did I."

"I'd better go."

"Good idea."

Rue pulled on his stocking cap but avoided making eye contact. "If Montana wants to come by after school, Don and I will be working at Night Hawk all day. I'll show him how to use the sander."

Ivy let Rue out and locked the door, then watched through the window as he brushed a new layer of powder snow off his windshield, got in the Explorer, and backed up to the road.

She went over and lowered herself into the rocker and stared at the embers in the fireplace, unsure which was more surprising: that she had felt desire or that she had exercised self-control. It occurred to her that she'd had little experience with either.

# 18

JUST AFTER SIX on Tuesday morning, Flint pushed open the front door of Jewel's Café, the delicious aroma of warm fruit muffins causing him to forget for a second that Jewel wasn't there.

"Hey, Sheriff," Rita said. "Want your usual?"

"Yeah, thanks. That'd be great."

Flint sat at the table closest to the moose head and wondered how many times he had eaten at the café in the past twenty years, and how many times he had been the first customer of the day.

Rita filled his mug with coffee and then set the plastic pitcher on the table. "I saw Jewel last night. Her bruises look worse, but she's not so out of it. Said you'd been over there, trying to help her put her thoughts together. She doesn't seem all that confused to me."

"She's coming around." Flint blew on his coffee. "Sometimes painful memories have holes in them for a while. We need to know every detail to help us nail this guy."

The front door opened, and a few customers walked in, followed by Bobby Knolls.

Bobby nodded at Flint and came over and sat at the table. "I don't know how you can eat this early."

"Years of practice. What I need is a quick rundown on what you found out yesterday. I'm meeting Kyle Redmond in an hour, and then I'm locking myself in my office before that stack of paperwork gets higher than Jacob's Peak."

"It took some footwork, but the team talked to dozens of male guests who stayed in White Top, Mt. Byron, or Jacob's Ear over the weekend. Most had solid alibis. We're takin' a closer look at those who didn't, includin' a fella named Rue Kessler who's workin' out at Three Peaks."

"I'm not familiar with that name. Tell me about him."

Bobby blew a pink bubble and sucked the gum into his mouth. "Elam Griffith authorized the hirin' of Kessler and a guy named Don Freeman through a Christian organization called My Brother's Keeper. As I understand it, this outfit finds jobs for recoverin' substance abusers once they get right with Jesus." Bobby smirked. "Like who *wouldn't* say he got religion if he thought it would get him a job?"

"Go on."

"Kessler and Freeman arrived Monday of last week and plan to stay through the winter, refurbishin' cabins. Both have carpentry skills. Brandon Jones said they seem to be real nice guys and are doin' a bang-up job."

"So why does Kessler stand out?"

"Because of the absurdity of what he claims he was doin' at the time of the assaults."

"Let's hear it."

Flint warmed his hands around his coffee mug and listened as Bobby relayed the conversation he'd had with Rue Kessler and Don Freeman outside the dining hall at Three Peaks, and Kessler's insistence that he'd been out stargazing at the time of the beatings.

"And you don't believe him?" Flint said.

"Come on, lookin' at stars out in the middle of nowhere, and without a telescope?" Bobby chortled. "Can't imagine anybody doin' that all night. But I have other concerns. Kessler was at Grinder's with Ivy Griffith till eleven the night Jewel was attacked. Who's to say he didn't hang around after Ivy left? He can't prove he was up on Tanner's Ridge the night

Deke and Roscoe were attacked either. Claims he got back to the cabin around three in the morning—same time as the attack. It's a little too tidy, if you ask me."

"Can't Kessler's roommate verify when he came in?"

"No. Freeman heard him come in but never looked at the clock. For all we know, it might've been a lot later than three."

"What motive would Kessler have had to assault the victims?"

"Maybe he's just plain mean."

"That's unlikely, since everyone working at Three Peaks has to go through a background check and a drug test. Someone with that kind of pent-up anger would've shown signs of it before."

Bobby leaned forward, his arms folded on the table. "All I can tell you is, Kessler acts like he's hidin' somethin'. He's also taller than Deke. And except for the black clothes and a ski mask, that's the only description we have of the perp."

"Deke's five eight. How many of the men you talked to were taller than five eight?"

"Most. But we also know that perp's vehicle may have a big motor." A grin spread across Bobby's face. "Guess what? Kessler drives an old model Ford Explorer that's in dire need of a new muffler."

"Good, then maybe someone else at the camp heard him come in."

"Nah, there's no one out where Kessler and Freeman are stayin' at Deer Run, which is the first cabin when you turn on—"

"I know exactly where it is, Bobby." Flint took a sip of coffee. "Which tells me that no one can verify whether or not Freeman was home on those nights either. Am I right?"

"Yeah, but I'd bet my 401(k) that he's tellin' the truth."

"Did you question Luke Draper so we don't get criticized for profiling the rehabbers?"

Bobby nodded. "We talked to him over at the medical center. There's no way he's capable of this."

"Okay. But if you've got a bad feeling about Kessler, you're going to have to come up with something more incriminating than he can't prove where he was. I suggest you look for a motive."


Ivy arrived at work ten minutes early and immersed herself in typing guest comments into the computer, hoping neither Brandon nor Kelsey nor Rue would come in and confront her with anything that had happened the night before. She still hadn't come to grips with her unexpected attraction to Rue and certainly didn't want to have to defend it to either of the Joneses.

The door leading back to the offices opened, and she pretended to be concentrating on the computer screen.

"Ivy, sorry to bother you," Brandon said. "Lieutenant Knolls would like to ask you a few questions. Why don't you go to my office, and I'll watch the front desk for you?"

Ivy turned and saw Bobby Knolls, the tension of her past interrogations turning to perspiration under her wool sweater.

She shot Brandon a questioning look, then went through the door and down the hall to his office and sat in a vinyl chair.

Bobby shut the door and pulled a chair up next to her. "Relax, Ivy. We're conductin' a routine investigation of all male guests who were stayin' in the area the nights of the beatings. Rue Kessler said you spent time with him this past weekend. Would you mind tellin' me where you were and in what time frame?"

"Not at all."

Ivy told him everything she did with Rue from the time he approached her after work on Friday until they left Grinder's on Saturday night."

"So you and Mr. Kessler parted ways around 11:00 p.m.?"

"We did. He invited me to go stargazing with him, but I didn't want to sit out in the cold. I didn't want to be up late because of church the next day."

"Have you ever been stargazin' with him?"

"Actually, no. Rue did take my son, Montana, out Sunday after dinner and pointed out a couple of the brightest stars—Betelgeuse and something else. I forgot the name of it. Rue's really passionate about astronomy."

"Yeah, I heard. So why do you suppose he would forget to bring his telescope? I mean an avid fisherman never goes far without his tackle. Or a golfer without his clubs."

Ivy shrugged. "Maybe he never considered he'd have the chance to get out at night. He did come here to work."

"You said he took your son out to look at stars on Sunday? Did you spend time with him on Sunday too?"

*Here we go again.* "Yes, Rue met us at church, then we made peanut-butter-and-jelly sandwiches and went snowmobiling. The three of us had a very pleasant day. We played Chinese checkers and had dinner at my place. And then Rue sat with Montana in the waiting room at TCMC so I could go visit Jewel Sadler."

"That was Sunday night?"

Ivy nodded. "Why are you asking me these questions?"

"Like I said, it's just routine. Let's back up a minute. When you left Grinder's Saturday night, you drove down Main Street and took Three Peaks Road back to the camp, right?"

"Yes."

"Mr. Kessler says he drove down Main Street and got on Three Peaks Road. But instead of going all the way to the camp, he turned on Road G-7 to look at the stars again. Did you see him behind you—his headlights, I mean?"

"No."

"If he left Grinder's when you did, wouldn't you have expected him to be right behind you?"

"Not necessarily." Ivy wondered if Bobby Knolls thought she was too stupid to see what he was doing. "He might've stopped to get gasoline. Or to look at Christmas lights. Or get something from Quick Mart. I could've been three minutes in front of him the whole time. But I'm sure a professional like you must've thought of all that."

"So what did you two talk about in all those hours you spent together?"

Ivy was tempted to ask why her private conversations were any of his business but thought better of it. The last thing she needed after being released from jail was to antagonize the sheriff's right-hand man.

"Rue and I talked about lots of things. Astronomy. Work. Personal struggles. Victories. I'm sure you're aware that we've both overcome addictions."

"I suppose Mr. Kessler shared a great deal about his background."

Ivy bit her lip and decided enough was enough. "Lieutenant, this line of questioning doesn't seem at all routine to me. Is there something you're not telling me?"

Bobby popped a pink bubble. "I'm just tryin' to tie up all loose ends."

"Could you explain to me how Rue Kessler is a loose end?"

"Simply that he was a guest in the area who doesn't have an alibi for the nights of the beatings."

"For what it's worth, when he talked to me Friday after work, he told me he was going stargazing and would probably be out till early morning. And when my son and I met him on Saturday morning, he went on and on about how clear the sky had been and what all he had seen. His excitement was contagious. I believe he did exactly what he said he did. And Saturday night when we left Grinder's, he said he was going stargazing again. I have no doubt that's what he did."

"I'm certainly not suggestin' Mr. Kessler is guilty of any wrongdoin'. We're just coverin' all bases. To do less wouldn't be fair to your friend Jewel, now, would it?"

"No one wants you to find that monster any more than I do. But if you have the slightest thought that Rue Kessler could've done it, you're on the wrong track. He's a sensitive guy with his sights set on a bright future. He's walking the straight and narrow trying to get his life back. He's even got a construction foreman job waiting for him when he returns to Denver."

"Well, if that's the case, he has absolutely nothin' to fear from us. All I'm doin' is contactin' and eliminatin' potential suspects."

"Well, I've told you everything I know. Can I go back to work now?"

"Absolutely." Bobby reached out and shook her hand. "Thanks for talkin' to me."

Flint took off his glasses and walked over to the window. He looked out at the shimmering white peaks of the San Juans and promised himself that he'd take Betty and Ian skiing as soon as this case was solved. He heard footsteps and turned around.

"I'm glad it's you," he said to Bobby. "The soil composition results just came in on the mud sample we took from Deke and Roscoe's carpet. It's there on my desk. Read the last paragraph."

Bobby picked up the report and seconds later a toothy grin overtook his face. "Contains high concentrations of sand and silt consistent with sediment commonly found on the flood plain of the Missouri River in Kansas City and surrounding areas." Bobby laughed. "Looks like Maxfield just got put back on the suspect list. Lends a whole new meanin' to the term *pay dirt,* doesn't it?"

"Not if we can't put him at the scene, it doesn't. Were any Kansas City residents on your list of weekend lodgers?"

"I'll go get the list." Bobby set the report on the desk and left the office.

Flint looked up at a hawk soaring overhead. Maybe there was hope that they would catch this guy before he hurt someone else.

Bobby came back a few minutes later and stood next to Flint, the list in his hand. "Looks like we had at least a dozen skiers from the Kansas City metropolitan area. Each one could account for his whereabouts. There were only three guys we didn't feel good about. Two of them were skiers from Illinois. The other was Rue Kessler."

"All right. Go back and find out if any of these guys have made a trip to Kansas City in the recent past. We already know Huck Maxfield's story. Let's see if one of these three leads anywhere."

Bobby nodded. "By the way, I just got back from talkin' to Ivy Griffith about Kessler."

"Please tell me you didn't lean on her too hard," Flint said. "All I need is Elam on my case right now."

"Nah, I was polite. I just coaxed her into tellin' me everything she knows about Kessler. To hear her talk, he's just a heck of a nice guy."

"Maybe he is."

Bobby rolled his eyes. "You'll have to excuse me if I'm underwhelmed. But a recoverin' wino who dates a recoverin' crackhead and enjoys sittin' alone in the dark all night starin' at the stars has lost one too many brain cells."

"I'm not interested in his brain-cell count, Bobby. Just find me motive and opportunity."

There was a knock at the door, and Investigator Buck Lowry stepped in the office. "Bad news. We've got another beating."

# 19

FLINT TURNED OFF Main Street onto Silver Dollar and spotted the yellow crime-scene tape across the porch of Geoffrey and Morgan Dilly's gray Victorian house. A small crowd was standing on the snowy sidewalk outside the wrought-iron fence, and the KTNR-TV van was parked down the street.

Flint pulled his squad car around to the alley and parked behind the marshal's car. He walked in the back door and through the kitchen into the living room, his attention instantly drawn to the red letters smeared on the pale yellow wall: *Catch me before I kill someone!*

Flint's eyes moved from the wall to the blood-soaked couch to the bloody streak across the hardwood floor—and then to Bobby Knolls, who was walking toward him, shaking his head.

"MO's the same," Bobby said, "other than the victims are much younger. Morgan was conscious when we arrived. Said a man in a ski mask woke them up in the night and held a kitchen knife to her throat while proddin' Geoffrey into the livin' room. The perp shoved her on the couch and motioned for Geoff to sit next to her. He did. Begged the perp not to hurt them. Offered him cash, jewelry, valuable antiques—anything he wanted. The perp shook his head no, took a hammer out of his waistband and held it high over his head, then proceeded to brutalize them."

"What did he dip in the blood to write on the wall?"

"A sponge. We found a drawer open in the kitchen and think he might've gotten the hammer in there too. In both previous attacks he used somethin' from the house to attack his victims with."

Flint glanced around the room. "So what's missing this time?"

"A family portrait the Dillys took before movin' here from the UK. Morgan vaguely remembers seein' the perp grab it off the bookshelf. She passed out after that. Came to later and thought Geoff was dead. Tried to get up to call 911 and collapsed on the floor. Dragged herself with her arms, tryin' to get to that phone over there. Doesn't remember anything else till the EMTs brought her around."

"What about Geoff?"

Bobby blew out a breath. "Hasn't regained consciousness, and they think he has serious head injuries. He was air-lifted to Denver. Morgan's not as critical, but it's not good. The level of violence is definitely escalating. The perp's playin' us and enjoyin' every minute."

"Who found them?"

Bobby unwrapped a piece of bubblegum and popped it into his mouth. "Their assistant manager at the deli. He got worried when they didn't come in, and he couldn't get them to answer their home phone or cell. He came over and saw their cars in the driveway and pounded on the door. When he didn't get an answer, he called Kyle."

Marshal Kyle Redmond came over and stood next to Flint. "People are going to panic when this gets out. Can you spare more manpower?"

"Sure," Flint said. "But I can't put a cruiser on every block. Our perp just threw us a curve, and we don't really know who he's targeting."

"Well, he's darin' us to catch him before he kills someone," Bobby said. "I don't think he's kiddin' around."

Flint clenched his jaw. "Me either. Let's go ask those four guys without alibis where they were last night."

Ivy came back from lunch and started to open the front door to Three
Peaks Lodge when she heard someone behind her whistle.

"Ivy, wait!" Rue ran up to her. "I just wanted to apologize for last night.
I don't know what got into me. Kissing you that way was completely over
the top."

"Yes, it was."

"Does that mean I blew my chances of seeing you again?"

"I didn't say that." Ivy felt her cheeks get hot and hated that she was
blushing. "I certainly kissed you back, and with equal passion. I just don't
think that's the way we ought to begin whatever it is we're beginning."

"I agree. I'm really sorry." Rue glanced at her and then looked away.
"So what *is* it we're beginning?"

"I'm not sure. But it could be a really good thing. I thoroughly
enjoyed the time we spent together over the weekend. I haven't had that
much fun in a long, long time."

"Me either. I was so upset last night when I left your place that I drove
around for hours, kicking myself. I almost came back to apologize but was
afraid I'd wake you up."

Ivy pushed her hands deeper into her coat pockets and stared at her
boots. "Actually, I couldn't sleep. I wondered if I'd given you mixed sig-
nals. Just because I have a son and never married his father doesn't mean
that I'm interested in a sexual relationship."

"I never thought that."

"I think I need to set the record straight so there won't be any misun-
derstanding. I like you—a lot. I enjoy being in your company and appreciate the interest you've taken in Montana. I can tell he's fond of you."

"The feeling's mutual."

"So why don't we concentrate on becoming good friends and see if
that grows into something more?"

"Okay."

Ivy lifted her eyes and held his gaze. "I *don't* want to end up in bed
with you, Rue. We need to do this right."

"We will." He pulled back his coat sleeve and glanced at his watch. "You're gonna be late."

"I know. Let's talk more later. I need to tell you about the conversation *I* had with Lieutenant Knolls this morning."

Flint decided to let Bobby take care of questioning Huck Maxfield and the two skiers from Illinois while he drove out to Three Peaks to eyeball Don Freeman and Rue Kessler.

Flint pulled up in front of the second cabin, Night Hawk, and cringed when he saw Elam Griffith's maroon Suburban parked behind an older model white Ford Explorer. He got out of the squad car and walked up on the stoop and started to knock on the door just as Elam opened it.

"What're you doing out here?" Elam said.

*Nice to see you too.* "We've had another break-in and assault—that couple from England who bought Barton's Deli."

"Morgan and Geoff Dilly?"

Flint nodded. "You know them?"

"Sure. Carolyn and I eat in there at least once a week. Were they hurt badly?"

"I'm afraid so. Geoff has severe head injuries and was flown by helicopter to Denver. Morgan looks about like Jewel, but she also fell and broke her arm when she tried to get to the phone and call for help."

"You think this was the same guy who hurt the others?"

"Same MO."

"So why are you out here?"

Flint looked over Elam's shoulder and saw two men talking to Montana Griffith. "We're talking to all males who were staying in the area over the weekend. I'd like to talk to Don Freeman and Rue Kessler."

"You know we do background checks on everyone we hire."

"I'll try not to keep them long."

Elam turned around and went over to Montana. "The sheriff needs to talk to Rue and Don right now. Why don't we ride over and say hello to your mom and then get something from the vending machine?"

"Can we come back?" Montana looked over at Flint and waved.

"Sure. The sheriff said it wouldn't take long. Rue and Don can show you how the sander works later."

Flint winked at Montana as the boy squeezed by him and deliberately avoided making eye contact with Elam. He closed the door when they left and went over and introduced himself to Don and Rue.

"I know you guys are on the clock, so I'll cut to the chase. There's been another break-in and assault, and I need to know where you were this morning between midnight and two."

"I was sawing logs," Don said. "My truck died on me yesterday afternoon, and I was stuck at home all evening. Went to bed right after the ten-o'clock news."

"Can anyone confirm that?" Flint said.

"I guess not. But I called a mechanic yesterday afternoon and made arrangements for him to come tow my truck. He came for it after lunch today. His name's Jim Speck. I can have him call you."

"That won't be necessary," Flint said. "I know Jim. I'll ask him. What about you, Mr. Kessler?"

"I was at a friend's house till eleven thirty. After that I drove around for a while."

"Define *a while*."

"A couple hours."

"Where'd you go?"

"No place in particular."

"Were you alone?"

Rue nodded.

"I'll tell you what," Flint said. "I'd like to pursue this a little more, but I don't want to keep Mr. Freeman from his work. Why don't we go out to my squad car and finish our conversation?"

Flint thought he saw Rue shivering in spite of the heat pouring out of the vents in his squad car.

"Mr. Kessler, tell me again why you didn't go back to your cabin after you left Ivy's?"

"I had something personal on my mind regarding my relationship with Ivy. I needed to clear my head, so I took a ride."

"Did you drive into Jacob's Ear?"

"Yes sir. I did."

"Where'd you go when you were in town?"

"I came in on Main and looked at Christmas lights. I never got out of the car except at Spruce Park to use the public restroom. I just drove around."

"At any point, were you on Silver Dollar Street?"

"I didn't pay attention. Maybe."

"It's just around the corner from Spruce Park."

Rue folded his arms. "Seems like everything in Jacob's Ear is just around the corner from Spruce Park."

Flint smiled. "I guess it is at that. Have you ever been to Jewel Sadler's house?"

"No, but I drive by there all the time, since it's on Main Street."

"What about Deke and Roscoe's house?"

Rue shook his head. "I don't even know where it is."

"It's on Tanner's Ridge Road. And you had to have passed right by it on the way up to Tanner's Ridge, where you claim you were stargazing the night they were assaulted."

Rue massaged the back of his neck. "Sheriff, I told Lieutenant Knolls everything. I had nothing to do with those beatings. I've always spent a lot of time alone. It's not out of the ordinary for me."

"Do you travel alone too?"

"Sometimes. Not real often."

"Ever been to Missouri?"

Flint was sure Rue shifted his weight.

"When I was a kid, my parents took me to St. Louis to see the arch."

"Have you been there recently?"

"No sir. I just saw the arch that one time."

"I mean to Missouri."

"No, not recently."

"Ever been to Kansas City?"

Rue cracked his knuckles. "I'm sure I have. It's on the way to St. Louis."

"Yeah, I guess it is. So you're saying you haven't been to Kansas City recently?"

"That's right." Rue turned to Flint. "I don't know why you're asking *me* all these questions, but all I'm trying to do is keep my nose clean and get on with my life."

"I understand. And all I'm trying to do is put away the piece of garbage that's brutalizing my friends and neighbors. It may seem to you like I'm coming down hard, but you've been conveniently off the radar during the time each of these assaults took place."

"But I'm telling the truth."

"Then you have absolutely nothing to lose by answering questions. But make no mistake, I *am* going to get this guy."

"I'm not violent, Sheriff. I wasn't even a violent drunk. Can I get back to work now?"

# 20

AFTER DINNER THAT NIGHT, Ivy pulled her legs up on the couch and relished the sound of Montana reading *Green Eggs and Ham* to Rue for a second time.

She tried to imagine what it might be like to be married to someone like Rue for fifty years. How many kids and grandkids would they have? Would they still find each other attractive? Would they have anything to talk about? Would they be spiritually mature? Would they have more joys than sorrows, more satisfaction than regret, more money than bills to pay? Would they be wise enough to give advice and smart enough to wait till they were asked for it?

Ivy closed her eyes, daring to believe that in spite of her history of failure and brokenness, she might still have a chance at a normal life.

The doorbell rang. Who would be at her door this time of night? She got up and looked through the peephole and saw her father on the stoop. For a split second she thought about not opening the door, but she knew he had seen Rue's car parked outside.

She manufactured a smile and opened door. "What a surprise. Come in."

"I see you've got company. I recognized Rue's car."

"He came over for dinner, and Montana's reading to him. What brings you out?"

"Maybe I should come back another time."

She took his hand and pulled him inside. "Rue and I are just hanging out. How about some hot chocolate? Or I could make coffee."

"Thanks, but I'm not staying that long."

Montana scrambled down the ladder from the loft and ran over to Elam and hugged his legs. "Hi, Grandpa."

"Hi, yourself." Elam lifted Montana by his elbows, then set him down again. "I think you've grown since five o'clock."

Montana flexed the muscle in his arm. "Rue says I'm superstrong in arm wrestling. I can even beat him sometimes."

Rue, who'd followed Montana down from the loft, held out his hand and shook Elam's. "Hello again."

"I thought you were going over to the dining hall with Don."

"I was, but Ivy invited me over for meat loaf. That was an offer I couldn't refuse."

Elam's eyes were probing. "Does Ivy know what Sheriff Carter talked to you and Don about?"

"Of course I know." Ivy put her hands on Montana's shoulders. "Sweetie, why don't you go change while we talk to Grandpa for a few minutes? I put a pair of clean p.j.'s on top of the dryer."

"Okay. Don't let Rue leave till I finish reading *Green Eggs and Ham*."

When Montana was out of earshot, Ivy looked at her dad and said, "Lieutenant Knolls came out to Three Peaks and talked to me this morning."

Elam tugged at his mustache. "How come nobody told me?"

"It was no big deal. The lieutenant has been questioning all males who were guests in town over the weekend. He just wanted to know if I could vouch for where Rue was."

"Why would he ask *you*?"

"Because Ivy and Montana were with me quite a bit over the weekend."

Rue told her father about his love for astronomy and what a hassle it had been that he wasn't able to account for where he was during the times of the attacks.

"Well, I can see how that would be frustrating," Elam said. "Flint can be downright obnoxious when he's pushing the envelope."

"He's wasting his time pushing me," Rue said. "I don't have anything to hide, but it's kind of embarrassing. I sure hope you're not sorry you hired me to come here."

"No way. Jake and Brandon are thrilled with your work. Sounds like you just got caught in the middle of an investigation. We've had a little experience with that ourselves." Elam glanced over at Ivy. "I really don't like Bobby Knolls talking to you without anyone else present. I don't trust anyone down there anymore. Maybe I should rehire Brett Hewitt."

"To do what? I'm fine, Dad. I certainly don't need a lawyer."

"Mr. Griffith, the bottom line is, I can't prove where I was. That's just the nature of stargazing. I'm used to spending long stretches of time alone. Lieutenant Knolls acted like he thought I made it up, especially since I forgot to pack my telescope when I came here. But I assure you, I do this all the time."

Montana suddenly reappeared, his pajama shirt on inside out. "Yeah, Rue showed me Betelgeuse and Rigel! Those are the very brightest stars in O-ri-uhn." Montana flashed Rue a smile of satisfaction. "He's the Great Hunter. Rue's gonna draw me what he looks like because it's kind of hard to see him with all the other stars out."

The corners of Elam's mouth twitched. "So you're into astronomy now, eh?"

Montana's head bobbed. "Rue's gonna take me again."

Jewel looked beyond the plethora of cut flowers, potted plants, and cards from well-wishers into the inky blackness outside her window. The doctor suggested she wait a day or two to go see Morgan Dilly. Jewel had heard on the news that Morgan was in serious but stable condition. But how stable could the poor thing be after being bludgeoned by an intruder and separated from her husband, who might never regain consciousness? She hoped that Morgan had not been aware of her attacker using their blood to write his awful message on the wall.

A tear inched down Jewel's cheek and dripped onto her hospital gown. It had been easier when she couldn't remember the details of her own attack, when she felt distanced from the horror. But now every detail played over and over again in her mind with gruesome clarity. For the first time since Mel died, she didn't feel safe anywhere.

She heard someone cough and quickly wiped her eyes and turned around and saw Luke standing with Brandon and Kelsey.

"Hey, why the sad face?" Luke said softly, taking her hand.

"I feel so sorry for the Dillys."

"Everybody does," Kelsey said. "I can't even imagine what they've been through. What all of you have been through."

"Their lives will never be the same," Jewel said. "Even if Geoff survives. They were so excited about living in Colorado. And now…" Jewel put her face in her hands. "I'm sure they wish they'd never left England."

It was as though no one knew what to say. Jewel hid in the silence for a moment and pulled herself together. "Well, enough about sad things. I'm glad to see the three of you."

"We bumped into each other in the parking lot," Luke said. "Lots of people are asking about you, even if they haven't come over to see you."

"How's the café running?"

Luke smiled. "I was down there all afternoon and am happy to report that Rita and Laura are holding it together *fine*. But everyone wants you back. It's not the same without Deke and Roscoe either."

"Those two are mending surprisingly well," Jewel said. "I finally got up the gumption to push my darned walker down there this morning so I could see them. I must've been quite a sight. I'm glad I didn't have to see myself."

"It's just temporary," Brandon said. "It's great you're able to be up and around. Did the doctor say when you could go home?"

"Probably before weekend. Apparently, my injuries aren't as bad as they look. I'll have one of those home-care nurses look in on me every day. I should be fine as long as I sleep in the downstairs bedroom for a while."

Luke sat on the side of the bed, his hands clasped between his knees. "I could bring you meals from the café."

"I'd be glad to clean your house," Kelsey said.

Brandon glanced at Kelsey and then back to Jewel. "I've got Saturdays and Sundays off. I can run errands or do odd jobs, whatever you need."

Jewel's eyes welled again. "You're such good friends. And here I was thinking I had to go through this alone."

"No chance of that." Luke rose to his feet and set her walker in front of her. "Come on. I want to take a stroll down the hall with my favorite girl."

Jewel smiled in spite of herself. "I know you're just funning me, but thanks for making me feel special when this face of mine could stop a pit bull in his tracks and send him running the other way."

Ivy hugged her father good-night, closed the door behind him, and went back to the couch and sat next to Rue.

"Well, at least that's out of the way," she said. "I wasn't sure how he'd respond to Lieutenant Knolls's questioning me. And I knew he wouldn't like the idea that you were being singled out either, or that you and I are seeing each other."

"He doesn't approve of you seeing me?"

"It's not personal. My parents don't think I should date someone who has the same addictive temperament. And they think I need time to figure out who I am first."

Rue smiled. "If you don't know who you are, then who does?"

"Exactly. But in all fairness, I haven't always been the best judge of character. Pete was the worst thing that ever happened to me. I was a new Christian when I started dating him my senior year. I let him talk me into everything I knew was wrong—sex, drugs, deceiving my parents, skipping out of youth group. I was miserable, but I was so desperate to be accepted that I went along with anything he wanted. I was afraid if I didn't, he would get some other girl to wear his ring. Talk about dumb."

"I did plenty of dumb things in high school."

"But you didn't cover up a murder. That choice cost me a decade of my life. And aged me beyond my years."

Rue reached for her hand. "I told you, the new you I see coming out is beautiful."

"I'm glad you see me that way. But the truth is, I'll never fully recover from the effects of the drugs, especially the meth. Did you know I'm only twenty-nine? Bet you thought I was much older."

"I like the way you look, so stop putting yourself down, okay?"

"You're right. I do that a lot."

"Well, stop. Today's a new day. I don't care where you've been or what you've done."

Ivy paused and considered Rue's words. She believed he sincerely meant them, but she would never be brave enough to test them. "I have trouble forgiving myself sometimes. Don't you ever think back on the worst things you've ever done and, deep down inside, wonder if God's punishing you for it?"

"Not really. I'm pretty new at this Christianity thing. The Bible says if we confess our sins, He forgives us and cleanses us, so what's left for Him to punish?"

"Nothing. I just struggle with it sometimes, that's all." Ivy stole several well-spaced glances at Rue's face. Maybe he didn't find it hard to forgive himself or to believe that God had. But could he forgive the dirty little secret she had confessed over and over but couldn't seem to turn loose of? Could any man?

"I don't know how we got off on this," Ivy said. "We were talking about me not being a good judge of character. It wasn't just in high school. Last spring I started dating a guy I knew a long time ago. I was impressed at how Bill had changed for the better and treated me with more respect than any man ever had." She hesitated and then just decided to say it.

"He's now doing life in prison with no chance for parole. I really don't care to relive the whole thing, but you can read the newspaper articles at the library, if you want to know more. The point is, I was dating a murderer and was clueless."

Rue pursed his lips. "I get it, so you're afraid to trust me?"

"It's not that I sense anything dishonest about you. You seem like a terrific guy, but I thought the same thing two times before and was wrong. Plus I've done things I still can't talk about. You could do better."

"Neither of us were saints, Ivy. Does that mean we shouldn't even give this a chance? Or can we work at it, believing God's in control, and see if goes anywhere?"


Flint took off his reading glasses and rubbed his eyes, unable to shake the image of the bloody letters smeared on the Dillys' wall. *Catch me before I kill someone!* Each time he repeated the phrase, it seemed more of a taunt to him than a cry for help.

His phone call to Geoff Dilly's brother in London had been emotional. The man didn't have the money to fly to Denver to be with Geoff, which added to the heaviness. Flint felt tightness grip his chest and hoped it was just the pressure of the job and not a heart attack waiting to happen.

"Flint, are you okay?" Betty said.

He looked up and forced a smile. "I'm fine, hon. Just can't sleep. This case is working on me."

"I didn't even hear you come in."

"I tried not to wake you."

"Well, as long as I'm awake, talk to me. I don't want Ian subjected to any of this. The phone's been ringing off the hook since this hit the news." Betty sat on the couch, her arms folded. "There's no way you can shelter me, so let's hear it."

"All right. I went out to Three Peaks and talked to Rue Kessler, the guy I told you about. He didn't give me anything solid. I feel sure he was lying about not having been to Missouri recently. I don't have enough for a warrant, but I found out he's dating Ivy Griffith. Until we know more, I don't want Ian over there."

Betty sighed. "What about the two skiers from Illinois?"

"Bobby drove over to White Top and talked to them. They were nursing bad hangovers and claimed they'd been up partying all night. At least twenty people confirmed that. We've pretty much eliminated them."

"What about that crazy guy?"

"Bobby paid Huck Maxfield another visit and pushed him just short of violating his rights and got nothing. But this time when Maxfield told him to search the house, truck, and shed, Bobby jumped on it. Unfortunately, it probably won't yield anything. Trying to collect usable DNA in a trash heap like that is next to impossible. Cat hair collected in the house might lead somewhere if it matches the feline hair we found at Jewel's. The orange and white cat I saw perched on Maxfield's shoulder was nowhere to be found for a DNA sample. When Bobby asked Maxfield to produce the cat, he insisted that 'Mr. Whiskers' was hiding somewhere and that cats won't come when you call them."

"Well, that's true."

"Yeah, but Bobby thinks he was lying, that maybe he did away with the cat. Truthfully, our best hope of finding usable DNA is probably the hair, soil, and fibers collected from Maxfield's truck. Unfortunately, they couldn't find a trace of blood, inside or out. Then when they opened the door to the shed, a thick layer of dust on the floor was a dead giveaway that no one had set foot in there for a long time. And missing altogether is the black ski mask, clothes, shoes, and gloves the perp was wearing during the attacks."

"He could've buried them out there on his property."

"Anything's possible. But Bobby couldn't find a trace of blood on Maxwell's person or any of the disgusting clothes, shoes, or socks piled on his closet floor. For a guy who looks and smells like he hasn't washed since Jimmy Carter was in the White House, that would be pretty hard to pull off. I mean we'd expect to find blood spatter somewhere."

Betty heaved a sigh and leaned her head against the back of the couch. "What now?"

"I really don't know yet." Flint popped two Tums and chewed them. "But I'll tell you this: figuring out who's doing this isn't as important tonight as figuring out where he's going to strike next."

# 21

IVY FOLLOWED MONTANA up the front steps of her parents' home and walked inside. "It's just us!"

Carolyn came out of the kitchen, drying her hands with a towel. She hugged Montana and looked at Ivy. "I didn't expect to see you so early on a Wednesday. Did Jake call a staff meeting?"

"No. I wanted to talk to you for a few minutes. Maybe Montana could watch a DVD while we visit at the kitchen table?"

"Yay!" Montana shot into the living room.

Carolyn laughed. "Well, that was a crowd pleaser. You want some coffee?"

"That sounds good. Thanks."

Ivy followed her mother into the kitchen and sat at the table. Half a minute later she had her hands wrapped around a warm mug of coffee.

"So what'd you want to talk to me about?" Carolyn said.

"Rusty."

"Why do you look so grim?"

Ivy reached in her purse and handed her mother the note she had gotten from Rusty. "This came Monday."

Carolyn put on her glasses, her eyes slowly moving down the page. Finally she sighed, took off her glasses, and wiped her eyes. "Honey, I'm so sorry. There's no excuse for this."

"Mom, I didn't show this to you so Rusty would be in trouble with you and Dad. He said there's no reason to drag you into the reasons why he didn't want Montana and me associated with Christmas. But I don't want to keep any more secrets. I think you need to know exactly how Rusty feels and respect it."

"Respect it? Your father and I could never go to Albuquerque and exchange gifts under these circumstances."

"Why not? There's no reason why Rusty's feelings about me should have to spoil your relationship with him—and especially Tia and Josie. Painful as it is, Rusty isn't going to accept us, at least not right now."

"I'd like to shake him."

Ivy put her hand on her mother's. "I know. Sometimes I feel that way too. But I betrayed him—all of you—and for a long time. It's unrealistic to expect that all three of you would process that in the same way or in the same time frame. I think you and Dad should go."

"Have you said anything about this to your father?"

Ivy shook her head. "Why don't you keep the note and show it to him? Please try to convince him to go to Rusty's without us. I've been responsible for enough pain in this family…" Her voice cracked, and she continued. "This is all part of my punishment."

"The Lord doesn't punish people who've repented, Ivy. You and God have dealt with your past. Your rift with Rusty is just part of the natural consequences you have to work through. Your dad and I can help."

Ivy took a sip of coffee. "Not if he never forgives me. You can't change his heart."

"We can try. I think once he sees the consistency in your life, he'll come around."

"It hurts me more for Montana than for myself. I'm just grateful that Rue's so good with him."

Her mother started to say something and then didn't.

"What's wrong?" Ivy said.

"I should probably just keep my feelings to myself."

"Dad talked to you about Rue, didn't he?"

Carolyn held her gaze. "Yes, he did. And I think you need to tread very carefully, honey. It would be a good idea if you just backed away from seeing Rue until Flint catches the man who's guilty of the assaults."

"What you're really saying is he might be guilty, and you don't trust my judgment."

"No one knows who's guilty. That's my point."

"Mom, the only reason Sheriff Carter is talking to Rue is because he's new in the area and can't prove where he was at the times of the assaults. I'm sure Dad told you he's into astronomy and spends a lot of time alone at night. He's really a great guy. Montana adores him. We even talk about spiritual things."

Carolyn blew out a breath. "Ivy, why can't you set your sights on someone who isn't carrying a lot of the same baggage?"

"Did you ever stop to think that maybe Rue's family would think the same thing about *me*?"

"How much have you told him about yourself?"

"Everything." *Almost.* "He said he doesn't care where I've been or what I've done."

"That doesn't mean he's right for you or that he's the only man who will ever feel that way. You have so much love to give, and I have high hopes that someday you'll find a nice, stable man and live happily ever after."

"So do I, Mom. But realistically, anyone willing to build a relationship with me is taking a chance. I could fall back into my addiction. I've never been involved in a healthy relationship with a guy, and I've spent exactly one month raising my son on my own."

Carolyn reached across the table with her gaze. "The past does not have to control your future."

"I agree, but you can't deny that most people would consider me a high-risk option."

There was a long, uncomfortable pause, and then Carolyn said, "Ivy, you're too grown up for me to tell you what to do. If you insist on building a relationship with Rue, promise me you'll be open with us. You can come to us with anything. There's so much more to consider than just your happiness. Montana's future is at stake too."

*Like I haven't thought of that?* "All right, Mom." Ivy downed the last of her coffee and stood. "I'd better get to work."

Ivy drove down the long, snowpacked drive from her parents' house and turned left into Three Peaks Christian Camp and Conference Center. She glanced at the clock on her dashboard. It was only seven forty.

She drove past Three Peaks Lodge and around to the back of Building A, then parked the car and trudged beyond the tall pines to the scenic overlook. She stood on the wooden platform, her arms resting on the snowy railing, and drank in the magnificent, unspoiled beauty of Phantom Hollow. As far as she could see, winter's pure white blanket had been draped over the jagged peaks and spread out across the valley floor.

About thirty yards from where she stood, and not quite hidden under a layer of new snow, was a row of smooth boulders that seemed to rise up out of nowhere. It didn't seem all that long ago that she and Rusty had left their footprints all over them. Sometimes they pretended the biggest boulder was an island, other times, a fort. They had even imagined it to be a mighty ship, a magic carpet, a cloud—just about anything that struck their fancy at the moment. And how many times had they crawled up there and lain on their backs, resting in the warmth of the sun and the quiet of the wide-open spaces?

In those days there was nothing out here but pine and aspen forests, open range, and the bulwark of rugged peaks that surrounded it. Her parents owned this pristine piece of paradise and could have kept it exclusively for themselves.

When Ivy came home after being away ten years, she had been shocked to find a camp and conference center standing in the heart of what was once her childhood playground. Not only was its presence intrusive, but she could hardly believe her parents had chosen to make any part of the family homestead available to strangers.

It didn't take long to realize that the grandeur of this vast expanse had not been compromised and that Three Peaks simply offered a place where people from all over the country could come and enjoy the Creator's handiwork.

The wind whipped around her, and for a moment she was a kid again, galloping with Rusty across Phantom Hollow on their horses, the wind tickling their faces and the sense that at any second they might sprout wings and take flight. Ivy clung to that childhood memory for a moment, all too aware that her relationship with Rusty had been irreparably damaged. The cold, harsh honesty of his note had left no question in her mind.

She swallowed the wad of emotion that rose in her throat and turned her thoughts back to this morning's conversation with her mother. Not that thinking about her parents' lack of confidence in her decision making was less painful. But was it fair to fault them for not trusting her judgment when she didn't trust it herself? What if Rue was wrong for her? What if her sudden attraction to him was nothing more than a repeat of the dysfunctional cycle that would eventually heap more misery on her? Or what if, despite what her mother thought, God was punishing her for the awful things she had done, and no matter what choice she made now or in the future, she wasn't going to find a man who would love her and be a fitting dad for her son?

*I know the plans I have for you…plans to prosper you and not to harm you, plans to give you hope and a future.*

Ivy thought it ironic that she could remember Jeremiah 29:11 so readily and yet found it hard to believe it applied to her.

A Cooper's hawk seemed to come out of nowhere and swoop down on the snowy range a few yards in front of her and then lifted off the ground, a field mouse writhing in its talons.

She glanced at her watch and hurried back toward the car, certain of only one thing at the moment: she was late for work.

The sheriff sat in his office, going over the details of all the assault cases with Lieutenant Bobby Knolls, Investigator Buck Lowry, and Marshal Kyle Redmond.

"Face it, guys," Flint said. "We've got almost nothing to go on. We know the perp had Missouri mud on his shoes. And that he wore black from head to toe, including a black ski mask."

"And that he's meaner than a grizzly," Kyle added.

Bobby popped a pink bubble. "We didn't find anything incriminatin' at Huck Maxfield's place either, but the guy's hidin' somethin'."

"That's what you said about that guy out at the camp," Kyle said.

"Yep. Somethin's off about Kessler too, but provin' it's another story."

Flint got up and paced in front of the window. "We've got to stop this nut before he kills someone. I think he wrote on the Dillys' wall to taunt us. I don't think it was a cry for help. I've got six cruisers out there. That should at least slow him down till we can figure out our next move."

"I don't want to 'slow him down,'" Kyle said. "We need to get him off the street! My phone's ringing off the hook. People are scared."

Buck threw up his hands. "We can't be everywhere, Kyle. What do you suggest we do that we haven't already done? It's not like *you* can do anything."

"Knock it off," Flint said. "We need to stay united on this. Here's what I think we should do next. We have to start taking a closer look at residents, not just in Jacob's Ear, but in nearby communities—adults *and* juveniles. Talk to each of the marshals. Find out who the violent domestic abusers are and the school bullies. Even their victims could be time bombs. Let's start pushing a few buttons and see if we can't get some leads."

"What do you want us to do about Kessler and Maxfield?" Bobby said.

"Dig deeper into their backgrounds. I want to know everything, right down to what brand of toothpaste they use. And let's keep them under surveillance."

"It'll be impossible to be discreet," Bobby said, "considerin' where they live."

"Tough. I don't want either of them making a move without us knowing it."


Ivy walked up on the stoop and stomped the snow off her boots. She started to open the door to her house when she heard a car motor. She turned and saw Rue's Ford Explorer pulling into her drive.

Rue waved and then got out and walked over to her. "I'm getting ready to have lunch over at the dining hall and wondered if you'd like to join me."

"I'm only taking thirty minutes. I was late for work this morning. I don't know that I'd be very good company anyway."

He put his hands on her shoulders and looked into her eyes. "Hey, what's wrong?"

"Nothing."

"I know you better than that. I thought we decided last night that we were gonna give this thing a try."

"We did. I'm just a little beat up today. I talked to my mom before I came to work, and it's obvious she's no more excited about me pursuing this relationship than my dad is."

"So who's in the driver's seat?" Rue said. "Them? You? Or God?"

Ivy exhaled. "You want to have a sandwich here? I don't feel like going to the dining hall. All I've got is peanut butter and jelly."

"Sounds great to me. I'm starved. You're not worried that someone on staff might see my car and think something's going on?"

"I'm tired of worrying about what everyone else thinks."

Ivy opened the door and laid her coat across the back of the couch, then went over to the kitchen and got out a jar of peanut butter and a jar of grape jam. "Have you been working hard this morning?"

"Yeah. Don and I are making good time." He smiled sheepishly.

"Not that I'm in a hurry to finish this project. Now that I've met you and Montana, I'd really like to hang around as long as possible. I even found an AA group that meets on Tuesdays in Mt. Bryon. Don and I are gonna start going."

"Good for you. I went to support-group meetings for a couple years after I got out of rehab." Ivy reached for the loaf of bread. Why did she feel so comfortable with Rue? She thought back on her relationship with both Pete and Bill. She started out feeling comfortable in both instances, but it didn't last long. Had she listened to her inner voice, she would probably have saved herself a great deal of grief.

"Don and I got a kick out of showing Montana how to use the sander." Rue laughed. "Sometimes kids have more fun playing with adult stuff than their own toys."

"He had a ball." Ivy smiled. "I'm not sure if it was because he got to use the sander or because he got to hang out with the guys."

"He's a great kid. You gonna let me take him out to look at the stars Friday night—assuming the sky's clear, that is?"

"Sure. He'd love that."

"I made a diagram of Orion for him to keep. It'll help if he can see what the Great Hunter is supposed to look like. Why don't you go with us?"

"I don't know. It's freezing out there at night."

"You can sit in my car with the heater on. You'd be amazed at what you could see. Better yet, we could find an open spot and build a fire. Even make s'mores. It'd be fun."

"In the snow?"

Rue rubbed his chin. "Why not? I could throw some logs in the back of my Explorer. I'll even bring the marshmallows, Hershey bars, and graham crackers."

"I hate being cold."

"Just dress for the arctic and you should be fine." Rue winked. "Come on, beneath that dainty exterior is an adventurer begging to get out. At least think about it."

"I thought you couldn't see the stars if you're too close to other light."

"When you're out there in the pitch-black, you can walk fifty yards away from the fire, turn your back, and see more stars in one minute than most people see in a lifetime."

Ivy put the sandwiches on plates, cut them in two, and brought them to the table. "I admit it sounds like fun. You want some milk to go with that?"

"Sure." Rue reached over and took her hand. "I have a really good feeling about us, Ivy. I really wanna see if we can build something, but I don't want your relationship with your parents to go south because of it."

"Neither do I, but it's my choice. If they're uneasy, they're just going to have to live with it."

# 22

JUST AFTER LUNCH, Brandon Jones drove to the boys' cabins and pulled up in front of Night Hawk. He walked in the front door and took in the fresh new look. A cheery shade of yellow had been painted over the wood-paneled walls, and the bunks and built-in drawers had all been refinished and stained a rich golden brown. The nondescript beige linoleum had been replaced with laminated wood tiles.

He poked his head in the bathroom. The fixtures were new, and a storage cabinet had been mounted above the toilet.

The door opened, and Brandon turned around. "Hey, Don."

"So does it meet your expectations?" Don Freeman asked.

"You kidding? None of the camps I've seen looked this nice. You guys did a great job!"

Don's smile spanned his face and made his glasses appear crooked. "Glad you like it. Mr. Griffith almost didn't go for painting the wood paneling, but we convinced him yellow would brighten the place up—and it's completely washable."

"That's good. Sure makes it seem cheerier in here. So you're pleased?"

"Yeah, it's been fun getting back to doing what I love."

Brandon looked around the room again, impressed that he didn't see a speck of yellow paint on the refinished wood. "By the way, did you and Rue get over to the dining hall and try the Frito pie?"

"I did. Rue told me to save him a place while he went to find Ivy, but he never came back. Too bad. He really missed out."

Brandon looked at his watch. "He's never late. I wonder where he is."

"Oh, I expect he's down at Bald Eagle. That's where I was headed when I spotted your SUV. We're ready to get started refinishing all the wood."

"Okay, don't let me keep you. Tell Rue I'll catch up to him later." Brandon shook Don's hand. "Great job."

"Thanks."

Brandon got in his car and headed back to the main road and noticed a sheriff's department SUV parked on Three Peaks Road just outside the stone entrance. He turned left and exited the camp and pulled up alongside the car, his window rolled down. "I'm Brandon Jones, the camp director. Can I help you find something?"

"No, thanks. We're just going to sit here awhile."

"Is there a problem?"

"Nothing for you to concern yourself with. Just go about your business."

Brandon smiled. "Well, part of my business is making sure the conference attendees who'll be arriving this afternoon feel comfortable. It could be a little unsettling to have a sheriff's department cruiser sitting outside our gate."

"I understand."

"Any idea how long you plan to be out here?"

"I really can't say."

"Can you at least tell me what this is about?"

The deputy looked him squarely in the eye. "No sir. It's not your concern. I'd appreciate it if you'd just go back to your job and let us do ours."

Brandon wondered if Jake or Elam knew about this. He stuck his arm out the window and handed the deputy his business card. "If there's anything I can do to help you, stop in at the main lodge. That's where the offices are."

The deputy tipped the rim of his hat. "You have a nice day."

Brandon made a U-turn and drove back toward the main lodge, a sick feeling in his gut that this had something to do with Rue Kessler.

Flint unlocked his office door and flipped on the lights. The Rueben sandwich he'd barely taken the time to chew already felt like a hot brick in his stomach. He reached in his top drawer and popped two Tums just as the intercom clicked on.

"Sheriff, Elam Griffith is here to see you."

"Do you know what he wants, Tammy?"

"No sir"—his administrative assistant lowered her voice—"but he's been in the waiting room pacing for the past twenty minutes."

*Great. That's all I need.* "All right. Send him this way."

Flint picked up the chairs he had rearranged for this morning's meeting and moved them back in place.

There was a knock, and then Elam stepped into his office and closed the door. "You want to tell me just what you think you're doing?"

*Hello to you too.* "Could you be more specific?"

"Jake Compton called me and said two of your deputies were parked outside the entrance at Three Peaks. Why?"

"It's official business, Elam. I don't want to get into it."

"Well, it's my camp. And I do!"

"All right, sit down and cool off."

Elam flopped into a chair, his arms folded tightly across his chest.

"Would you stop glaring at me?" Flint said. "I'm not the enemy here. I'm trying to keep people safe."

"Well, people *are* safe at Three Peaks. We've never had trouble."

"Maybe not, but the cause of *my* trouble could be right under *your* nose."

"You're talking about Rue Kessler?"

Flint gave a nod and leaned back against his desk. "Look, I have an obligation to protect the public. Mr. Kessler is one of two potential suspects in the assaults, neither of whom can be eliminated because they can't prove where they were at the time. And because of another factor I can't get into. All I'm doing is keeping an eye on him."

"Does he know that?"

"He will, once he leaves the camp. But you're the only one I've told. And I'd appreciate it if you kept it to yourself. I'm not even close to charging Kessler with anything, but I just can't take the chance that he might be our perp. I want him tailed any time he leaves the camp."

"For how long? That seems like harassment."

"You have a better suggestion, Elam? The level of violence is escalating. We believe if the perp gets another chance, he's going to kill his victim. I'd rather be criticized for harassment than leave the door open for another friend or neighbor to be victimized."

"You're really that uncomfortable about Rue?"

"Let me put it this way. If I were Ivy, I'd think twice about dating him while he's under suspicion, especially after I just got out of jail. If nothing else, she doesn't need the bad publicity."

Elam's eyebrows formed a single bushy line. "Don't you even think of talking to Ivy about this again unless Brett Hewitt is present! I'm not going to stand back and watch her get railroaded just—"

"You can stop right there!" Flint shouted. "I don't care how much weight you think you have around here, this is *my* investigation. I'm not out to get Ivy. I'm out to get this worthless piece of garbage off the street! And if your toes happen to be in the way, I apologize in advance for stepping all over them! But I'm keeping a tail on Kessler until I've either eliminated him or have enough evidence to arrest him."

Elam's face was redder than the checks on his flannel shirt. "Do what you have to do with Rue Kessler," he said through gritted teeth, "but Ivy's off-limits unless Brett is present. You got that?"

Flint slowly counted to ten and then said, "Elam, listen to me. You have my word that I haven't got a hidden agenda. I don't suspect Ivy of any wrongdoing."

"You'll have to excuse me if your word doesn't mean a whole lot. I've heard all this before."

"Not from me you haven't. I *never* told you Ivy wasn't a suspect when she was."

"No, you were real sneaky about that."

Flint put his hands in his pockets and started pacing. "We've already been over that, and I'm not rehashing it. What I *am* telling you is that right now Ivy's not under suspicion for anything, but she is in the middle of a criminal investigation. I can't ignore that, especially since she's closer to Kessler than anyone. I just wish she'd stay away from him until we figure this thing out."

Brandon walked in the front door of Bald Eagle just after four and saw Don Freeman stirring something in a small plastic container and Montana Griffith watching closely as Rue prepared to start stripping the old finish off a set of drawers.

"How's it going, guys?" Brandon asked.

Montana flashed him an Opie Taylor grin. "We've gotta get this old varnish off. It's gonna take lots and lots of elbow grace."

"That's elbow *grease*." Rue reached over and punched Montana on the arm. "We've got a ways to go before we can use the sander again, that's for sure."

"I hate to spoil the party," Brandon said, "but I need to talk to Rue for a few minutes."

Montana's face fell. "Oh, man…every time I come to help, somebody has to leave."

"I'll have him back in ten minutes."

"Not to worry," Don said. "I just happen to have an extra Snickers bar in my pocket. Why don't you and me take a little break while they're gone?"

"I *love* Snickers!"

Don grinned. "I knew that."

Rue got up and put on his ski jacket and stepped outside on the stoop, and Brandon came out behind him and shut the door.

"Why don't we sit in my car where it's warm?" Brandon climbed in the driver's seat and waited till Rue was situated in the passenger seat.

"What's up?" Rue said.

"Is there anything you need to tell me?"

"About what?"

"About why the sheriff has two deputies parked outside the entrance to the camp?"

"I didn't know he did."

"He does. And they won't tell me anything."

"And you assume it's because of me, since I'm the one Lieutenant Knolls and Sheriff Carter have questions about?"

Brandon traced the steering wheel with his finger. "Is it?"

"I don't know, but I haven't done anything wrong."

"I have no reason to doubt you, but why do you think they would go to such extremes to keep an eye on you?"

"They never said that's what they were doing."

"It doesn't take a rocket scientist to put two and two together. If there's something I need to know, you'd tell me, right?"

Rue cracked his knuckles. "Just because I can't prove where I was when those assaults happened doesn't mean I had anything to do with them. The only thing I'm guilty of is spending too much time by myself."

"Did you have lunch by yourself today?"

"No, I had lunch with Ivy."

"At her place?"

Rue leaned his head against the back of the seat and exhaled. "Yes, at her place. Everywhere I go lately it's like big brother is watching me. What is it with everyone?"

"My concern is simply that the two of you being there alone over the lunch hour could be misconstrued as something other than lunch."

"For crying out loud, Brandon. We had peanut-butter-and-jelly sandwiches and planned an outing for Friday night. We talked about stargazing and campfires and making s'mores. The moral Gestapo who came running to you should mind his or her own business."

"Don't get upset. It wasn't like that, and no one is accusing you of anything inappropriate. I just wanted to remind you that this is a Christian camp and conference center, and part of our commitment as staff members is to uphold the integrity of this establishment by guarding ourselves from anything that would give the even slightest hint of impropriety."

Rue was quiet and seemed to be thinking. Finally he said, "Yeah, you're right. It probably wasn't the best choice. But just so you'll know, there's nothing sexual going on. Ivy and I are trying to build a solid friendship and see if it goes anywhere. We both have the same basic goals for the future."

Brandon started to say something and didn't, and then decided just to jump in. "Rue, have you and Ivy given any thought to the downside of two people with addictive temperaments trying to build a future together?"

"Sure. But neither of us is giving up on the idea just because of it. Ivy's been clean a long time, and next month it'll be a year since I've taken a drink. We just need to put God first and take one day at a time. I decided it was good idea to stay plugged in to AA while I'm here and found a group that meets in Mt. Bryon on Tuesday nights. Don and I are gonna start going next week."

"What about Ivy—is she planning to join a support group?"

"I don't think so. She went to one in Denver for a long time, then stopped going when she moved here. She's done okay."

"She seems fragile to me," Brandon said.

"Only because she lets other people make her feel guilty about stuff she needs to put behind her. I'm never gonna do that."


Flint stacked the silverware and salad bowls on top of the dirty dinner plates and let his son carry them ever so slowly to the sink.

"I'm a good helper," Ian said.

"You're an excellent helper. Mom appreciates it when the men in this house pitch in."

"Will you help me with my spelling words?"

"I'm going to talk to Mom for a little while, and then I'll come upstairs and help you with your spelling words."

"Okay," Ian said. "Montana and me are the best spellers in the whole class. We have more gold stars than anybody." He started to walk out of the kitchen and then turned around. "Can I go to his house for a sleep-over Saturday night? His mom said it's okay."

Flint glanced over at Betty and then at his son. "Not this weekend."

"But I didn't get to go last weekend."

"Let's talk about it later."

Ian pushed out his lower lip and stomped his foot. "You never let me do *anything*!"

"And acting like that won't get you anything either," Flint said. "I suggest you go take your bath and adjust your attitude before I start taking away privileges."

Ian turned and ran up the stairs and shut a door harder than he needed to.

Betty's eyes widened. "At least he didn't slam it. So what are we going to tell him, that Montana's mother is dating a really bad man and we're afraid to leave him over there? That'll go over big at school."

"Right now I'm not interested in whether my decisions go over big!"

Betty took his hand. "Tell me what's going on. You've been wound tighter than a tick since you got home."

Flint sat at the table. He explained his decision to keep a close watch on Rue Kessler and Huck Maxfield while the department was checking deeper into their backgrounds. And he recounted the conversation he'd had with Elam.

"Well, that explains a lot," Betty said.

"Elam just won't let go of his anger at me for interrogating Ivy without a lawyer present. He seems obsessed with throwing it in my face, like I've been redefined and can never be trusted again."

"He'll get over it. Give him time. But you're done talking to Ivy, right?"

"For the moment," Flint said, "but I can't promise I won't need to question her again. That's the kind of call I have to make minute by minute. As far as I can tell, Ivy's doing a good job at the camp and keeping her nose clean. She's not even on the radar. Kessler's another story."

"You really think this guy could be the perp?"

Flint took his hand and massaged the back of his neck. "I haven't been able to find a motive yet. The guy's half likable, but I've never met a drunk that could be trusted, and I'm not letting down my guard."

"He's a *recovering* alcoholic, right?"

"Yeah, but Bobby thinks he's hiding something, and I've learned to trust Bobby's gut. He thinks Maxfield's hiding something too. That's enough for me."

Betty sighed. "What are we going to tell our son about seeing Montana? Those boys are two peas in a pod. They shouldn't have to be separated because of this investigation."

"They'll see each other at school, but until I know where this is going, there's no way I want Ian at Ivy's house. Kessler's over there all the time."

"What about having Montana come here for a sleepover?"

"No." Flint folded his hands on the table. "As long as Kessler is under investigation and he's seeing Ivy, we need to distance ourselves."

"How do we explain that to a seven-year-old without trashing his mother's boyfriend? Ian said that Montana talks about Rue all the time and is really excited about going out with him to look at the stars."

"And that's exactly what I don't want—Ian getting pulled into that. As far as we know, Kessler could be using stargazing as a ruse."


"Montana, it's time to go to bed, sweetie," Ivy said. "Can you tell Rue good night?"

"Just five more minutes—pleeease." Montana looked up at her with those pleading puppy eyes.

"I already gave you an extra five minutes. I don't want to have to pry you out of bed in the morning."

Rue winked at Ivy. "Your mom's right. Come on, I'll go up with you."

Ivy kissed Montana and hugged him good-night, then sat on the couch, basking in the warmth of the fire and the contentment she was starting to feel every time Rue spent time there. If he was misrepresenting himself in any way, she couldn't see it. And she was looking closely.

A loud growl startled her, and then Montana shrieked and started belly laughing. It sounded as though Rue were tickling him.

She relished the happy sounds for a few moments and then hollered, "Hey, you two, tomorrow's a school day. Lights out."

The laughter subsided and then stopped. She heard the drone of voices but couldn't make out what was being said. A couple of minutes later Rue came down the ladder from the loft and sat next to her on the couch.

"So what were you *boys* talking about?" she asked.

"Oh, just how much fun we're gonna have Friday night. And then we prayed together."

"Really?"

"Yeah, Montana said his prayers, and I added a P.S. and thanked the Lord for bringing the two of you into my life." Rue smiled and took her hand in his. "This feels so right to me. I can't remember when I've been more content."

"Funny, I was just thinking the same thing."

"I'm so glad you didn't let anyone else make up your mind for you," Rue said. "I promise I'm not gonna disappoint you."

"Let's don't start out making promises," Ivy said. "Let's just let things unfold, okay?"

"All right. By the way, my first hunch about having lunch over here was right on. Brandon pulled me aside and gave me a talking-to about not doing anything that might look inappropriate."

Ivy sighed. "How'd he know you were over here?"

"He never said, but he asked me outright. I told him the truth, right down to the PBJs. He was nice about it."

"Brandon's always nice."

"I got the feeling he's not too keen on us seeing each other, though. Since we've both been addicts and all."

Ivy stared at the flames in the fireplace. "And how do you feel about that?"

"Like he and everybody else is making too much of it. You and I aren't gonna forget where we've been. Just knowing what it's like to fight addiction could help us to help each other stay clean."

"I feel that way too."

Rue brought her hand to his lips. "I don't wanna blow this, Ivy. We need to do everything right."

# 23

FLINT FINISHED DRESSING for the day and went into the living room and flipped on KTNR-TV just as the news came on.

"Good morning, Southwest Colorado. This is Jillian Parker."

"And I'm Watson Smyth. Welcome to *Daybreak*. Residents of Jacob's Ear are still reeling after Tuesday morning's gruesome discovery of two more assault victims by a man who is now being called the Masked Maniac.

"The brutal beating of Geoffrey and Morgan Dilly, the owners of a local deli, has everyone on edge, and not just because of the increased level of brutality. In this latest incident, the attacker used the victims' blood to write a message at the scene. And his victims were in their early forties, decades younger than those who were targeted in two previous attacks. Everyone here feels at risk now, and residents are demanding answers.

"The town's marshal, Kyle Redmond, told reporters late yesterday that he's working directly with the Tanner County Sheriff's Department on the case, since two of the three attacks occurred within the city limits. Redmond made it clear that Sheriff Flint Carter is heading up the investigation and is the only spokesperson authorized to release information to the media. Jillian, you spoke with the sheriff. What did he have to say?"

"Well, that's just it, Watson. The sheriff declined to comment regarding possible suspects or what was actually written on the wall in the Dillys' home, citing the ongoing investigation. He did say that his department is working 24/7, following up on leads, and that he has put six department cruisers on the streets of Jacob's Ear in order to deter future attacks.

"Last evening, roving reporter Jessica Monrovia went to Jewel's Café, which is one of many landmarks in this small community, in an effort to find out from residents how they feel about what's been happening. Jessica, what kind of response did you get?"

"As you'll remember, Jillian, the owner of the café, seventy-year-old Jewel Sadler, was the third victim attacked by the Masked Maniac and has been in Tanner County Medical Center since Sunday morning after she was discovered beaten in her home. Customers here had plenty to say, beginning with Millicent Remington, a lifelong resident, and the widow of philanthropist Whitaker Remington.

"Ms. Remington, have these assaults affected you personally?"

"Oh my, yes. This is the first time in eighty-two years that I've been frightened to stay in my own home. I'm terrified of going to sleep. What are we supposed to do when locked doors aren't enough to stop this crazy man? Really, I'm a basket case. I've had to get a prescription from my doctor just to calm my nerves."

"Mr. Gentry, what about you? You've owned the hardware store for thirty years and developed quite a reputation for the banter that gets batted around the old potbelly stove. How has this affected you?"

"Haven't had a good night's sleep since it all started. The first two victims, Deke and Roscoe, have been like surrogate fathers to me over the years. It's beyond me how anybody could inflict that kind of pain on two old-timers—and for a jar of change, no less. I've always known the world *out there* was sick, but now it's here. And nobody knows how to stop it."

"Mr. Draper, you're here on vacation. Has this had an effect on you?"

"Yeah, it's depressing. I fell in love with this place, and three of the victims I consider friends. It breaks my heart to see how this madman has not only beaten their bodies but broken their spirits. They need our support and our prayers, and so does Sheriff Carter. I sure wouldn't want his job."

"Jillian, everyone I talked to had similar comments. There's no doubt that people here are feeling scared and helpless and that they're waiting expectantly for Sheriff Carter to get this Masked Maniac off the streets. This is Jessica Monrovia, reporting from Jewel's Café in Jacob's Ear. Back to you."

Flint turned off the TV and tossed the remote on the chair. So much for reelection. In all his years as sheriff, he had never made an arrest just to appease the public, and he wasn't about to start now.

The thought that the perp might be laughing at him wasn't as maddening as the fear that he might not be able stop the guy before he killed someone. At least Maxfield and Kessler couldn't make a move without his knowing it.


Ivy walked in the lobby of Three Peaks Lodge and over to registration. She lifted the hinged section of counter and walked through to the other side, then hung her coat on the hook and turned on her computer.

A few seconds later, the door to the administrative offices opened, and Kelsey Jones came out and strolled over to her.

"Hey, girlfriend," Kelsey said. "I've hardly talked to you all week. How are you?"

"Doing really well, thanks."

"Still liking the job?"

Ivy nodded. "It's great living out here and also not having to deal with the drive every day."

"I know. Brandon and I love it." Kelsey seemed to be examining her fingernails and then looked up. "Are we okay after our last conversation? I sense that I hurt your feelings."

"I know you meant well. I'm just trying to gain confidence in my ability to make good decisions, and people treat me like I haven't learned anything since high school."

"I'm sorry," Kelsey said. "I just care so much what happens to you."

An uncomfortable silence stood like a wall between them, and Ivy decided to knock it down.

"Kelsey, if you're concerned about Rue because Lieutenant Knolls and Sheriff Carter have been talking to him, don't be. I can honestly say that my first impression of him was completely wrong. Rue's a gentle, sensitive person, and he's great with Montana."

"I'm glad to hear that."

"I'm enjoying his company immensely. Which I'm sure has ruffled some feathers around here, but I can't live my life to please other people. When I talked to you the last time, I told you that what I had with Rue could hardly be called a relationship, which was true. But things have changed. I've never had an attraction like this to any man. And I'm not talking about a physical attraction as much as…well, I'm not sure exactly. I'm just drawn to him. And he never makes me feel guilty about my past."

Kelsey held her gaze. "So Rue knows about all that?"

"Yes. He says he doesn't care where I've been or what I've done."

"That's good because openness and honesty are so important. The worst thing either of you could do is hang on to secrets. They always manage to come out sooner or later."

"Well, Rue's not a hang-on-to-past-mistakes kind of guy. He hasn't been a Christian long, but he really trusts God. He's positive all the time. Knows what he wants out of life. He's really good for me."

"And are you good for him?"

Ivy bit her lip. "What's that supposed to mean?"

"I didn't say it to make you feel defensive. *Any* person building a relationship should ask if he or she has something valuable to contribute."

"Rue must think so."

"I'm sure he does." Kelsey leaned on the counter and looked into Ivy's eyes. "But do *you*? What you think of yourself matters just as much as what he thinks of you. We're supposed to love others as we love ourselves."

"I never thought about it that way."

"I hadn't either. It was something I learned when I was dating Brandon. It's so important to love and respect ourselves if we want to be a good partner."

Ivy sighed. "I never said I was going to marry him, Kelsey. What's your point?"

"My point is that God's in the process of restoring you. If you're building a relationship that has the potential to get serious, why not take time to find yourself before you try to lose yourself? I just don't want you to settle for less than He wants for you."

"How do *you* know Rue isn't exactly what God wants for me?" Ivy hated that she sounded defensive.

"Obviously, I don't. My prayer is that you seek the Lord with all your heart and let things with Rue *evolve*. If he's the man God's picked out for you, you're not going to lose him by taking some time to get your bearings."

Flint swallowed the last bite of a sub sandwich, wadded up the wrapper, and threw it in his trash can.

"There was a knock at the door, and Bobby Knolls waltzed into his office, waving some papers in his hand. "Wait'll you see this!"

"What?"

"The fax that just came in." A grin spread across Bobby's face and seemed to connect his ears. "I couldn't find anything new on Maxfield, so I decided to see what we could dig up on Kessler. I called the Denver PD and talked to a sergeant friend I dated years ago. Gave her everything I have on Kessler and asked her to nose around and see if anything surfaced." Bobby handed the fax to Flint. "Eighteen months ago, Kessler quit his job and moved to Missouri to live with his mother. Wanna guess where?"

"Kansas City?"

"Bingo. Then one morning two months later, Kessler allegedly found his mother dead on the kitchen floor. Bludgeoned with an iron skillet. He called 911 and later told the K.C. police he couldn't even remember where he'd been the night before, that he must've come home and passed out. Claims he never saw his mother till one minute before he called 911."

"Was there a sign of forced entry?"

"Yep. A broken window on the back door. The place had been ransacked. Kessler identified a ceramic bank smashed on the kitchen table and said his mother's grocery money was missin'. But he could've staged the whole thing after he killed her. The cops questioned him at length and never charged him with anything. His clothes tested negative for blood. And the iron skillet had been wiped clean of fingerprints—same as the knob on the back door. The case is still open."

"Did he have a motive?"

"According to Kessler's sister, he was hittin' the bottle pretty hard, and their mother was on his case about it, but the sister didn't believe Kessler was capable of violence."

"They never do."

Bobby stuffed a piece of bubblegum into his mouth. "He moved back to Denver after that. Lived with a buddy while he was on the skids for a few months and then landed in rehab."

"Okay, so how'd he bring Kansas City mud into Deke and Roscoe's house more than a year later?"

"When Kessler lived in Kansas City, he was doin' construction work. I'm thinkin' mud can get caked and dried on work boots for a long time, especially when they're sittin' in a closet, which they probably were, since he wasn't workin' when he came back."

Flint smiled. "Kessler packs the boots when he comes here to work at the camp."

"And the dirt on his boots gets mixed with snow and turns into mud evidence on the carpet. It's enough for a warrant, any way you cut it."

Brandon stood with Jake Compton and Rue Kessler while Bobby Knolls and some other deputies executed the search warrant by going through Rue's belongings at Deer Run and searching his Ford Explorer.

"You okay?" Brandon said to Rue.

Rue seemed to stare at nothing, his hands in his pockets. "I swear I had nothing to do with the assaults. You gonna send me back to Denver?"

"Let's don't get ahead of ourselves, okay?" Jake said.

"They aren't gonna find anything incriminating because I wasn't there when any of the attacks happened."

Brandon saw a white Jeep Liberty pull up. *Oh, boy.*

Ivy got out and ran over to Rue. She linked her arm in his and glared at Jake and Brandon. "How can you two just stand there and let them do this?"

"They have a warrant," Jake said. "There's nothing *we* can do. Your dad's on the way, but he's not going to be able to stop the search either."

"This is so unfair." Ivy looked up at Rue. "I'm sorry this is happening. I don't know why they won't let up on you."

Rue exhaled as if it took every ounce of strength he had just to let it out. "They must've found out about my mom. I kept hoping they wouldn't because I knew this is exactly what would happen."

# 24

THE SHERIFF STOOD on one side of the two-way mirror and observed Bobby Knolls's interrogation of Rue Kessler.

Bobby sat across from Rue, his arms folded on the table. "Tell me again why you told the sheriff you hadn't been to Kansas City recently."

"Because it'd been over a year. That's not recently."

"Why'd you mislead him into thinkin' the only part of the state you'd been to was St. Louis?"

"I already told you I wasn't misleading him. I answered the question he asked. I didn't wanna bring up what happened to my mom. I didn't see the point."

Bobby blew a pink bubble and sucked it into his mouth. "The *point,* Rue, is that we found mud at the first crime scene, and our soil specialists say it came from Kansas City."

"That doesn't prove I was at the scene. This is a tourist town, for crying out loud. There must be dozens of people from Missouri."

"But you're the only one who carefully avoided any mention of Kansas City."

Rue raked his hands through his hair. "Look, my mother was beaten to death. It's all I can do to say the words out loud. I sure didn't wanna relive the nightmare, especially when it had nothing to do with what the sheriff was asking me."

"Yeah, I'll bet. I understand the Kansas City police grilled you long and hard about it."

"Then you also know they didn't charge me."

"All that means is they couldn't get you for it." Bobby leaned forward and put his face in front of Rue's. "But we've got your number."

"I'm not hiding anything."

"Why don't I believe you?"

"I don't know, but I'm telling the truth!" Rue sighed. "This is exactly why I didn't mention my mom's murder in the first place. I knew you'd try to connect me to the assaults here."

"You've gotta admit it's a chain of bizarre coincidences."

"Coincidences aren't proof."

"Not till we find out where you slipped up." Bobby's gaze was penetrating. "It's just a little too convenient that you happened to be passed out the night your mother was beaten with an iron skillet. Just happened to be stargazin' the nights Deke and Roscoe were beaten with a fire log and Jewel Sadler was beaten with a fire poker and lead paperweight. Just happened to be drivin' around by yourself when Geoffrey and Morgan Dilly were beaten half to death with a hammer."

Rue threw up his hands. "What motive would I have to hurt those people? I'm trying to get a job reference from Three Peaks so I can get on with my life. Every minute you waste talking to me, this psycho is out there planning his next move."

Flint knocked on the window, and Bobby excused himself and came out of the interrogation room.

"We've held him long enough," Flint said. "Let him go before he decides to lawyer-up. Keep him under surveillance and see what he does."

Flint heard someone whistle and then saw Buck Lowry rushing down the hall toward them. "Hate to bust up the party, but we've got a body."

—

Brandon closed the door to Jake Compton's office and pulled up a chair next to Elam Griffith and Rue Kessler.

"So are you sending me back to Denver?" Rue said.

Elam folded his hands between his knees. "Why don't you just tell us what's going on?"

Brandon listened intently as Rue recounted the details of Bobby Knolls's interrogation and the painful details of his mother's murder.

"I know it looks bad," Rue said, "but I'm innocent. I loved my mom and could never have hurt her." He paused and swallowed hard. "It nearly killed me when I saw what someone did to her! I started drinking day *and* night after that. I went back to Denver and ended up in rehab a few months later. I haven't been back to Kansas City. And whatever mud they found at the crime scene didn't come from my shoes because I was never there."

"The sheriff's deputies took all your shoes when they executed the warrant," Jake said.

Rue nodded. "Good. Maybe they'll see I'm telling the truth."

"Don Freeman doesn't think you have a mean bone in your body," Elam said. "He's pretty shaken by what's happened. Thinks it's crazy."

"I'm glad Don feels that way, but I'm more interested in what you think. Are you sending me back to Denver?"

Elam glanced at Jake and then at Brandon, and then tugged at his mustache. "I'm not deciding anything till I've had a chance to talk to the sheriff. I've had personal run-ins with Flint's department, and I know how pushy he gets when he's under pressure."

"Mr. Griffith, I swear to you I had nothing to do with any of this." Rue looked into Elam's eyes. "Please, I really need to finish the refurbishing project here so I'll have a recent job reference. I've got a chance at a construction foreman job in the spring. I don't want this mix-up to blow my chances. I've worked so hard to move on with my life."

"If Flint can't link you to any wrongdoing," Elam said, "I don't see how we can penalize you."

Rue nodded. "Thank you, sir. That's all I'm asking."


Flint pulled up behind Bobby's squad car and saw the yellow crime-scene tape marking a stand of trees about half a mile from the entrance to Jacob's mine. He got out of his car and walked over to Buck Lowry.

"What have we got?"

Buck pulled the collar of his jacket up around his ears. "A dead male zipped up in a nylon sleeping bag. Stab wound to the chest. The body's frozen. It's hard to say how long it's been out here. Maybe the CSIs can tell us that."

"Who found it?"

"Four Mt. Byron Junior College students on a photo shoot. The bag was covered with snow, and one of them tripped over it. Heck of a find."

Bobby walked over and stood next to Flint. "I doubt this is related to the assaults. This is probably what our anonymous caller was alludin' to. Don't know how we missed it."

"You couldn't cover every square inch of this area," Flint said. "Besides, you were looking for suspicious *activity,* not a bag buried under the snow."

"Well, I'm goin' back and talk to our buddy Huck Maxfield and see if he flinches when we tell him what we found."

Flint glanced over at the CSIs snapping pictures of the victim. "I'll follow you over there. It'll be a while before they're finished here."

Flint got in his car and followed Bobby about two miles to Huck Maxfield's place. He raised his hand to acknowledge the surveillance team parked on the side of the road as he slowed and turned into the long drive, which had all but disappeared under a new layer of powder snow.

He pulled up behind Bobby and got out of the car, aware of a face in the front window. A few seconds later, Huck Maxfield came out on the porch wearing the same obnoxious grin and a Siamese cat perched on his shoulder.

"Morning, Sheriff. Lieutenant," Huck said. "Don't tell me there's been *another* beating in town?"

Bobby shook his head. "This isn't about the assaults. We're investigatin' a homicide."

"And once again you thought to check with me," Huck said. "I'm truly flattered, but I can save you a lot of time. I don't know anything about a homicide. Who died?"

"Some guy stuffed in a nylon sleepin' bag about half a mile from the entrance to Jacob's mine."

"How unfortunate. Was he a hiker?"

Bobby closed the gap between him and Huck, seemingly to invade his space. "We don't know yet. He was stabbed in the chest and his body zipped up in the bag. Guess someone figured he'd never be found."

"That's really cold." Huck's grin seemed plastered on. "Sorry. No pun intended."

"So have you seen anything unusual out this way? Vehicles? People? Lights? Sounds? Anything out of the ordinary?"

"No. I hardly ever go outside. But then you know that, since you've got two of your people watching my house."

"Well, see there, you noticed *them*," Bobby said. "So I have to ask myself what else you saw."

Huck shrugged. "Nothing. It's quiet out here. That's what I love about it."

"Must be frustratin' now that you can't go anywhere without us knowin' about it."

"Not at all. You can plant your people out there as long as you want and follow me anytime I leave. I don't really care. But I would think the taxpayers would be screaming by now. I really am a dead end. All I can figure is, you're incredibly desperate to solve your cases, or just not very good at what you do."

"Keep talkin', moron, and I'll haul your sorry—"

"Forget it, Bobby," Flint said. "Mr. Maxfield has answered our questions. Let's go. Thanks for your time."


Ivy put on her coat, then lifted the hinged counter and walked to the other side. "Good night, Suzanne."

"Good night."

Ivy pushed open the front door of Three Peaks Lodge, the icy wind feeling razor sharp against her cheeks. She went out to her car and started to get in when Rue's Explorer pulled up beside her, his passenger-side window rolled down.

"Are you still speaking to me?" he said.

"Of course!" Ivy leaned on the open window. "I've been worried sick about you. I had visions of the sheriff keeping you down there half the night, bombarding you with questions. Did you get a lawyer?"

"I don't need a lawyer. I'm innocent. They finally let me go after a couple hours, and I went back to work this afternoon. Your dad was really calm about it. Why don't you get in here where it's warm, and I'll tell you everything?"

Ivy climbed up in the passenger seat and let the blast of heated air from the vents warm her cheeks. She rolled up the window and listened as he told her the details of his interrogation and of his meeting with her father, Jake, and Brandon. And also the grim details of his mother's brutal attack and death.

Rue leaned his head back on the seat. "I probably should've told you about my mom before, but it's painful talking about it. I was working up to it."

Ivy reached for his hand. "That's okay. I understand. What an awful thing to go through. I can see why it's hard to talk about."

"I didn't have anything to do with my mom's death or the assaults here. And now I'm scared that the two of us might lose what we've started because of it."

Ivy held his hand to her cheek. "We won't. I believe you."

Rue was quiet for a few moments and then turned to her. "It means everything that you believe I'm telling the truth. But it'd probably be best for you if we stopped seeing each other till this thing's resolved. The cloud of suspicion hanging over me won't be good for your reputation, especially since you just got out of jail."

"I don't care. People are going to think what they want. I'm used to it. I sure don't intend to throw away a chance at something that feels so right just because some people might judge us."

"It does feel right, doesn't it?"

Ivy nodded. "I admit I'm still afraid of trusting my feelings, but I don't want to shut them down either. I'm ready to see where this goes."

Rue leaned closer and slid his arm around her. "Me too. There could be some rough spots till the sheriff makes an arrest."

"I know. And I'm liable to get even more resistance from friends and family. We might as well brace ourselves for that. I guess we just have to trust God to open this door wider or close it."

Flint sat at his desk and chomped on a couple of Tums just as the phone rang.

"Flint Carter."

"It's me," Betty said. "I heard on the news about the body that was discovered. Just what you needed right now, eh?"

"Like a hole in the head, but it keeps life interesting."

"You coming home for dinner, or do you have to work late?"

Flint glanced at the clock on his desk. "I could be home by seven. Is that too late?"

"No. I've got a pot of beef stew on the stove, and it's ready any time you are. I'll put the corn bread in the oven at six thirty. Ian already took his bath. I think he's wanting a little dad time before he goes to bed."

"Sounds good to me too. I sure hope he doesn't start in again about wanting to have a sleepover with Montana. I'm not changing my mind while Rue's under investigation. And I don't want to be put in the position of having to tell Ian the hard facts."

"So how'd Rue's interrogation go?"

"We couldn't trip him up. We worked on him a couple hours and then let him go just about the time the call came in about the John Doe. We've been wrapped up in this new case ever since. But we're keeping Kessler and Maxfield under surveillance. I don't have a good feeling about either of these guys."

Bobby waltzed into the office with a folder in his hands.

"Hon, I've got to go. We'll talk more later. I'll see you around seven. Love you."

"Love you too."

Flint hung up the phone. "What's up?"

"The lab just called. None of the cat hair we collected from Maxfield's truck or house matches the cat hair we found at Jewel Sadler's. In fact, nothin' we collected from Maxfield's property matches anything at any of the crime scenes. Couldn't even find good old Missouri mud on his shoes."

"Could just mean that he's darned good at not leaving evidence."

"Yeah, I know." Bobby spit his gum in the trash can and popped a fresh piece into his mouth. "I'd just like to pin *somethin'* on him and get that smug grin off his face."

"Well, harassing him isn't going to get us anywhere."

"You're right. Sorry. What else did I come to tell you? Oh yeah, our handwriting expert can't make an accurate analysis of the bloody letters written on the Dillys' wall because the strokes were formed with a sponge. So that's out. And we put a rush on everything we collected at Kessler's. We might know somethin' tomorrow."

"I find it interesting that there haven't been any more assaults since we started our surveillance on Maxfield and Kessler. It's looking more like one of those two is guilty, or our perp's moved on."

## 25

IVY PUT THE LAST of the dinner dishes in the dishwasher and turned it on. She went over to the table and sat down next to Rue, who was losing a game of Chinese checkers to Montana.

"I'm telling you, kid, you're a prodigy," Rue said.

"What's that mean?" Montana jumped three of Rue's marbles.

"It means you're amazing, maybe even a genius at this game."

Montana made a fist and pointed at himself with his thumb. "*I'm* the champ."

"Indeed you are," Ivy said. "And the champ needs to go take a shower and start winding down so he's not too wired to sleep. Tomorrow's a big day at school with the spelling contest, and then tomorrow night—"

"We get to see Orion! Yippee!"

"The sky's supposed to be crystal clear. Which reminds me"—Rue reached in his shirt pocket and pulled out a piece of paper and unfolded it—"I drew a diagram for you. That's what the Great Hunter would look like if you could connect the dots."

Montana took the paper, his eyes wide. "Cool! Look, Mom."

"How neat," she said. "I think maybe even I can find him with this."

Rue nodded. "As program director, let me remind you that dressing warm will make all the difference in how much fun you have."

"Don't worry. Montana has long johns," Ivy said. "And I'm borrowing my mother's thermal underwear. But you promised we would have a fire going."

"We will."

"And s'mores," Montana said. "We made some in Brandon and Kelsey's fireplace. Those're yummy."

"Well, they taste even yummier when you make them outside."

Montana cocked his head and looked up at Rue. "Why? Don't you make the outside kind just the same as the inside kind?"

"Ah, but it's the fresh air and wide-open sky that makes them taste better. You'll see. Okay, champ. Go take your shower, and I'll let you read me a story before you hit the sack."

"Okay." Montana charged down the hall toward the bathroom and hollered over his shoulder. *"Green Eggs and Ham!"*

"I knew that." Rue looked over at Ivy, his face beaming. "I love that kid."

She savored the words for a moment and assumed he meant it as a figure of speech. Yet how wonderful it was hearing a man besides her father say those words.


Brandon threw another log on the fire and then went back to the couch and sat next to Kelsey.

"Honey, we have to stop talking with Ivy about Rue and let her make her own decisions."

"Are you trying to say I was out of line?"

"Let's just say you were bold. I know how much you care about Ivy and want her to make good decisions. But if she's determined to pursue a relationship with Rue, trying to counsel her will probably end up ruining your friendship. Which would be really sad because you've had more of a positive impact on Ivy than anyone."

"I don't think anything I said should've been perceived as an attack on Rue. I emphasized that she should take some time to find herself before she tries to lose herself, and that she shouldn't settle for less than what God wants for her."

Brandon stoked her hair. "Sound advice for a healthy person. I'm not sure Ivy even knows what you mean. And I'm sure she knows you're not wild about Rue."

"I always felt he was hiding something. Now that he's opened up about his mother's murder, maybe that feeling will go away. I'm surprised Elam is letting him continue his work at the camp, though. You'd think he would welcome any excuse to keep Rue away from Ivy."

"Well, the whole point in hiring guys from My Brother's Keeper was to give them a chance to start over. Rue denies any wrongdoing, and no one's proved otherwise. Elam feels it would be a slap in the face to terminate the agreement with MBK and send him back based solely on speculation."

"Has Elam said anything about Ivy and Rue dating?"

"Not a word. He seems to like Rue, but I can't imagine that he's too keen on Ivy getting involved with someone who's been in recovery."

Ivy nestled with Rue on the couch, enjoying his presence and the warmth of the fire and only half listening to the music playing on the radio. Now that she'd made a clear-cut decision to build a relationship with him, she knew she'd have to tell him the truth about Montana's father. The timing almost seemed right, especially after Rue had opened up his heart and his past to her. What if he couldn't handle it? What if it was too repulsive for him to accept? What if it changed the way he saw her? Wasn't it better to find out now, before she let herself fall for him, whether or not he could handle the baggage she brought to the relationship? The sound of the disc jockey's voice interrupted her thoughts.

"I've been meaning to ask what you and Montana are gonna do about a Christmas tree?" Rue said.

"My parents told us to explore the property and pick one, so I guess

we're going on a Christmas-tree hunt. There must be a million trees out
there to choose from."

"Need some help?"

"I'm sure we do. You offering?"

Rue smiled and played with her hair. "Yeah. I'd love it. I don't even
remember last Christmas. I was totally sloshed through the holidays. My
sister tried to coax me into going to Kansas City and spending Christmas
with her and my nephews. But I was so messed up about my mom that I
never sobered up till January, when I finally got into rehab."

"That first Christmas without your mom must've been so hard."

"Yeah, but no harder than any other day. I couldn't get the image of
her lying in her own blood out of my head. Still can't."

"It must bother you horribly that her killer got away with it."

"You bet it does. And it bothers me that anyone would believe I'm
capable of doing something like that to any human being, especially my
own mother. Hey, let's talk about something happy, okay? When do you
wanna get the Christmas tree?"

"How about Sunday after church? We'd have all afternoon to go pick
out a tree, bring it home, decorate it, and then just enjoy looking at it. I'll
make some hot chocolate and have sugar-cookie dough ready to pop into
the oven. It'd be fun."

"Yeah, could be the start of a new tradition."

*A new tradition?* Ivy liked the implications of that. "I need to check
with my parents. I'm sure they're assuming Montana and I are going out
tree hunting with them, not that we ever said we were."

"Maybe you should. You don't wanna get on your parents' bad side."

"Since I haven't done this with them in ten years and Montana never
has, I doubt they have any great expectation about it."

"But maybe you do."

"Not really. It'll never be the same as when I was a kid, and I know
better than to try to duplicate the event or the feelings. It's really more
about Montana and getting him into it."

"Well, I'm open either way. I won't get my feelings hurt if you decide to do it with your folks."

"All right. I'll feel them out first. One thing we definitely need help with is buying lights and picking out new ornaments and a tree stand. Maybe the three of us could do that on Saturday."

Rue's face lit up the way Montana's did when he had something fun to look forward to. "Sounds like fun. If somebody would've told me last Christmas how positive I'd feel this Christmas, I would've told them they were nuts." He put his arm around Ivy and drew her close and let his warm lips melt into hers. He pulled back slowly and gently brushed the hair off her face. "I'm glad you know about my mom. It's a big relief to have that out of the way. I wanted to tell you but wasn't sure how to bring it up."

"I know what you mean."

"Is somethin' wrong?"

Ivy shrugged. "There're some things I haven't known how to bring up with you, either."

Rue put his fingers to her lips. "I know everything about you I need to know. You got mixed up with Pete. Witnessed Joe's murder. Kept the pact. Got messed up on drugs. Finally got clean. Came back here. Recommitted your life to the Lord. Confessed the truth to the sheriff. Did your time. And found me. I don't have to know everything that happened between the lines."

*No, just the one thing I'm scared to tell you.* "You've never asked me much about Montana's father."

"You said he wasn't involved in your lives. I didn't see the point in pressing the issue."

"You're not curious about him?"

"Should I be?"

"Well, I am."

"If you're curious, why don't you go looking for him?"

*Come on, Ivy. Just say it and get it over with.* "Because I…I don't know who he is. I never asked his name."

"I'm not following you."

"I know." Ivy got up and stood in front of the fire, her back to him. "There'll never be an easy way to tell you this, so I'm just going to force myself to say it. It would be wrong to keep it from you. You can hate me if you want."

"I could never hate you. I told you I don't care where you've been or what you've done. I'm serious about that."

"I believe you mean it, but you haven't heard what I have to say either." Rue came up behind her, his hands on her shoulders. "Try me."

Ivy stood shaking, her stomach feeling as though a herd of tiny stallions were trapped inside, trying to kick their way out. "In my darkest days on the street, the next fix never came fast enough. I never had enough money, and I wandered around half crazed and desperate. That's when—" She choked on the words, which suddenly seemed stuck to the roof of her mouth like a wad of peanut butter. Did she really need to admit the one thing she was most ashamed of, especially when she had already confessed it to God, and Rue said nothing she'd done mattered to him?

Ivy stared at the flames, her pulse racing and guilt taunting her. She'd spent a decade of her life in bondage to a secret that had nearly destroyed her. Was she going to build a future based on deception? "I…I began to…use my body to get drug money. I don't remember a lot of detail, just these horrible flashbacks that make me want to throw up." Ivy wiped the tears off her cheeks. "It's really hard to talk about this. I'm so ashamed."

"That was then. This is now." Rue kissed the top of her head.

"I know, but I can't seem to turn loose of it. I got arrested for soliciting and for cocaine possession. I had no choice but to call my parents. My dad hired some hot-shot lawyer who got the charges dropped with the stipulation that I go through rehab."

"Which you did. And you got clean."

"For a while. I found out I was pregnant and couldn't bring myself to get an abortion. I stayed clean through the whole pregnancy and decided to keep the baby. I don't know what I was thinking, probably that I was going to stay clean and make a new life. But shortly after Montana was born, I couldn't take the pressure of being home with him and went back to doing drugs."

"Is that when your friend Lu came along?"

Ivy nodded. "She knew I was high and half the time not even aware that Montana was there. I'm surprised she didn't report me. She just came over and got him and took him over to her place. That's how it was for the next four years until I ended up in rehab the second time, and they told me if I didn't get off drugs I was going to die. I never told any of them I had a son. I knew he'd be safe with Lu."

"So did your parents pay for the second rehab?"

"Yes, I called and pleaded with them and promised I was serious about kicking the addiction. So they footed the bill again, and this time it took. When I got out, I never even called them. I think I was too ashamed. Lu let me move in with her. I worked as a waitress, and she helped me raise Montana. Between what I made and her Social Security, we barely had enough to scrape by. I realize now what an incredible blessing she was."

Rue turned her around and looked into her eyes. "Ivy, when did your parents find out about Montana?"

"Not until last spring when I called them and asked if I could come home. Lu was dying, and I brought her with us. My parents helped me through that crisis, and they've been wonderful with Montana. And very supportive of both of us while I was in jail."

Rue took her hand and led her back to the couch and sat next to her. "So are you trying to tell me that Montana's father was one of the guys who paid you for sex?"

"Had to be. I wasn't seeing anyone."

"What have you told Montana?"

Ivy's eyes clouded over, and the flames in the fireplace were a big yellow blur. "I told him that I don't remember his father's name, which is technically true. And that his father wasn't around when he was born. But I also said that if he knew Montana, he would love him."

"Was he satisfied with that answer?"

Ivy wiped the tears that escaped down her face. "Only because he can't stand to see me get upset when we talk about it. The child is so desperate to feel like he belongs somewhere."

"Mom?"

Ivy's heart sank. *Oh no. How long has he been standing there?*

"Hey, champ," Rue said. "Come around here where we can see you."

Montana crawled up on the couch and sat between them. "I had a bad dream that these giant creepy-looking robots came and took Rue away, and I never got to see him ever again."

"Well, I'm right here." Rue slid his arm around Montana. "So you can tell those silly robots to stay out of your dreams. And that they're full of baloney."

"But how long *are* you gonna be here? Grandpa said you're going back to Denver when you're finished working on the cabins."

"Well, not for months, and things can change. Why don't we just take it one day at a time?"

Ivy looked over at Rue just as he looked at her. It had never occurred to her that Montana was already more attached to him than she was.

# 26

ON FRIDAY MORNING, Flint sat at the table in his office with Bobby Knolls, waiting for Buck Lowry to get back from the medical examiner's office with the findings concerning the John Doe.

"We don't have the staff to keep this up," Flint said.

"At least the assaults have stopped. Maybe trace'll find somethin' on Maxfield or Kessler. I'm bettin' one of those guys is really sweatin' it."

There was a knock, and Buck breezed into the office and sat at the table and handed Flint a folder.

"Okay," he said, "the ME estimates our John Doe's age between fifty and fifty-five. Cause of death was a stab wound to the torso. The guy bled out. We've got his DNA, but it doesn't match anyone's in the system. Fingers were degraded, so we don't have prints. But before the body was frozen, it showed signs of decomp consistent with exposure to warmer temperatures. They have to do more testing and study the weather logs over the past few months to determine how long he's been dead, but it was definitely sometime before the cold weather settled in. We're working with the missing persons database to match his DNA."

Flint lifted his eyes and looked at Buck and then at Bobby. "The feds have more manpower and resources than we do. I'd like them to assist on this so we can concentrate on the assault cases. You guys think you can handle working with Nick Sanchez again?"

Bobby popped a pink bubble. "I'll wear my thick boots. Just keep him off my toes."

"Okay with me," Buck said. "It'd be nice to start getting home before my kids go to bed."

"All right. I'll call Nick when we're done here. What's the latest from the surveillance teams?"

"It's been deader than a doornail," Bobby said. "Maxfield turned out the lights about ten, and Kessler never left the camp. I don't know how long it's gonna take us to nail one of them, but I think we're on the right track."


Ivy dropped Montana off at her mother's house, then drove down to the camp, past Three Peaks Lodge, and around to the scenic overlook behind Building A.

She got out of her car and climbed up on the wooden platform. She looked out across the lustrous landscape to the jagged peaks capped in pearly white—mighty and steadfast like the One who made them. She stood silent and drank in the splendor until she was nearly breathless and could feel God's presence.

*Lord, I'm really scared. I thought I felt You prodding me to be honest with Rue, but now I wonder if it was just me. What if he can't handle my past, once the full impact hits? And what if Montana overheard what we were talking about? How am I supposed to explain that kind of vile behavior to a seven-year-old?*

Ivy spotted a doe and her fawn ambling out of a brushy area onto the open range about fifty yards from where she stood. They appeared to be vulnerable to predators, but she knew that their God-given instincts rendered them neither helpless nor unaware.

Maybe she was fretting for nothing. Rue's good-night kiss had been tender and sincere. Maybe her sordid past hadn't fazed him and never would. Montana might not have overheard any of her conversation with Rue. He might have slipped downstairs half asleep and paid no attention to what they were saying. He seemed okay at breakfast.

*Lord, I can handle whatever happens, but please don't let Montana suffer because of my mistakes. If I'm never going to have a man to share my life with, I can accept that. But if Montana is never going to have a dad, at least help him to feel good about himself.*

Ivy glanced at her watch and stood for another minute, trying to prepare emotionally for whatever the day would bring. She walked back toward her car, sure of only one thing: if Rue couldn't handle the truth about her past, it was better for her to know it now.


Jewel sat on the side of the bed and signed the forms the nurse had brought to her.

"I'll bet you're ready to get home," the nurse said. "Have you got enough help once you get there?"

"Oh, sure," Jewel said. "More than I need. I really don't want to be waited on. I'm a little nervous about being alone in the house, though. I'm hoping that the attack hasn't spoiled my happy memories there. I had Gene Gentry from the hardware store put deadbolt locks on the doors. But I'm having an alarm system installed, just to feel safe." *If that's even possible now.*

"Well, you're free to leave anytime. I assume someone is picking you up?"

Jewel smiled. "Uh-huh. My friend Luke, who's one of my best customers, and Rita, my right-hand gal. I think they've gotten sweet on each other this past week. At least *something* good has come of all this."

"You're not thinking of going back to work yet, are you?"

"I doubt I'll last twenty-four hours at home. Even if I go in just long enough to make muffins and chicken salad, it would be great getting back to some semblance of normalcy. It seems a lifetime ago that I was attacked. It's amazing how something like that can turn your whole world upside down."

The phone rang, and Jewel reached for the receiver. "Hello."

"Jewel, it's Ivy. How're you feeling?"

"Like a punching bag that's fighting back." She laughed. "They're releasing me, doll. Luke and Rita are on their way over here to pick me up and take me home."

"That's wonderful! So when can I come clean your house?"

"You were precious to offer, but I think you need to spend time with that sweet little boy of yours. A customer offered to do it, and I'm giving her free meals in trade. Should work out dandy."

"Well, is there something else I can do?"

"I think I'm all set. Should be back in the café before you know it."

There was a long pause, and she could hear Ivy breathing.

"Jewel, I'm sorry I never got back to the hospital. It's been a crazy week. Montana really wants to see you. We're going to be shopping in town tomorrow. Could we stop by your house late morning?"

"Of course. I'd love it. But if I'm not there, check at the café. I'm serious about getting things back to normal."

"Did the doctor say you could go back to work?"

"Said I could do whatever I felt like doing."

"All right. I just don't want you to take on too much too quickly, especially when so many of us have offered to help."

"Listen, doll. The best medicine for me is to roll up my sleeves and get back to work."

Jewel looked up and saw Luke and Rita walk through the door. "Looks like my taxi's arrived. See you tomorrow. Give Montana a hug for me."

"I will. Don't overdo, you hear me? By the way, are Deke and Roscoe being released too?"

"Actually, they've been moved over to the convalescent home, just till they're strong enough to take care of themselves. They're coming around as well as can be expected, but it's going to take a while for them to get their zip back. And their spirit. It's hard to explain what something like this takes out of you."

Flint sat at the table in his office reviewing the results of the trace evidence collected from Rue Kessler's car and cabin.

"Bobby, nothing here matches anything found at the three assault crime scenes," Flint said. "Not even the mud found on Deke and Roscoe's carpet. Now what? We don't have anything on Maxfield *or* Kessler."

There was a knock on the open door.

Buck Lowry came in and sat at the table and let out a sigh. "Geoffrey Dilly just died. It's all over the news. Man, we did not need *this* right now."

"I guarantee you Mrs. Dilly didn't either." Flint's mind flashed back to the crime scene and the blood writing on the wall. "I want this animal locked up!"

Bobby pushed his chair back from the table and stood. "I'm gonna revisit the evidence we collected from Maxfield's place before Sanchez arrives and sets up his throne."

"I suggest you cut the sarcasm," Flint said. "It'll be a relief not having to deal with the John Doe's murder while we're still putting together the pieces of this one. And let us not forget that our perp has dared us to catch him before he kills someone."

"A little late for that," Buck said.

Bobby stopped chewing his gum. "Not really. He didn't know Dilly wasn't gonna make it when he wrote that message on the wall. Hard to say what else he's plannin'."

"So why do you want to revisit the evidence from Maxfield's place?" Flint said. "There wasn't anything incriminating there."

"There's just somethin' *off* about Maxfield."

Buck smirked. "Do you think?"

"The guy's a weirdo," Bobby said, "but he's not crazy. And he knows somethin' about somethin'. I just wanna dig a little more before Sanchez questions him about the John Doe."

"All right." Flint rose to his feet. "I'm going to go prepare a statement for the media. The public's going to be screaming for somebody's head now that one of the assault victims has died."

Ivy heard the door to the lodge open and felt a cold draft. She looked up, surprised to see Rue walking up to the registration desk, his face beaming.

"Hi."

"Hi, yourself," she said.

"I just wanted to nail down the details for tonight." Rue leaned on the counter. "Not supposed to be a cloud in the sky. Thought I'd run into town after work and pick up what we need to make s'mores. Maybe get some takeout so you don't have to cook dinner."

Rue's face bore the same kidlike excitement she had seen when he suggested they go stargazing.

"What kind of takeout did you have in mind?" Ivy said.

"How about chili? Don said it's the special at Jewel's today. I could bring it to your place, and we could eat before we head out."

"Mmm. Sounds good. Want me to make a thermos of coffee to take with us?"

"Sure. Make it extra strong." He hesitated a moment and then said, "How was Montana this morning?"

"He seemed fine. I don't think he overheard our conversation. I think he just had a bad dream."

"Seemed like it. I was surprised, and definitely flattered, that he'd miss me if I weren't around. I want you to know I don't take that lightly."

Ivy met his gaze and held it. "Rue, are we okay? I mean, I dropped a bomb on you last night, and you're acting like nothing's changed."

"As far as I'm concerned, it hasn't. I'm not hung up about your past. I told you that."

Ivy blinked the stinging from her eyes, but not before a tear escaped down her cheek. "I'm really not a bad person."

"Of course you're not. You would've never done that if you hadn't been desperate for a fix."

"I was so afraid you'd hate me."

Rue tilted her chin and wiped the tear with his thumb. "That's not gonna happen."

"I had to tell you before I could let our relationship go any further. I thought you deserved to know."

"It's good you got it off your chest, but it doesn't matter to me. However, the way you handle the subject with Montana could make a huge difference in how he sees himself. And that *does* matter."

"I know. He's much too young to understand, especially since he doesn't even know how babies get here. I think for now it's enough for him to know that his father had problems and couldn't be a part of his life."

"Okay." Rue played with her collar. "So tell me where *our* relationship is so I don't overstep with Montana. He's starting to feel attached to me, and vice versa. I don't want him getting hurt."

"If you're asking me how I feel about you, I don't know yet. I think I've been holding back because I was afraid of how you'd react to my past. I'm incredibly drawn to you and want to pursue this and see if it develops into something serious."

Rue picked up her hand and kissed it. "Good, then we're on the same page."

The door to the administrative office opened, and Brandon came out. "Oh…Rue. I didn't realize you were here."

"I stopped by on my morning break." Rue let go of Ivy's hand. "I'll bring the chili between six and six thirty."

"Actually, you'll want to hear this too," Brandon said. "Jake just heard on the news that Geoffrey Dilly died this morning. So the Masked Maniac is now wanted for murder."

Ivy's face fell. "That's depressing."

"Apparently, as soon as Morgan's able to travel, she's flying back to England and having Geoffrey's funeral held there. I heard the deli's for sale again."

Ivy glanced over at Rue. "Pete's family owned it before the Dillys bought it last summer. With all the dark history attached to it, they may never find a buyer."

She squirmed in the silence that followed, aware that Brandon seemed to be sizing them up.

"Well," Rue finally said. "I guess I'd better get back to the site. See you tonight, Ivy."

"All right."

Brandon watched Rue go out the door of the lodge and then turned his gaze on her. "Is everything okay?"

"Why would you ask me that?"

"You look like you've been crying."

"Everything's fine. Rue just stopped by to double-check our plans for tonight. We're taking Montana stargazing. The big goal is to pick out the constellation Orion. We're going to build a fire and make s'mores. Montana will definitely be in his element."

Brandon smiled. "Sounds like fun. So he and Rue get along pretty well, eh?"

"Very well. Rue's wonderful with him."

"So you guys are officially dating?"

"We definitely are." *Please tell me you didn't come out here to lecture me about that.*

Brandon came over and stood by the counter. "Ivy, are you aware the sheriff is tailing Rue?"

"What?"

"Any time he leaves the camp, he's going to be followed."

"That's insane. He hasn't done anything. Does my dad know?"

"He does. Flint asked him to keep it to himself, but he told Jake and me. I think you should know that if you're going on a date, you may have company."

"They're wasting their time. But thanks for the heads-up." *I think.*

# 27

IVY LEANED AGAINST Rue's Ford Explorer wrapped in a stadium blanket and sipping hot coffee. She was enjoying the stargazing adventure far more than she ever imagined.

Rue stood with his hands on Montana's shoulders. "Good job! You've got the North Star and the Big and Little Dippers down pat. Now, turn this way and look over here. See if you can pick out Orion."

Montana paused a few seconds and then pointed to the sky. "I see the three stars on his belt!"

"Good. Now can you use your imagination and picture the Great Hunter looking like this?" Rue shone the flashlight on the diagram where he had used a pen to connect the stars that made up Orion.

Montana looked up to the heavens, a blank look on his face. "Not really."

"Okay, keep your eyes on his belt. Now find Betelgeuse and Rigel like we did the other night. Once you do that, you'll be able to picture the Great Hunter."

Montana turned to Rue, his eyes two black olives under the band of his stocking cap. "There's too many stars up there. I don't remember which ones they are."

"I'll give you a hint: Betelgeuse is very bright and looks reddish, and you have to look higher than Orion's belt and to the left."

Montana studied the diagram and then looked up and seemed to be searching. Finally, he pointed to the sky and shouted, "I see Betelgeuse there—on his left shoulder!"

"Good job! Now find Rigel."

Montana's grin overtook his face. "Man, this is really, really hard work." He seemed to be studying the diagram as if his whole future depended on his answer.

"Need another hint?"

"No, I wanna do it by myself." Montana focused on the sky for what seemed an eternity and then bellowed, "Rigel is there—on his right foot! I can see him, Rue! I can see the Great Hunter!"

"Yee-haw!" Rue picked Montana up off the ground and whirled him around three hundred and sixty degrees and then set him down again.

"Can you see him, Mom?" Montana said, sounding almost out of breath.

Ivy nodded, her eyes fixed on the heavens, the image on the paper clear in her mind. "I actually can. It's amazing."

"And there's so much more to see," Rue said. "You won't believe the detail you can see through a telescope. What gets to me is the size of every-thing we're looking at. Remember, if we could measure across just Rigel, it would be about sixty times larger than the sun and at least forty thou-sand times brighter. And yet it's just a dot out there. Blows my mind."

"Mine too. It's enough to give you goose bumps." Ivy drank in the splendor and tried to comprehend the vastness of what she was seeing.

"Okay, champ"—Rue tugged on the scarf around Montana's neck—"let's drive back to the campfire and let your poor mother thaw out."

"And make *more* s'mores!"

"That too."

Rue followed Ivy to the Explorer, put his hands around her waist, and boosted her up into the passenger seat. "Fascinating, huh?"

"Breathtaking. I've never taken the time to marvel at the heavens before. At least not like this."

"I'm glad you decided to come with us." Rue leaned inside the car and pressed his lips to hers.

"Are we gonna make s'mores? Or are you guys gonna get all kissy-kissy?" Montana let out a husky laugh that turned into a cloud of white vapor.

Rue put him in a headlock and started tickling him. "Kissy-kissy, eh? You spying on us?"

Montana and Rue's converging laughter infused her soul, and Ivy recorded the sound and filed it in her memory to be replayed later.

Rue finally let up on Montana and hoisted him up into Ivy's lap. "There you go, champ. Keep your mother warm. We'll be sitting by the fire in two minutes."

She watched Rue walk around to the driver's side. Surely, he was an answer to prayer.

Somewhere nearby a car motor was running, and she figured the sheriff's deputies were probably freezing their tails off. At least she hoped so.

Jewel sat in her living room sipping a cup of Sleepytime tea.

"You and Rita were sweet to stay with me this evening," she said to Luke Draper, "but I'm really fine. It's only nine o'clock. Why don't you go out and do something fun? I can take care of myself."

"I'm sure you can," Luke said, "but should you? Seems like it would be smart to have somebody stay with you for a few days."

"I've lived alone for twenty years. I wouldn't know how to act if somebody stayed with me." Jewel looked at the glow on their youthful faces. "It's Friday night, for heaven's sake. Go look at Christmas lights and take a sleigh ride. Have some of that wonderful eggnog at Grinder's. You really don't need to baby-sit me. I'm just going to watch an old movie."

Even as she said it, Jewel shuddered, remembering that that's what she had been doing just before she was attacked.

"I'd really feel better if you let me sack out on the couch for a few nights," Luke said. "Just till you're sure you feel okay being here by yourself."

"It's really not necessary."

"Well, *I'd* sleep a whole lot better, knowing you weren't alone."

Jewel could hardly believe how much Luke's deep blue eyes looked so much like Mel's when he was young.

"I'm not trying to scare you, Jewel, but this guy's still out there. Why don't you let me stay here at night, at least until you get the new alarm system installed next week?"

"Couldn't hurt," Rita said. "I'd offer to stay myself, but my mom is terrified about the whole thing and won't close her eyes till I get home."

Jewel wrinkled her nose. "I guess the next stop is the nursing home."

Luke smiled and went over to the couch and sat next to her. "Listen to me. You're a lively, fun lady with a couple decades still left in her, but you're not going to get over this thing in one week. What happened to you was a big deal. The guy could've killed you."

Jewel's eyes filled unexpectedly, and it would have felt good to cry. Instead, she swallowed hard. "I just don't want to be afraid to live my life. I can't let him do that to me."

"Of course you can't. So why not let a friend who's got nothing but time on his hands sack out on your couch so you can sleep soundly and get your strength back? No one is going to get by me. Not only that, I turn into a barbarian if someone starts messing with my women." He flashed that charming smile.

"I think you should take him up on it," Rita said.

"And *I* think you two young people should be out having a good time."

Rita stood. "Not tonight. I have to open in the morning, and I promised my mom I'd be home before ten."

"You're running out of excuses," Luke said.

"Oh, all right." Jewel pushed her shoulder against Luke's. "But only until I get my alarm system installed."

—

Flint poured a cup of coffee and handed it to FBI Special Agent Nick Sanchez.

"Déjà vu, eh?" Nick said.

"Yeah, unfortunately. I'm really glad you're here."

"I heard the Griffith girl is out of jail."

Flint nodded. "Yeah, she seems to be on the straight and narrow, other than she's dating one of the suspects in the assault cases. Not that we can find anything on him."

"Which one?"

"Rue Kessler."

"The fella working out at the camp." Nick blew on his coffee and took a sip. "You know I'm more interested in this Masked Maniac than I am the perp who killed the John Doe?"

"I figured."

"You want me to roll up my sleeves on this one too?"

Flint sighed. "I don't know, Nick. Bobby and Buck are on top of it. I really don't need any additional tension around here."

"You think *I'm* going to ruffle their feathers?" Nick's cup couldn't hide his grin. "Hey, it's your call. But if you invite me into the investigation, I promise to use great tact and finesse."

Flint laughed. "And if you believe that, I've got some beachfront property for sale in Telluride."

"Well, the offer stands if you change your mind. It took me a while last time, but I think I learned how to work with them without stomping on their turf. You do want to get this guy, right?"

"That's all I can think about. And to tell you the truth, I'm completely baffled. Not that I haven't been baffled before. But this perp doesn't even steal anything of value…well, you already read the files."

"Intriguing." Nick sat back in his chair. "That just tells me he's skilled, experienced, and arrogant like me—only bloodthirsty as a shark.

I believe he's going to go in for the kill once he's through bloodying the waters."

"I believe it, and that's exactly what I'm trying to avoid."

"Well, if you want help, holler. Like I said, it's intriguing. And I'd love to help you nail this guy."

"Let me think about it." Flint's cell phone rang, and he put it to his ear. "Sheriff Carter."

"You're not gonna believe this," Bobby said. "I just found a cardboard box out here on the front steps of the courthouse. Looks like it contains Deke and Roscoe's jar of nickels, Jewel's Tiffany lamp, and the Dillys' family portrait—everything the perp took from the crime scenes."

"Was there a note with it?"

"No, and there's nobody out here."

"Okay, Bobby. Take it to the lab and see if our perp left any trace evidence behind."

"Will do."

Flint disconnected the call. "The assault cases just get weirder by the minute."

"How's that?"

"The perp returned everything he stole from the crime scenes. Put them in a cardboard box on the courthouse steps. Bobby just found it. No note. No indication of why he returned it. Nothing."

The lines on Nick's forehead deepened. "That's not a good sign. I think he's trying to tell you that he's through playing games, that he's ready to go in for the kill."


Ivy relaxed on the couch while Rue followed Montana up the ladder to the loft and tucked him in for the night. A few minutes later, Rue came back and flopped on the couch next to her.

"He crashed the second his head hit the pillow," he said. "What a great evening!"

Ivy smiled. "It was perfect, other than the sheriff's deputies following us."

"It's their problem. One of these days they'll figure out that I'm not the Masked Maniac."

"It doesn't bother you that they followed us?"

"I refuse to let it get to me. I hope Montana doesn't catch on. There's no reason he needs to know this stuff. I'm surprised the sheriff's son hasn't said something."

"They could be watching my house," Ivy said. "How would we know?"

"And why would we care, as long as we can be together?" Rue slid his arm around her.

"Well, I'd be lying if I said it doesn't bother me"—Ivy leaned her head on his shoulder—"but it didn't spoil anything. It was absolutely amazing out there."

"Told you."

"Montana had so much fun. Thanks for being so tuned in to him and for building his self-esteem. He's just never had that from any man other than my dad."

"Not hard to do. He's respectful. Smart. Interested. The kind of kid people love being around."

"Everyone but my brother, Rusty."

"It's Rusty's loss. He's the one missing out."

Ivy shivered. "Is it cold in here or is it just me?"

"I'm comfortable." Rue took her hands in his. "Your fingers are like ice."

"So are my toes."

"Why didn't you say so? Let me warm them up."

"How?"

"I'll massage your feet."

"You don't have to ask me twice." Ivy took off her hiking boots and socks and leaned her back on the arm of the couch and swung her feet up in Rue's lap.

He wrapped his hands around her toes. "Good grief, Ivy. They're like icicles."

"I know. I can't believe how warm your hands are."

"They're always like that. For some reason, the cold doesn't affect them."

Ivy closed her eyes and relaxed as Rue's hands gently massaged her feet and the warmth began to return to them. "That feels wonderful. Thanks."

"Once your feet and ankles are warm, you'll start warming up all over." Rue pushed up the elastic leg bands of her sweatpants and wrapped her cold ankles in his warm hands. "I didn't know you had a tattoo."

"When I was in college, I got impulsive one weekend and had it custommade. I wanted it to look like an ankle bracelet made of ivy. I was trying to make some kind of statement about who I was."

Rue picked up her leg and studied the tattoo more closely. "Do you have others?"

"No, that's it… You hate it, don't you?"

"I didn't say that."

"You didn't have to. I can tell."

"It's no big deal, Ivy."

"I can always have it removed."

Rue set her leg down, his eyes seemingly fixed on the tattoo she suddenly wished she had never gotten, and continued massaging her foot.

"Are you upset?" Ivy said.

"No, I'm not upset."

"Well, *something's* wrong."

"Why do you say that?"

"Ouch!" Ivy winced. "Because all of a sudden you're kneading my foot like a lump of bread dough."

"Sorry. I've got a monster headache."

"Why didn't you say so? I'll get you some Tylenol."

"Actually, it'd be better if I just go. I've got medication back at the cabin that'll work better."

"Is it a migraine?" Ivy set her feet on the floor and hurriedly put on her socks and boots, aware that Rue had already zipped up his ski jacket and was standing at the front door.

She got up and walked over to him. "Are you sure you're okay to drive?"

"I'll be fine. I had a great time tonight. I'll call you tomorrow." Rue opened the door and left without kissing her good-night.


Flint sat in his easy chair and thumbed through a back issue of *High Country Sportsman,* holding little hope he was going to get a good night's sleep.

Why did he feel so inept every time he was stumped? It's not as though it was his fault the perp left no incriminating evidence. The Masked Maniac was cruel and calculating and meticulous. Even the smear of mud on Deke and Roscoe's carpet proved only that the attacker had, at some point, been in Kansas City.

Flint closed the magazine and tossed it on the end table. It was too late to take a sleeping pill. Maybe he'd just turn off the lamp and rest his eyes. His cell phone vibrated, and he picked it up.

"Flint Carter."

"Sheriff, it's Buck. I'm over at the Remington mansion. Looks like our perp acted on his threat—times two."

# 28

FLINT TURNED INTO the wide circle drive of the Remington mansion and parked behind Buck Lowry's squad car. He got out and jogged up the front steps to the beveled glass and wooden door that had been framed with lighted Christmas greens and red velvet.

He went inside, instantly aware that the palatial elegance had been gauchely upstaged by the battered corpse slumped on a blood-spattered white sofa.

Flint walked over to where Bobby Knolls and Buck Lowry were standing and realized the victim was not Millicent Remington but an African American woman.

"Have you made an ID?"

Bobby popped a pink bubble. "Name's Lily Augustine. She was just hired as Mrs. Remington's live-in nurse. Looks like her skull was crushed with that marble statue over there."

Flint sighed and shook his head. "Where's Mrs. Remington?"

"Body's upstairs in the master bedroom. Head bashed in with some kind of antique iron tool. It's not pretty."

"Who called it in?"

"Anonymous caller at 12:17. Prepaid cell. Distorted male voice. Gave the address and said it was a twofer, that we should've caught him first. Then he laughed this ghoulish laugh and hung up. A real freak."

"How'd he gain entrance?"

"Broke a window in back and climbed in."

"Do we know if he took anything?"

"The safe was open," Bobby said, "but he didn't take the jewelry."

"Any idea what else was in it?"

"Can't be sure, but Mrs. Remington popped off for years about keepin' two million bucks in it because she didn't trust the banks to be there if the economy went bad. Don't know how true it was. People here didn't take her seriously. You know what an eccentric she was."

*Was.* Flint couldn't remember a time when Mrs. Remington wasn't a pillar of this community. Among the many projects she and her late husband had funded was the civic center, the library, the miner's museum, and the ice rink and bandstand at Spruce Park. They had also donated the gaslights and flower boxes that dressed up Main Street and the quaint pedestrian bridge that spanned the white water of Phantom Creek and connected the downtown to the nature trail that led up to Tanner Falls. It was their generosity that had made Jacob's Ear one of prettiest old mining towns on the western slope.

"You comin'?"

Flint was jolted back to the moment by Bobby's question. "Uh, yeah."

He followed Bobby and Buck up the polished wood staircase to the second floor, and then down a hallway hung with rich oil portraits to a room with an elegant marble fireplace and canopy bed—and a dead body lying on the floor, half in and half out of the closet.

Marshal Kyle Redmond walked over to Flint, his eyes red-rimmed, his demeanor dazed. "Millicent was a personal friend. All she ever wanted to do was help people."

Flint patted Kyle on the back. "I know. Where's the safe?"

"In the closet. Her jewelry's still in it."

Flint knelt down next to Mrs. Remington, whose white satin nightgown was drenched in red, and saw a gaping wound in her head. He quickly blinked away the image and decided he wasn't going to remember her that way.

Flint rose to his feet and walked around her body and into a clothes closet bigger than his son's bedroom. He saw the door to the safe was wide open. "I wonder if the perp beat the poor thing till she gave up the combination, or if he picked the lock and bludgeoned the life out of her just for the fun of it." He clenched his jaw. "I want this gorilla's head on a stick!"

"Since there're no survivors this time," Bobby said, "we don't know if the perp took anything inconsequential. But we assume he got whatever he wanted from the safe. Wonder why this guy keeps changin' his MO?"

"I don't know, but we've been looking for an outsider all this time. Tell me how an outsider would know about Mrs. Remington's claim to have two million in the safe?"

"Probably wouldn't. My guess is the Masked Maniac saw her on the news when they did that interview down at Jewel's and decided she was next. Maybe he just got lucky and hit the jackpot."

Flint rubbed the stubble on his chin. "Or maybe this wasn't the same perp. Maybe it was someone who decided to steal the money and let us think it was the Masked Maniac."

"Could be. But it'd be pretty risky beatin' two people to death unless he was sure the money was in the safe."

"Exactly. Mrs. Remington's attorney would've known for sure whether or not the money was there."

"You're thinkin' the *attorney* did this?"

"I don't know what I think." Flint folded his arms across his chest. "But as long as Nick Sanchez is already here, I want him to help us investigate this."

"Yeah, I figured."

"Don't sound so glum. We can use all the help we can get."

Bobby gave a nod. "Okay by me. I sure don't want any more 911 calls like this one."

Ivy lay in bed staring at the ceiling, wondering if Rue was all right. His strange and sudden change in behavior had almost frightened her. But then again, she knew migraines could be horrific. He probably knew what was coming and wanted to get to his cabin as quickly as possible.

She thought back on the evening and how wonderful it had felt with the three of them having such fun together. She knew better than to think beyond today to what the future might hold, but her affection for Rue had grown significantly over the past couple of days. It wasn't romantic love. It could be if she'd give in to it, and that both excited and terrified her.

*Lord, I trust You to guide me while I'm still thinking clearly. If this relationship is not what You want for me, please close the door on it before my heart takes over.*

As scary as it was allowing herself to be vulnerable again, she knew she could never move forward with her life as long as she was afraid to trust her own judgment. And no matter what her parents or Kelsey and Brandon thought, Rue Kessler seemed to be the answer to her prayers.

Flint sat at the table in his office with FBI Special Agent Nick Sanchez, Lieutenant Bobby Knolls, and Investigator Buck Lowry going over what they knew so far about tonight's murders.

"Nick, we're all in agreement that you need to take the lead on this," Flint said. "We've given it our best shot, and we're no closer to finding our perp."

Nick took a sip of coffee. "After my CSIs have finished going over the scene, we'll know more. They don't miss anything. Not a crumb."

Bobby raked his hands through his hair. "Why does this perp keep changin' his MO? He's messin' with us, right?"

"Actually, his MO regarding the assaults *has* been consistent." Nick made a tent with his fingers. "All the victims were beaten with something from their own home. And for the purpose of inflicting terror, not death. The perp wrote the bloody message on the wall to warn you he was going to intentionally kill someone. Which he's now done. Mr. Dilly's death was not intentional. In fact, it probably ticked him off and caused him to kill *two* victims in order to recapture the feeling of being in control."

"So why'd he take Mrs. Remington's money and leave her jewelry? That's a new twist."

Nick smirked. "Hard to pass up a chance to pocket two million dollars or however much was in there. He left a lot of very expensive jewelry behind because this guy's all about control. He wanted to show us that he gets to choose whatever he wants to take or leave, and whether his victims live or die."

"So tonight was the night he made good on his threat," Flint said.

"Precisely. And we know that Kessler and Maxfield didn't commit this murder. Your deputies were tailing them all evening."

Flint shook his head. "Nick, are we even sure this *was* the same perp who did the beatings? What if it was a copycat, someone who knew the money was in the safe and wanted us to think the Masked Maniac took it? We should talk to Mrs. Remington's attorney and find out whoever else knew about her claim to have two million in the safe."

"Don't worry, we're already on it."

Bobby rubbed his eyes. "Okay. Somethin' about Maxfield's really buggin' me. Earlier today, I took another look at all the evidence we collected at his place. We found two distinct sets of prints all over his house: One set was his. We don't know who the other set belongs to, but we assumed his grandfather. Thing is, the prints we found in Maxfield's truck don't match his. They match the other set. So why aren't Maxfield's prints in the truck when he's the only one drivin' it?"

Nick's eyes grew wide and pushed back his chair and stood. "I can think of one explanation, Lieutenant: the guy isn't Huck Maxfield! Radio your surveillance team and tell them to pick him up!"

Flint took a sip of freshly brewed coffee, his eyelids heavy with the sleepiness that had evaded him earlier.

"Okay, I blew it," Bobby said. "Everyone feel better?"

Nick shook his head. "I'm not here to point a finger, Lieutenant. From what I read in the case file, I didn't think Kessler *or* Maxfield looked good for this."

Nick's cell phone rang, and he picked it up. "Sanchez… Well, for crying out loud. How'd he get past them?… All right. Get the bloodhounds on it!" Nick disconnected the call and put his phone on his belt clip.

"What happened?" Flint said.

"Maxfield bolted. The surveillance team went up to his door and couldn't get a response, so they entered the premises and discovered he'd gone out the back door on foot. They followed his tracks in the snow but lost his trail in the woods. No way to know how long he's been gone."

Bobby swore under his breath.

"You know what I think?" Nick said. "I think our John Doe is Huck Maxfield. And whoever's living in that house killed him."

There was a stretch of silence, and everyone seemed to be processing.

Finally Bobby's face relaxed, and he said, "Makes perfect sense, and it never even occurred to me."

"Me either." Flint set his coffee mug on the table. "But we need to take a look at the evidence we collected from the John Doe and see if we can match it to anything we collected at Maxfield's house."

"We already know we can't match his fingerprints," Bobby said. "The John Doe's fingers were too degraded."

"Well, there's always dental records," Nick said. "And I'll bet we can find the real Maxfield's DNA in the house if we go looking for it. I'll get the CSIs right on it."

"But if you're thinkin' the guy livin' in Maxwell's house is the Masked Maniac, think again," Bobby said. "The impostor *stinks*. His BO is enough to gag you. None of the victims mentioned the smell."

"Good point," Flint said. "They couldn't have missed it. And the odor would've lingered at the scene. It's that bad."

Nick nodded. "Well, it makes more sense that we're looking for two different perps anyway. The John Doe was killed back when the weather was warmer, which means long before the beatings started. MO's are completely different." He glanced at his watch. "Why don't you guys go home and get some sleep. The CSIs are going to be at it all night. By morning, we should know what we're dealing with."

# 29

IVY GRIFFITH OPENED her eyes to the sound of Montana's laughter
and cartoons playing on the TV in the living room. She smiled and let the
sound seep deep into her soul. The high decibel level of nonstop noise at
the jail had been almost as difficult to cope with as being locked up. But
this sound was soothing…healing…one she never wanted to be deprived
of again.

Her thoughts turned to Rue, and she wondered if his headache had
gone away or if he'd been up all night in terrible pain. And if he might be
down for the day and unable to go shopping for Christmas ornaments.
She glanced at the clock: eight forty-five. She wondered how long she
should wait before calling him.

The sound of the phone ringing startled her, and she picked up the
receiver. "Hello."

"Honey, it's Mom. Have you heard the bad news?"

"No, what happened now?"

"Millicent Remington and her live-in nurse were murdered last night.
Beaten like the others—only fatally. This time the guy robbed her safe and
called 911 to report the crime and to gloat. I can hardly believe this is happening here."

"Oh, Mom. That's horrible. What time did it happen?"

"Around eleven."

*Thank heavens Rue was here.* "Everyone must be so upset."

"They are. Your dad and I are at the café having breakfast. Jewel's here, believe it or not. Poor thing still looks dreadful, but she's got grit. She's devastated about Millicent. She had been a customer ever since Jewel opened."

"I remember when she used to come in. I got a kick out of somebody that rich eating at the café instead of hiring her own cook. Did the nurse have a family?"

Carolyn exhaled into the receiver. "I don't know yet. They haven't even released her name. We're all dazed."

"It's getting scarier all the time. I thought this was going to be a safe place to raise Montana. At least we haven't had any trouble out here at the camp."

"Speaking of camp, how was your stargazing and campfire adventure last night?"

Ivy smiled without meaning to. "Spectacular. We had *so* much fun. Montana is really into it, and Rue's wonderful with him. We were out until eleven thirty and then came back here. If the murder happened around eleven, Sheriff Carter can finally take Rue off his suspect list because he was here with us. But then he probably knows that, since his deputies tailed us all evening."

"They followed you?"

"The minute we drove out of the camp. Oh, they tried to be subtle, but we knew they were there. It's so stupid. Rue wouldn't hurt a flea."

"Your father told me what happened to his mom. Must've been terrible."

"It was. And it's hard for him to talk about it. I think being under suspicion for her murder was almost as hard as losing her."

"Police always suspect family members first. Isn't that the usual protocol?"

"I guess. But it was devastating. Why don't we talk about something pleasant? Rue offered to take Montana and me out after church on Sunday to cut down a Christmas tree. I didn't know if you and Dad assumed we'd all go together, or if it made any difference."

There was a long pause.

"Well, I…I guess it really doesn't. Of course Elam and I *assumed* we'd all go together, but it's not as though it's been a family tradition in a long time."

"We could start a new family tradition and take two cars. I'll ask Rue to come along."

"Actually, it might be good for you and Montana to start your own tradition."

*Why don't you just admit you're not ready to meet Rue?* "We will, but part of it could be helping you find and decorate your tree. Montana's going to flip when he sees the size tree you guys always put up."

*Beep.*

"Mom, that's my Call Waiting. Do you want to hang on?"

"No, I'll catch you later, after I get your dad's ideas about going to get a tree."

"All right. Call my cell if I'm not here." *Click.* "Hello."

"Ivy, it's Rue."

"How are you feeling?"

"Not too great. I'm gonna stay in and take it easy today. I'm sorry to flake out on shopping for tree ornaments, but I wouldn't be good company."

"So do you get these a lot?"

"Not really. I just need to sleep it off."

Ivy played with the cord on the phone. "Can I bring you breakfast or lunch or something?"

"No. I'm sick to my stomach. I'll do better by myself. But thanks."

"Is Don around today to check on you?"

"He went skiing. Honestly, I'm glad. I need the quiet."

"Sorry," she said. "I'll let you go. But I have good news. Well, actually it's horrible news, but it's good news for us. The Masked Maniac struck again last night around eleven. Since you were with me, that means you're off their suspect list."

"I knew they'd wise up eventually. So who'd he hurt this time?"

Ivy sighed. "Actually, there were two victims, and he beat them to death: a rich old widow, Millicent Remington, and her live-in nurse. Pretty horrific."

"No kidding."

"You sure I can't do anything to help you?"

"I'm sure."

"How long do these headaches usually last?"

"A couple days."

"So you won't be able to help us get the tree on Sunday?"

"Sorry. You better make other plans."

Ivy thought his voice sounded cold, as if he were distancing himself. "Are you sure there's not something else going on?"

"Like what?"

"Like my tattoo is a turnoff?" Even as she said the words, they didn't ring true. Wasn't this the same man who accepted the fact that she had sold her body for drug money?

"I'm not that petty, Ivy. Don't put your own spin on it. I told you what's wrong with me."

"Okay, I'm going to hang up and let you rest. I had a wonderful time last night. I'd love to go stargazing again some time."

"We'll talk later."

"Okay, call if you need something. Bye."

Ivy hung up the phone and lay staring at the beam of sunlight that had squeezed through the crack in the curtains and found its way to the ceiling. Why couldn't she just take Rue at his word? Why did she have this uncomfortable feeling that he wasn't telling her everything?

Flint sat at the table in his office studying the case files and captured a yawn with his hand.

"I saw that." Nick Sanchez came in, a smug grin on his face. "You ready for this? The strands of human hair we collected from Maxfield's house match the DNA found on our John Doe. And the saliva found on an envelope addressed to Gus Maxfield from Huck. The dead guy is definitely Huck Maxfield, no question."

"So who's the impostor, and what was he doing out there?"

"Don't know yet. His prints aren't on file at NCIC, and he doesn't have a Colorado driver's license. He could've lived out there indefinitely if you hadn't gotten your anonymous 911 calls. His living in filth could've been to cover up evidence, though it'd take someone with a strong motive to pull that off."

"Yeah, it was totally disgusting."

"Unfortunately, the bloodhounds lost the guy's scent on that long stretch of Miner's Highway. Maybe a trucker picked him up. It's hard to say how long he'd been gone. I've got an APB out with his description. Maybe we'll get lucky."

"Especially if he doesn't take a bath." Flint took the last gulp of lukewarm coffee. "So what now?"

"We're having the FBI lab process all the trace evidence found at Maxfield's place. If there's anything there that'll tell us who the impostor is, we'll find it." Nick glanced up at Flint. "Don't kick yourself over this. It would've been baffling to the best of them. This guy's clever."

"Okay, so what do we do about the Masked Maniac? You think he's moved on now that he's shown us he's in control?"

Nick shook his head. "Not by a long shot. His violence is escalating with each assault. We need to step up the presence of law enforcement. Except for the first assault, all have taken place within the city limits. This guy is flaunting his ability to outsmart us. Truthfully, he acts like a pro. I can't imagine this is someone who lives here. I'm hoping he got careless during last night's attack and left his DNA. But he's been meticulous so far. And the way he covers up his body for the attacks, he's managed to keep his DNA to himself."

"I'm really baffled," Flint said. "Right after the first two assaults, we checked all male guests staying in motels, lodges, and B and Bs in the region. The only ones without alibis were two guys from Illinois and Rue Kessler, and they've been cleared now."

Ivy pushed open the exit door at the Christmas Store and let Montana squeeze past her and then almost ran headlong into Brandon and Kelsey.

"Oops." Ivy smiled, tightening her grip on the plastic bags of tree decorations she was carrying. "Looks like we're on the same wavelength."

"We heard this place has the best assortment of Christmas ornaments in the area," Kelsey said. "We want to add to what we started last year. And find something neat for the mantel."

"Well, as you can see, we found lots of stuff."

"Yeah," Montana said. "My grandma and grandpa are gonna help us cut down a tree tomorrow. Rue's got a bad headache."

Brandon raised his eyebrows. "I'm sorry to hear that."

"It's a migraine," Ivy said. "Rue says they usually last a couple days. He was really sorry he couldn't help us." She turned to Montana. "Sweetie, would you put these packages in the car for me? I'll be right there." Ivy loaded him down with sacks. "Have you got them?"

Montana giggled. "They're almost bigger than me. But I'm really, really strong."

"I know you are. Watch your step." Ivy waited until Montana was out of earshot. "I guess you heard about Mrs. Remington and her nurse?"

"Unfortunately," Kelsey said. "I'm glad we're not living in town. I'd be terrified."

"Just in case you were wondering, Rue was with Montana and me until early this morning. We were out stargazing. And the sheriff's deputies were tailing us. So that should clear him once and for all."

"I never thought he was guilty of anything," Brandon said.

*Yeah, right.* "So when are you guys going to get your tree?"

"Elam told us to take one from the property, so we may do that tomorrow after church."

Ivy glanced at her watch. "I need to scoot. It was good seeing you. Have fun in there."

"We will." Brandon gently took her arm. "Hey…I'm really glad Rue's out from under suspicion. Too bad about the headache. Maybe I'll stop by there later and check on him."

"He said he'd rather deal with it by himself. Don went skiing. I think I'm just going to honor his wishes and let him rest."

"Have you taken him over to your parents' house?" Kelsey said.

Ivy forced a smile, thinking she knew where this was going. "That was supposed to happen tomorrow when we all went to cut down a tree. But I guess it'll have to wait a few days. I'll see you later. Montana and I are going to stop by Jewel's for a few minutes."

Ivy sat with Montana at the round antique oak table in Jewel Sadler's kitchen, enjoying hot apple cider and gingersnaps.

"I'm so glad you stopped by," Jewel said. "It's been a hard morning, what with the horrible news about Millicent and all. I just don't want to dwell on it, especially at Christmastime and when I have such wonderful company."

"I hate it that you're here alone," Ivy said.

"Actually, I'm not. Luke offered to spend his nights on my couch until I get my security alarm installed. So Montana…" Jewel said. "Tell me what you want for Christmas."

"A puppy."

Ivy laughed and turned to him. "This is the first I've heard of it. What kind of puppy?"

Montana cocked his head, an elfish grin on his face. "A cute kind."

"Big or little?"

"All puppies are little, Mom."

"Well, they don't stay that way."

Montana took a sip of cider, his eyes peeking over the top of the cup. "Well, could I have a Sasha puppy?"

"Oh, sweetie, I don't know. Siberian Huskies are expensive. And we're both gone all day. A puppy might get lonely. I'm not sure that's a good idea."

"You could go home at lunch and give him a hug. And I would take care of him all the rest of the time. Grandma said I'm a very responsible young man."

"You are, but—"

"And I've never ever had a dog." Montana pushed out his lower lip, his eyes pleading.

"Well, we need to discuss this some more." Ivy caught Jewel's gaze, hoping to elicit some support for her reluctance.

"I just had a thought," Jewel said. "The county animal shelter has hundreds of puppies that need homes, and it's very inexpensive. Does it have to be a Sasha dog?"

Montana shrugged. "Not really. I just want a puppy that will stay with me till I'm big and follow me around and stuff."

"Thanks, Jewel," Ivy said. "You're a real rabble-rouser."

"Just think about it, doll. Little boys and puppies seem to be made for each other. And dogs are really protective. I wish I had one right now.'

"I honestly hadn't thought of that."

Montana cupped her face in his hands. "So can I have a puppy? Pleeease?"

"Why don't we run this by Grandma and Grandpa first and see what they think, since the chalet belongs to them? I'm not saying no, but I'm not ready to say yes, either."

"Okay. Can I go outside and play in the alley?"

"If you promise to stay right there."

"I will." Montana got up and walked over to Jewel. "Will it hurt if I hug you?"

Jewel chuckled. "It'll hurt a darned sight more if you don't."

Montana put his arms around her and gently squeezed. "I hope all those blacky-bluey places go away soon and you start to look like you used to."

"That's two of us, sweetie."

Ivy's eyes followed Montana out the back door, and she realized it was the same door the intruder had used to break in.

"He's a wonderful boy, Ivy."

"Thanks. I'm realizing it more every day. So how are you *really* doing?"

Jewel's white eyebrows came together. "I'm scared. There, I said it. Me, Jewel Sadler, scared. Terrified is more like it. I've never been scared a day in my life till now. It's not that I'm afraid to die, you understand. But I'm sure not excited about anyone besides the Lord helping me along."

Ivy covered Jewel's hand with hers. "I can't even imagine how horrifying it must've been for you."

"You really can't. I'm a nervous wreck. I woke up more than once last night and heard doors creaking and footsteps in the house and was scared to death the masked man had come back to finish me off. Then I remembered Luke was staying here with me. What a relief."

"It's really sweet of him to do it."

"I think so." Jewel smiled. "I get tickled with him. I think he's sweet on Rita."

"Really?"

"Yes, she was here with him the other night. I detected a little spark there. Truthfully, I was hoping the two of you might hit it off."

"I'm dating someone, Jewel. His name's Rue Kessler, and he's doing some refurbishing work out at the camp. He's great with Montana, and he's introduced us to a whole new hobby: stargazing."

Ivy took a few minutes and told Jewel about Rue's love for astronomy and the details of their big outdoor adventure the night before.

"Well, doesn't that beat all?" Jewel said. "I'm thrilled for you, doll. Sounds promising."

"I don't know if it's going anywhere, but it sure feels right."

Ivy heard the front door open and then footsteps across the hardwood floor.

"Oh, excuse me," Luke said. "I didn't realize you had company. Hello, Ivy. Sorry I haven't gotten around to snowmobiling yet. So much has been happening. Did you hear about Mrs. Remington?"

"I did. I was sick."

Luke nodded. "Me too. I don't know what's taking so long to catch this crazy man, but I insisted on staying with Jewel until she gets her alarm system installed. No sense in her being afraid."

"I couldn't agree more." Ivy pushed back her chair and stood. "Well, I hate to leave, but I still need to go to the grocery store before I head back to Three Peaks. It's good to see you looking so much better. And now that Luke's staying with you, we can all rest easier."

# 30

ON MONDAY MORNING, Ivy drove down the road to the youth cabins and slowed when she passed Bald Eagle, Rue and Don's current work site. She saw Don's truck and Rue's Explorer and was torn between anger and relief. She had left two messages on Rue's cell phone on Sunday and never heard back from him. After that she got stubborn and decided it was up to him to call her.

Ivy turned around and drove back to Three Peaks Lodge, confused and disappointed at Rue's sudden indifference. She thought about driving out to the scenic overlook to calm down, but she needed to be at work in five minutes. Why was he being so inconsiderate? Did he think she wouldn't worry? Or that Montana wouldn't be disappointed that he had backed out of his offer to go shopping with them on Saturday and tree hunting on Sunday?

At least the time she and Montana had spent with her parents hunting for the perfect tree had been fun. But in the back of her mind all day had been the nagging question about Rue's well-being and this odd change in his behavior.

Ivy parked her car and went into the lodge, glad to see a roaring fire in the huge rock fireplace. She lifted the counter and went on the other side and turned on her computer, looking forward to the organized chaos of checking in a new group today. At least she would be busy enough to forget how disgusted she was.

The door to the administrative offices opened, and Brandon Jones came out and went over and poked the logs in the fire, then turned to her.

"Hey, Ivy. How was your tree-finding adventure?"

"Great. We found a beautiful six-footer that fit perfectly in the corner to the right of the fireplace. The piney smell is wonderful. Montana's never had a fresh-cut tree before and wanted to sleep on the couch so he could be near it." Ivy smiled. "Of course my parents cut a *ten*-footer for their living room."

"I remember the one they had last year," Brandon said. "The thing was huge."

"Always. You wouldn't believe what they go through to get it home. So did you and Kelsey get yours?"

"Actually, we did. It's about the size of yours, though we haven't decorated it yet. What did Rue think of your family tradition?"

Ivy looked at her computer screen and pulled up the list of guests expected to arrive today. "He was down with his migraine all weekend."

"That's a shame. Guess it's good I decided to follow your lead and not bother him. Maybe I'll run out to the work site later and see how he's doing. I'm sure he or Don would've called if he wasn't coming to work. I've got to hustle. I'm due in a meeting. Would you throw another log on the fire when it needs it?"

Ivy nodded and kept her eyes on the computer screen. "Sure."

She waited until Brandon was out of earshot and then picked up the phone and keyed in Rue's cell number, determined not to leave another message.

*Come on, pick up before your stupid answering machine goes on.*

"Hello."

"There you are. How're you feeling?"

"A lot better, thanks."

"Why didn't you return my calls? I've been worried."

"Sorry. I turned off my cell and didn't even check for messages. I told you I was gonna stay down."

Ivy played with the phone cord. "Montana and I really missed you."

"I missed you too. Did you get the tree?"

"Yes, it's up and decorated. We hated going ahead without you."

"Sorry."

"What are you doing for lunch today?" Ivy said. "You want to meet me at the dining hall?"

"I can't. I have some errands I need to run since I was down all weekend. You gonna let Montana come to the work site this afternoon? I promised to let him stain the trim."

"Uh, sure. I didn't know if you'd feel up to it."

"I'm fine."

"You want to bring him home and stay for dinner? I'm making chicken and dumplings from my mother's recipe. If mine is half as good as hers, you'll be glad you did."

"Okay."

*Could you try showing just a little enthusiasm?* "Rue, are you sure you're okay?"

"Yeah, why?"

"You just seem blah, that's all."

"The headaches take a lot out of me. I'll bring Montana home when we're done out here. See you around five fifteen."


Flint stood at the window in his office, looking out across Phantom Hollow, and felt as if an invisible demon were hovering over the valley, sucking up all the oxygen. He heard footsteps and turned around just as Nick Sanchez came into his office and sat at the table between Bobby Knolls and Buck Lowry.

Flint, anxious to hear what Nick had to say, went over and sat next to Kyle Redmond.

"I appreciate all of you meeting me here. I've got some pretty startling news: we know who our Masked Maniac is. The DNA from an eyelash found on Millicent Remington's satin nightgown belongs to Johnson McRae, who just happens to be one of the slickest jewel thieves in the world. Authorities in Kansas City suspect he and three accomplices pulled off a near-flawless jewel heist during an exhibit at the Nelson Art Gallery last month—rare jewels valued at six million bucks. It's believed that he shot and killed his three accomplices at a nearby warehouse and fled with the goods. The feds there think he could be lying low until the dust settles."

"Are you absolutely sure it's this McRae?" Bobby said.

Nick smiled. "Oh yeah. The eyelash is a beauty. It's the only DNA evidence we found. But it's all we need." Nick reached inside his folder and gave each person at the table a photograph. "That's what Johnson McRae looked like when he was caught on camera at a museum in Paris last year. He eluded authorities then. And he did it again in Kansas City after beating a security guard to death and disabling the security cameras and the alarm system. He's one of only four guys in North America capable of pulling off a heist that sophisticated, and the other three are dead. It's him, all right."

Flint studied the photo. "I haven't seen this man."

"I have to believe he's altered his looks quite a bit," Nick said. "He's six feet tall. Nature gave him red hair. Brown eyes. And a reddish star-shaped birthmark the size of a quarter on the back of his left calf. I'm working on getting an artist's sketch of his face. This is all we've got at the moment."

"So you think he did all the assaults?" Buck said.

"Yeah, I do. The Kansas City mud on the carpet at the scene of the first assault fits. McRae's wanted in several states and in France and England for a number of violent crimes. Our profiler thinks the beatings here are his way of letting off steam, almost as if to entertain himself until it's safe to move the jewels. Somehow McRae found out about the Remington woman's claim to have two million in her safe, and he couldn't resist."

Bobby popped a pink bubble. "Do we know for a fact that she had two million in the safe?"

"According to her attorney and against his advice, she did."

Flint sat back in his chair, his weight balancing on the balls of his feet. "So how do we catch a pro like that? If he's lying low, how do we find him?"

"The only way I know is to learn to think like him."

"How do we do that?"

Nick's eyes widened. "Study every move he's made. Leave that to me. Each of you guys is too valuable for me to tie up here in the office. You know the people in this town. You know what feels right and what doesn't. I need you working with my agents. Since we don't know for sure what McRae looks like now, we need to start looking at all males between five feet eleven and six feet one. That'll narrow down the field considerably, and that's the group we need to get DNA swabs from."

Ivy finished putting the dinner dishes in the dishwasher, aware of Montana's monotone reading voice coming from the loft.

She went in and sat on the couch, glad when Rue finally climbed down the ladder and sat beside her. He had been wonderful with Montana all evening but somewhat aloof with her. Or was she imagining it?

She put her hand on his. "Did you have a good day at work?"

"Yeah, Don and I got a lot accomplished. All we have to do now is paint and get the new flooring down. And then we're done at Bald Eagle. How about *your* day?"

"It was okay. Busy. So...do you like our Christmas tree? You've hardly said a word about it."

Rue looked at her, his face void of expression. "I told you I did when I came in. It looks real nice. Smells great."

"Thanks. It was a big deal getting it home, but my parents loved helping. Montana and I really felt your absence, especially after such a fun start to the weekend. We loved looking at the heavens and can hardly wait for you to take us out again and show us more stars and constellations. We're definitely hooked."

"I'm glad." Rue reached over to the end table and picked up the remote. "Do you mind if we watch a little TV?"

Rue turned the TV on and started surfing channels, and Ivy sat fuming. Was this what she had to look forward to?

Finally, she snatched the remote from his hand, turned off the TV, and glared at him till he looked at her. "If I wanted to do something mindless, I'd have done it by myself." She searched his eyes. "Rue, what's wrong? You're like a different person all of a sudden. And don't blame it on your migraine, because I'm not buying it."

"I don't know what you want me to say." He stared at his hands.

"The truth about what's bothering you. What changed you from a fun, exciting, enthusiastic date to a dud who would rather watch anything on TV than talk to me?"

"I never said that."

"Are you denying that something's different?"

"I told you I'm wiped out from the migraine, but you don't want to hear it."

"Well, you seem just fine with Montana." Ivy sighed and leaned her head back against the couch. "Are you afraid of hurting my feelings? Is that why you won't tell me what's wrong?"

Rue started to say something and then didn't.

"Whatever it is, I want to know. Anything is better than indifference."

There was a long, agonizing pause, and the only sound was Rue cracking his knuckles.

Finally, he said, "I guess I'm not as ready as I thought to pursue a serious relationship."

Ivy threw up her hands. "And you decided this why? Because you found out I had a tattoo?"

"That's not it at all."

"Then what is? Because that's when your whole attitude changed. You couldn't get out of here fast enough."

Rue got up off the couch and stood in front of the fire, his thumbs hooked in the pockets of his jeans. "I can't handle the intensity of this kind of relationship right now. I thought I could, but I was wrong. I just don't want to hurt you. I promised myself I'd never hurt you."

"Well, too late." Ivy wiped the tears off her cheeks. "You're the one who coaxed me into this. I trusted you. I finally opened the door to my heart, and now you're closing it."

"Please don't cry. I'm not closing it. I…I just need a little time to sort things out."

"What things. My *past*?"

"Will you stop with that? I told you it doesn't matter to me where you've been or what you've done. *I* have some stuff I have to work out, all right?"

"And you can't talk to me about it?"

Rue kept his eyes fixed on the fire. "Not right now."

"Then why are we even spending time together? I have zero interest in a relationship that isn't open and honest."

"Ivy, don't take what's going on with me as rejection. It's not."

"Then what would you call it? Because it sure feels that way to me."

"I just need to put on the brakes and work through some stuff. I need a little space, that's all."

"Fine. Take all the space you need, but take your indifference somewhere else."

"Can't we agree to put this on hold till I work some things out?"

"Don't you understand?" Ivy said. "I can handle just about anything but secrets. I've lived my entire adult life shrouded in secrets. No more. Not for you. Not for anyone."

"Yeah, I get it." Rue stood silent for several seconds, never once look-ing at her, and then walked over to the door and put on his ski jacket. "You gonna keep me from seeing Montana?"

"No. It's not fair to punish him because you've disappointed me. But don't expect me to hang out with you."

# 31

ON FRIDAY AFTERNOON, Flint stopped by Jewel Sadler's house, a box under his arm, and rang the doorbell. He was surprised when the door opened and Luke Draper appeared.

"Hi, Luke. Is Jewel home?"

"Yes, she just got back from the café. Come in." Luke held open the door, and Flint went inside.

Jewel came into the living room dressed in a housecoat and fuzzy slippers that made her look much older than she was. "Please tell me you don't have bad news."

"Actually, I have good news. I brought your Tiffany lamp back." Flint opened the flaps on the box so she could see.

Jewel put her hands to her face and sucked in a breath. "Oh my goodness." Tears began to run down her bruised and swollen cheeks. "I never thought I'd see it again. Can you put it over here on the table?"

Flint followed her to a small table adorned with a doily. He set the lamp on the table, plugged it in, and turned it on. "Look at that. Good as new."

Jewel took a tissue out of the pocket of her housecoat and wiped her eyes. "Thank you, Lord."

"The feds wanted to keep it longer, but I talked them out of it."

Jewel shook her head in disbelief. "I didn't even know you found it."

"I can't really get into details about how we got it back, either. We haven't made that fact public, so please don't tell anyone. You either, Luke."

Luke flashed a smile of approval. "I won't say anything. Isn't this great, Jewel?"

"Oh my, yes." Her eyes brimmed with tears all over again. "It's the only thing I own that I couldn't bear to part with. My sweet Mel gave it to me, you know."

Flint put his hand on her shoulder. "It's wonderful being able to return it to you."

"I heard on the news today that you're following up on some solid leads in the case," Luke said. "So are you close to getting this guy?"

"I hope so. We're working on it 24/7. Listen, would you object to giving us a DNA swab? Don't take it personal, but the feds want—"

"Say no more. I'll be glad to do it. When?"

"Would you mind dropping by my office in the morning?" Flint said. "It'll just take a minute, and then you can be on your way. By the way, have you seen Deke and Roscoe lately?"

"Yes, just this morning. They're getting stronger by the day but won't be home for a while yet. So…did the Masked Maniac return their money jar too?"

"I've already said more than I should."

Luke arched his eyebrows. "Sounds like a yes to me."

"Well, I need to get back to work. I wanted to be the one to return Jewel's Tiffany lamp."

Jewel slipped her arms around him. "Thank you, Flint. With all the awful things that have been happening, I consider this a real blessing."

On Friday night Ivy left the mall in Mt. Byron loaded down with shopping bags of Christmas presents. She put the packages in back of her Jeep, then got in the front seat, picked up her cell phone, and dialed home.

"Hello."

"Hi, sweetie, it's Mom. How are things going?"

"Rue and me are having fun!" Montana said. "I got to paint with the roller. Then we ate spasketti at the dining hall with Kelsey and Brandon, and then we went snowmobiling. We couldn't see the stars because it's cloudy, so now I'm beating him at Chinese checkers."

Ivy started the car. "Well, I'm leaving the Mt. Byron Mall and should be home in about thirty minutes. Tell Rue, okay?"

"I will. Did you buy me a puppy for Christmas?"

"Listen, mister. We haven't decided on that yet."

"Well, maybe I'll tell Santa Claus that's what I want."

"I thought you and Ian didn't believe in Santa anymore."

Montana giggled. "Rue's tickling me, Mom. I've gotta go."

"All right. See you soon."

Ivy disconnected the call and dropped her cell phone on the passenger seat. She had muddled through the week by staying busy at work during the day and Christmas shopping in the evenings while Montana spent time with Rue. And except for Tuesday night, when Rue went to his AA meeting, Montana had seemed happier than she'd ever seen him.

More and more she found herself resenting Montana's relationship with Rue and hating herself for feeling that way. Why hadn't she just broken off all ties with Rue? Montana was getting increasingly attached, and she was just prolonging the inevitable. And she was growing weary of feeling like the "odd man out."

Ivy blinked the stinging from her eyes. *Lord, I was so sure You had opened the door to something good with Rue. What went wrong?*

The old feelings of guilt and condemnation settled on her heart, and it took all the energy she had just to breathe in and let it out. She should have known better than to trust her own judgment when it came to men. How was she ever going to sever ties with Rue and not wound her son?

Flint sat at the table in his office, studying the case files. His cell phone rang, and he groped for the receiver.

"Sheriff Carter."

"Is your stomach growling?" Betty said.

Flint glanced at his watch. "Sorry, hon. I told you two hours ago I was on my way home and then got engrossed in something. I totally lost track of time."

"I figured. Don't worry about it. I made corned beef and cabbage, and you can have yours when you get home."

"Boy, does that sound good. I've done all I can do here and might as well leave. I'm not too thrilled about spending another weekend down here, though."

"No breaks in the case, eh?"

Flint sighed. "No. But we're sure eliminating suspects right and left. We know McRae is six feet tall, so we're asking for DNA swabs on guys between five-eleven and six-one. But there are hundreds of county employees coming and going every day in different shifts. It's a huge task to get to everyone."

"Have any men objected to giving a DNA swab?"

"Oh yeah. A few felt their rights were being violated. Said if we want their DNA, we'd have to get a warrant…blah blah blah."

"Maybe McRae knows what you're doing and has left town."

"That's what I said, but Nick doesn't think so. He's desperate to find him before he strikes again. In fact, Nick thinks he's planning to end his spree with something big and then try to elude us. It's a control game. I've racked my brain to figure out what kind of disguise a pro like him would use, but how would I know? We're looking hard at visitors and county employees and not just in Jacob's Ear, but the entire area. Nobody's standing out."


Ivy pulled into her driveway, grateful that Rue had parked his Explorer on the street so she wouldn't have to come out and move her car when he left.

It was hard to believe that it had been just one week since Rue had taken her and Montana out stargazing and she had actually believed he was the kind of man she could get serious about. Now she just wanted him to stay away from her and prayed that Montana's fascination with him would fizzle out soon.

She walked up to the front door and paused, then went inside.

Montana came running to her and wrapped his arms around her waist. "Hi, Mom. Where are the Christmas presents?"

"What Christmas presents?"

A slow grin spread across his face, and he cocked his head. "Did you pick out my puppy?"

"*You* are entirely too nosy." She tousled his hair, aware of Rue standing there. "I guess you guys had fun?"

"Yeah, we did," Rue said. "You need help with anything before I go?"

"No, thanks."

Montana went over and clung to his hand. "I don't want you to leave."

"We've had some great time together this week, right?"

Montana bobbed his head. "But we didn't get to look at the stars."

"We'll do it again soon when it's not cloudy."

"Mom can go too. Like last time." Montana turned, his eyes seeming to search hers as if he knew something was wrong. "We can have a campfire and make s'mores again."

"Oh, sweetie. Mommy has a lot of things to do to get ready for Christmas."

"Listen, champ." Rue put his hands on Montana's shoulders. "I'm gonna drive back to Denver in the morning so I can get my telescope. I probably won't be back until Sunday night."

"Oh, man. I wanted us to do something fun when I don't have school."

"You're gonna love looking through the telescope," Rue said. "Why don't you help your mom this weekend? Santa's making his list and checking it twice. You gonna be naughty or nice?"

"My mom is Santa Claus."

"Well, if that's what you believe, then you better be extra nice to her, don't you think?" Rue winked.

He put on his jacket and said his good-byes to Montana. Ivy closed the door behind him, thinking this must be how awkward it was for divorced couples. How in the world had a relationship with a man she had never even loved come to this?

Jewel sat in the living room with Luke, enjoying a cup of tea. "You should be out with some nice young lady instead of baby-sitting me."

Luke smiled. "Who'd you have in mind—Rita?"

"Well, she's certainly a lovely girl."

"Ah, but she has to get up at five to open the café at six. It's not like we can do a whole lot in the evenings."

Jewel set her cup and saucer on the coffee table. "Do you ever think about settling down, Luke?"

"Sometimes."

"Forty will be here before you know it."

"You sound like my mother."

Jewel laughed. "More like your grandmother."

"I never had a grandmother. But I always thought it would be neat to be spoiled."

"Instead, you're the one spoiling everyone. You're a fine young man and a good friend, Luke. I can't tell you how much I appreciate all you've done for me."

"Can I get you some more tea and cookies?" he said.

"Goodness, I'm not used to being pampered."

"Well, enjoy it while you can. I'll be right back."

Jewel watched him walk into the kitchen and felt a pang of regret that she and Mel had never been able to have children.

She looked over at the Tiffany lamp that once again adorned the small table. It was almost too good to be true that it had been returned to her. She didn't want it to remind her of the horrible beating she took and was determined not to allow fear to spoil the attachment she had to it.

At least for now she could rest easy, knowing Luke was in the house. She had grown fond of him and wasn't looking forward to the day when he would go back to Denver.

"Here you go." Luke set a cup of tea on the coffee table and, next to it, a napkin with two gingersnaps. He sat in the chair across from her and popped the last bite of a gingersnap into his mouth. "These are incredible."

Jewel smiled and took a sip of tea. "It's my great aunt's recipe. It's been in the family for years."

Luke glanced at his watch. "How about us watching *It's a Wonderful Life*? It's on in five minutes."

"Oh my, yes. It's my very favorite Christmas movie."

"Mine too." He picked up the remote and turned on the TV. "As soon as you finish your tea, why don't you curl up there on the couch and I'll get your afghan?"

"You're so good to me." Jewel sipped her tea until it was gone and then lay on the couch and put a throw pillow behind her head. "It does feel chilly in here to me."

Luke got up and spread the afghan over her. "How many times have you seen this movie?"

"Oh, I don't know, dozens I suppose."

He sat in the chair and turned up the sound. "It's the kind of movie you never get tired of."

Jewel watched the first couple minutes of the movie and glanced over at Luke every so often, thinking how nice it was to share his company. All at once, she heard a buzzing sound in her head, and it seemed as if one side of the floor had been raised at an angle, and she was slowly sliding off. Her lips felt thick and rubbery and her mouth as dry as cotton. "I don't know...what's wrong with...me... I don't...feel at all...well..."

Luke got up and stood next to the couch and said nothing. She looked up at him and tried to focus, but he had two faces that kept joining together and then separating. She had a terrible feeling he had put something in her tea but couldn't imagine why he would do such a thing.

As he stood over her, she had a flashback of her attacker. His stance. His demeanor. His eyes. *Oh, Luke...*

"Sorry to leave this way. But if I let myself get any more attached to you, it's going to get me caught. Good-bye, Jewel."

Ivy put the worn copy of *Green Eggs and Ham* on the nightstand and tucked the covers around Montana.

"Good night, sweetie. Maybe tomorrow we can stop by and see Grandma and Grandpa and then go shopping so you can pick out the Christmas presents you want to give them."

"Okay." Montana's big brown eyes seemed full of questions. "How come you don't want to be with Rue anymore?"

"I've been busy. You can have fun with Rue without me."

"But I like it when you're with us."

Ivy brushed the hair off his forehead. "Why?"

Montana rolled his eyes, the corners of his mouth twitching. "You know."

"No, I don't. Tell me."

"Because then I can pretend I have a mom *and* a dad."

Montana's words pierced her, and she fought hard not to show any reaction. "Sweetie, I know it's hard not knowing your father. But Rue is only going to be here until spring. He can be a very good friend, and you can have lots of fun together. But he's going to have to leave. You know that."

Montana cupped her face in his hands. "If he married you, he wouldn't ever have to leave. He could live here with us."

"Rue and I are not getting married."

"Why not?"

Ivy sighed. Was it foolish to try to reason with a seven-year-old about something this serious? "God wants marriage to last forever. And I don't love Rue with a forever love. Can you understand that?"

"Does he love you with a forever love?"

*Hardly.* "No, he doesn't."

"Then why did he kiss you?"

"Montana, you're asking questions that are difficult for a little boy to understand."

"I'm seven, Mom. I'm not so little anymore."

Ivy combed his hair with her hand. "Okay. Rue and I started out thinking maybe we could fall in love the way people who want to get married fall in love. That's why he kissed me. But we don't have those kinds of feelings for each other, and we never will."

Montana's face fell. "So you're not getting married?"

"No. I'm sorry if you thought we were. But I never said that."

"It's not fair."

"What isn't fair?"

Montana shrugged, his arms folded tightly across his chest.

Ivy bent down and kissed his cheek. "It's not fair that you don't have a dad. I wish things were different. But you do have me, and I love you very, very much. And think of all the others who care so much about you: Jesus most of all. And Gramma Lu in heaven. And Grandma and Grandpa. Brandon and Kelsey. Your friend Ian…"

"And Rue."

"Yes, Rue. For now. But friends come and go, and very few last forever. Your family is forever."

Montana seemed to be processing her words, then sat up and put his arms around her. "I'm glad you're forever, Mom."

"Me too."

Ivy tucked the covers around him and got up. She started to turn off the lamp and noticed his jeans on the floor. She picked them up and saw what appeared to be blood smeared in several places."

"Did you cut yourself?"

"No."

"Where'd the blood come from?"

"What blood?"

Ivy held up the jeans. "This blood."

Montana shrugged, the all-too-angelic look on his face telling her he was hiding something.

"Sweetie, I'm not going to be mad. What happened?"

He looked away and didn't answer.

"Why are you acting so strange about this?" She tilted his chin and looked into his eyes. "Tell me what happened."

"I can't."

"Why not?"

"Because then it won't be our secret."

"Whose secret?"

"Me and Rue."

Ivy's pulse quickened. "I don't want you keeping secrets from me."

"I have to or it won't be special anymore."

Ivy put her hands on his shoulders and gently squeezed. "I need you to tell me! *Right now!*"

Montana's eyes brimmed with tears. "I just don't want to. Please don't make me."

# 32

IVY WENT INTO HER bedroom, closed the door, sat on the side of the bed, then picked up the phone and dialed Rue's cell phone. The phone rang three times, and she decided if the voice mail clicked on, she would hang up and keep calling all night until he finally answered.

"Hello?"

"I want to know what secret you and Montana are keeping from me!"

"What are you talking about?" Rue said.

"There's blood on his jeans, and he won't tell me how it got there because if he does, it won't be your *secret* anymore!"

"Calm down, Ivy. I can explain. We did this harmless blood brother ritual that was supposed to make him feel special. But I never told him not to tell you."

"From the looks of his clothes, this was a lot more than a finger prick."

"We stuck a pin in the top of our hands. Montana had already done the finger prick with his friend Ian, and I wanted to do something different—as a symbol that I promise not to forget him when I go back to Denver. He bled a little more than I thought he would. I applied pressure to the spot and then had him put his glove back on. It was no big deal."

"Then why didn't he want me to know?"

"I'm not sure. Maybe it feels more special to him if it's just between the two of us. But I never told him not to tell anyone. I swear."

"Well, I resent not knowing what's going on with my own son!" Ivy raked her hand through her hair. "And how do I even know your blood is *safe*? You had no right to do this without telling me. I want you to stay away from Montana."

"Come on, Ivy. Don't overreact."

"Stay away from him, Rue. I mean it!"

Ivy hung up the phone and realized she was shaking.

The doorknob turned, and then the door slowly opened. "Why did you yell at Rue?" Montana said. "He's my bestest friend, Mom."

"Rue told me how the blood got on your jeans. Now I want you to tell me in your own words." She patted the bed. "Come up here."

Montana climbed into her bed. "When we were out in the snowmobile, Rue said he wanted me to always remember he thinks I'm special, even when he doesn't live here anymore. He poked the top of his hand with a pin and poked the top of mine with a pin, and we rubbed our hands together. Now we'll always be blood brothers. Montana held up his left hand and showed her a tiny mark on the top. "See?"

Ivy examined the mark. "How did the blood get on your clothes?"

"I just bleeded a lot, and we didn't have a Band-Aid. Rue pushed on it, and it stopped. It doesn't even hurt. I'm telling the truth. Why do you look mad?"

Ivy pulled Montana into her arms and held him. "I just want to protect you. There's absolutely nothing you can't tell me, you hear? You can always come to Mommy if something scares you. Or confuses you."

"But I'm not scared of Rue. Are you scared of Rue?"

*I don't know,* she thought. *Maybe I should be.*


Flint sat at the kitchen table with Betty enjoying a cup of hot chocolate and trying to wind down after the intensive investigation of the past week.

"About the only rewarding thing that's happened was being able to return the Tiffany lamp to Jewel. You should have seen her eyes. You'd have thought I brought back her wedding ring or something."

"How's she doing, Flint?"

"Okay, I think. I doubt the fear is going away any time soon, but at least Luke Draper is staying with her at night."

Betty took a sip of hot chocolate. "Why do you suppose a guy his age would enjoy spending his vacation getting involved with the people in this town, especially ones much older than he?"

"It's a total change of pace. The guy's the CEO of a big computer firm. Maybe he's enjoying just being laid back for a change. I know Deke and Roscoe and Jewel have appreciated his looking after them."

"He seems almost too good to be true."

"Well, the world needs a few heroes these days. Sure aren't many around."

Flint's cell phone vibrated and startled Betty, who spilled her hot chocolate down the front of her bathrobe. "Sorry, hon. I've got to take this…Sheriff Carter."

"It's Nick. A 911 call just came in from our perp. He said we'll find two dead bodies at 430 Post Office Road. And to tell Sheriff Carter good-bye, that it's been fun."

Flint clenched his jaw. "I hate this guy."

"That's two of us. I'll meet you over there."

"All right, Nick."

Flint disconnected the call and quickly relayed to Betty everything Nick had said.

"Oh, Flint. After all he's put us through, now he's going to get away?"

"Not if I can help it." Flint kissed her cheek. "Don't wait up."


Flint pulled up in front of 430 Post Office Road and felt sick inside. He recognized the house as Rita Benson's, the gal who worked at Jewel's Café.

Flint got out of his squad car, and Bobby Knolls ran up to him. "They're both alive! The perp didn't lay a hand on them."

"What?"

"Come inside. You need to hear this from them."

Flint followed Bobby inside and saw Nick Sanchez standing next to a couch where Rita Benson sat with a gray-haired woman. Both ladies were visibly shaken.

"Rita, thank God you're okay." Flint looked at Nick and then at Rita. "What happened?"

"Mother and I were watching TV when a man in a ski mask just appeared out of nowhere." She let out a sob and then seemed to inhale it. "I thought he was going to kill us."

"What did he do?"

"He just stood there. His face was covered, but it felt like he was smiling. He tied us up and taped our mouths. And then went out in the kitchen and used the phone."

"What time was that?"

"Ten thirty. I looked up at the mantel clock."

"Could you hear what he was saying?"

Rita nodded. "He called 911 and said there were two dead bodies at 430 Post Office Road. And to tell Sheriff Carter good-bye, that it's been fun." Rita's eyes brimmed with tears. "And then he left and didn't hurt us."

"Can you describe his voice?"

"His voice reminded me of Luke Draper's," said the gray-haired lady.

Rita shook her head. "Mother, he may have sounded a little like Luke, but it wasn't him. Luke's one of the nicest guys I've ever met."

Nick glanced over at Flint. "I've already sent agents over to Jewel Sadler's to see if Draper's there."

Flint sat on his haunches next to the couch and extended his hand to the elderly lady sitting next to Rita. "I'm Sheriff Carter, ma'am."

"I'm Dorothy Benson, Rita's mother. I'm sorry if I got Luke into trouble, but I'm quite sure it was his voice."

Nick's cell phone rang, and he put it to his ear. "Sanchez. Yeah…I figured… She okay…? All right, thanks." Nick put his phone back on his belt clip. "Jewel Sadler's been drugged. She'll be okay. There's no sign of Draper."

"Man, I never saw it coming." Flint shook his head from side to side. "He gave me his business card. My deputies contacted his company and confirmed he's on vacation. I never once suspected him."

"Don't kick yourself too hard," Nick said. "McRae's a pro. He probably killed the real Luke Draper and used his identity to lie low for a while. Guess he got bored being Mr. Nice Guy and decided to entertain himself. Looks like he's gone now."

"But why would McRae go to all this trouble to create a grand finale and not even get in the last lick?" Flint said. "Just doesn't fit."

Nick got that intense look he got whenever he was processing, and then his eyes grew wide. "You're right. He didn't! He baited you to come over here because he's gone to *your* house!"

Flint climbed in the passenger seat of Nick's car and hit the auto dial for home. *Come on, hon. Answer the phone!*

"What took you so long, Sheriff?" said a familiar male voice. "I've been waiting here with your lovely wife and little boy, hoping you'd call."

"McRae, be reasonable," Flint said. "You have nothing to gain by hurting my family."

"Oh, but I do. I like to win."

"This is not a game."

"Of course it is. And it's your move."

"Come on, McRae. What do you really want? You didn't pull off a six-million-dollar jewel heist only to get caught doing this."

"I'm too smart to get caught. Haven't you figured that out yet? I think you should talk to Betty. She looks distressed…"

"Flint, help us." Betty's voice was a frightened whisper. "He's going to kill us…"

"I'd put Ian on the phone," McRae said, "but the poor little guy's crying."

"Tell me what you want."

"I want one hour in your house with your family, without you or the feds making a move. One hour."

"No way."

"It would take only seconds to slit their throats. And that would be such a waste. Sit tight for one hour, and I promise not to hurt them."

"You expect me to believe that?"

"Guess you're going to have to trust me, Flint. I like you. And I really have no reason to hurt Betty or Ian. I just want to experience the thrill of holding the power of life and death in my grasp, while you and the feds sit by and wait helplessly for an hour. That's the deal."

"And what happens when the hour's over—you take them hostage?"

"You can come in and get them. I don't need hostages. I know how to disappear into thin air, remember? Oh, and one more thing, don't call again or try to communicate in any way for the entire hour. Violate the agreement or cut it short by even one second, and they're dead. The hour starts right...now." *Click.*

Flint paced next to his squad car and pounded his fist into the palm of his other hand. "You have no idea how badly I want to take him out."

"Of course I do," Nick said. "But it's his game, and he's in the driver's seat."

"What if he's bluffing? What if he's planning to kill them anyway?"

"What options do we have?" Nick said. "McRae knows exactly how SWAT teams work. He's not going to give us a clear shot, and there's no way to outsmart him. If we could somehow manage to get inside, he'd hear us and slit their throats before we could make a move. We can't risk it. It's a control game, and winning is all he cares about." Nick pulled his collar up around his ears. "But he can't get away. We've got the house surrounded and every road in or out of town barricaded."

"He's a jewel thief, Nick. Getting away is what he does."

"Not on my watch."

"You think if we corner him, he'll kill himself?"

Nick smirked. "You kidding? The guy's too in love with himself. But he's also too smart to get backed into a corner. He's got something up his sleeve."

Flint wiped the sweat off his lip. "Why me? Why my family?"

"He's been playing you from the start. Pretending to be friends with his first three victims. Showing up at the hospital day after day. Staying at Jewel Sadler's so she wouldn't be scared. It's all fun and games to him."

"I suppose Luke, I mean McRae, realized the game was over when I asked him to give a DNA sample."

"Yeah," Nick said. "But he wasn't about to leave until he played his final hand. I know it's torture waiting out the hour, but I think it's our only shot."

"He's liable to kill them anyway! He could be hurting them right now!"

"Let's stick with what we know for sure. He's promised to kill them if we make a move. And I believe he means it."

"We're the top guns, Nick. We should be able to do something more than kowtow to his demands and sit on our thumbs while he puts Betty and Ian through an ordeal that, even if they survive, they'll never get over! I feel so helpless. I hate this!"

"I know you do." Nick put his hand on Flint's shoulder. "But I can honestly say that if it were my family in there, I'd do the same thing. I might puke my guts out while I waited, but I'd do what he said. With a guy this slick, there's really no way to save your family unless we do what he wants. We've got thirty-two minutes left."

Flint looked up at the house. It appeared as if every light in the place were lit. Where in the house was McRae holding them? What was he doing to them? Suddenly, he felt more desolate than he ever had in his life.

*God, I'm sorry I've been too busy lately to pray. Please don't let McRae hurt my family.*

Flint heard a familiar whistle and turned around. He saw Elam Griffith standing behind a barricade, waving his arms.

"Nick, that guy's a friend of mine. Would you tell your guys to let him through?"

"Sure." Nick went over and said something to one of his agents.

A few seconds later, Elam jogged over to where Flint was standing. "Carolyn and I heard a news bulletin on TV that something was going on. The details were sketchy, but I came right over. I figured you could use a friend, and that it's about time I started acting like one."

Flint blinked the stinging from his eyes. "I'm glad you came. It's serious." He told Elam about Luke Draper's real identity and about the "deal" he had made, and how scared Betty sounded on the phone.

Elam tugged at his mustache and looked up at the house. "How much longer?"

"Twenty-seven minutes."

"Well, I'm sure Carolyn's already got the prayer team on their knees."


Ivy heard an obnoxious ringing noise and realized it was the telephone. She groped the nightstand and picked up the receiver. "Hello."

"Ivy, it's Rue. I'm sorry if I woke you up, but it's important to me that we get this settled. Did you talk to Montana?"

"Yes. He gave me the same story you did. But I'm not changing my mind about you not seeing him anymore. There can be only one end to this: Montana's going to get hurt when you go back to Denver. And the more time he spends with you, the more attached he's going to get. It's better to end it now."

"Can I tell you why I don't think that's a good idea *before* you hang up on me? Because you know I genuinely care about Montana, and that I'm good with him. You know I can boost his self-esteem and teach him guy things you can't. And even if it's just for a few months, my presence in his life could have a very positive effect on him."

"But a negative effect on me. I hate being the odd man out, and it's awkward with you and me being at odds."

"I'm not at odds with you."

"Well, I'm at odds with you."

"Because I asked for a little time to put on the brakes and work through some stuff?"

"No. Because you won't talk to me about what your *stuff* is, and I detest secrets."

"So not wanting me to spend time with Montana is really about your resentment toward me, not about what's best for him?"

"That's not what I said." *But that's certainly part of it.*

There was a long stretch of dead air, and Ivy thought they had been disconnected.

"Rue, are you there?"

"Yeah, I'm here. Give me till next Friday."

"For what?"

"To talk to you about what I'm trying to work through. If you still don't want me around after that, I'll leave you alone."

# 33

FLINT GLANCED AT HIS watch and then at his house, and tried not to let his imagination take him to what might be happening behind those walls. He felt a hand on his shoulder.

"How're you doing?" Elam said.

"Lousy." Flint swallowed hard, wishing he had something for heartburn. "In another thirteen minutes, I may find out I've lost everything. I've never in my life wanted to kill someone before now, and I hate it that McRae has the power to bring out that kind of raw instinct in me."

"You just want to protect your family," Elam said.

Flint blinked rapidly to clear the moisture from his eyes, thinking he didn't dare get weak. "What if he kills them while I'm standing out here like a dupe? How am I going to live with that?"

"He didn't hurt Rita and her mom," Elam said. "There's a good chance he'll do exactly what he said if you do exactly what he wants."

Flint blew on his hands and rubbed them together, aware that it had begun snowing. "I've always been the one in charge, Elam. I've never been a victim before. I've seen how people suffer when their loved ones, especially their kids, are hurt or threatened. I knew it was tough. But I had no idea it hurt this much."

"It's the most helpless feeling in the world."

Flint lifted his eyes and caught Elam's gaze. "I can't imagine how much you suffered with Ivy throughout her ordeal."

"Probably took ten years off my life."

"I'm sorry I was so insensitive. As sheriff, I honestly believed I was doing the right thing when I allowed Ivy to be interrogated when she didn't ask for legal counsel. But as a friend, I should've been more sensitive to what you were going through. Instead, I dug in my heels and blew it off. I decided it was your problem and you just needed to get over it." Flint heaved a heavy sigh. "I avoided you when Ivy was in jail because I didn't want to admit I'd hurt you. I'm sorry. If I could, I'd go back and do some things differently."

"Yeah, I know you would." Elam put his hands in his pockets and looked down at the ground. "Doesn't seem like much compared to what you're dealing with at the moment."

"But it was big at the time. And I should've dealt with it then instead of letting it come between our friendship."

"I was wrong to hold a grudge," Elam said. "I'm ready to put this behind us. Can we do that?"

Flint nodded. "Done."

Nick Sanchez came over and stood next to Flint. "Ten minutes left. How're you holding up?"

"Don't ask."

"We're doing the right thing."

Flint turned his gaze back on the house. *Only if they make it out alive.*


Ivy got up off her knees and crawled back into bed after pleading with God to spare Betty and Ian Carter and to comfort the sheriff. She had been wide awake since her mother called to tell her of the horrific situation at the Carters'. She couldn't imagine how she would feel if Montana's life were threatened or how she was going to break the news to him if Ian was murdered.

She reached over and picked up the receiver on the phone and dialed her parents' number.

"Hello, Elam?"

"It's just me, Mom. I take it Dad hasn't called back?"

"Not yet. There're only six minutes left."

"And then what?" Ivy said.

"This McRae character told Flint to come in and get Betty and Ian after an hour. He promised not to hurt them."

"The guy's a cold-blooded killer. Does Sheriff Carter really believe he won't?"

"Your dad said the FBI special agent in charge was adamant that they had no other option but to comply. McRae threatened to slit their throats if anybody made the slightest move."

Ivy felt a cold chill crawl up her spine. "If only we'd invited Ian to spend the night over here, he wouldn't be subjected to this horror show." Ivy wiped the tears that ran down the sides of her face. "Have you heard how Jewel's doing?"

"Only that whatever drug McRae gave her wasn't life threatening. Listen, honey, I'm going to get off the phone and keep praying. I'll call you when I know something."

"Did you call Brandon and Kelsey?"

"Of course I did—and the prayer team at church."

"I'll let you go. When you know something, call me on my cell phone. I'm going to climb into bed with Montana. I want him close to me right now."

Ivy hung up the phone and put her cell phone in the pocket of her pajamas. She climbed up the ladder to the loft and tiptoed over to Montana's bed and lay beside him, her cheek next to his. She thought back to Thanksgiving weekend when Luke Draper or Johnson McRae or whatever his name was carried her packages into the house. It could have been her and Montana that he chose to victimize.

She snuggled closer to her son and listened to the peaceful sound of his breathing. *Thank you, Lord, that nothing ever came of that relationship. Please protect Betty and Ian. Don't let him hurt them.*

Flint glanced at his watch, his stomach feeling like a ball of fire, his pulse racing so fast that his temples throbbed. "Four minutes to go."

"Here's what I think we need to do," Nick said. "Let's give it *five* minutes, just to be safe. Then I'll send in the SWAT team. Elam and I will wait here with you."

"No, I'm going in," Flint said.

Nick shook his head. "Not a good idea."

"There's no way I'm staying out here."

"Flint, we don't know what McRae's going to do, but he isn't going to surrender. Wait with us. Just until we know if Betty and Ian are all right."

"Or if they're dead." Flint turned to Nick. "I'm going in. No matter what's happened, I have to face it."

"Not like that, you don't," Elam said. "Listen to Special Agent Sanchez."

"If your family was in there, would either of you wait around with your hands in your pockets?"

Nick dropped his cigarette on the ground and snuffed it out. "All right. But we're going in *behind* the SWAT team."

"Fair enough."

Nick picked up his walkie-talkie and put it to his ear. "Eagle Scout, this is Sanchez. Prepare to move when I tell you. I'm going to wait an extra minute to be on the safe side. Sheriff Carter and I will go in right behind you. Do you read me? Over... Yeah, copy that. Out." Nick glanced at his watch and then looked searchingly into Flint's eyes. "You sure you want to go in?"

"Yeah, I'm sure."

Elam put his hand on Flint's shoulder and squeezed. "I've been praying like nuts."

"Thanks. If this thing goes south, I'm not sure I can handle it. I'm going to need all the prayers I can get. I really appreciate your coming..." Flint's voice cracked. "It means a lot."

"Here," Nick said. "Put on your vest. All I need now is to lose a good man."

Flint put the bulletproof vest on over his jacket and thought for a moment about how dramatically his life might change in the next few minutes. He glanced down the street at all the Christmas lights and wondered if there would ever be peace on earth.

"Two minutes," Nick said. "Come on, let's go get positioned."

Flint looked over at Elam, and in the next instant, he was drawn into a bear hug.

"You're not alone," Elam said. "God's with you. And people are praying. Don't lose hope."

Flint nodded and swallowed hard.

"Come on," Nick said.

Flint felt almost as if someone else were occupying his body. He felt apprehensive and at the same time detached. He followed Nick Sanchez over to where the SWAT team stood.

"McRae isn't about to surrender," Nick said to the team. "I have no idea what he's got staged. But if he so much as blinks, take him out."

The seconds ticked away, and Flint realized perspiration was running down his temples, and the fire in his gut burned hotter than ever.

Finally, Nick gave the signal, and the SWAT team advanced stealthily toward the house like a pride of lions sneaking up on a wildebeest. Within a matter of seconds, they were inside.

"McRae," Nick shouted, "this is Special Agent Nick Sanchez of the FBI! We did exactly what you asked. The hour is up. We're here to get Betty and Ian."

The silence in the house screamed with possibilities Flint didn't want to think about.

"McRae, do you hear me?" Nick motioned for the SWAT team to proceed.

"Clear," he heard someone say.

Nick held out his arm and stopped Flint from taking another step. "Let's wait."

"Clear," someone called from the kitchen.

"Clear," called a voice from the family room.

Flint had a bad feeling about this. What if Nick had been wrong about McRae? What if his final hand had been killing Betty and Ian and leaving Flint holding the joker?

"Clear," called a voice from the dining room.

Flint glanced over at Nick and saw the lines on his forehead deepen. He had to be thinking the same thing. Suddenly short of breath, Flint wondered if he had enough strength left to cope if his worst fear had happened.

"Clear," called a muffled voice from the direction of Ian's room.

Flint felt as if his heart were falling down an elevator shaft. There was no way McRae could have escaped with Betty and Ian without being seen. They had to be dead.

"Master bedroom!" someone shouted. "Both subjects alive!"

Flint charged down the hall to the master bedroom where he saw Betty and Ian sitting in the closet being untied by a member of the SWAT team.

"Mrs. Carter, where's McRae?" Nick asked.

"I don't know," Betty said. "He left right after he talked to Flint."

"An hour ago?"

"Yes."

In the next instant Flint was embracing his wife and son, barely able to contain his emotion. When he finally pulled himself together, he noticed Nick pacing in front of the dresser, his face red and his fists clenched, swearing under his breath.

Finally, Nick took off his hat and threw it on the floor. "We've been had. McRae knew that we had no choice but to do what he said. And he used it to give himself an hour's head start."

Flint bent down and lifted Ian with one arm and then pulled Betty close with the other. At that moment, he couldn't have cared less that Johnson McRae had escaped, or that he'd tricked them. Flint was filled with gratitude that the two people he loved most in the world had been left unharmed. And somehow everything else seemed small compared to that.

# 34

THE NEXT MORNING, Flint enjoyed time with his family and waited until ten o'clock to go to work. When he arrived at his office, Nick Sanchez was sitting at the table flipping through case files.

"So how're you doing?" Nick asked.

"Okay. I'm not sure it's even hit me yet."

"Well, you dodged a big one. I guarantee you McRae would've slit your wife's and son's throats without batting an eye if it'd served his purpose. Want some good news?"

"Sure, let's hear it."

"We've got Huck Maxfield's impostor—some guy named Bernie Acres. A Durango patrolman spotted a hitchhiker who fit the description on the APB and brought him in. They contacted the bureau, and our guys worked on him and got him to admit to killing Maxfield."

"Did he say why?"

"Yeah, said he'd been down and out for a long time and saw this as his chance to stay warm through the winter and get three squares a day. Apparently, he met Maxfield at an all-night diner over in Mt. Byron, and they got to talking. Maxfield told him he had inherited his grandfathers' place and had recently moved to the area. Must've blabbed enough for Acres to see him as an easy mark. Found out everything he could about

Maxfield and what it would take to step into his shoes. Then he came back a couple weeks later and killed him. Should be a slam dunk for the DA. Acres is being transported back here this afternoon."

"Did he have a record?"

"No. But I have a feeling this isn't the first time he's pulled a stunt like this. He's just never been caught before."

"So he turned Maxfield's house into a dump."

"And any way you cut it, it was a great ruse to cover up the fact that he wasn't Huck Maxfield. He looked just enough like him to pull it off."

"This is starting to make sense," Flint said. "When Bobby and I questioned him, he was cooperative until we asked what he did for a living. He said he was between jobs but refused to tell us about any previous job. Maybe he didn't know about Maxfield's teaching career. Or not enough to talk about it without hanging himself."

"Could be. At any rate, case solved."

Flint pulled out a chair and sat across from Nick, his arms folded on the table. "That was a brave judgment call you made last night."

"Sorry we got outsmarted, but I wasn't willing to take a chance with your wife and son."

"I appreciate that, Nick. *And* you talking me through it. It was the longest hour I ever remember."

"I'm just glad you drew the long straw this time."

Flint nodded. "So when are you headed back?"

"I thought I'd hang around here a couple days and make sure we leave everything in order. See if anything else surfaces. I don't know whether or not we'll ever get McRae. He's probably changed his looks, got a new ID, and a new car. He could've left the country, for all we know."

"What makes a person so evil?" Flint said. "Do you ever think about that?"

"All the time. Don't have an answer. But nothing people do surprises me anymore. I don't know if that's good or bad."

"How do you keep from getting cynical?"

Nick clasped his hands behind his head, a smile tugging at the corners of his mouth. "A shortstop named Daniel, and a ballerina named Destiny—my twelve-year-old twins. They keep me grounded. I can't solve the world's problems, but I know that if I raise my two to be responsible, caring people, they'll make a positive difference instead of adding to the craziness."

"Well, after last night, I just thank God that I still have my kid to raise."

Brandon sat in his SUV outside the chalet Luke Draper had occupied, his hands wrapped around a plastic coffee cup, and watched as the FBI investigative team took pictures and bagged evidence.

He glanced over at Kelsey. "It's like watching a movie. It would've been so easy for this McRae to victimize someone here. It could've been us."

"Believe me, I've thought about that." Kelsey looked down at her hands. "I feel so ashamed. I suspected Rue because he'd been in rehab and had been questioned by the sheriff. But I never once suspected Luke Draper—I mean Johnson McRae—simply because he drove a Corvette and was a sharp dresser and I thought he was the CEO of a computer firm."

"Yeah, same here. I'm glad I at least gave Rue the benefit of the doubt. I wonder how he and Ivy are doing?"

"Truthfully, I don't remember her mentioning him all week. She really didn't have a lot to say about anything."

Brandon set his cup in the holder. "I doubt Ivy's going to talk about her relationship with Rue to anyone. I can't really blame her. It's obvious no one's jazzed about it."

"Well, I think my advice that she learn to love herself before she gets into a serious relationship was sound, and it was certainly given in the right spirit. I could be wrong, but I see Ivy and Rue as two very wounded people who are bringing empty hearts to the relationship and expecting the other to fill it. That's a recipe for failure, and they'll end up hurting each other. But I *am* relieved Rue's no longer on anyone's suspect list."

"You still get the feeling he's hiding something?"

Kelsey shrugged. "I don't know. Maybe I was looking for something to criticize when I should've been trying to see what it is Ivy sees in him."

"Well, I'll tell you one thing, Montana idolizes him."


Ivy sat in an overstuffed chair at her parents' house admiring the Christmas tree that had swallowed up a quarter of the living room and trying to let go of the fear she still carried from the night before.

"I clung to Montana all night," Ivy said to her dad, "even after Mom called back and told me Ian and Betty were all right." She glanced outside and saw Montana riding his sled down the hill, Sasha barking playfully and running in circles. "I was afraid to leave him up in the loft by himself. I'll rest easier when McRae is in jail. No one's been able to keep him from breaking in. I can't believe he was actually in our house."

Elam shook his head. "Me, either. Gives me cold chills if I dwell on it. Special Agent Sanchez thinks he's long gone. Maybe even left the country already. There's no reason for him to ever come back here."

"He sure left a trail of victims," Carolyn said. "Thank heavens Betty and Ian weren't physically harmed."

"I'll bet they broke down when Flint found them," Ivy said.

Elam shook his head. "Actually, they were fine. McRae had tied them up and left, and they knew he wasn't coming back. Flint's the one that I practically had to scoop up off the sidewalk. I've never seen him so shaken. I'm really glad I went over there."

"So are you friends again?" Ivy asked.

Elam tugged at his mustache. "Sure. All I had to do was swallow my pride and stop acting like an imbecile. Should've done it months ago. I know better than to rub someone's nose in his past mistakes when he's sincerely asked my forgiveness. I don't know who I thought I was. Even God doesn't do that."

Carolyn covered her smile with her hand. "Hey, you said it, not me."

Elam tossed a couch pillow at her and chuckled, and then got quiet for a few moments. Finally, he looked over at Ivy. "Your mother and I have decided not to go to Albuquerque the week after Christmas. We simply aren't willing to accept the way Rusty's acted toward you and Montana. The note he sent you was unconscionable."

"But that doesn't have to ruin your relationship with him," Ivy said.

"Ruin is a strong word, honey. We love Rusty. That hasn't changed. But we're not going to allow his bitterness to spoil another holiday, especially the one with such spiritual significance. We don't want to go too long without seeing Tia and Josie, so maybe we'll drive down there in a few weeks. But not during the holidays."

"I'm really sorry you're in the middle of this." Ivy glanced outside and fluttered her eyelashes to clear the moisture. "Sometimes I wonder if it's even possible to be free from the awful things I've done. Even if I could completely forgive myself, which I haven't been able to do, my past is like this festering wound that can get opened up by a careless word or a disapproving look and make me feel dirty all over again. And sometimes I have the most awful feeling that God is punishing me, that He doesn't even want me to be happy. I know that's not true. But it feels that way."

"We've talked about this before," Carolyn said. "You need to stop replaying in your mind everything you did wrong and start focusing on the things you're doing right."

"Your mom has a good point, honey. It took time to get so far off track, and it's going to take time for the Lord to redirect your steps. You have to be patient."

Ivy started to say something and then didn't, and then decided she might as well be honest. "What if God doesn't think I'm worth redirecting? What if the things I did were so disgusting to Him that He's given up on me?"

"Then the God you're serving isn't the God of the Bible." Elam got up and stood in front of her and tilted her chin. "Ivy, look at me. Psalm 103 says God's removed our sins as far as the east is from the west. Forgiveness is a done deal. You don't have to keep confessing the same sins. God doesn't punish us for what we've confessed. If He were going to do that, what would be the point of sending Jesus to die? You know all this."

Ivy brushed a tear off her cheek. "You're right." *So why don't I feel any better?*

"Honey, what's brought all this back?" Carolyn said.

"I'm not sure I've ever been able to completely turn loose of it. And Rusty's rejection just rubs salt in the wound." *And so does Rue's.*

"Well, Montana's never seemed happier," Carolyn said. "You must be doing something right. So when am I going to get to meet this Rue Kessler I keep hearing about?"

"He's gone back to Denver for the weekend to pick up his telescope."

"Well, maybe one night next week we should have the three of you over for dinner, and I'll make my special lasagna. What do you think?"

"Uh, sure. I mean, we can talk about it. I don't know what his plans are." *Or if we'll even be speaking.*


Later that day, Ivy sat in Jewel's living room, relieved that the drug McRae had put in Jewel's tea had worn off without serious side effects.

"I'm so sorry this McRae turned out not to be the person you thought he was," Ivy said.

Jewel shook her head from side to side. "And to think I actually wanted the two of you to get together."

"And to think I actually felt slighted that he never took me up on my offer to take him snowmobiling. Rita's lucky he didn't kill her."

"Luke—sorry, but I just can't call him anything else—had a tender side." Jewel's eyes brimmed with tears. "I can hardly believe he's the savage that beat me. I'm not sure I'll ever be the same. Most nights I'm afraid to close my eyes." A tear trailed down Jewel's cheek, and she wiped it off. "What hurts most of all is the betrayal. I feel so foolish to have trusted him."

"But why wouldn't you? He seemed genuinely fond of you and Deke and Roscoe. I'll never understand what drove him to attack you."

"I just hope they find him before he hurts someone else," Jewel said. "Why don't we talk about something more pleasant? How's Montana doing?"

"Fine. He's spending the day at Mom and Dad's."

"So have you picked out his puppy yet?" Jewel covered her smile with her hand, but her eyes gave her away.

Ivy laughed. "Nooo. I keep hoping he'll change his mind, but Christmas is only ten days away. I guess I'm going to have to make a decision."

"So tell me about this young man you're dating."

"Rue and I aren't exactly dating anymore." Ivy took a sip of coffee. "I'm not even sure we're compatible."

"Oh? I got the impression last weekend that you were having a lot of fun together."

"We were. Kind of. But I don't think he's my type. I did at first, but now I have my doubts."

"I didn't mean to pry." Jewel pursed her lips. "Oh, who am I kidding? Of course I did. I can hardly wait for you to find someone to love."

"Well, don't hold your breath. I don't think I'm all that lovable."

"Listen, doll. You're plenty lovable. What's gotten into you? Last weekend you were all aglow, and now you seem to have a gray cloud hanging over you."

"I'm not sure I'll ever find the right guy," Ivy said. "I have baggage that few guys would be willing to accept."

"Any man who loves you would."

"Well, like I said, I'm not all that lovable."

The room throbbed with an awkward silence. Finally, Jewel said, "I don't know what's going on inside you. There's nothing to be gained by looking over your shoulder. I don't know anyone who hasn't made mistakes, Ivy."

*Not like the ones I've made.* "You're right. I just need to work on it." Ivy got up out of the love seat and went over and put her arms around

Jewel. "I have to get going. It's a relief to see you looking so well. Are you sure you're going to be okay by yourself?"

"Of course I'm not," Jewel said. "I may never be okay by myself after what's happened. But I'm sure not going to let it stop me from being independent."


Ivy pulled her Jeep into the scenic overlook on Tanner's Ridge and sat for a few minutes enjoying the silence and hoping the couple in the Chevy Tahoe would drive away and leave her to her own thoughts.

*Listen, doll. You're plenty lovable.*

Jewel's words echoed in her head, but her heart refused to accept it. Obviously, she wasn't lovable enough to offset the stain of her past. Rusty couldn't forgive her. And if Rue had run the other way because he couldn't handle the truth about her, what hope did she have that any man wouldn't do exactly the same thing?

So much had happened since last night's conversation with Rue that she'd hardly had time to think about it. But she was going to have to make the choice whether to allow Montana to keep seeing him. And she couldn't put it off for long.

The Tahoe finally pulled out of the overlook and continued up the mountain road, and Ivy got out and trudged up to the lookout point. She leaned on the railing and drank in the splendor of the majestic white peaks that surrounded Phantom Hollow like a circle of mighty angels. How she had missed the beauty of the San Juan Mountains all the years she was away in Denver. There had been clear days when she had a good view of the Front Range, but none as pristine and inspiring as this. She wondered if there was anywhere on earth where a person could feel closer to God than here. And how desperate she was to feel close to God.

Emotion clouded her eyes, and the jagged peaks became a ghostly blur.

*Lord, I need a touch from You, something to let me know You haven't given up on me. It's so miserable feeling this worthless.*

# 35

BY THE FOLLOWING Thursday, Ivy was merely going through the motions at work and had little hope that her relationship with Rue could be salvaged. Activity at the conference center had come to a halt, and she was eagerly awaiting the Christmas break and a chance to focus her thoughts on the joy of the season.

She didn't know whether to be grateful or disgusted that Rue hadn't called Montana. She couldn't imagine what it was he planned to talk to her about or why he had opted to wait until Friday to do it. Probably because it was the last workday until Christmas, and he could dump her and not have to see her again for the long weekend.

She was prepared for the possibility that Rue might not come talk to her at all. She hated that she was becoming so cynical and that she had felt compelled to make excuses for him each time her parents had suggested she bring him to dinner.

The door to the administrative offices opened, and Ivy came back to the moment and noticed Kelsey coming toward her.

"You think it could get any slower?" Kelsey said.

"I doubt it. Our only two guests just checked out, and no more are due to arrive until after New Year's. I've been putting guest comments into the computer, but I'm bored out of my mind."

Kelsey smiled. "I keep hoping Jake will tell us not to come in tomorrow."

"I wish. I've got something I need to pick up for Montana, and that would make it a whole lot easier."

Kelsey folded her arms on the counter. "You okay? You've been quiet lately, like you're really down."

"The holidays are harder than I thought they would be. I really miss Lu." *Though that has nothing to do with it.*

"Of course you do. I hadn't thought of that."

"She and Montana and I were a family for years. It just seems strange not having her around."

"Do you and Montana have plans for the long weekend?"

"Oh, sure. We'll spend most of it with my parents. Montana's Sunday-school class is doing a program at the candlelight service on Christmas Eve. And we want to go to movies, eat out, go ice skating, do some snow-mobiling, and then hit the after-Christmas sales. Should be a mini vacation. I'm looking forward to it." Ivy was all too aware that she had made no mention of Rue being included in her plans and hoped that Kelsey wouldn't inquire. "What about you and Brandon?"

"My sister and her husband are flying in Saturday to spend Christmas with us, and we're all going skiing the day after. Should be great fun. Well"—Kelsey backed away from the counter—"I'm sure I'll see you at church, but I just wanted to wish you a Merry Christmas. I know your mom and dad are ecstatic to have you here this year. I guess I'd better get back to my desk. Let's hope Jake decides to let us start the Christmas break tonight instead of waiting till noon tomorrow."

Brandon looked over his list of last year's camp counselors and started to eliminate those he knew wouldn't be available this year. He was aware of someone standing in the doorway and looked up, glad to see it was Rue.

"Thanks for coming," Brandon said. "Sit wherever you're comfortable."

Brandon got up and closed the door, then went over and leaned on his desk, his arms folded across his chest.

"I don't want to pry into your personal life, Rue, but something's changed in your performance this week. The work's slowed way down, and I sense that Don is doing more than his share. You want to tell me what's going on?"

Rue stared at his hands. "I've just got some personal stuff I'm trying to deal with."

"Can I help?"

"I don't see how."

"Are you in trouble?"

Rue shook his head. "Not with the law or anything, if that's what you mean."

"Whatever it is, it's affecting your job. I can't just ignore it. Might help to talk about it."

"There's nothing you can do to help."

"Are you drinking again?"

"No." Rue let out a desolate sigh. "But if I don't get this worked out, I'm afraid I might. It's eating me up."

"So talk to me. Anything personal you tell me stays between you and me."

Rue's eyes seemed to search Brandon's. "Anything?"

"As long as it has nothing to do with your work arrangement with us."

"It doesn't. Look, I really don't think I need to involve anyone else in this. I can work it out over Christmas break. I'll come back and give you a hundred and ten percent. I promise."

"Rue, we both know this is a tough season to stay sober, even if things are going well. Everybody needs a friend. Try me. I'm not here to pass judgment."

"You might change your mind if you knew what it was."

"I don't know, I'm pretty objective."

"What if it involves your boss's daughter?"

Brandon tried not to react. "You and Ivy having problems?"

"Nothing like the one we're about to have. And I'm not sure how to handle it."

"Well, maybe together we can figure something out."

Ivy stood at the registration desk, staring at nothing and bemoaning tomorrow's confrontation with Rue when her father walked in, Montana on his heels.

"Hi, Mom! I know what Grandma and Grandpa got you for Christmas!" Montana raced over to the counter and lifted himself by his forearms, his feet dangling. "But I'm not gonna tell you what it is."

"Good, because I like being surprised."

"How's your day going?" Elam asked.

"Dad, it is *so* dead around here that I can hardly wait to get sprung."

"Well, wait no more. Jake just shut it down. You are officially on Christmas break." His smile, half hidden under his mustache, shone in his eyes. "Your mother made her special lasagna and has invited the Carters over for dinner tonight. She'd like you and Montana to come. And Rue, if he can."

"Rue's got plans, but Montana and I would love to come."

Elam slipped his arm around her shoulder. "I can't tell you how wonderful it is having you home for Christmas again. I feel ten years younger. In fact, Flint and I are taking Montana and Ian ice-skating after dinner."

*"Ice-skating?"* Ivy laughed. "The last time I saw you on ice skates, I think I was about ten. What if you break something?"

"Well, then, I'll just have to brag about what a good time I had."

"I'm so glad you and Flint worked things out."

"Me too, honey. I'd almost forgotten how much I enjoy his company. So can you and Montana come over around six?"

"Sure. You need me to bring anything?"

"Just this little scamp." Elam grabbed Montana and started tickling his ribs.

The sound of Montana's laughter reminded her of the fun times with Rue, and she wondered if, by this time tomorrow, Rue would be just someone she used to know instead of someone she thought she could fall in love with.

# 36

ON FRIDAY MORNING, Ivy got an unexpected phone call from Kelsey and Brandon, asking if they could borrow Montana to help them pick out some age-appropriate gifts for two little boys on their Christmas list. Ivy was glad for the offer and decided to use the time to finish wrapping presents.

She had just gotten out the paper, ribbon, and bows and put them on the kitchen table when she heard a knock at the door. She looked out and saw Rue's Ford Explorer, and her pulse began to race.

*Lord, help me get through this. Please don't let him spoil my Christmas.*

Ivy went over to the front door and took a slow deep breath and let it out, then opened it. "I wasn't sure you'd show."

"I told you I would," Rue said. "Is it okay if we talk here?"

"I guess." Ivy let him squeeze past her and then shut the door. "You caught me just as I was about to start wrapping packages. I'd offer you something to drink, but I really don't have a lot of time." She went over to the rocker and sat, hands in her lap, anxious to get it over with.

Rue sat at the far end of the couch, cracking his knuckles.

"Okay," Ivy prodded. "I'm listening."

Rue stared at the Christmas tree, his face as somber as she'd ever seen it. Finally, he said, "Thanks for waiting a week. I know it's been a confusing time for you, and I'm really sorry. It's been confusing for me too. Please just listen till I'm finished, or I'll never get it out."

*If you're going to break it off, just do it,* Ivy thought. *Spare me the drama.*

"Remember I told you that for years I practically lived at Irving's bar after work? The guys I worked with hung out there. We played pool. Threw darts. Watched sports. Had a few laughs. I was drinking back then, but nothing like I was after my mom died. Anyhow, I was shy with women. I dated once in a while, but I didn't have any confidence and got razzed about it nonstop.

"One night a young gal came in the bar looking to earn some quick drug money. It's not like that'd never happened before, but the guys got their heads together and decided I should take her up on her offer. I was sloshed and not thinking too clearly, and the next thing I knew they stuffed bills into my pockets and said to go have a good time.

"The bartender winked and nodded toward the back room, and I went. I had never paid for sex before and haven't since, so I never forgot the incident, even though I don't remember the gal's face." Rue paused, his voice quavering. "But she had an ivy tattoo on her ankle, exactly like yours."

Ivy's gaze collided with Rue's, her mind screaming with the implications.

"So when I saw your tattoo the other night, I'm thinking, what are the odds our paths would cross again after all this time?" Rue's voice cracked. "And then I remembered Montana saying he was gonna be eight in March, and I started doing the math. The incident happened on June 10, 1998. The reason I remember is because we had just celebrated my mom's fiftieth birthday the day before."

"Rue, what are you saying?"

He reached in his coat pocket, took out a piece of paper, unfolded it, and gave it to her, his hand shaking.

"What is this?" Ivy said.

"The results of a paternity test." Rue's face suddenly looked scalded. "I knew it was a long shot, but I had to know. Ivy, he's mine… Montana's mine."

"*Yours?*" Ivy looked down at the test results, too stunned to make heads or tails of it.

Rue pointed to the text at the bottom of the page. "See…the test proves with 99.999 percent accuracy that the two DNA samples I submitted represent father and child. There's no doubt."

"You did a DNA test on Montana without even asking me?"

"All I did was swab his mouth, and then my own. I made it part of the blood brother ritual the other night. He had no idea what I was doing."

"How'd you even know how to go about it?"

"I called a friend in Denver, and she looked up 'paternity tests' on Google. She found a genetic testing lab that promised fast results and told me exactly how to do the swabs. I put the two samples in separate envelopes, filled out a request form for a paternity test, and put it all into a mailer with a check for one hundred and fifteen dollars. Then I dropped it into the night deposit at the lab this past weekend. I never in a million years expected it to come back a match." Rue sat forward, his hands folded between his knees. "I still can't believe it."

"*You* can't believe it?" Ivy stared at the paper. "I…I don't even know what to say."


Ivy had no idea how long she had sat there mute, unable to recall even the slightest detail of the alleged sexual encounter with Rue. She regretted more than ever that her drug habit had left gaping holes in her memory about behaviors she could neither deny nor defend.

"You okay?" she heard Rue ask.

"Hardly."

"Look, I know this is a big shock. But you also know I'm crazy about Montana. I'll do right by him. And my feelings for you haven't changed."

Ivy studied his expression and saw no reason to doubt him. She blew the bangs off her forehead. "I'm totally overwhelmed."

"That's two of us."

"So what now? You've had more time to think about this than I have."

Rue patted the couch cushion. "Come sit with me."

Ivy got up and sat next to him, pleased when he slipped his arm around her.

"Why don't we continue building our relationship," Rue said, "just like we were doing before this happened? I'm not expecting any special treatment because we found out I'm Montana's biological father. I'm hoping someday you and I will get serious about each other. But regardless, that little boy can't help but do better with two parents who care about him."

"Do you have any idea how strange that sounds? In all these years, I never once considered that I would ever know who Montana's father was, much less that his father would actually care about him."

"Well, I sure do care about him. It's killing me that you don't want me to see him anymore." Rue paused and seemed pensive. "I don't think we should tell him I'm his dad till *we're* comfortable with it and have figured out how much he really needs to know."

"I agree, but we have to tell my parents."

"Seems to me it'd be a lot easier for them to accept it if they like me. Maybe we could spend time with them first, and then tell them when it feels right."

"Mom's been all over me to bring you to dinner, though I'm not sure I can handle being social right now." Ivy shook her head. "I can't believe this is happening. How do we explain this to a seven-year-old?"

"I don't know. I've been struggling with it for days." Rue turned and looked into her eyes, his own brimming with tears "I can't tell you how much I've missed you. I'm sorry I couldn't tell you what was going on. It's been the longest week of my life. But you know what I finally realized? If the paternity test had come back negative, I'd still feel exactly the same about both of you."

# 37

THE NEXT MORNING, as the sun rose over the craggy peaks and turned the snow-covered valley into a sea of shimmering diamonds, Ivy drove her Jeep on the unplowed highway to Woodlands Community Church. She pulled in the parking lot, glad when she didn't see any other vehicles.

She trudged over to a wrought-iron bench in the courtyard and brushed off half a foot of fresh powder snow, then sat down and basked in the quiet. How many times had she come here to think when she first got saved? Some of her best conversations with God had happened on this very spot.

How dramatically her life had changed in the past twenty-four hours! She didn't know if Rue was ever going to be anything more to her than Montana's father, but she knew their relationship would never be healthy unless she dealt with her own sense of unworthiness. Kelsey was right. It was important to love and respect herself if she had any hope of being a good partner.

She noticed deer tracks in the snow, a red-tailed hawk soaring overhead, and a pair of rabbits huddled underneath an evergreen tree. Everything here was unspoiled and pure—everything except her. Why was it so hard for her to feel as if she had been washed clean?

Hadn't she given her heart to the Lord and accepted His forgiveness?

Didn't she believe with all her heart that she would spend eternity with Him? Why then was it so difficult to accept that His sacrifice on the cross was sufficient to cover her sins, even the ones that caused her the most shame?

Ivy moved her eyes to the life-size nativity scene that her parents had donated to the church when she and Rusty were little. She had never seen another like it anywhere. The beautifully crafted characters seemed so life-like that she could almost hear them whispering in the stillness.

The roof of the stable had captured most of the snowfall, and Mary and Joseph nestled together on a bed of straw, their backs propped against the far wall, and baby Jesus cradled in Joseph's arms. The look of joyful exhaustion on their faces seemed a more realistic indicator of what their true emotions might have been than the overly pious expressions typically depicted on the faces of these two unlikely parents.

She wondered what had been going through Mary's mind during the months she was pregnant. Did the realization of the angel's announcement hit before or after she felt the baby kick? Did people gossip about her? Was she scared? Did she even know how to take care of a baby? Did she instantly love Jesus, or did that come later?

Ivy thought back on the night Montana was born and how afraid she had been without a husband and without parents or a friend to hold her hand. She remembered her son's first wail drowning out every other sound in the delivery room and her thinking that she'd made the wrong choice to raise him by herself. And hadn't she?

How long had it taken for the pressure to cause her to start using drugs again? Three months? Four? By then, Montana had fallen through the cracks, and no social worker came calling to hold her accountable— only Lu Ramirez, who lived in the apartment next door. Lu came and got Montana and cared for him when Ivy was too high even to remember he was there.

God had used Lu to protect Montana and then had given him back to Ivy. This beautiful little boy, conceived in the sleaziest of circumstances, was the purest gift she had ever received. So why did she still feel dirty?

*Though your sins are like scarlet, they shall be as white as snow.*

The words of Isaiah resounded in her mind. Either God's Word was true, or everything she believed was a lie. How long could she keep picking and choosing which Scriptures to accept when God's promises were given for every believer?

Ivy got down and knelt in the snow and then lay on her back, her arms outstretched as if she were going to make a snow angel. She looked up at the clear blue December sky.

*Lord, I need to feel white as snow if I'm ever going to be the person You made me to be, if I'm ever going to love myself enough to make a good wife and mother.*

Ivy closed her eyes and, for the first time in her life, dug deep into the foul, messy mire of her past and took hold of her darkest sins, the ones she had asked God to forgive, even though *she* couldn't. She pictured herself placing each of these shameful failings—one by one—in His nail-scarred hand until they formed a mountain of muck.

When she was finished, the mountain seemed to turn to clay, and the Lord simply crushed it and blew the dust to the four winds. Peace like nothing she had ever known before infused her.

She lay still for a long time afterward, feeling weightless and serene and as clean as the spray of blowing snow the breeze had picked up and swept across her face.

# 38

ON CHRISTMAS EVE, Ivy strolled through the vestibule of Woodlands Community Church with Montana and Rue just before the candlelight service. She moved her gaze across the group gathered there until she spotted her mother waving.

"There you are." Carolyn zigzagged around several people and made her way over to them, Elam trying to keep up. "We saved you seats near the front."

Ivy put her lips to Montana's ear. "Why don't you introduce Grandma to Rue?"

Montana looked up at her with puppy eyes and a wry smile that looked surprisingly like his father's. "Now?"

Ivy nodded.

Montana reached for one of Rue's hands and then one of his grandmother's and stood between them, looking as if he were confused about what to say.

"Tell Grandma who we brought with us," Ivy said.

"We brought Rue, me and my mom's very bestest friend. He knows more about stars than anybody except God. And he knows how to use all kinds of really cool tools. But he's not very good at Chinese checkers." Montana hit Rue with his elbow and let out a husky laugh.

Ivy covered her smile with her hand and was proud of Rue for staying focused.

"And who is this nice lady?" Rue asked.

"My Grandma Carolyn. She teached me how to cook and bake cookies, and she sticks all the pictures I draw on her frigerator. She lives in a humongous log house with Grandpa Elam. You already know who he is."

Elam winked and extended his hand to Rue. "Glad you're here."

"It's good to finally meet you," Carolyn said. "Ivy and Montana have told us so much about you that I feel as if I know you. You're invited out to the house after church. We'll have eggnog and hot cocoa and all kind of munchies. Sing Christmas carols. And if Montana has anything to say about it, I imagine we'll sing silly songs around the piano."

"Yay!" Montana said. "And Rue's gonna show me the big, shiny moon through his telescope."

"Wonderful." Carolyn glanced at her watch. "It's about to start. We'd better take our seats."

The four adults sat together near the front of the church, and Montana scurried off to join his Sunday-school class on the stage, where several children in costumes were getting positioned to act out the traditional Christmas story.

When the teacher gave the signal, Montana, looking adorable in his red turtleneck and tan trousers, stepped up to the mike and began to narrate the story, reciting his lines from memory.

Ivy silently coached his every word as if that would somehow keep him from stumbling. She stole several well-spaced glances at Rue, careful not to be too obvious, and was touched by the unmistakable that's-my-son expression on his face. She sensed that it was all he could do to keep it to himself.

Montana projected his voice and looked out at the people the way his teacher had taught him. At one point he seemed distracted and, for a few agonizing seconds, seemed to have lost his place. Rue clutched tightly to her hand and finally exhaled when Montana continued reciting his lines without faltering. Ivy turned to Rue just as he turned to her, and for the very first time, she felt a parental connectedness that transcended whatever feelings she had for him.

After the kids' program, Pastor Rick Myers gave a wonderful sermon, and then the congregation sang Christmas carols and celebrated the Lord's Supper together. The service ended with the lighting of the candles and the congregation singing "Silent Night" a cappella.

By midnight, the laughter and feasting and singing had wound down at the Griffiths', and the peace of this holy night seemed to have fallen softly over the entire house. Montana was asleep on the couch, his head in Rue's lap. Ivy and Carolyn and Elam sat on the floor in front of a crackling fire and sipped eggnog and admired the tree.

"What a great evening." Ivy breathed a sigh of satisfaction. "I'd almost forgotten how much fun it is having Christmas Eve at your house."

"Well, it hasn't been this much fun in a long time," Elam said. "It's nice to have you home, honey."

Ivy was relieved that no one mentioned Rusty, but they had to feel the void as much she did.

Carolyn put her cup in the saucer and looked over at Rue. "It's been delightful having you here. Not everyone would be as enthusiastic about our silly songfest around the piano. It's obvious Montana's taken with you."

"The feeling's mutual."

"You're very good with him. I can tell you've been around children."

"Just my nephews, actually. But I like kids. This one…well, he's special. We hit it off right off the bat. I love this age. They're so full of questions and so interested in everything."

"It's great you've hooked him on stargazing," Elam said. "It's nice for a boy to have a hobby he can enjoy for a lifetime. I don't imagine you ever run out of things to learn in astronomy."

"You really don't." Rue brushed his fingers through Montana's hair. "And he's a fast learner. Or as he likes to put it, he's 'a good rememberer.'"

Carolyn smiled. "It's hard to believe I'd gone my whole life without looking through a telescope until tonight. I enjoyed seeing the craters on the moon. I had no idea they could be seen so clearly."

"It's surprising what we miss if we don't know how or what to look for."

Ivy got up and sat next to Rue on the couch, pleased when he slipped his arm around her.

"I'm really glad you came too," she said. "It was a special evening all the way around, and Montana was beside himself that you came to watch his program. And as much as I hate to spoil the magic, I need to get home. You know he's going to be up with the sun, and that means you and I need to move the you-know-what into the you-know-where."

"What in the world are you two elves plotting?" Elam said.

Ivy laughed. "You'll find out soon enough."

# 39

IVY DRIFTED IN AND OUT of wakefulness the way she always did when she needed to be up at a certain time and was afraid she would turn off her alarm and fall asleep again.

She heard the sound of slippered feet shuffling across the wood floor and then felt a gentle tapping on her shoulder.

"Mom, it's Christmas!" Montana whispered. "There are *so many* presents under the tree!"

Ivy smiled and forced her sleepy eyes to open.

Montana's nose was almost pressed against hers, his brown eyes the size of nickels. "You have to get up!" He climbed into her bed and started to bounce up and down as if it were a trampoline. "My tummy feels all fizzley like Coke bubbles, and I'm really, really hyper."

Ivy laughed. "Yes, you are."

"I want you to open your present I got you."

"You have a present for me under the tree?"

Montana jumped off the bed and tugged on her arm. "I saved the money Rue paid me for helping him make the cabins look pretty. And he helped me find the bestest present for you. Come on."

"I didn't even know he paid you." Ivy covered a yawn with her hand and sat up on the side of the bed. She glanced at the clock and put on her bathrobe and slippers and let Montana lead her by the hand out to the Christmas tree.

"Oh my!" she exclaimed. "Just look at all those gifts. Santa Claus must've found out you moved."

Montana cocked his head, his button nose dotted with freckles. "You put them there."

"Hey, mister. You're growing up much too fast. Whatever happened to pretending?"

"I don't hafta pretend." Montana got down and started touching the packages. "It's Jesus's birthday, but we get all these presents. How cool is that?"

"Very. Let's call Rue and get him over here. We don't want to start without him."

Montana ran into the kitchen and dialed the phone. "Hello, Rue? It's Montana. Mom said to come over so you can open presents with us. Okay, hurry. Bye." He went over and crawled up on the couch next to Ivy. "He said he'll be here in a flash."

Just seconds later, there was a knock on the door.

"That was quick," Ivy said.

Montana raced to the door and opened it. "How'd you get here so fast?"

"I've been waiting in the driveway," Rue said. "I even shoveled the walk. Merry Christmas." He tousled Montana's hair, then walked over and flopped on the couch next to Ivy. "Mission accomplished."

Ivy smiled. "Thanks. Who wants to go first?"

"You do!" Montana picked up a package and handed it to her. "It's from me. I wrapped it myself, only I messed it up, so Rue helped me."

Ivy pulled off the ribbon and slowly removed the crumpled paper, relishing the joy in Montana's eyes and wondering how she ever managed to raise a child who thought of her before himself on Christmas Day. She popped the tape on the top of the box, pulled out something wrapped in bubble wrap, and carefully unwound it. "Oh, sweetie, this is beautiful," she said. "A crystal snowflake."

"It's a sun catcher you can hang on the window with that plastic thing," Montana said. "Did you know that every single snowflake is special, and in the whole wide world, there's not even two alike?"

"I did know that."

"And since there's no other mommy like you in the whole wide world, that makes you special too."

"What a sweet thing to say." Ivy blinked rapidly to clear her eyes. "Thank you for such a beautiful and thoughtful gift." She pulled Montana close. "I absolutely *love* it."

"I have a present for Rue too." Montana picked up a package wrapped in green tissue paper and a red bow and gave it to Rue.

"Well, I wasn't expecting this," Rue said. He carefully unwrapped the soft package and discovered an orange stocking cap. "This is great, thanks. It's just like yours."

"So now we'll match."

"We sure will."

"Okay, my turn!" Montana sat on his heels and tore the paper and ribbon off one of the packages and opened it. He looked up at Ivy, a smile playing with the corners of his mouth. "A dog collar?"

Ivy lifted her eyebrows up and down. "You never know when you might need one. Open something else."

Montana ripped open a foil-wrapped package containing a dog bowl. And another containing a leash. And another a pet brush. And finally he opened the largest package, which contained a huge sack of Puppy Chow.

The child's face beamed and his eyes danced. "Where is it?"

"Where's what?"

"My puppy."

Ivy looked at Rue, stifling a grin. "You know anything about a puppy?"

"Puppy?" Rue sounded totally clueless. "He wanted a puppy?"

Montana got up on his feet and stood in front of the couch looking from one to the other. "I know you got it! Where is it? Where's my puppy?"

Rue put his hand to his ear and sucked in a breath. "Listen...did you hear that?"

"What?"

"That barking noise."

"Where?"

Rue got up and acted as though he were following the sound. He opened the front door, Montana and Ivy following close behind, and walked on the newly shoveled path to his SUV. He put his hand to his ear again, and then opened the back hatch and reached inside. He turned around holding a wiggling, yapping ball of fur in his hands.

"Is this what you were hoping for?" Rue said.

"It's a Sasha dog! You got me a Sasha dog!" Montana took the puppy into his arms and giggled with delight as the dog swiped his cheek with its tongue. "This is all I ever wanted!"

"It's a gift from me *and* your mom."

"Is it a girl dog or a boy dog?"

It's a female," Ivy said.

Montana nodded. "That's what I meant. Where did you find her?"

"At the animal shelter. She's part Siberian husky like Sasha. And part something else. We thought she was adorable."

"Hey, why don't we go inside and get out of this wind?" Rue said. "Before you freeze to death."

"We need to think of a name," Ivy said as they walked back in the house.

Montana knelt on the living room floor and set the puppy down and scratched her ears, his voice suddenly an octave higher. "Hi, girl. This is your home now. You need a name, don't you?" He picked the puppy up with both hands and held her in front of his face and studied her. "I know...why don't we call her Windy."

"That's an interesting name," Ivy said. "What made you think of it?"

"I like the way her coat got all fluffed up when the wind blew on it."

Rue chuckled. "Works for me."

"Then I guess Windy it is."

Montana got up and threw his arms around her, and then Rue. "Thanks. This is the very funnest Christmas in my whole life!"

# 40

ON NEW YEAR'S EVE, Ivy dropped Montana off at Ian Carter's house for a sleepover, and then she and Rue went to her parents' house and told them about the results of the paternity test.

*Would somebody please say something?* Ivy held tightly to Rue's hand, trying to remember that her sins were white as snow and she wasn't going to dredge up the guilt.

Elam tugged at his mustache and then cleared his throat. "I have to tell you, this is the last thing I ever expected to hear. Of course it's good news for Montana. But it's a shock."

"Believe me, I know," Ivy said. "I never in a million years thought I would ever know who Montana's father was, much less that he'd actually be a good and decent guy."

"What I did with Ivy wasn't decent," Rue quickly added, "and it's always bothered me, though it never once occurred to me that I'd fathered a child. Thank heavens Montana won't have to spend the rest of his life wondering who his father is and thinking he didn't want him."

"When are you going to tell him?"

"We've decided to wait until his birthday," Ivy said. "That seems like the most natural time to bring it up. And it'll give Rue and me a few months to build our relationship and see where we are."

Elam leaned forward, his hands folded between his knees. "How are you going to explain something this heavy to a child his age?"

"We've discussed it at length," Ivy said. "I've told Montana all along that the drugs affected my memory and I couldn't remember who his father was. We think it's enough for him to know that Rue is his daddy and loves him with all his heart. And that it was a miracle that God sent Rue to find the both of us. I think that's all the explanation he needs right now—maybe ever."

Carolyn's eyes brimmed with tears. "This is so like the Lord to do the impossible. Ivy, didn't you tell me you had prayed to God and asked for a sign that He hasn't given up on You? I think you just got your answer. If God Himself has enough confidence in the two of you to bring you together to raise Montana, then I'd say you should be able to turn loose of past failures and start trusting that God knows what He's doing.

At five minutes until midnight, Ivy and Rue nestled together on the couch in her living room, Windy asleep on Rue's lap and Dick Clark's *New Year's Rockin' Eve* playing on the TV.

"You've been awfully quiet since we left my parents' house," Ivy said.

"I can't stop thinking about what your mother said. It's awesome to think that God set this whole thing up. The concept of Him actually being involved in every move we make is pretty new for me."

"It had to be Him. What are the odds that we would both wind up working at Three Peaks and that you would figure out who I was—by recognizing a tattoo, no less?" Ivy laid her head on his shoulder. "What I can't stop thinking about is how obvious it is that the Lord wants both of us involved in Montana's life, in spite of what we did. We are the two least likely people to deserve such a wonderful child, and yet God has chosen us to raise him."

"*Chosen?* Wow, that's a powerful word."

"I know." Ivy dabbed the corners of her eyes. "It's taken me until now to believe that God still loves me and has forgiven me for all the disgusting things I've done—not only forgiven, but forgotten. It seems too good to be true, but that's what the Bible says He does. And His bringing you to us was an added bonus I would never have even thought to pray for."

"I'm excited about being a dad. It's so weird, but if I could've hand-picked a son, I'd have picked one just like Montana."

"He has your smile," Ivy said.

"You think so?"

She nodded. "Definitely. I've seen it several times." Ivy relished the proud look on Rue's face and then glanced over at the TV and saw the ball was starting to drop for the ten-second countdown. "Well, it looks like we're about to say good-bye to this year."

Rue put his arm around her and drew closer, his lips within inches of hers. "Happy New Year, sweetheart. Something tells me things are just gonna get better and better."

# 41

A FEW WEEKS LATER Ivy sat nestled between Rue and Montana on a huge boulder on Tanner's Ridge, captivated by the late-night sky.

She pulled the stadium blanket up around her neck. "I wonder how many stars there are."

"Well, from what I've read," Rue said, "there could be more than ten billion trillion. But even out here where it's pitch-black, you can see only about three thousand stars without using binoculars or a telescope."

"Really?"

"Yeah, but think about this: Betelgeuse is about five hundred light-years from earth, and just one light-year equals about 5.88 trillion miles! Astronomers have discovered galaxies that are twelve to sixteen *billion* light-years away. Blows your mind even trying to comprehend how far away that is. Should give us a clue how powerful God is, since distance is nothing to Him and He knows every star by name."

"How many star names do you know?" Montana asked.

"I don't know, champ. Quite a few. But it's like a grain of sand compared to ten billion trillion."

Ivy exhaled in awe. "This is fabulous, Rue. I might have gone my entire life without realizing what was up there."

"Well, thanks to the light bulb, people in cities rarely get a good view of the night sky. Most have no idea what they're missing."

"Could we bring Ian sometime and let him see?" Montana asked.

"Sure we can." Rue inched closer to Ivy. "You cold?"

"Yes, but I'm loving every glorious minute of this."

"So this is a hobby, right?" Montana said. "Because that's what I told Ian."

Ivy smiled. "I guess so, since a hobby is anything we love doing every chance we get. But for me, it's much more that. I almost feel as though I'm sitting at God's feet out here."

"Whoa!" Montana exclaimed. "Did you guys see *that*?"

"That was a shooting star," Rue said. "I'm hoping we'll see more of those tonight. How about you and me going to the car and getting a couple packages of foot warmers? Looks like we might be out here for a while."

"Okay." Montana jumped to his feet and pulled Rue's stocking cap down over his eyes, then giggled and started scrambling up the hill.

Rue repositioned his hat, then let out a ferocious growl and started chasing him. "When I catch you, I'm gonna tickle your little belly till you beg for mercy!"

Ivy sat hugging her knees, the playful sounds of father and son filling her heart with laughter and hope. She rested in the peace of the moment and the presence of the One whom she couldn't see but sensed in everything around her.

A few minutes later, the guys returned, and Rue opened two cellophane wrappers and put a foot warmer in each of her boots, and then Montana's.

"That ought to help," he said.

Ivy reached for his hand. "Thanks. I'd really like to stay out here awhile."

Rue nestled between her and Montana and pulled the blanket up around all three. They sat for a long time in comfortable silence, and Montana finally fell asleep, his head in Rue's lap.

"What are you thinking about?" Rue whispered.

"Do you realize I've spent my entire adult life looking back, longing for what *was* instead of what *could* be? And God, in this incredible act of divine mercy, brought it all right to my door. Me, Ivy Griffith, the most unworthy vessel in the universe, and He gave me my heart's desire. I never realized He loved me that much." Ivy wiped away a runaway tear.

"Same here. And I really don't know why." Rue looked down at Montana and gently stroked his back. "But I'll tell you what I do know: God wants the two of us to focus on raising our son and never look back on what we were before."

"Amen to that. From now on, the only direction we need to look is up."

Ivy lifted her eyes and reveled in the lavish display of royal jewels spilled out across the black velvet sky. It was too wonderful to comprehend that the King of kings and Lord of lords knew each one by name, and that He had never lost sight of anything that belonged to Him, not even a pair of seemingly hopeless addicts or a little boy who desperately needed a dad.

# AFTERWORD

*As far as the east is from the west,*
*so far has he removed*
*our transgressions from us.*

PSALM 103:12

Dear friends,

The longer I walk with the Lord, the more intently I marvel at His matchless mercy and grace. There are numerous scriptures that speak to us of God's forgiveness, but none states it any clearer than 1 John 1:9: "If we confess our sins, he is faithful and just and will forgive us our sins and purify us from all unrighteousness." There is no condition attached to that promise other than our confession.

How then is it that so many believers, like Ivy Griffith in this story, find it difficult to turn loose of guilt and shame even after they accept God's forgiveness? Perhaps it's because our human tendency is to categorize certain sins as much less acceptable than others, when the truth is that *all* sin is offensive to a holy God, and even those sins *we* consider minor cannot be forgiven and removed apart from Jesus's death on the cross. There are different kinds of sins, but only one remedy. But that remedy is all sufficient. For those of us who have trusted Jesus Christ as Lord and Savior, we have the assurance of salvation, and our sins have been removed as far as the east is from the west. There is nothing we can add to the finished work on the cross. Nothing.

The astounding reality for Ivy and for all who profess the name of Jesus is that we have been made holy and blameless in the sight of God, and He no longer holds our offenses against us—not even those we still find it hard to talk about. Let us never be deceived into thinking that the magnitude of our sin negates His grace, for grace just abounds all the more.

Join me for the dramatic conclusion to the Phantom Hollow Series in book three, *The Grand Scheme,* where we will find out what happens to Ivy, Rue, and Montana. Count on a few twists and turns, and hold on to your hat. Mystery and suspense abound!

I love hearing from my readers. You can write to me through my publisher at WaterBrook Multnomah Publishing Group, 12265 Oracle Boulevard, Suite 200, Colorado Springs, CO 80921, or directly through my Web site at www.kathyherman.com. I read and respond to every e-mail and greatly value your input.

In His love,

*Kathy Herman*

# DISCUSSION GUIDE

1. Do you believe 1 John 1:9, "If we confess our sins, he is faithful and just and will forgive us our sins and purify us from all unrighteousness," should be taken literally? If not, what do you think this verse means? Do you believe there's any other way to be forgiven by God than confessing our sin?

2. Are there sins you've confessed that you don't feel forgiven for? If so, can you identify the reason why you have doubts? Does your reasoning line up with Scripture? Is it possible it's actually you who haven't forgiven the sin and not God?

3. Is there a difference between deeply regretting your sinful past and being guilt-ridden? If so, can you explain the difference? What is the biblical remedy for guilt and shame?

4. Is there a sin in your past that you've confessed but live in fear of someone else finding out? If so, are you still carrying the shame? According to 1 John 1:9, has God forgiven you? Can anything positive come from your carrying the shame? What do you think God wants you to do?

5. When a believer continues to struggle with guilt, do you think confiding in a trusted brother or sister in Christ could be a powerful tool for letting it go? Can you think of some cautions a person should consider before doing this?

6.  Can you think of a situation when you heard someone share something surprising about his or her struggle with sin and you actually found yourself respecting that person more for having had the courage to admit it? Were you able to empathize with his or her weakness? Did the person seem more real to you afterward?

7.  Can deeper healing result from knowing we're loved and accepted in spite of our sin? Do you think God can use your sinful mistakes as a means of teaching you empathy for others who also struggle?

8.  Do you believe God always forgives a person who has repented and asked His forgiveness? If so, do you believe His grace would be given in equal measure to someone like Ivy Griffith for a decade of abusing her body, as it would to Elam Griffith for harboring a six-month grudge? Explain your answer.

9.  In Matthew 18:22, Jesus tells us to forgive others "seventy-seven times." Do you think that statement should be taken literally? If not, what do you think it means? Do you think there's value in applying that same principle when forgiving ourselves?

10.  Do you think God punishes us if we don't repent once we realize we're sinning? When you've experienced hardship, have you ever secretly feared that God was punishing you? Is it possible He was disciplining you as outlined in Hebrews 12:7–11?

11.  Have you ever experienced this type of godly discipline? Did it make you fearful or remorseful? Did it eventually cause you to grow more Christlike?

12.  Do you believe Psalm 103:12, which reads, "As far as the east is from the west, so far has he removed our transgressions from us,"

should be taken literally? If not, what do you think it means? If so, should we ever dredge up the sins we've already confessed?

13. Is there ever a time when we have the right to hold someone else's sin against him or her? If you think there is, find biblical support for your answer.

14. What are some of the faulty perceptions a person might have that create stumbling blocks to accepting God's forgiveness? Do faulty perceptions change the truth of 1 John 1:9?

15. Who was your favorite character in this story? If you could meet that person, what would you like to say to him or her?

16. Did God speak to your heart through this story? Was there a particular thought or principle you took away?

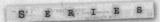
# THE BAXTER SERIES

## *by Kathy Herman*

Welcome to Baxter: the very best of small-town America. Life here is good. People are bonded by a proud heritage—and a hundred-year history unstained by the violence that has seeped into nearly every other American city. But when a powerful explosion shakes not only the windows, but the very foundation on which they've based their safety and security, the door is left open for evil to slither in. The death of innocence is painful to endure, but with it comes the resurgence of faith and hope.

Suspenseful, unforgettable stories that inspire, challenge, and stay with you long after the covers are closed!

**TESTED BY FIRE**
*Book One*

**DAY OF RECKONING**
*Book Two*

**VITAL SIGNS**
*Book Three*

**HIGH STAKES**
*Book Four*

**A FINE LINE**
*Book Five*

LEARN MORE ABOUT THESE NOVELS FROM BESTSELLING AUTHOR KATHY HERMAN

LOG ON TO WWW.KATHYHERMAN.COM TODAY!